BEFORE SHE FINDS ME

A NOVEL

HEATHER CHAVEZ

MULHOLLAND BOOKS

Little, Brown and Company
New York Boston London

Copyright © 2023 by Heather Chavez

Mulholland Books / Little, Brown and Company
Hachette Book Group
1290 Avenue of the Americas, New York, NY 10104
mulhollandbooks.com

First Edition: June 2023

Mulholland Books is an imprint of Little, Brown and Company, a division of Hachette Book Group, Inc. The Mulholland Books name and logo are trademarks of Hachette Book Group, Inc.

The publisher is not responsible for websites (or their content) that are not owned by the publisher.

The Hachette Speakers Bureau provides a wide range of authors for speaking events. To find out more, go to hachettespeakersbureau.com or email hachettespeakers@hbgusa.com.

Little, Brown and Company books may be purchased in bulk for business, educational, or promotional use. For information, please contact your local bookseller or the Hachette Book Group Special Markets Department at special.markets@hbgusa.com.

ISBN 9780316531351
LCCN 2022946267

10 9 8 7 6 5 4 3 2 1

MRQ-T

Printed in Canada

For my mom, Norma, and dad, Ron:
Thank you for encouraging my love of books.
And thank you for not raising me to be a hired killer.

BEFORE

SHE

FINDS

ME

CHAPTER 1

JULIA

The afternoon Julia Bennett was supposed to move Cora into the dorms, she thought the worst that would happen was she would openly cry and embarrass her daughter. That, and Cora's father would be late.

As predicted, she did get teary-eyed, and Eric was late. But she didn't predict Eric would bring along his new wife, Brie.

In her thirty-eight years, Julia had experienced her share of Very Bad Things—in her mind, it was always capped like that—and the rational part of her understood that Brie's unexpected appearance didn't rise to that level. It was more a moderately irksome thing.

Still, as she watched her ex-husband and his wife of six months stalk across the lawn under a harsh midday sun, their steps plodding and in sync, Julia could nearly hear the horror movie soundtrack. She half expected Brie to drop onto all fours and skitter across the courtyard like the vengeful spirit of a girl who'd died while chained to a basement pipe.

Julia should've grabbed Cora then, taken her far from that wide-open courtyard. She should've heeded the bone chill she would later recognize as her first warning.

Instead, Julia stole a quick glance at Cora's face to see if she'd spotted

Brie, but her daughter seemed unaware of her new stepmom's approach. Julia dug into her purse for her emergency chocolate. It had melted. Of course.

She held out the foil-wrapped square. "Squishy chocolate?"

Cora wrinkled her nose. "Tempting, but no."

Julia dropped the chocolate back in her purse and looked around, trying to enjoy their last Brie-free moments. Anderson Hughes College had only about five thousand students, but the crowd gathered for move-in day was still enough that Julia felt claustrophobic. She liked to track the movement of those around her. Watch their faces for signs of shifting emotion. Possible danger. She'd developed the habit as a teen, but it was hard to keep watch when there were hundreds of people pressed close enough that she could feel their heat.

Anderson Hughes was also where Julia taught botany as an assistant professor. Despite the break in tuition, Cora had been slow to warm up to the school. Eventually, the arts program and the fact that her best friend, Evie Fournier, was also attending won her over. The ocean view didn't hurt either.

Julia nudged Cora with her shoulder. "Since you'll be on campus, we can have lunch every day."

"We will not be doing that."

"But I get to walk you to your classes, right?"

"Absolutely not."

"Then what will I do with the matching T-shirts?" When Cora groaned, Julia squeezed her arm. "This is going to be so much fun."

"Think there's still time to transfer to San Diego State?"

At that moment, the line of families and students waiting to check into the dorms compressed. The man behind them, wearing a plaid button-up and a thick smear of sunscreen on his nose, inched closer. Julia's skin buzzed.

She felt a sudden poke in her ribs. Then Cora nudged her a second time with their cart, containing most of her belongings. Apparently, her daughter had snuck in a couple of items when Julia hadn't been paying attention.

Julia cocked an eyebrow. "We agreed throw pillows aren't essential."

"If only one of us believes that, can you really say we agreed?" Cora extracted one of the pillows and held it so her mom could read the imprinted slogan: THAT'S A TERRIBLE IDEA…WHAT TIME? "Tell me this isn't essential."

"It's not essential."

Cora made that face that got Julia every time: wide eyes and flushed cheeks that were half earnest, half *Don't test me.* Then she pointed to the second pillow, still in the cart. "That other one is the cat wearing sunglasses. A cat, Mom. Wearing sunglasses."

Julia sighed deeply. It wasn't about the throw pillows. "You've made a *purr*suasive case."

"Stop."

Julia feigned innocence. "What?"

"I heard what you did there. You punned."

"That's an ap*paw*lling accusation."

The corner of Cora's mouth twitched.

Studying her daughter's face, Julia felt a swell of pride. Cora had been born eight weeks premature, weighing not quite four pounds. Her skin slightly fuzzy. Her bones soft. Her nails not yet fully formed. Eighteen years later, Cora remained as determined as she'd been those first weeks in the NICU. Still fighting for her place in the world. Fearing nothing. When Julia had been just a little younger than Cora, her life had been contained within a few city blocks. But her daughter's world held no such dark boundaries.

As Julia stared beyond the crowd and toward the ocean, it was easy to imagine that Cora could do anything. Go anywhere.

That terrified Julia. The world wasn't always a welcoming place.

Cora tapped her mom with the pillow before tossing it back in the cart. "I'm going to miss you and your corny puns," she said.

"And I'm going to miss you and your unhealthy obsession with throw pillows."

Cora must've noticed the break in her voice. "Don't worry, Mom. I left you the one with the flying monkeys."

Thinking of *The Wizard of Oz* reminded Julia of the Wicked Witch, which snapped her focus back to Brie. Closer now. Cora still unaware of her presence. Would she be okay with Brie being here? The day before, Cora had canceled what was supposed to be Eric's day with her at the last minute. She wouldn't say why, but Julia sensed tension between Cora and her stepmom.

Around them, the crowd undulated like a snake digesting. Julia's skin itched again. So many people.

Deep breaths, Julia.

When the crowd spit out Eric and Brie a moment later, they were less than thirty feet away.

Julia shifted, putting herself between them and Cora. "I hope your roommate brought only a toothbrush and a blanket, because otherwise, I'm not sure you'll both fit in the room."

"Says the woman who packed her purse today for a monthlong trip."

"Everything in my purse is necessary."

"Like the melted chocolate?"

Julia's gaze landed on Brie, less than ten feet away now. "Especially the melted chocolate."

Cora's eyes tracked hers, and then she saw them. Her face brightened, then clouded. Julia reached for Cora's hand and gave it a quick squeeze. A few seconds later, Eric arrived at Cora's side. He looked around and whistled, long and low. "This place is nice."

Julia and Eric had been divorced for years, long before Julia had started teaching at Anderson Hughes, and he'd missed Cora's first official campus visit. Brie had arranged a wine-tasting getaway the same week. An oversight, she'd claimed. Julia knew better.

Located in Point Loma, Anderson Hughes College was flanked by white-capped waters and scrubbed by a salty breeze. The sheer sandstone cliffs beneath it contained dinosaur fossils, or so Julia had been told. If someone had shown her a clay mold made from a possum's bones, she wouldn't have been able to tell the difference.

From his blond hair to his square jaw, Eric had the frat-boy-turned-finance-professional look down. Only Julia knew he'd started as a nerd. Sometimes she missed that version of him.

Eric turned his aging-frat-boy smile toward her. "Good morning, Julia."

The smile didn't work on her anymore. "Afternoon, actually. Morning officially ends when the little hand reaches the twelve."

He waved off the comment and hugged Cora. Brie kept her distance behind him, looking uncomfortable at the display.

Eric eyed the overfilled cart. "I see you brought both guitars. Sure you'll have room for books?"

Cora brightened, grinning at her father, and it occurred to Julia how long the road to this moment, this peace, had been. Eric looked so damn paternal that Julia's breath caught.

"Mom said only the essential stuff."

The man in plaid suddenly bumped up against Julia, and her breath hitched.

"Sorry," he said.

She turned to find him standing next to a young woman in glasses, a strawberry blonde braid trailing down her back. Probably his daughter. Her attention focused on the sign-in table up ahead, the girl wore the same expression as Cora: contemplative and ardent. The effort of restraining her excitement was causing the muscles in her face to spasm.

Julia softened and nodded once. "It's fine."

When she turned to face Cora again, Eric's arm was slung around her shoulder, and Cora was describing all the spots on campus she already loved. That left Julia and Brie to face each other in awkward silence. There were only two topics they'd ever been able to discuss for more than thirty seconds: Cora, and Julia's poor taste in wine.

"So, screw cap or cork?" Julia finally asked.

Brie's brow furrowed. "What?"

"Nothing. I didn't know you were coming."

"I hadn't planned on it—headache—but Eric insisted." Brie shifted. "And it's nice to be able to support Cora on her big day."

That last part sounded prepared.

Though the two women had met on many occasions, the same thought hit Julia each time: *Eric definitely has a type.* She and Brie were both tall, and they shared the same toothy smile. The same dark hair. Even the same creases at the corners of their eyes. They could've been the pre- and post-makeover versions of a character in a romantic comedy. Julia would've been the woman hiding behind her glasses, while Brie would've been that same woman after discovering the transformative powers of lipstick.

Julia was suddenly grateful she'd cut her hair and added highlights the previous weekend.

When she tucked a strand behind her ear, Brie scowled. "You've cut your hair." She said this in the same way she might've said, *You've stepped in a pile of dog shit.* "Why?"

"Why'd I cut my hair?" She forced a smile. "It was easier than growing my head, I guess."

"You had such beautiful hair."

"Same hair. Just shorter."

Brie stared at her for a moment, as if trying to decide whether Julia had made the comment at her expense, then made a show of checking her watch.

"How long do you think this will take?"

"Who knows?" Julia smiled brightly. "We could be here for days. Weeks, even."

Brie craned her neck to see past the crowd. "I need coffee."

Thank God. "The food court is on the other side of the courtyard," Julia said helpfully.

Brie squinted and managed a reluctant "Thank you," but when she tried to push past Eric, he looked away from Cora to touch his wife's elbow. Julia felt an unexpected pang at the affection in the gesture. Though she'd stopped feeling more than friendly toward him long before, every so often, a memory would sneak up on her. There had been a time when she knew Eric better than anyone. Now, though they'd grown closer again in recent months, Julia remained on the edge of his life. Brie was its center.

Julia was still adjusting to that.

Eric leaned in so his mouth hovered near his wife's ear. "You're not leaving?"

"Just going to get a latte."

"You couldn't have had one before we left?" He tried to blunt his sharp tone with a smile.

Brie pulled her elbow away and whispered—loud enough that it was clear she wanted Julia to hear—"I want to be here for Cora, but maybe it's better if I left."

Eric looked over at Julia with pleading eyes. "Julia's fine with you being here. Tell her, Julia."

Julia's irritation flared. She wasn't about to let either of them ruin this milestone for Cora. "Why don't you *both* go grab a coffee?" Silently, she added, *And come back when you've remembered whose day we're celebrating.*

Hand back on Brie's elbow, Eric leaned in again, his mouth inches from Brie's ear. "We talked about this."

Brie tried to maneuver around him, but the man in the plaid shirt scooted closer again, now forcing Brie into Julia. Brie's expression grew panicked. Julia recognized the feeling. Maybe her skittishness wasn't about Julia? At least not entirely. Maybe it was about the crowd. Or maybe Brie just wanted to get away from her husband. Frankly, Julia could relate either way.

Brie planted her palm against the man's chest and gave him a slight push. His eyes widened in shock. Eric's too.

Eric glanced down at Brie's hand. "What the—"

Cora interrupted, suddenly as distressed as her stepmother. "Mom, where's my phone?"

Julia turned her attention back to her daughter, whose eyes were now as wide as Brie's.

"Did you check the cart?"

Cora continued to pat her pockets. "I wouldn't have put it in the cart," she said, even as she burrowed through the pile of bedding, clothing, and mementos. The cherished throw pillows were discarded onto the concrete.

Julia took out her own phone. "We'll track it."

"It's a new phone, Mom." Her pitch sharpened. She'd gotten the phone from Brie two weeks before, and two days after Julia mentioned to Eric that she'd planned the same gift. "I haven't set that up yet."

Julia wanted to reassure her daughter that it was just a phone, but she knew what kind of reaction that would get. So instead, she made a quick mental inventory of all the places they'd visited before getting in line earlier.

"The library. You were taking photos." With her fingertips, Julia grazed Cora's hand, white-knuckled as she clenched the edge of the cart. "Be right back."

Julia turned. She took a couple of steps. Extended her hand uneasily to part the crowd. The day had started out with such promise and now—

A sudden chill shot through her.

She'd believed the same thing a few days before her fifteenth birthday, when she'd found the new pair of sneakers her parents planned to give her. A major haul, considering their financial circumstances. There had even been talk of a cake with cinnamon sprinkles. Then, a day later, her entire universe had shifted.

From that experience, Julia had grown to distrust days that were too bright. Too happy.

Or maybe it wasn't that at all. Maybe her subconscious had already recognized a threat.

Her neck tingled a heartbeat before she heard the *pop*, abrupt and sharp.

In the hum of the crowd, the sound was nearly lost. No one screamed. Not right away. In those first seconds, the crowd reacted as they would to a dropped soda can or backfiring car.

They didn't understand.

But Julia understood. She was silent too, but only so she could hear better. She knew from experience that listening was what saved you. That, and action.

The sound came again.

Pop.

At last, the crowd began to react, more out of confusion than horror, becoming one clumsy, pulsating knot.

Instincts firing ahead of conscious thought, Julia had already grabbed Cora and forced her to the ground. At first, her daughter struggled, as confused as everyone else. But then she went limp as Julia pulled her behind the cart.

Prone on the concrete, they were alone. Everyone around them remained upright.

No, not alone. The man in the plaid shirt had fallen beside them, eyes closed, hand clutching his stomach.

Julia wrapped herself around her daughter. She wedged their bodies against the cart's undercarriage. She held on to it tightly. Prayed the crowd wouldn't stampede.

Pop pop pop.

Julia felt Cora's rabbit-fast heartbeat. Good. Her pulse was strong, if too quick.

Julia glanced up. Tried to find Eric and Brie.

There. Both still standing.

But how?

How was Brie still standing with that hole in her forehead? Blood trickled from it, into eyes grown flat.

Slowly, Brie crumpled on top of the man in the plaid shirt.

Julia held Cora tighter so she wouldn't see.

Then the screaming began.

CHAPTER 2

REN

Ren Petrovic selected a belly band holster from the gun shop rack and strapped it around her waist. Or, rather, the spot where her waist had been. She grimaced. In the past few weeks, her formerly flat stomach had become swollen, a tiny stranger mounting an aggressive campaign to expand its territory. Ren patted the hard lump, still indistinguishable from a big breakfast unless she wore a snug T-shirt. Unfortunately, she owned far too many snug T-shirts. Time to rethink her wardrobe, starting with her holster.

"What do you think, tiny stranger?" Ren whispered. "Belly band or shoulder holster?"

The lump offered no advice.

Ren adjusted the straps on the belly band, but its fit remained awkward. She twisted it farther back on her hip. To test the band's comfort, she squatted until her backside came within inches of her heels. The strap cut into the flesh beneath her rib cage. She stood, adjusted, then bent again, this time wobbling on her way down. How much longer would she be able to duplicate that particular move? She already felt slightly off-balance.

Ren took off the holster and returned it to the rack. She scanned the gun shop, a habit she'd picked up from her father.

Check your surroundings. Don't let people drift into your blind spot.

The squat shop with barred windows was located in Burbank, across from a gas station and wedged between a nail salon and a community hall. Just past noon on a weekday, she was the only customer. Even if she hadn't been, Ren knew the squirrel-cheeked man near the register would eventually make his way to her. Since she'd entered the store a few minutes before, he'd telegraphed his intentions with frequent swipes of his tongue across his lower lip, as if she were a meal he was considering.

Even without a weapon, Ren could think of at least three ways to disable him.

Keeping the man pinned in her peripheral vision, Ren surveyed the rack. Shoulder holster or belly band? She wished the choice were an easier one, like deciding between *Clostridium botulinum* and ricin, two of the first poisons she'd ever studied.

C. botulinum had always intrigued her. Its toxin blocked nerve signals, which made it useful for smoothing wrinkles and treating migraines, excessive sweating, and leaky bladders—and for killing someone. Kind of hard to breathe if your muscles can't get the message.

It wasn't the bacteria itself that killed, of course, but the toxin the body produced in response, to protect itself, which Ren found poetic. Just several grams of it would kill everyone on the planet.

Tiny but fierce. Ren's fingertips grazed her stomach.

She was more familiar with ricin, having used it in a couple of early jobs. She'd actually considered returning to it for her current target. Ricin was nearly as deadly as *C. botulinum:* while it took the pulp of many castor seeds to kill someone if eaten, only a couple of milligrams would do the trick if injected. Less deadly than botulinum, sure, but when she was on the job, Ren only ever needed to kill a single person. Two at most.

Ricin was also so much easier to get. Plus there was no antidote, and it came from *Ricinus communis,* a flowering perennial. She'd always loved plants.

Ren blew out a sharp breath. She would much rather have been shopping online for foxglove or monkshood, or even ricin, but she refocused her attention back onto the holsters. Someone in her line of work needed to have options.

Out of the corner of her eye, Ren saw the clerk begin his approach, and she bit the inside of her cheek to keep from scowling. When he stopped beside her, he introduced himself as Steve, despite the name tag that made the introduction redundant.

"You look a little lost," he said. He smiled, and his teeth reminded Ren of the kernels on a cob of baby corn, small and pale yellow. "Can I help you with something?"

Ren kept her expression neutral. *Always be polite. Strangers remember you if you're rude.*

"I'm good."

"Really, it's no trouble. Kind of why they pay me." The corn-kernel smile stretched. "What do you carry?" He immediately held up a finger to stop her response, though she had made no move to offer one. "No. Wait. Let me guess. SIG Sauer P365, right?"

Ren didn't have her husband Nolan's long-range skills, so the .45 had always been her go-to gun. Specifically, the Walther PPQ 45. It was no vial of artfully crafted toxin, but as far as guns went, it had the perfect blend of capacity and stopping power. The big-bore round improved her chances of hitting an artery or an organ or something else that would bleed. The recoil was manageable too, and the grip fit well in her hand.

"Good guess," she said dryly.

Steve's pale-yellow grin grew smug. "I knew you were a SIG Sauer."

Ren turned away, but Steve lingered. From the rack, he pulled out a holder intended to be worn around the waist. "This is a popular one. Or a thigh holster?"

She pictured herself: nine months pregnant and reaching around her bloated stomach to access her pistol.

When she didn't respond, he grabbed an ankle holster. "Will it be for your primary weapon, or a backup?"

Her thoughts strayed again to her collection of powdered roots and crushed leaves. "Backup," she said.

He waved the holster in his hand. "This one's on sale."

Her stare was hard, her smile thin. "I'll consider it." Another brush-off.

Undeterred, he shifted his gaze to her left hand. Specifically, her ring finger. Though she and Nolan had been married for close to a decade, she wore no ring.

Steve's smile widened. Then his eyes found her stomach, and the lump that the tiny stranger made.

He pulled his eyes away from her stomach. "If comfort's an issue, you could always stash it in a fanny pack or purse."

Ren bit hard on her tongue. Even she knew better than to carry her weapon off-body.

"Hmm," she mumbled.

"What about a bra holster?"

Her breasts were tender enough without being pinched. "Another interesting option."

He finally took the hint. "Well, if you need anything…" He motioned to the counter.

"Thank you," she said, staring at the rack and wishing it was filled with vials of powder, liquid, and pills, instead of sheaths of leather, thermoplastic, and nylon.

Ren's phone buzzed in her pocket. She pulled it out and checked the display. Nolan.

She walked briskly toward the exit. Outside, a four-lane road carried a steady stream of traffic. Farther down the block, the wide crown of a lone oak shaded the sidewalk, but Ren stayed near the shop in direct sun, back pressed against the building's stuccoed exterior. She hit the button to connect, catching the call right before it rolled to voicemail.

Though no pedestrians were within earshot, she kept her voice low. "Shoulder holster or belly band?"

"Shoulder holster will hold up better." Though Nolan had spoken only a single sentence, Ren read his mood clearly. His pitch was higher than usual, verging on manic. It dripped with adrenaline.

Suddenly on edge, she spoke slowly. "Having a good day?"

"It'll be better when I get home to you guys."

Ren's hand fell to where her stomach bulged. She pressed against it. It was only a small slip, mentioning the baby like that. But still, even if Nolan sometimes bristled at her precautions, he was usually more careful.

"I'm headed to the gym now, but I should be home soon," she said. "You?"

"Give me a few hours." His voice was husky—the way it got after a job.

They were opposites that way: after she killed someone, Ren preferred solitude. Darkness. Silence. The first time they'd worked together, Nolan had misread the blackening of her mood as guilt. Offended, she'd asked if he would think the same of a veterinarian who'd just euthanized a sick animal.

In contrast, Nolan vibrated. The need to affirm life, he said. The tiny stranger had been conceived in an Olive Garden bathroom after one of Nolan's assignments.

Ren took a moment to respond, and when she did, she chose her words carefully. "I didn't know you were working today."

"Just helping a friend out."

"A favor?" They didn't do favors.

At a nearby stoplight, a car tapped its horn, three quick bleats. The driver on the receiving end flipped a middle finger out his window before turning left. Despite Nolan's ribbing when she spoke of such things, Ren believed the universe returned to you what you gave it. That's why their work was so important.

"I'll tell you about it later. Promise."

"I'll hold you to that."

He chuckled. "I'm sure you will, love." He muted the call for several seconds. When he unmuted, Ren thought she heard sirens. "Anyway, I just wanted to hear your voice, but I've got to go."

The call dropped. Nolan was superstitious about goodbyes.

There had been dozens of such check-in calls over the years: *I'm okay. Things went according to plan. Be home soon.*

Except Nolan wasn't supposed to be working.

Ren was struck by the same off-balance sensation she'd experienced while trying on the holster—as if she might be in danger of tipping. She planted a hand against the wall to steady herself, the warmth of the stucco transferring to her palm, and watched the cars streak by. The flashes of white, silver, blue, and black made her momentarily dizzy. Her nostrils flared as she breathed deeply, the air acrid with exhaust fumes and hot asphalt.

Though the roles within their marriage might've been considered nontraditional, they were still clearly defined. Nolan secured the jobs. Ren planned them.

So why hadn't she known about this one?

Inside Ren's womb, the tiny stranger wriggled.

CHAPTER 3

JULIA

The salty breeze that wafted in from the sea mingled with the tang of sweat and death. Clocking the momentary silence, Julia separated from Cora and scooted toward Brie. She reached out to roll Brie off the man in the plaid shirt. She touched the other woman's neck. No pulse. She held her fingers beneath Brie's nose. Watched Brie's chest for movement. She was as still as stone.

A surge of adrenaline shot through Julia. Turning back, she grabbed Cora's face between her hands and studied it for signs of shock. Her daughter's skin remained dry, but her eyes were all pupil. "You hurt?"

Cora's breath quickened. She didn't respond. Blood stained the right side of her T-shirt.

Heart thrashing, Julia lifted Cora's hem to inspect the skin beneath. It appeared unbroken, though with its crimson smear, it was hard to be sure. She probed Cora's side with her fingertips. Nothing. The blood must've wicked into her shirt from Brie's body, or from the fallen man, who'd gone silent.

Julia found Cora's eyes again and repeated her question. "You hurt?"

Cora shook her head slowly, but Julia suddenly noticed more blood on her arm. Gently, she rolled her daughter so she could better see the skin beneath her right shoulder. Jagged lacerations seeped blood. Had Cora's arm scraped the concrete when they'd gone down?

An instant later, Julia recognized it for what it was: a bullet wound. Her daughter had been shot.

Cora had been *shot*.

Julia struggled to swallow a greasy swell of fear and an anger darker than she'd ever known. She held Cora tighter, but her daughter wriggled against her, growing agitated. "Dad?" A frantic edge to her voice. "Where's Dad?"

Julia maintained her grip, afraid Cora might bolt, as she scanned the nearby masses for Eric. He'd been standing beside them before. Where was he now? And, more importantly, where was the shooter?

A moment later, she found Eric, hunched a few feet away, next to a forgotten throw pillow. A shoe print sullied the cat's face. Eric was staring at his dead wife, frozen, his breaths coming in ragged bursts. *Shock.*

Pulling Cora along, careful not to jostle her wounded arm, Julia scuttled toward Eric. She strained to listen beyond the rumbling of the crowd. A woman a few feet away was on the phone with 911, speaking in frantic whispers.

Julia screwed her eyes closed, focusing. How long had it been since the last shot? Several minutes? Longer? Or had it been only seconds? Time both blazed as if afire and drifted, like floating ash.

Near her, Julia heard sobbing, screaming. Others made no sound at all, lying as still as Brie. Julia couldn't tell if fear or death had silenced them.

Julia had studied guns the way she would any enemy. So she had immediately recognized the high-pitched crack. *A rifle.*

While others continued scanning the crowd, Julia looked up. From where would he have taken his shot?

The arts building? Tall enough but too far from an escape route.

Her head whipped left toward the closest parking structure, but the sniper wouldn't have set up there. Trees would've blocked his view of the courtyard. It was the same with the dorms.

Behind them, the Pacific Ocean thrashed against the cliffs, a steady violence matched by her own heartbeat. Nothing in that direction but the track and soccer field.

That left the office buildings just beyond campus—or the roof of someone's home. If it was the latter, what might've happened to the family inside? Julia squinted, but the buildings were too far away to see without the aid of a sniper's scope. Somewhere in that jagged skyline, the shooter had concealed himself.

Might still be concealing himself.

"Emily."

Julia startled at the rasp from the man in the plaid shirt.

Emily? Then Julia remembered: the earnest girl with the strawberry blonde braid.

Julia couldn't bring herself to follow the man's gaze. She didn't want to see. With her own injured daughter cradled in her arms, she had no room for another parent's pain.

She took a breath and forced her eyes to search. But she couldn't find the girl with the braid.

The man shifted.

"Emily." More urgent this time. He tried to stand, bleeding, but before he could get to his knees, he crumpled as if crushed by an unseen boot. His eyes rolled back, exposing milky crescents.

Julia again focused her attention in the direction he'd been staring. Finally, Julia found her. The girl had curled in on herself. Frightened, of course, but had she also been shot? Trampled? Except for the smaller target the girl had made of herself, nothing else protected her. Julia thought she saw a dark smear on the girl's neck.

She looked again toward the distant buildings, but they offered no reassurance. The sniper could still be there. Her eyes burned. She blinked to clear sweat from them.

She yanked Eric's arm. Gestured to Cora. "Stay with her."

At first, she wasn't sure he'd heard, his eyes glazed, but then he nodded. He scooted closer and replaced Julia as their daughter's shield.

With Cora protected, Julia forced herself upright. Half-hunched, she darted toward Emily, knowing that her awkward gait provided no protection. The only thing that would help her was speed.

She ran faster.

A sharp crack split the air, and Julia flinched. But darting a glance, she caught only the glint of a large metal case, which had apparently fallen from one of the carts onto concrete. No time for relief; she forced herself forward. As she passed a cluster of students, she caught the faint scent of urine, and the acrid tang of sweat. A smell she'd long ago come to associate with fear.

The girl wasn't far from their cart. Less than fifteen feet. But in that courtyard, without cover, it felt more like miles. Seconds stretched, Julia's exposed back on fire, but then she was there, next to Emily. The girl was half-conscious. Alive. The dark smear on her neck was blood, but not her own. Probably her father's. Or Brie's.

Or Cora's.

There wasn't time for kindness. Julia yanked the girl from the ground. Half carried, half dragged her back. But as she lurched toward their cart, the shelter seemed laughably inadequate. A bullet would easily pierce the cotton and paper inside on its way toward her daughter.

At last, Julia dumped Emily next to her father, and dropped, winded, next to Eric and Cora. She checked Cora's arm again. Her wound continued to ooze, but less now. She thought of how much worse it could've been. The bullet could've hit an artery or ricocheted off bone. But it was hard to take comfort when inches from them, Emily sobbed against the chest of her silent father.

When Julia glanced at the man again, with the slope of his nose and his face half turned away, a resemblance to her own dad struck her, and Julia's chest tightened.

Holding Cora's hand, Julia steeled herself for another assault. She'd long ago come to understand that truth about violence: it seldom ended when you hoped. And it usually happened when your guard was down.

She glanced again at Emily, who, despite her sobs, seemed oblivious to the way her dad's jaw had gone slack, or how his fingers jutted from her hand like sticks of driftwood.

Soon the first San Diego Police officers arrived. Other agencies converged on the scene too. Emergency Medical Services. The fire department. The college's department of public safety. Julia also caught the flash of an FBI windbreaker.

As the crowd began to stir, Julia reached out toward Eric, frozen around Cora. Her impulse was to pull Cora back to her, but she reluctantly let her ex-husband continue holding their daughter. His need was greater. When Julia touched his arm, he winced.

"Eric." It was both comfort and a question.

He looked away from her. No, not from *her,* she realized. Away from his wife's body.

"Why?" he asked. The single word held infinite anguish.

She had no answers, so she squeezed Eric's arm, ignoring how her own shoulder throbbed where she'd landed on the concrete. "I'm sorry, Eric."

Within the first hour, a command center had been established at the edge of campus, ambulances had arrived to carry victims to local hospitals, and Cora's wound had been cleaned and bandaged by a paramedic. Law enforcement began lining up witnesses for interviews.

As Julia watched Cora's report, waiting for her own turn, she kept an eye on Eric, who sat stiffly, silently, on a planter behind her. As she did, she overheard two women comparing stories. A blonde claimed she'd seen a short man in a dark blue sweatshirt fleeing toward the ocean, but the brunette countered that he had been a student taking refuge. The brunette was certain the shots had been fired from within the crowd. A third woman joined, insisting the shots had come from the dorms. She'd even seen the flash from a window.

Each conversation Julia overheard went like that—contradictions wrapped in confusion. As she waited to be interviewed, she began to question her own memories.

When it was finally Julia's turn, the SDPD officer assigned extended her hand, offering a card. Her name was Sandra Lee. Black hair worn within an inch of her scalp. A small hole in her nose that suggested a piercing. Officer Lee looked the type to get cranky if you called her Sandy.

She pulled out a notepad and pen. "Walk me through what you saw."

Julia sorted through her memories for details that might help, but all she could see was the wound just below her daughter's shoulder.

"Cora—my daughter—was shot," she said.

Lee's face was sympathetic. "Did you see it happen?" When Julia shook her head, Lee asked, "What else? How about before the attack?"

It took a couple of breaths before Julia's head cleared enough to answer. She told her how Cora had forgotten her cell phone, and how she'd volunteered to return to the library to get it. How she'd started to walk in that direction and then—"My back was turned, so I was looking away when the first shot was fired."

"How many shots did you hear?"

In her head, each shot rang clearly. *Pop. Pop. Pop pop pop.* "Five."

"You say you were looking away. From what?"

"The shooter."

Officer Lee perked up. "You saw the shooter?"

Something twisted in Julia, releasing an echo from twenty-three years before: *Did you see the shooter?*

Julia shook her head, half in response to Lee's question and half to silence the memory, which only made her unexpectedly dizzy. "I meant, from the direction where he must've fired."

"How do you know where that might be?"

Another echo, slithering up from the past: *I didn't see it. I didn't see any of it.*

"I just assumed."

The shots had come from above. She was sure of it. Even with the slight ocean breeze, a person trained in long-distance marksmanship could've hit his targets from half a mile away, or farther. Then he could've packed away his rifle before the first person screamed.

"Your daughter says you pulled her to the ground. She says she didn't know what was happening, and that everyone else seemed confused too. Yet you knew."

"Like I said, I heard the shots."

The adrenaline gone, a tremor ran through Julia's hand. Only the right one. Was there significance in that?

"Others heard them too, but you were first to the ground, according to your daughter. You sure you didn't see something?"

Julia didn't want to talk about her heightened reflexes, or the reasons for them. "I'm sure."

"And where were Mr. and Mrs. Bennett?"

It was odd, hearing Brie referred to as Mrs. Bennett, a title that had once been hers. There was no Mrs. Bennett now.

"Brie was standing next to the cart."

"So she hadn't yet been shot?"

An image flashed: the hole in Brie's head. Her eyes gone flat. Julia chilled, rubbing her arms for warmth. "No, she had been."

"But she remained standing?"

"For just a second." Despite herself, Julia pictured Brie as she had been in the next moment: collapsing, as if all her bones had been pulled from her body at the same time. "Then she fell."

Lee scribbled on her notepad. "How about Mr. Murphy? Did you see him get shot?" At Julia's puzzled expression, Lee added, "He was standing next to you. Plaid shirt. You saved his daughter, Emily."

"I didn't save anyone. The shooting had already stopped." The floaty feeling intensified. If her head weighed no more than a balloon, why was her neck struggling to support it?

"But you couldn't *know* the shooting had stopped. That's only something you realize in hindsight. Even *we* weren't sure the shooting had stopped when we first arrived."

Julia remembered those first moments. The police had proceeded cautiously, herding the crowd away from the center of the courtyard.

Now she wondered, *What if they were all wrong?* What if the sniper remained, hidden on the roof or behind a distant window, waiting, his finger even now resting near the trigger?

"There hadn't been a shot fired for several minutes." She realized the officer hadn't told her how the man in the plaid shirt was doing. "Emily's dad—is he okay?"

"I don't know." Lee sounded tired. "But you must've thought Emily was in danger. Otherwise, why go after her?"

Julia flushed, uncomfortable. She'd managed not to think of that other interview, decades earlier, for so long, but now it kept rearing its horrible head.

You're a very lucky girl, Julia. And brave.

She pushed down the memory. She hadn't been a hero then, and she wasn't one now. "I couldn't leave her alone out there."

Lee nodded, as if Julia had given the correct answer. Then she repeated her earlier question: "So did you see Mr. Murphy get shot?"

Julia shook her head.

"How about any of the other victims?"

"No." Not even her own daughter. "Do you know how many there are?"

Lee's eyes clouded. "We're still assessing the situation."

Assessing the situation. Casualties uncertain. Suspect still out there. The same morbid fascination that had allowed Julia to recognize the killer's weapon also brought to her a list of cities. In Arkansas. Indiana. Louisiana. Mississippi. Texas. Some attacks lasting minutes, others lasting hours. Even days. For years, Julia had focused on remembering the names of the victims, but by now, there were too many.

Brie was now a name on that list.

"I know this is hard, but is there anything else you saw, maybe before the shooting?" Lee said. "In the minutes leading up to the attack, did you notice anything that struck you as unusual?"

Julia clawed through her cotton-soft memories but couldn't find anything useful. "Nothing."

"How about after?"

The muscles in Julia's forehead tightened as she replayed each moment, but the images grew blurry at their centers, like out-of-focus photos. "No."

"Did you record video at any time in the courtyard?"

"No."

"You're sure?" Lee prodded. "It's a big deal, your daughter moving into her dorm. You didn't take a video to mark the day?"

"I'm sure." And if she had, she would've erased every frame.

"Notice anyone else recording?"

"No. But there are security cameras around campus." She gestured toward the surrounding buildings. "Barclay Hall has one, as does the administration building and library." When Lee cocked her head, Julia added, "I'm a professor here. For three years now."

Lee flipped her notepad to the next page, then dropped her hands to her side. "I know this has been difficult, so I appreciate you taking the time to answer my questions." She offered a weary half smile, then quickly swallowed it. "You have my card. If you think of anything, call me."

Officer Lee nodded once, then moved on to Eric. She had to call his name twice before he responded, rising slowly to his feet. Julia fought the urge to squeeze his hand in passing.

While Julia waited with Cora, neither of them comfortable leaving Eric, Julia's attention drifted back to the courtyard. Though Brie's body had been removed, if Julia squinted, she could just make out the small, dark stain where Brie had fallen.

CHAPTER 4

REN

Anthony's Gym on West Pico Boulevard wasn't fancy. Unlike some of the multistoried fitness centers in L.A., it didn't offer Bollywood dance or pole fitness classes. There was no valet or on-site café. The closest thing to a kids' club was a mat in the corner where some of the regulars' children did homework while Mom or Dad squeezed in a quick workout. Located in an older building, the gym was small but not cramped, with gray painted-brick walls, exposed ducting, and serviceable equipment. A place where members came to sweat and then go home, grateful for the low monthly fees that were never advertised. Anthony's didn't draw attention to itself.

Like Ren and Nolan, its owners. *At least,* she thought, *that's how it's always been before.*

The television over the welcome desk broadcast news about a shooting on a loop. A sniper, the blond field correspondent reported. At least one dead, but more casualties expected.

Darien, the gym's manager, noticed she'd stopped to watch. He walked over and took up a spot next to her, arms folded across his chest, his attention on the TV too.

"It's horrible."

His flat voice contradicted his words. But that was just Darien. Ren

27

knew that some members were put off by the way he talked. The way his large eyes protruded. His slightly odd grin. Ren would often catch members staring at her manager's left ear, its lobe mangled in childhood by a Pomeranian. When talking to members, Darien attributed the injury to a street fight. He'd once told Ren that by making people uncomfortable, he could more easily enforce rules with members twice his size.

Plus, he'd said on more than one occasion, *women love crazy dudes.*

On the TV, the blonde motioned behind her, to a stone sign with the college's name. She used words like "carnage" and "fear" and "justice." "It is indeed horrible," Ren said, keeping her own voice neutral.

"What sick fuck would do something like that?"

At the obscenity, Ren's hand fell to her stomach. She hated lying even more than she did swearing, so she left the question unanswered. Though Nolan hadn't mentioned any details, the timeline fit with his phone call. And she recognized his skill set. Her husband had a talent with all guns, but he had few equals with a rifle.

"I mean, who'd take a shot at a school like that?" Darien said. "They're just a bunch of kids."

On the screen, the banner confirmed that an unidentified woman had been killed, but there was no news yet about whether any students were among the injured. Darien's question bothered her. Her hand continued to cradle her stomach and the lump made by the tiny stranger.

They're just a bunch of kids.

Nolan would have an explanation.

Ren changed the subject. "Did you check on that broken elliptical?"

If Darien was surprised by the shift, he didn't show it. "Guy's coming out to fix it this afternoon."

Ren nodded once. "Great," she said. "I'll be in the office if you need me."

Sitting in her office in the back of the gym, Ren turned the mason jar of coins over and over in her hands. The rattle of pennies, nickels, and quarters she kept as mementos didn't soothe her as it usually did.

She put the jar back in its desk drawer and pulled out a blue file folder.

Before opening it, she looked around at walls that needed painting, noticing that one of the fluorescent bulbs needed replacing. She and Nolan hadn't put any money into the place since buying it from her father a few years before, and it showed. Their clientele didn't seem to mind, but the gym had stopped attracting new customers.

Not that it mattered. The gym existed solely to launder money and provide an answer to that question—the one asked at every dinner party and on every application: *What do you do for a living?* Because it was never acceptable to say *I kill people.* Even if those people deserved it.

Ren locked the drawer and opened the blue folder. To distract herself from thoughts of the shooting, she decided to focus on her plans for the next job, the one originally scheduled for the following day but that she would now delay because of Anderson Hughes.

When planning a job, Ren tried to store as much information as she could in her head. Paper could be dangerous. So the folder contained only a single oversized sheet folded into a rectangle. She stood and unbent the paper so that it took up most of the desk's surface, careful not to smudge the pencil as she smoothed the creases. On it was drawn the kill map. Buildings and open spaces were represented by simple geometric shapes. Tracking lines were bolded and dotted. Dates and times were recorded in careful script.

Most people were creatures of habit. They left for work at around the same time each day, restricted themselves to their neighborhoods or cities, ate at the same restaurants. There might be an unexpected trip to pick up a gift for a nephew's birthday, or a workday cut short to meet the cable installer. But in Ren's experience, even those events could often be predicted if you studied a subject for long enough. The latest target completed most of his errands on Friday afternoons, for example, and in the month Ren had been surveilling him, he'd left his home after 9 p.m. only once.

Each of the latest target's habits was meticulously recorded on the map. Ren touched the paper, clean despite the frequent handling. She'd completed her first such map when she was only twelve years old. Her father had burned her first two attempts, calling them sloppy, but he'd beamed when she shared her third.

You've really developed an eye for scale, he'd said.

Two weeks later, she'd witnessed her first kill. An adulterer whose body her father had dumped in a reservoir near Castaic. Though her father could've easily handled the corpse's weight on his own, he'd made Ren carry the feet.

If you've taken part in the planning or the killing, you should take part in the cleanup, he'd said.

The door to the office opened abruptly. Ren's pulse rarely topped sixty, according to her Garmin, but for a few seconds, it raced.

Darien entered carrying a stack of what Ren guessed were invoices.

Darn it. She could've sworn she'd locked the door. She always locked it.

She stepped around her desk, blocking Darien's view, and quickly started folding the map just as his eyes landed on it.

"You planning a remodel of the gym?" he asked.

"Thinking about it." Not a lie exactly. The idea had crossed her mind on occasion. Nonetheless, the words tasted bitter on her tongue.

"My cousin's a contractor, if you decide to go ahead."

"Friends and family discount?"

Darien bared his teeth in that odd grin of his. "Nah. He hates me. But he does good work." He handed her the stack of invoices. "Forgot to give you these earlier."

"Thank you."

Her words were clearly a dismissal but he lingered, his attention on the hastily folded map.

"You want me to take a look at the sketches? I worked with my cousin for a summer, so I might have some ideas."

Ren put the paper back in the blue folder and closed it. "I thought he hated you?"

"That's why he hates me. It was a rough summer."

"I'll keep your offer in mind." Ren reached a finger into the folder and touched the uneven edge of the map, fighting the urge to refold it properly. She worried she'd smudged a line, or poked a hole with a fingernail.

As Darien stared at her, his eyes bulged more than usual. Finally, he said, "You thinking of changing locations?"

She matched his flat stare with one of her own. "Why would you say that?"

"Thought I saw Eissler Elementary. That's Bakersfield."

Ren tried to read Darien's face. She couldn't kill him. It would be hell finding a manager half as reliable, and killing someone just because they were curious wouldn't be ethical.

Unless the curiosity led him to blackmail her, or threaten her family.

Is that where this was headed?

"I wasn't aware you were so familiar with the Bakersfield school system," she said.

"I have a niece who used to go there."

"First a cousin, now a niece. You have a lot of family."

His grin stretched. "It would be criminal not to pass along these genes. I plan on having at least five kids myself."

Ren couldn't tell if he was joking. She rarely could with Darien.

"We're not relocating," she said.

Darien considered her answer. Then he tilted his chin toward the blue folder. "Well, let me know if you want a second opinion."

After Darien left, Ren locked the door behind him. The shooting had left Ren rattled, which surprised her. Even at twelve, carrying that first body with her father, she'd remained calm. She hadn't slept that night, sure, but she'd eaten her pizza without throwing up.

Like skipping a rock on water, Ren paused only a second on that memory before landing on what actually troubled her. Planning mattered. Being careful and ethical mattered. Nolan, far less patient than Ren, often teased her about spending too much time on her maps. Still, he'd never rushed her. He trusted her.

Yet today, without telling her, Nolan had completed a job—one that had ended up on CNN.

Ren pulled the map from the blue folder and stashed it in her purse, no longer certain it was safe even in the locked drawer.

CHAPTER 5

JULIA

The police asked everyone to stay on the scene until all witnesses were questioned. Eric's interview was one of the last and took longer than the others. His pallor worried Julia, as did the way his body swayed, as if even the gentle coastal wind might knock him down.

Julia worried for Cora too. As they waited, Julia tried to convince her daughter to go to the hospital. Cora refused. "There are injuries worse than mine," she said before drifting into a dark silence.

Yes, Julia wanted to say, *but those wounds aren't my daughter's.*

By the time they were allowed to leave, it had been hours since Brie's death, and the reality of it seemed to have settled on Eric. Under the weight, Eric's shoulders hunched, his feet shuffled.

They stopped at the library to retrieve Cora's phone. Cora didn't want to go inside, so she and Eric sat on a bench while Julia went in alone.

After returning, Julia motioned toward the parking lot. Watching Cora lead Eric off campus, Julia couldn't look away from her daughter's tense stride, the way she kept peering over her shoulder. Julia recognized her wariness; suddenly, her daughter looked so much more like she herself had when young.

While Cora knew some details about how her grandparents had died—

with the internet, there was no getting around that—Julia had shielded her daughter from the full truth, meeting Cora's occasional questions with careful responses or, more often, avoidance. Julia had wanted her daughter to grow up vigilant but unafraid, and right up until the sniper's first shot, Julia had been sure she'd made the right decision. But now she wavered. Should she have better prepared Cora for how ugly the world could be? Should she have shared the lesson she herself had learned as a teenager—that safety was an illusion easily shattered?

Cora now recognized that truly horrible things could happen to her. That was a much more serious and permanent wound than the one on her arm.

Julia was ashamed at how relieved she felt after they'd crossed the lot, and the need for action took precedence again. Apparently, Eric and Brie had driven to Anderson Hughes in Brie's Lexus, which still smelled faintly of jasmine and vanilla as Cora opened the driver's-side door for her dad. Eric climbed in slowly. When he reached to adjust the seat to fit his longer legs, his hand froze on the trackpad. For a minute, he sat there, body tensed, door open, until Julia stepped up to touch his shoulder and urge him back out of the car.

"Let Cora and me take you home."

He shook his head but got out anyway, holding so tightly to the door that his knuckles blanched. Julia took his keys, slipped off the spare to Brie's car, and tucked the key ring into his coat pocket.

"We'll come back for Brie's car," she said.

He shook his head again but took a step. Cora snaked her uninjured arm around him, and rested her head briefly against his chest. Then, in silence, the three of them headed toward Julia's Honda Civic.

On the drive to Encinitas, Cora sat in the back seat, eyes locked on her phone screen, her expression blank in a way that drew Julia's gaze to her rearview mirror every few seconds. Would the gift always remind Cora of what had happened to Brie? Would she relive the horror of that day every time she got a text or opened an app? Julia fought an urge to snatch the phone and throw it out onto the highway.

As they made their way north on I-5, Eric also stared blankly, gazing out the windshield from the passenger seat. Thirty-five minutes in, he tilted his chin toward an off-ramp. "Exit here," he said, voice hoarse, as if Julia hadn't dropped Cora off at his curb every other weekend for the past six months.

When Julia flicked her blinker, her hand trembled. She forced it to still. Brie would've hated that Julia was the one driving Eric home. But even more, she would've hated the indignity of her death—face ruined, destined for a stainless steel table. A victim.

Julia tamped down an inconvenient surge of emotion and refocused on the road. Brie had died—maybe others had too—but with Cora's face cast in the warm slant of sunshine, Julia focused on how much worse it could've been.

When Julia finally pulled her car into a spot in front of Eric's town house, she felt like an intruder. She'd heard that Eric and Brie were renovating the place, but she'd never been invited in.

Brie wouldn't want me here. Especially now, when her husband is vulnerable.

The three of them got out of the car and headed up the walkway. The Spanish-style town house was one in a row of identical homes, each sharing a single wall and featuring a traditional red tile roof, stucco walls in pale yellow, and iron sconces. Eric's hand shook as he tried to unlock the front door, and Julia took the keys from him. After the click, she stepped aside to let him enter first, watching as he crossed the threshold. He seemed to be breathing fine, and his skin was only a shade paler than normal. Other than the tremor in Eric's hand, a stranger might have no indication that he'd just watched his wife die.

The town house was a short walk to Moonlight Beach, but Julia knew it was the proximity to Anderson Hughes that had finally sold the newly-weds on the place. Eric had been in and out of his daughter's life since he and Julia divorced six years before, but in the past year, he'd been making more of an effort. The move to Encinitas after the wedding was part of that. He was committed to spending more time with Cora, and Brie had gone along with it, maybe hoping it would help her bond with her new stepdaughter, or at least convince Eric she was trying.

The news of their sudden marriage half a year before had shocked Julia, but she'd been relieved too, as it clarified their boundaries, making a friendship finally possible. Of course, Julia had also been curious about the new woman in Eric's—and Cora's—life, but Brie had quickly made it clear she had no interest in her husband's ex.

Still, Julia had insisted that Cora give Brie a real chance, suggesting the two of them do something on their own, in a neutral space, to which her daughter had responded, "What if I don't *want* to grab a latte with her?"

Julia had pointed out that it didn't have to be a latte. Cora could instead choose green tea.

So Cora had gone, and the coffee dates had become a regular thing. Once a month, usually on a Saturday morning. Until they'd stopped without explanation the month before. She'd figured it was because her daughter had been so busy preparing to move out, but Julia hadn't been able to get an answer out of Cora.

Now Julia paused in Eric's arched doorway, Cora beside her. Inside, there was no hint of the Spanish exterior. According to Cora, Brie had supervised an interior remodel, putting in wood floors, Calacatta marble, woven blinds, and a Viking range even though she seldom cooked. Cora said that only the downstairs guest bathroom remained untouched, boasting the original tile floors. Brie had planned to rip them out the following month. She'd probably already bookmarked a dozen design sites on her phone.

Julia's shoulder still throbbed, and she gave it a half-hearted rub. It was no worse than the time she'd hit the mat too hard in one of her self-defense classes, and it was a welcome distraction. As she straddled the threshold, it was strange seeing the place herself for the first time.

Finally, she took a step, Cora trailing. But once inside, she felt a chill, as if entering a space where spirits lingered, like a cathedral or graveyard. Her eyes landed on the bandage on her daughter's arm. She leaned in. "How're you holding up?" she whispered, wary of disturbing the imagined dead.

Cora didn't answer. When Julia searched her daughter's face, her pupils were black disks, and her body trembled. From shock? Pain?

After Julia's parents died, she'd fallen so far into the abyss that she'd nearly disappeared. It had been the same after she'd lost her friend Cordelia. She watched for signs that Cora might be teetering on that same edge now.

"Does your arm hurt?" she asked quietly.

Cora still said nothing, focused suddenly on a small patch of her arm and the flakes of blood that had dried there.

"Let's get you cleaned up."

Julia placed her palm on Cora's back and urged her forward. On the short walk to the bathroom, Cora continued picking at the flakes on her arm until a small circle of skin was clean, raw.

Julia sat Cora on the edge of the bathtub and then foraged through the cabinets until she found a washcloth. She turned on the tap, letting the water warm. She soaked the cloth, squeezed out the excess water, and touched it to Cora's skin.

At the contact, Julia flashed to the first time she'd bathed Cora as a newborn. The curve of her stomach. The chubby, bowed legs. Julia had tested the water on her own wrist a dozen times before pouring small handfuls of it over Cora's shoulders. When Julia had stroked the damp washcloth across Cora's cheeks, across tiny bumps of neonatal acne, Cora had blinked, eyes bluish gray and unfocused. Julia had been so careful bathing her newborn daughter, afraid she might break.

Cora's eyes looked the same now. Julia's fear was the same too—that her daughter might be close to breaking. Or, worse, already broken.

Julia dabbed at Cora's arm. When she neared the edge of the bandage the paramedic had applied, Cora flinched. She jerked her arm away and held it in a protective gesture, as if cradling a broken bone.

Cora's voice was weary. "I'm tired."

"I know."

Julia led Cora down the hall, finding the guest room on the first try. She settled Cora into bed, though her daughter's widened eyes and enlarged pupils made Julia doubt her ability to rest. She left the blinds open. She wasn't sure Cora would be okay in the dark.

When Julia bent to kiss Cora on the top of her head, she noticed a spot of blood on her own shirt. Brie's blood.

She returned to the bathroom to scrub away the stain.

Back in the front of the house, Julia found Eric staring at the closed refrigerator.

"You hungry?" she asked.

He shook his head.

"Tonight we were supposed to have salmon," he said, still facing the refrigerator. "I should put it back in the freezer so it doesn't go bad." He made no move to open the door.

She reached around him, opened the door, found the salmon, and put it in the freezer.

"You want to talk?" she asked.

He shrugged. She thought of Cora nearby, and motioned toward the patio where they might have privacy. "Let's go outside."

He stepped away from the refrigerator and followed her toward the slider.

On the patio, Julia sat in one of the two cast-iron chairs. Eric lowered himself into the other. Between them, a pitcher plant had started to brown, a few of the once-yellow, red-veined tubes collapsing altogether. She reached over to touch the soil, a mix of peat moss and perlite. Too wet. Overwatered. Probably from the tap too, instead of the distilled water it needed. Julia made a note to prune it. Worst case, she could clone one of hers and replace it. It wasn't healthy for Eric to be alone with his dead plant.

"Brie always hated that thing," he said.

Probably reminded her of me. "It was Cora's gift, not mine."

"Cora and you are two halves of a whole." He paused, slumping in his chair, as if even sitting, his body was too heavy. "Her arm's okay? I wasn't…I should've talked to the paramedics too."

The haze that had shuttered Eric's eyes earlier had lifted. They'd grown bright, like headlights switched on after an extended period of darkness. Too bright.

"She'll be fine. She *is* fine." She wasn't, of course, but Eric was only asking about the physical wound.

"Thanks, by the way. For insisting Cora spend so much time with Brie. It meant a lot to her." His voice was distant. His expression too.

"It meant a lot to Cora too."

"You're a terrible liar."

There was a time when she'd been quite good at it, but she'd fallen out of practice.

Eric's face clouded. Julia had spent years reading him, but she couldn't read him now. "I was a shit husband, wasn't I?"

Julia shook her head. Not because he hadn't been a shit husband, but because she didn't want to talk about this. She wanted to make sure Eric was situated, and then head back home herself. She wanted to clone him a new pitcher plant. That she could do. The current conversation wasn't good for either of them.

"We've moved past all that," she said.

"Everything's always ending." He dropped his head into his hands and rubbed his forehead. "I still don't like thinking about the way we ended. It makes me feel like an asshole."

"Then stop."

"Looking back, or being an asshole?"

"Looking back. I know you can't help the asshole part."

Head still buried in his hands, Eric exhaled so deeply his chest shuddered. "Thanks for looking out for our girl today."

"It was instinct."

"To see Brie like that…I should've let her get her damn latte." His voice cracked, and when he looked up, his face was red from rubbing, his eyes glassy. "Is that what it was like for you?"

She knew what he meant. *Her parents.*

"It's not about me. It's about you. If there's anything I can do to help…"

She studied his face, waiting for him to break down. For the glassy eyes to dissolve into spontaneous tears. But Eric had never been the type. On the day he'd packed up the U-Haul to leave them, he'd been dry-eyed even as their daughter had begged him to stay.

"Do you want Cora with you tonight? It was supposed to be your week with her."

He shook his head. "I need to be alone."

Julia wasn't sure that was a good idea. "What about your family? Do you need me to reach out?"

He shook his head again. "I called them while you were being interviewed. My parents will be here in a few days. Brother might come the middle of the week if he can. But he's got the baby now…"

Julia's phone buzzed, and she checked the screen. A text from Mike. You and Cora ok?

She'd also missed a campus-wide alert and a call from her department chair.

She scanned the alert—campus closed, updates coming by email—and ignored the missed call. To Mike she typed, we're ok.

Need to talk?

She thought, *Yes. Very much.* But she didn't want to get into it over text. Not home. Tomorrow.

She folded her phone in her hands and rested it on her lap.

Normally, Eric would've asked who it was, and Julia would've lied to avoid an argument. Eric wasn't Mike's biggest fan. Instead, Eric's gaze wandered toward the line of the Pacific Ocean, just visible above the red-tiled roofs of the houses below them. "Brie was a good person. She didn't always show that to you, I know, but she made me happy." His eyes grew fuzzy again. "When I was sick, she made me soup."

Julia thought of the spotless Viking stove. "I didn't know she liked to cook."

"Hated it. But she went to three different stores to get the lentil soup I like. Turns out most places don't stock it."

Julia remembered the soup. It smelled and tasted like sweaty towels. "Can't imagine why."

"I hate that we had that stupid argument this morning. That *that* was the last thing..." His gaze shifted from the ocean back to Julia. "Last week, Brie and I bought Cora a gift for her dorm room. A lava lamp, but with jellyfish." He tried to disguise the catch in his voice by clearing his throat. "I guess I'll save it. Who knows when that'll be, now."

"Just don't forget to feed the jellyfish in the meantime."

"They're not—oh. You're joking."

"Sorry. It's what I do when I'm stressed." Her skin started to burn, the memories she'd suppressed years before suddenly as close as the ones from earlier that day. "You sure you don't need anything? Some of that sweaty towel soup?"

"I'm good." His chest seized, and when he spoke again, his voice rasped. "What kind of questions did the police ask you?"

"The usual."

"Like?"

Julia fought the urge to stand. She wanted to check on Cora. Take her home. Have a shower. Burn the T-shirt that was now stained with Brie's blood.

"You sure we should be talking about this?"

Eric grew agitated. "I asked the question, didn't I? Of course I want to talk about it."

Julia knew that what someone *wanted* to do and *should* do were often diametrically opposed. But Eric was an adult. He wasn't hers to protect. Not anymore. "Officer Lee asked what I saw. What I heard."

"What did you tell her?"

"Obviously, I told her what I saw, and what I heard."

He released a long, pained breath. "Julia."

She studied his face, chilled to no longer see the grief in him.

40

She immediately chastised herself. *Don't be an idiot, Julia.* In grief, no two people were alike. "You were there too," she reminded him.

He shook his head. "For me, it's all fuzzy."

She sighed. "I told them how many shots I heard. At least five. Lee also asked if I noticed anything unusual."

Julia left out the part where she'd told Lee about seeing Brie collapse, dead. Eric shifted closer, eyes growing feverish. "So? Did you see anything unusual?"

Julia shook her head.

"Did they ask about me?"

Julia's hands tightened around her phone. She leaned back into her chair, the cast-iron slats pressing into her back. "Why would they ask about you?"

"They always ask about the husband, don't they?"

"Not this time."

Eric nodded, slumping again, his gaze wandering from her to the sliver of ocean visible beyond the roofline. When he spoke, his voice dropped to a whisper. "No one would want to kill Brie."

"Of course not," Julia said, even as she thought, *Who'd suggested otherwise?*

CHAPTER 6

REN

Ren waited under dim light in the lounge chair that faced the front door. Modern in style, the chair was her favorite piece of furniture in the condo, so much so that she'd designed the rest of the downstairs around it. Its cushion, deep and wide, allowed for her to tuck her feet beneath her as she sat, and its sculpted backrest provided firm support for hours spent waiting.

As someone who took craft seriously, Ren appreciated the chair's construction. Solid. No stray threads, no uneven seams. The dark poplar frame and deep blue fabric were also stain-resistant, as she'd learned a month after she brought the chair home, when Nolan had transferred a spot of blood from his hand to the accent pillow. His own blood, from a small cut on his thumb. Not a target's. Nolan would never be so careless.

Ren shifted slightly in the chair, no more than an inch. She'd long ago mastered the art of stillness. She could sit for hours with nothing to occupy her but her thoughts. Her mind, though, never rested. Though she'd been waiting less than an hour, her brain buzzed with a ferocity unusual even for her.

Why had Nolan taken a job without telling her?

A breeze from an open window caused one of the sheer curtains to flutter. A few minutes later, Ren heard him at the front door. He unlocked the dead bolt and pushed hard so that the door flew in, hitting the stopper on the wall. He always opened doors this way, in a sudden burst. He'd once told her he liked to get the clearest view of any room he entered as quickly as possible. But, really, he was like that in everything—bold, quick, confident.

Seeing her in the chair, Nolan smiled—his usual grin, wide and disarming. Oblivious to Ren's doubts. He held a brown paper bag. Too small for takeout. Unless it was the pork dumplings she liked?

As he went through his routine—removing his sneakers, placing them in the closet, adjusting the overhead lights to three-quarters brightness— Ren appreciated the fluidity of his movements. The way his muscles contracted, then relaxed. The strength in him.

"How long have you been waiting?" he asked.

Ren untucked her legs and placed her bare feet on the floor. Nolan had wanted to install heated floors, but Ren liked the way the cool tile felt on the soles of her feet.

She checked her watch. "Fifty-three minutes. What's in the bag?"

Nolan crossed to her and kissed the top of her head. "I've missed you." His voice was low, guttural. As he handed her the paper sack, his fingertips brushed her stomach, a quick greeting for the tiny stranger too, before he pulled away.

Ren opened the bag and immediately felt a tingle of warmth. Nolan had brought her flowers. Or, rather, flower bulbs.

A fairly common plant, death camas grew across the western states, so it was one of the plants she'd been able to see in the wild. Their clusters of delicate white flowers and grasslike leaves grew along slender stalks. The bag Nolan had handed her contained three bulbs. She sniffed to confirm. The death camas bulb looked similar to the wild onion, but only a beginner wouldn't be able to tell the two apart. One smelled like onion. The other didn't. A mistake could lead to frothing at the mouth, dizziness, seizures, and, as its name clearly stated, death.

Ren looked up from the bulbs, caked in dirt, stripped of everything but small bits of stalk and clumps of roots. "They're beautiful."

"I would've liked to get you something more exotic." He knelt beside her, his face inches from hers. His breath was hot on her face, his pupils dilated. "I wish you'd seen it this morning. Every shot hit its target. It was fifteen hundred meters, at least. Nearly a mile. And there was a breeze too, and so much movement on the ground, but still: Every. Fuckin'. Shot."

Her mouth tightened at the expletive, but she allowed him his moment uninterrupted. As Nolan described his morning—the last-minute research, the execution, the escape from the rooftop of an office building—his eyes blazed, the angular planes of his stubbled face accentuated by the tension in his jaw.

When his lips found her neck, bristles grazing her skin, he inhaled. "You smell good."

That close, he did too. Because of their profession, neither of them wore fragrance, so nothing masked the scent of him—clean, like concrete after a heavy rain, with the sharp hint of sweat long since dried.

She reached around him to place the bag on the floor, then pinned his eyes again. "Why did you shoot those people?"

Nolan pulled back, grin in place. "Right to it, then." At her serious expression, his smile slipped. "You can't be angry?"

"I'm curious."

"We've both worked solo before. You don't trust me to do a job without you?"

Of course she trusted him. He was one of only two people she trusted, the other being her father. But though both were expert marksmen, if Ren had wanted a man shot at two thousand yards when a slight wind blew, she would've hired her husband. Nolan could calculate in seconds how the bullet's trajectory would be affected by changes in weather or altitude. He was eerily skilled at anticipating a target's movements. In the field, he was invisible. In the time they'd worked together, Nolan had never missed a shot, and he'd never come close to getting caught.

Her instincts hummed nonetheless.

"You should've told me."

Nolan exhaled deeply, expression softening again. "I would have if there'd been time." His voice regained its husky quality. He placed his palm on her stomach. "How's the little guy?"

"It's fine. Why wasn't there time?"

"I just got final authorization yesterday."

"At which point we could've started planning."

"It had to be today."

He moved his hand from her stomach to her neck, stroking her skin with the back of his fingers. She usually enjoyed the athletic, sweaty sex that followed one of Nolan's jobs. Immensely enjoyed it, in fact. But at the moment, she would've been more aroused had she been unclogging the toilet.

His tone was playful when he said, "Besides, you were asleep when I got home last night."

Though he meant nothing by it, Ren frowned. It was exhausting work, growing a baby.

"You could've woken me."

He cocked an eyebrow. "And risk an elbow to the gut?"

That happened once. "A job can always be rescheduled."

"Not this one. The targets were related, and this was the only time they were guaranteed to be in public together."

So two dead, then, even if only one had been reported on the news.

Ren supposed it made sense to stage a public attack. A shooting that appeared random drew less attention to the victims, and more to the crime itself. The Anderson Hughes attack was being labeled a "senseless tragedy." Calls for gun reform were being revived. No one was peering too deeply into the victims' lives. As, apparently, the client wished. Still, Ren's jaw tensed.

"If they were related, what about an inhalation poisoning while they were sleeping? Or a home invasion?"

"Like I said, my instructions were to make it public."

Nolan leaned in again so his mouth was only an inch from her ear, his breath warming her neck. His lips landed on her cheek, but she pulled back. "On the phone, you said it was a favor?" she said.

He sighed. "Is this an interrogation?"

She crossed her arms and waited for his answer. His pupils had eclipsed all but a thin rim of iris.

"It was a favor for Oliver Baird," he said.

"Baird hired you for two jobs in a row?"

"He's involved in most of our work. You know that."

It was a conversation they'd had before, but still she couldn't stop herself from asking, "You don't find it…curious?"

"This again."

"We agreed we would never take assignments unless the target deserved it."

"We don't," he said earnestly.

"How can one client know so many people worth killing?"

"Haven't you met just as many?"

True enough. But she'd been raised by a father who killed people for a living, and she and her husband did the same. Her social circle was limited.

"What did today's victims do to deserve to die?"

Nolan scowled at her use of the word "victims." They usually referred to the people they were hired to kill as targets. Neither of them used the v-word. A habitual drunk convicted in multiple fatal DUIs, a man who abused his children, a woman who shot her business partner—these weren't *victims*.

"Only two died, and neither of the *targets* was innocent."

"What about the guy in the hospital?"

"If there weren't injuries too, the police would look even more closely. He'll be fine."

"How do you know that?"

"Because I'm the best at what I do."

"And you're certain they were ethical kills?"

He hesitated, as if weighing his words, then said, "These are contract killings. People who pissed off someone enough that we're paid tens of thousands to kill them. We're not knocking off kindergarten teachers."

Unless the kindergarten teacher had it coming, Ren thought. *That's the point.*

Nolan touched his forehead to hers. "I did a good thing, Ren. I promise."

She tried to decipher his eyes, with their too-large pupils and half-hooded lids. "I'm going to need more than that."

He pulled away. "The primary target killed someone."

"Someone important to Baird?"

He shrugged. "I don't know all the details."

"What about the second target? What was Baird's motivation with that one?"

"Both targets were culpable." His brow furrowed. "Why the sudden interest in Baird? You've never cared much before."

Nolan had always secured the jobs, while Ren had handled the surveillance—the tracking of schedules and habits, each a fragment in a mosaic that only revealed its larger picture the longer you stared at it. Nolan was right: she'd always preferred the art of the approach. With little effort, she could recall details of every kill map she'd ever drawn. She could remember how many milligrams of monkshood she'd used on the banker from Santa Fe, and how he'd complained about a burning in his mouth before his breathing grew ragged. After his death, the police found the skeletal remains of three elderly men buried in his yard. She could recite every name. Every sin.

But with the Anderson Hughes shooting, all she had was the news coverage, with nothing to weigh the deaths against.

Nolan reached out and cradled her face, tracing her lower lip with his thumb. "It was thoughtless of me, not to tell you. I should've woken you and risked the elbow." He smiled and settled on the sofa across from her. "If you want to talk more about this later, we can. But right now, we need to focus on Karl Voss. You sure you don't need me on this one?"

Reluctantly, she allowed the shift in conversation. She shook her head. "I'm ready to move on him next week. Voss takes his Labradoodle to a small dog park midday every Friday, which isn't usually busy. That's probably why he goes at that time."

Divorced and recently fired from his hotel job, Voss was a bit of a recluse, rarely venturing from his home, except for walks with his dog and visits with his eight-year-old son every other weekend.

Nolan's brow furrowed. "Tomorrow's Friday."

"I'm aware."

"Why wait until next week?"

"You know why."

His sigh had an edge to it. "If anything, the media attention on Anderson Hughes will distract from the Voss hit."

"Honestly, I'm wondering if next week might even be too soon."

When he spoke, irritation finally clipped his voice. "You're too cautious."

"And you're too rash."

"I'm not being rash. We've been planning this for five weeks."

"It's too soon."

He wasn't ready to let it go. "There's no way the cops will connect a sniper attack in Point Loma with a poisoning in Bakersfield. And why would they? Other than Baird financing both jobs, there's no connection."

She shook her head. "We're the connection. It's too soon. Too risky."

Nolan leaned forward, his eyes blazing. "I told you why we should take the Karl Voss job, but I haven't actually given you all the details yet."

That wasn't unusual. Ren preferred to start her own surveillance cold, without Nolan's opinion influencing her own.

Now she stared at him and said, "Fine. Convince me we can't wait."

According to Nolan, Oliver Baird had taken an instant liking to Karl Voss. Baird thought he was a hard worker. Knew he had a wife and son. So when Baird bought the Malibu property, he hired Voss as night manager. Kept him on when the hotel closed for a major renovation. Family man Voss needed the money.

During the remodel, a janitorial crew would come in after the construction workers had gone home for the night. Some of the cleanup required specialized knowledge—certain days, hazardous chemicals were involved—but most times, it was the same group of three or four cleaners who'd worked for the hotel for years. They mopped the floors when the drywall was finished. They gathered and disposed of the smaller debris. Toward the end, they sanitized the surfaces. Baird could've hired an outside company to do it, but like Voss, these workers had families, and Baird felt a responsibility to keep them employed.

Turned out, though, that Voss wasn't such a great guy. Only later did Baird learn that when the janitorial staff came on-site, Voss would take away their cell phones. Then he would lock the doors, telling them that was what Baird had instructed. Voss would warn them that they would lose their jobs if they didn't comply. The charitable interpretation was that Voss figured the work would get done faster if they weren't distracted, and if they couldn't leave the building for unsanctioned smoke breaks or fast-food runs. Of course, that might earn Voss a fat bonus. Baird rewarded productivity.

But there was also the matter of the woman Voss was screwing. Turned out he was a pretty lousy husband too. For a while, it all worked perfectly for him. He would show up at the hotel, lock the workers in, then leave for a couple of hours to hook up with his girlfriend. The workers were too afraid of losing their jobs to complain.

Eventually, someone would've caught on. A surprise inspection, or the foreman returning for a forgotten tool. It would've been over for Voss. Unfortunately, before that could happen, the pool heater malfunctioned— and Voss had neglected to install the new carbon monoxide detectors.

Janice Stockwell. Juan Gomez. Teresa Reyes. Ray Osman. Those were the names of the hotel workers who died. Between them, they had seven children and three grandchildren.

Three of them never made it out of the hotel. But Teresa Reyes broke through a window before she collapsed in the parking lot. When Voss found Teresa, alive, he unlocked the door and dragged her back into the building. He returned the cell phones. And he waited for Teresa to die. Only then did he call Baird.

The police formally investigated, but by then, Baird had installed the carbon monoxide detectors, and there was no evidence to suggest what really happened. Except for the recording taken from a nearby business camera, which Baird had one of his people erase.

When Nolan stopped to take a breath, Ren spoke for the first time since he had started his story. "So Baird's choices were to come forward, possibly implicating himself and opening himself up to liability, or—"

He finished for her. "Hire us to erase Voss too."

The air in the living room had dropped several degrees. The day had turned cool, but neither of them moved to close the windows.

Because of her profession, Ren understood the mechanics of what had happened to the four workers. Carbon monoxide would've passed from their lungs into their blood, preventing it from carrying the oxygen their bodies needed. Cells would have suffocated and died. Organs shut down.

They wouldn't have realized what was happening until it was too late. It had likely started with a headache, or lethargy. But eventually, they would've known something was wrong. They would've felt nauseous. Likely vomited. Perhaps, like Teresa, the others had tried to escape too. If they were disoriented, maybe they didn't realize why the doors wouldn't open. They probably reached for their cell phones, maybe even searched for landlines that hadn't yet been installed.

How long had it taken for them to realize they weren't getting out? That they were dying inside that hotel?

If the carbon monoxide concentrations were high enough, they could've been dead within a few minutes, and unconscious before that. Ren hoped that's how it happened. It sounded as though Teresa died slowly, but Ren hoped the rest of them had died quickly.

While Nolan was talking, Ren's palm had settled on her stomach. Now she could feel the baby quickening.

Her husband was right. Karl Voss needed to die.

CHAPTER 7

JULIA

As Julia drove Cora toward home, she glanced sideways at her daughter, who was absorbed in her phone. Cora was supposed to be getting to know her roommate over a late dinner of dining hall pizza. Studying the campus map for the quickest route to her classes. Decorating her dorm room with her throw pillows and Polaroids and her new jellyfish lamp. Instead, Cora was returning to the home she hadn't planned on seeing again until she'd amassed enough laundry, with all her possessions again squeezed back into the Civic's trunk and back seat.

And she'd been shot.

Julia signaled her merge onto CA-163 S toward downtown San Diego. Cora was used to her detours—Julia took comfort in unfamiliar roads and unexpected routes. But this time, Cora shifted in her seat, putting her phone facedown on her lap.

"Where are we going?"

"We should eat something."

Cora shook her head, arms folded across her chest. "I'm not hungry."

"It's been"—Julia did the math—"ten hours since you ate."

"A human can go weeks without food."

"But how long can a human go without French fries?"

"My guess is longer." Her voice was distant. But when she spotted the

51

building with its familiar red palm trees and yellow arrow, she uncrossed her arms. "I suppose an exception can be made for animal-style fries."

Ten minutes later, Julia pulled the car beneath one of the parking lot lights and handed Cora her lemonade and fries, slathered in spread and topped with cheese and grilled onions, and a handful of napkins. Julia took a bite of her burger. Though it was wrapped in paper, she still managed to dribble sauce on her shirt. What was a little sauce compared to the blood she'd rinsed out earlier? The shirt was going in the garbage when she got home anyway.

Cora held her box of fries in her lap but didn't eat; she was staring at her phone. After a moment, she looked up. Her eyes were red and puffy. "His name's Bruce Murphy."

"Whose name?" Then Julia remembered: Officer Lee had mentioned him during their interview. The guy in the plaid shirt.

Cora held up her phone. Julia's eyes fell on the bandage on Cora's arm before moving to the screen. Though Bruce Murphy was smiling in the photo, Julia saw him as he'd been in the courtyard: unmoving, with his daughter collapsed beside him. She didn't know why she'd ever thought he looked like her own dad. The nose was all wrong. The forehead too broad.

"He's in critical condition," Cora said, her voice hitching. "There're also reports on social media that a student died."

Julia wiped her hands with a napkin and took the phone. She read the alert—Brie and a student dead. Murphy gravely injured, his name the only one released, by his daughter. Awaiting family notification on the fatalities, the alert said.

Julia handed back her daughter's phone. When Cora turned to face her again, the light from the lamppost caught the scuff at the edge of her eyebrow. The scar had faded so that it was nearly invisible, except for the few missing hairs that no longer grew there. She almost never noticed the scar anymore. Seeing the pale patch of flesh thrown into relief by the harsh light made her own skin tingle. She flashed to Cora at ten, racing across the kitchen in flip-flops, not realizing her mom had recently mopped.

Falling hard. Slicing her head on the corner of one of the cabinets. Holding a dish towel to her brow on the way to the ER. A towel that came away spotted with blood.

Julia reached out and touched the scar, her eyes falling again on the bandage on Cora's arm. Why were so many of their memories steeped in blood?

Julia took another bite of her burger, but now it tasted like dust. She returned the burger to the box she held on her lap.

"How's Dad seem to you?" Cora asked.

"He's devastated," Julia said, with too much conviction. Eric was grieving. Why did she think she could judge him for not doing it the way she expected? She of all people had no right to an opinion on that.

Cora nodded but said nothing, picking at her fries instead.

Cora had been born when Julia was not yet twenty. Sometimes she wondered if Cora had instinctively known how unprepared Julia was to become a mom, because even as a baby, her daughter went easy on her. At night, she rarely woke more than once. She always finished her mashed peas. Sometimes she could be prickly—if anyone but her parents tried to hold her, she would scream like a rabid howler monkey—but she was also curious and loving and quick with a toothless smile. And Cora's twos had been more inconvenient than terrible.

It broke Julia's heart to see Cora now, unsmiling, with eyes swollen from hours of silent crying.

"How about you?" Julia said. "How're you doing?"

Another question on the tip of her tongue: *What happened between you and Brie last month?* But she swallowed it, as she had dozens of times before. It wasn't the time to ask.

Cora dropped the fry she'd been contemplating and wiped her fingers on a napkin. The light now limned Cora's eyes, wide with grief.

She ignored Julia's question, instead asking one of her own. "How did you get over it?"

Cora wasn't asking about that day. She was asking about the one twenty-three years earlier.

When Julia spoke of Serena Bell, her mom—Cora's grandmother—

it was only ever through comments like, *Your grandmother loved dirty limericks* or *Your grandmother once set the kitchen on fire when she tried to fry some stuffed peppers.* The memories Julia wanted to recall.

And they talked about her dad, Vince, not at all.

Julia felt her lips pinch, deepening the worry wrinkles she passed off as laugh lines. "You should talk to someone."

Cora lapsed into silence. Julia waited while her daughter took another bite of fries, chasing it with a swig of lemonade. "Did you?" Cora asked. "Talk to someone?"

"Yes." It wasn't a lie. Not exactly. A counselor had been assigned. There had been an initial phone call. Further conversations had been scheduled. But Julia hadn't kept the appointments. Before she'd met Cordelia, seven months later, Julia had been slow to trust.

"Did it help?" Cora asked.

It might have, if she'd given it a chance. "Mike knows a great therapist. I'll make an appointment." Julia was pretty sure she still had the therapist's card, tucked in a drawer somewhere.

Julia's evasions usually mollified her daughter, but this time, Cora pushed. "How did you get over it?"

Cora's red-eyed stare was an unexpected pressure on Julia's chest. She struggled to find the right words. The ones that would fix this for her daughter. They wouldn't come—maybe they didn't exist.

"You don't get over it. You get through it, but it never goes away. Not entirely."

Julia shifted in the driver's seat, uncomfortable. She thought again about how Cora had nearly died. Inches and luck were all that had saved her. What if Cora had been standing closer to Brie? What if she'd leaned in for a hug, or her toe had caught one of the cart's wheels and she'd stumbled? What if the wind had been blowing more to the north, or the sniper had adjusted his hold on his rifle a second too late? What if the sniper had gotten off another shot before Julia knocked Cora to the ground, extinguishing all the promise and hope that lived in that amazing smile of hers? Julia shook loose the idea before it could take a firmer hold.

Cora returned her attention to her fries, and her brow knitted. They finished their now cold food in silence. When they were done, they wiped their hands and gathered the trash, Julia walking it to a nearby garbage can.

Back in the car, she secured her seat belt. "Your dad's pitcher plant might be dying," she said. "Think you're up for helping me clone a new one?"

Cora nodded. "Brie overwatered it. Pretty sure she meant to kill it." She flushed. "Sorry. That was mean."

Julia reached across the console and grabbed her daughter's hand, still slightly sticky from her fries.

Cora nibbled on her lower lip. Considering. Then she said, "In the beginning, I only went on those stupid coffee dates because you made me."

Julia had *encouraged* her, not forced her, but she didn't interrupt.

"I was angry. At Dad. At her. After so long, he was finally back in our lives. I thought if they weren't together, you guys might've tried again."

This time, Julia did interrupt. "We wouldn't have."

She and Eric had stopped loving each other before he'd started his first affair. Hadn't they? She couldn't quite remember. Did the fight at the aquarium come after the one at the grocery store? Did the Tahoe getaway meant to save their marriage come before she found the charge for the dress she hadn't bought? It had been nearly seven years since he'd walked out. She could no longer put the scenes of their marriage in their proper order.

"After a while, I didn't mind her so much, you know?" Cora said, shifting so that her scar caught the light again. "Brie could be pretty cool. She could be nice."

Her voice had grown fevered, as if she'd needed to sell the idea of a cool and nice Brie to soften what she would say next. She took a breath.

"But she wasn't always."

Julia waited for her to say more, but Cora turned away, her expression lost again to the night outside.

CHAPTER 8

REN

Ren rarely slept well, but her restlessness peaked the nights before a kill. She'd experimented with bedtime teas, cannabis-laced edibles, vigorous sex, and, once, sleeping pills. Now that she was pregnant, only sex remained an option. She glanced over at Nolan, snoring softly into his pillow. At least it had worked for one of them.

Ren got out of bed and pulled on a robe before heading into the office. She turned on the desk lamp and the computer, then grabbed the reading glasses she'd only needed since turning thirty-three a few months before. Even with her glasses on, she squinted. Something about the forty-watt bulb and the glare of the monitor. Probably the reason she'd needed glasses in the first place.

She leaned into the dim halo of light and navigated to her default browser, which came with privacy settings far more robust than the popular one it was modeled on. It blocked all cookies and trackers. Never logged her search history. When she clicked on a link, the referrer headers were blocked, making it impossible to pinpoint the web page where the request originated. The browser's built-in VPN also masked her IP address.

She typed a name into the search engine: Oliver Baird. Ren had researched the man a dozen times, but maybe there was something new, or something she'd overlooked previously. Unlikely, but it was still best to be thorough.

There was a lot on the internet about Oliver Baird. A billionaire, and a father with one of those rare marriages that seemed happy forty-five years in. Generous with his time and money. He was a popular keynote speaker. Volunteered with at-risk youth. If a Southern California nonprofit had an award recognizing philanthropy, it had at some point been given to Baird. Three community buildings bore his name, and he had dozens of properties, from hotels to office complexes to a strip mall in Valencia.

There was less to be found on Voss. The carbon monoxide poisoning had made the news, but only as a brief: DEATHS BLAMED ON POOL HEATER MALFUNCTION. Then nothing more.

After twenty minutes of searching, she typed in another name: Anderson Hughes College.

Not many more details than there'd been earlier. Two dead, though the second death was only being reported on social media. The news outlets were more cautious, using terms like "grave condition" and "nonresponsive," but stopping short of confirming the death. Still no suspects.

Searching the comments, Ren found the usual assortment of grief tourists—people who weren't at the college that morning, yet who nevertheless forced connections into their very public displays of grief.

I worked in the campus bookstore last semester. If the shooting had happened just a few months earlier, I might've been in the courtyard.

The college is less than a mile from my apartment. The sniper might've taken his shot from a roof on our street.

I planned on attending Anderson Hughes, but my financial aid fell through. Losing that scholarship turned out to be a lucky break.

A few stories broke through the noise. One was the firsthand account of a young woman named Emily whose father was the man critically injured.

The young woman described what had happened. The shots. The chaos. Standing next to another victim. The stranger who put herself in danger to save Emily's life.

"If not for her, I might've ended up like my dad, or that student who died," she said.

The reporter described the way the young woman's voice broke when she spoke.

The photo that accompanied the story showed a girl with a braid, palms pressed against her forehead in a universal gesture of horror.

Ren picked at the cuticle on her left thumb, considering. Should she switch to the other browser, the one that existed on that more complex network of internet relays, which would take her to the dark web?

She brought her thumb to her mouth, tearing off a small bit of loose skin, before resuming the scraping of her cuticle. The boards she occasionally visited in the darkest corners of the internet would certainly have information about the shooting. With such a high-profile attack, the trolls had to be sharing theories. Had any of them taken credit yet? Had anyone pointed a finger in Nolan's direction? Searches on the dark web were more cumbersome, the URL addresses random strings of numbers and letters that often changed. But Ren knew how to access the index to get where she wanted.

Most importantly, though, Ren wanted the victims' names. Needed them. While the media wouldn't speculate or share rumors, the dark web would have no such qualms.

Ren's cuticle started to throb.

She hesitated. She didn't like the greasy feeling she got in her gut when she visited these particular boards. She'd even been tempted to track down a few of the worst trolls. But to act out of anger would've violated her moral code. If she betrayed that, how would she be any better than the killers she punished?

Integrity wasn't just part of her code. It was a practical business model. It set her and Nolan far apart from the rest. She knew murder-for-hire scams flourished on the dark web. Since there were few repeat customers, once a would-be killer was paid, there was no incentive for them to finish a job. Even if a client held back half the contracted price, doing nothing for thousands of dollars was better than killing someone for double that. What was the disgruntled client going to do about it?

There was also a robust business built by blackmailing the potential clients. Again, it wasn't as if the would-be client could file a report with the Better Business Bureau.

After Ren left her father to start her own business, her earliest jobs had been found by scanning these forums for the people who'd already been cheated. She grew expert at identifying which hits were driven by greed or lust or petty revenge—most of them, honestly—and which were wrongs that needed to be righted. Ren would then offer her services for a small fee, payable only after the job was completed.

It took only a few such jobs to build her reputation. Third-party escrow services also helped reassure nervous clients, and word had circulated: anyone who hired them came away satisfied—but it had to be the right kind of job. They weren't the people you reached out to if you wanted a way out of paying alimony or if your business partner had discovered your thieving.

She took a breath, pushing the air as deep into her lungs as it would go. Her left hand fell to her stomach, which she stroked with her sore thumb. After another moment of deliberation, her fingers rose to her keyboard. She began typing.

In minutes, she found an active discussion about the Anderson Hughes shooting. As was standard here, most of the comments were posted anonymously. Ren scrolled through them.

Anonymous: whats the latest on AH shooting?

Anonymous: 2 dead. One's a college kid. Dozen or so injured.

Anonymous: lame. I wouldve taken out the whole fuckin campus

Anonymous: No way you could make that shot. My money's on ex-military.

Ren squinted, adjusting her glasses, but she wasn't too concerned. While Nolan was indeed a former Army Ranger, it was a natural assumption for the trolls to make given the complicated shot.

Anonymous: how do you know im not ex-military?

Anonymous: The same way I know you live in your mom's basement.

Anonymous: maybe I live in your mom's bedroom

Anonymous: You can have her. My mom's a bitch.

Anonymous: if more dont die this will be the lamest sniper attack ever

Ren wrinkled her nose in distaste as another troll joined the conversation.

Anonymous: Heard a bunch are critical. The number's going up for sure.

Anonymous: is there a pool?

Anonymous: There's always a pool.

He included a link.

Ren knew better than to click a link posted on the board. Besides, she had no interest in seeing how high the bettors were predicting the death toll would rise, and how much money they were willing to wager on it.

Not much here. She reached to log off, but her hand froze when one of the users uploaded a photo, accompanied by two words: *Kill shot.*

The image appeared to be a screen grab from video, enlarged to the point that it had become pixelated. Ren's cheeks flushed—her first glimpse of one of the victims. The woman had been captured mid-slump, limbs posed at odd angles. Her hair was long and dark, and she was thin, but other than that, her profile was a grainy blur.

The woman was half-lost in the crowd, and Ren's focus shifted slowly from the victim to a woman near her. Like the victim, this woman was already falling too, but there was an unexpected tension in her legs, and her hand was clamped to an arm of someone just out of the frame.

Ren couldn't see this second face any more clearly than she could the first, but she knew immediately who this was. The girl on the interview— Emily?—had described a woman who'd saved her life. This had to be that woman.

But who was she holding on to? Emily? No, it couldn't be. Too soon. This photo was taken immediately after the first shot. Which is what interested Ren. The victim had been caught as her body buckled, but everyone around her remained standing.

Except this woman.

Why did you react so quickly? Ren wondered, intrigued. *And who are you protecting?*

She reached out and touched the screen, willing the woman's secrets to be transferred to her through the layers of polarized glass.

CHAPTER 9

JULIA

As Julia pulled out of the parking lot, Cora changed the subject, as if suddenly worried that saying more about Brie would be disloyal. Julia didn't push. She listened as Cora talked about how cold it had gotten and how her favorite band was performing at a local club the following month. Though it was false comfort, Julia allowed herself to be lulled by her daughter's voice and the strobe of headlights on the freeway. While the specter of Brie's death remained a passenger in the car, it was pushed to the back seat. The night felt almost ordinary.

But by the time they got home, to their two-bedroom bungalow in Kearny Mesa, Cora had stopped talking. Julia offered her another ibuprofen for her arm and tried not to wince when she asked for a second. Then Cora grabbed her laptop from the kitchen table and retreated into her room to stream *Buffy the Vampire Slayer,* her TV equivalent of comfort food. In a break from habit, Cora flicked on the hall light as she passed. She left her door open.

Julia grabbed a glass of iced lemon water from the fridge and shook out one ibuprofen for herself, then settled on the slipcovered sofa with a charger and her phone. Their living room—sparsely decorated with thrifted furniture and overrun by houseplants—felt less cozy than usual.

The bamboo palm threw spidery shadows on the white walls. The striped leaves of the dracaena were knifelike in the dim light. Air trapped inside the house all day smelled faintly organic, and musty in a way that made Julia worry about the pipes.

She switched on a second lamp and cracked the window next to her. Then she turned on the TV with closed-captioning so she wouldn't disturb Cora. With the TV playing in the background, she searched her phone for an update on Bruce Murphy, and sucked in a sharp breath.

Murphy had died.

Though she'd only met him in passing, she blinked back unexpected tears—for the man, but also for the daughter he'd left behind. Did Emily have a mom? There had been no woman with the Murphys on campus. Stomach knotting, Julia scanned each line of the article, hoping to see mention of a mother. She clicked off the article and onto another, then another. It was the fourth article that finally mentioned a mom who lived in Reseda.

Relieved, Julia stretched her fingers, which had grown cramped with tension. But her relief was replaced quickly by anger. Two families intact one moment, shattered the next.

Julia kneaded her shoulder. So there were three dead now. That chill—*instinct*—wriggled up her spine.

Three dead.

She paused the TV and looked down at her phone. Hesitated.

I should call Mike instead. Give him a chance to talk me out of this.

If she shared her idea with Mike, he would remind her that she was a scientist. He would ask what evidence she had, knowing she had none. She'd have no reason to proceed.

She wanted Mike to talk her out of it, because she wanted to be wrong.

Still, she navigated to the browser on her phone.

Since her parents died, true crime had fascinated Julia as much as it repelled her. She'd studied shootings. Guns. How they worked, when they were used. At first, she'd even tried to get comfortable with them herself. When she turned eighteen, she'd visited a firing range. But her hand had shaken so badly, she'd never even taken a shot, and afterward she'd vomited in the parking lot. Since then, she'd kept her research academic.

She'd tried jiujitsu and tae kwon do then too, but she'd never liked strangers touching her. After she accidentally broke a man's wrist, she'd switched to empowerment self-defense instead—safety strategies, situational awareness—but even those classes quickly became uncomfortable reminders of why she'd first felt the need for them. After Cora's birth, she knew she needed to look forward, not back.

So she quit. She allowed herself to grow complacent. To believe that what had happened before couldn't happen again. That she could keep Cora safe.

For someone with more than a decade of higher education, she'd been profoundly stupid.

It's not worth it. Julia dropped the hand that held her phone into her lap. From her spot on the sofa, she could see into Cora's room. Her heart seized, for Cora and for Eric. For Brie too, though Julia doubted the other woman would've welcomed her grief. Brie had never wanted anything from her, other than her ex-husband.

Julia tried to dispel the thought. *Brie was a good person,* Eric had said. *She didn't always show that to you, I know, but she made me happy.*

Then, later: *No one would want to kill Brie.*

Julia lifted her phone and typed into the browser a phrase she hadn't searched in years: Sniper attacks.

Coverage of Anderson Hughes topped the results, of course, but Julia scrolled past these, to stories detailing older tragedies. Though many of the headlines were already familiar to her, she clicked on each one in turn.

The Beltway sniper attacks. Ten lives lost.

An Oakland shooting at a small college. Seven killed.

In Texas alone, five officers dead in Dallas. Twenty-three dead at a Killeen restaurant. Twenty-six at a Sutherland Springs church. Fifteen when a sniper opened fire from a university bell tower in Austin.

At a Las Vegas music festival, sixty were fatally shot.

Julia's stomach soured. *Sixty.*

There were other shootings too—far too many of them, some victims heartbreakingly young—each with its own list of names. Hundreds of rounds fired. Thousands. Ten minutes of terror. Twenty. In Austin, ninety-six.

At Anderson Hughes, three people had died. And it had been over in seconds.

Mouth dry, Julia reached for her water, the glass cool and slick against her palm, as she struggled to answer the questions troubling her: if the sniper attack was random, why did it end so quickly? And why weren't more people dead?

CHAPTER 10

REN

R en strapped on her ankle holster and stashed a fresh vial of curare-based poison and a syringe injector in the glove box.

When Ren prepared an injection, she always mixed in a little curare. A potent muscle relaxant derived from a South American vine, it paralyzed its target in minutes. First the eyelids stiffened. Then swallowing became impossible. And finally, the lungs froze too, leaving the target unable to breathe as the heart pumped a few final, futile times.

She would've used curare more often, but unfortunately, it only worked when it entered the bloodstream directly. As an edible, it was harmless.

After Ren double-checked her holster, she drove the hour to Malibu to get a final look at the Shearwater, the hotel Karl Voss had once managed. Most of the renovations had been completed since the night of the deadly accident. Now only a lone work truck was parked in the unloading zone out front. The hotel would reopen soon. Oliver Baird wanted Voss dead before that happened.

Ren spent twenty minutes surveilling the property from half a mile away, through a pair of Steiner binoculars. The hotel had no secrets left to offer her, but she hadn't come here to update her kill map. She'd come here for them. To remember.

Janice Stockwell. Juan Gomez. Teresa Reyes. Ray Osman.

Her gaze lingered on the spot where Teresa had collapsed, before Voss carried her back inside.

As she packed away the binoculars, she tried hard to focus on the four victims, and not the crouching woman she'd seen on her computer the night before.

The questions intruded anyway. What was her name? Was she ex-military, like Nolan? Was she a police officer?

Or could she be someone like Ren?

The woman didn't look like law enforcement, or ex-military. But could Ren be wrong about that? An unfamiliar uncertainty knotted the muscles at the base of her neck. She disliked surprises, but the woman's anomalous behavior also intrigued her.

Who are *you?*

Near the woman, three people had been shot. The man in the plaid shirt. The dark-haired woman. And the student. The night before, Ren had combed through all the cell phone photos and video she could find on the dark web, and it seemed clear that the crouching woman knew at least two of the victims—including the girl she'd pushed to the ground.

Was the woman a family friend? The girl's aunt? Her mom?

On impulse, she picked the clearest photo of the woman and forwarded it to her father with a brief message: You know her? They both used encrypted phones, but it was best to be vague. Though retired, her father still had connections. He would know who to ask.

Even as she hit send, Ren frowned. She needed to focus on Voss and the job, not on some stranger. A run would clear her mind. Already dressed for comfort in dark leggings and a T-shirt, she swapped her slip-on Converse for a pair of running shoes she kept in the trunk. She slipped off her gun and holster. Then she headed to a nearby section of the Backbone Trail off the Pacific Coast Highway.

Once her feet hit the packed dirt, she felt the surge of endorphins. She ran faster, but when she checked her watch, she saw her pace was off. The extra weight she carried in her midsection made her slow further when the trail grew pitted, and she felt a slight discomfort near her pelvis. She realized this was another thing she would have to give up in a few months. Irritated, she ran faster. She pushed herself until lactic acid burned in her legs, the discomfort in her pelvis bloomed into pain, and her T-shirt became more sweat than cotton.

With every footfall, the woman in the photo kept pace.

In Ren's experience, human beings behaved predictably. Yet when Nolan had started shooting, the woman had immediately been several steps ahead of everyone else in that crowd.

Why?

Eventually, concern for the tiny incubating stranger slowed Ren's pace, and she succeeded in pushing the woman from her mind. By the time she'd returned to the trailhead, her thoughts were again on planning Voss's death.

Whenever Ren planned a job, she thought of her father. As a child, Ren instinctively understood that Anthony Petrovic was different from other dads. He worked irregularly, and they moved a lot, often a few times within the same year. He also kept his bedroom closet padlocked.

Only once had Ren invited a classmate over to study. The girl was quite dull—she hadn't known a proton from an electron and thought Australia and Austria were the same country. But she'd shown unexpected curiosity that day. While Ren was in the kitchen pouring them glasses of juice, the girl had wandered into her father's bedroom. Then she'd asked Ren about that padlock. At the time, even Ren hadn't known what lay behind it, but she'd known enough to know she should never ask.

The overly curious classmate was the last person Ren had been allowed to bring into their home. Not that Ren minded. Most people bored her, and she and her father moved so often she never had time to develop deep connections anyway.

Besides, she much preferred the conversations she had with her father. They talked about what it meant to live a good life. The difference between justice and revenge. Whether humanity was headed in the right direction. And what they could do to be sure it was.

One afternoon, after her father spent an hour defining evil for her, he finally unlocked that closet and showed Ren what waited behind those doors. When he'd handed her his favorite gun, his SIG Sauer P220, her palms grew so damp she'd nearly dropped it.

Ren trained for nearly ten years before he let her eliminate her first target. Her mind drifted back to that day, and the look of pride in her father's eyes.

Anthony Petrovic was six foot four, with calloused hands and eyes that gave people the wrong impression. They were wide and blue and turned down at the corners. *Hangdog eyes,* he was told. *Kind eyes. Eyes that had seen things.* That last part at least was true enough.

While learning the trade, Ren had witnessed dying men mistaking the look in her father's eyes for remorse. More than once, she'd seen relief warp their expressions, belief that their would-be killer had changed his mind. Sometimes reality would dawn next, but often her father's victims died hoping.

That first time Ren killed a man—an adulterer who had twice broken his son's arm—his expression was just as easy to read. He'd been confused. Here was this attractive woman he'd hoped to sleep with, and she'd shot him instead.

After Ren had verified that her target was dead, she'd retreated to her father's gym, where he waited in his office. When her hands shook violently enough that she dropped the gun, her father knelt to pick it up. He placed the gun on his desk and then reached out, holding her hands so tightly his calluses abraded her skin.

"Do you regret it?" he asked.

She shook her head. "He was a horrible man." But her voice broke.

He released her hands and settled into a chair. She did the same, still trembling. Across from her, her father's eyes began to shine with a zeal she'd learned to recognize. "Say it."

She sighed, but she gave him the words he wanted. *"Shield the innocent. Kill the guilty. Defend the family."*

His mantra, not hers. Hers was simpler, and more complicated: *Do what's right.*

"Was the man tonight guilty?" he asked.

Ren nodded.

"And what do we do to the guilty?"

"We kill them."

He smiled. "Exactly right." He leaned back, his gaze drifting to her still shaking hands, and his eyes clouded. "Perhaps this isn't the path for you."

Ren felt as if she'd been kicked in the kidneys. How could he say that? She'd trained for this—sacrificed for this—since she was eleven years old. While other kids were at sleepovers or school dances, she was burying bodies and being homeschooled on how not to get caught. Instead of dissecting frogs in biology class, she learned about anatomy by cutting open her father's kills.

Perhaps this wasn't the path for her? It was the *only* path. There were no diverging roads, no alternate routes, only a single, linear highway with no exit ramps until the very end.

Besides, killing rapists, abusers, and murderers was a far nobler vocation than filing insurance claims in some cubicle.

When Ren frowned, her father's eyes went soft. "You shouldn't be ashamed." His voice was soft too. "Not everyone is capable of taking a life, even of a man so horrible."

"It's not that."

He reached over and squeezed her hands again, more firmly this time. Her fingers felt as though they might snap, but she took comfort in the pressure.

She tried to explain. "I know I've trained for this, but it…didn't feel right."

"You don't like guns."

"Not really."

Her father released her, picked up the gun, and locked it back in the safe under the desk. He helped her up and led her to the chair reserved for guests, then rolled his chair out from behind the desk. He positioned it so that their knees touched.

"What is it that bothers you about guns?" he asked.

Ren wanted to have an answer. She hated disappointing him. But her head felt as if it had been stuffed with wool batting, and her pulse was erratic.

Ren held her father's gaze. "It just felt…impersonal." She gestured toward the safe. "And then I was left holding the gun."

It had been warm and heavy, and she couldn't think where to put it. She should've been focusing on the target, but she was preoccupied as she fumbled to stash the gun in its holster.

Her father went silent for what felt to Ren like several minutes. Finally, he said, "What about poison?"

Ren squeezed her hands to stop them from shaking.

Poison.

She thought of her garden, begun two years before in the backyard of the duplex she'd rented, and the oleander that grew there. Narrow leaves and pale pink blossoms. All toxic. When she'd made the early mistake of stroking one soft pink petal, her skin had erupted into an angry rash that had lasted for days. Her rhododendrons too were poisonous, with their clusters of orange blossoms. Nearby she housed a bee colony, as bees that fed on either flower created a honey with enough neurotoxins to cause hallucinations and, if prepared correctly, death.

She nodded once, deciding.

The decision calmed her. When there came a sudden rapping at the door, she didn't even startle.

Her father stood. "That will be a colleague of mine," he said. "New to the profession, like you." His smile widened. "A former Army Ranger. Name's Nolan Frazer."

Ren stared hard at the door. When she looked back up at her father, she worked to keep her face from betraying her disappointment.

"We always work alone."

"Of course."

"Then why did you bring him here?"

Her father bent over so his mouth was inches from her ear. "Because, sweetheart, I want you to kill him."

At the memory, Ren felt a surge of warmth. That was what she needed to focus on: her family. The tiny stranger. The job she was planning. The workers who had died at the Shearwater.

Ren would've liked to get to know the woman in that screenshot—the first person to surprise her in a very long time—but Ren had spent decades without female friendship. She couldn't exactly talk about work over mojitos, and she now had her own locked closet to protect. Much safer to limit her relationships to her father, her husband, and the people she killed.

Ren took one last look down the Pacific Coast Highway, in the direction of the Shearwater. She could no longer see it, but she could feel it. Feel *them*. Then she slipped her ankle holster back on and threw her sneakers in the trunk, suddenly aware of the passing seconds. She had a long drive ahead of her, and she hadn't yet baked the cookies. It would do no good to meet Voss empty-handed.

CHAPTER 11

JULIA

The morning after the shooting, Julia made Cora's favorite breakfast—banana pancakes with chocolate chips. As if pancakes could cure gunshot wounds, or trauma. Or distract Julia from the idea that seemed even crazier in the early morning light.

What if the shooting wasn't random?

Hours of research the night before had shown no support for the theory, so Julia had finally pushed it aside. Now she poured Cora a glass of oat milk and placed two ibuprofen on the counter. When it became clear that her hovering was bothering her daughter, Julia put a fresh bag of cat treats in her purse and headed out into her small back garden to check on her carnivorous plants.

A patch of albino sundews grew in full sunlight, their tentacles tipped with sticky glands that lured in gnats and fruit flies. Nearby was a patch of Venus flytraps, and butterworts spread with their purple, flat rosettes. But Julia's favorite remained the pitcher plant.

Though Julia had been drawn to gardening since childhood, her fascination with carnivorous plants really began when Cora was a toddler, and their pantry had become infested with ants. She'd noticed the thick bands of pepper-grain bodies trailing from a pack of shortbread cookies.

73

Her shortbread cookies. When even tossing out the treats hadn't kept them away, she'd been tempted to set the entire kitchen on fire—that would show the little bastards—but Eric had suggested less dramatic alternatives. While researching natural solutions that *didn't* involve fire, Julia had stumbled across an academic article about a type of pitcher plant that used the vibration from raindrops to trap ants. Not a practical solution for the problem at hand, of course, but after Julia had nuked the ants with vinegar, she'd ordered her first pitcher plant. Being in the garden again had reminded her of the good times she'd spent with her mom, carefully weeding her beloved flower beds, and as she'd planted that first pitcher, Julia found a purpose beyond raising Cora. She applied to grad school a week later.

Enjoying the sunlight in her garden, Julia selected a sarracenia that had grown snug in its pot. She could've grown Eric a new plant from a cutting, or even a seed, but she lacked the patience. That old dead plant on her ex-husband's patio needed to be replaced as soon as possible. He should never have to look at the damn thing again. Impulsively, she also grabbed a potted Cape sundew she'd been meaning to transition into the earth. Its striking red flowers would complement the pitcher plant's bulbous caps.

She carried the pots into the garage and placed them on the table she used for transplanting, then returned to the kitchen for Cora.

"It's time to grow," she announced.

Cora stopped picking at her pancake and followed her mom into the garage. There Julia handed Cora a mask before donning her own. From one of the shelves, Cora knew to retrieve a bag of perlite, a volcanic rock Julia always used to improve soil aeration. Julia opened the bag of perlite, adding a small amount of water. The masks and the bit of water should keep them from coughing up perlite dust later.

As they worked, Julia studied Cora. "How're you feeling?" she asked.

"You asked me that earlier. Twice."

"And you grunted. Twice. A grunt is not an answer."

Cora sighed. "Unbe-leaf-able."

At least she was trying. Julia gave her daughter a quick shoulder hug, mindful of her wound. "That's my girl. But how are you really?"

Cora paused. "Did you hear that guy died?"

Bruce Murphy. "Yes."

"That sucks." Her voice breaking.

"It does."

"I hope they catch the bastard soon."

Julia let the word pass. There were far worse ones her daughter could've used. "I do too." She thought again of Emily, without her father now, and how hard Cora had taken Eric's frequent absences. She was more grateful than ever to have Eric back in their daughter's life. "Do you want me to take a look at the arm?"

"My arm's fine."

Julia felt helpless. An arm she could treat. Signs of healing, or infection, were obvious. "Hand me the peat moss?"

When Cora did, Julia mixed a little perlite and some peat moss in a bucket. "So...you want to talk about it yet?"

Cora stared at the table. Finally, she said, "Last night, I shouldn't have said what I did. About Brie."

Julia added a handful of washed sand to the bucket. She wasn't too careful about measuring. Pitchers were fairly hardy, and she'd been working with them long enough to be able to eyeball the mixture. The work helped steady her hands, and her thoughts. She waited for Cora to continue. When she didn't, Julia asked, "Does this have anything to do with why you stopped going on your coffee dates last month?"

Cora touched her bandage in what seemed an unconscious gesture, and Julia felt a phantom throbbing in her own arm. After a few minutes, Cora sucked in a breath. "I'm pretty sure Brie was hooking up with someone."

Julia's hand froze in the bucket mid-scoop. Toward the end of their marriage, Eric had been a serial cheater. She remembered the gut punch of Eric telling her he was leaving—not for one particular woman but for the freedom to choose from many. But Brie? She hadn't expected that. "Why would you think that?"

"Brie had a second phone."

Julia pulled her hand out of the bucket. Bits of washed sand scattered across the worktable. Her brain buzzed, but she tempered her voice. "That doesn't mean anything. Your dad has two phones. One for personal use, one for work."

"Brie didn't have a job."

Julia used her hands to sweep the scattered sand on the table into a tidy little pile, annoyed to notice that her unsteady arms sent a sprinkling of grains fluttering to the concrete.

Refocusing, Julia said, "Brie volunteered, and she was coordinating the remodel. Maybe she didn't want to give out her personal number."

"You really think the queen of Instagram would use a disposable flip phone? Besides, there were texts."

"What texts?"

Deep wrinkles creased Cora's forehead. "She was planning to leave Dad."

Julia felt her daughter retreating, her eyes downcast. Julia reached across the table and squeezed Cora's hand, trying to keep her own steady. She wanted to tell her daughter that they didn't need to talk about it, but a sliver of worry had wedged beneath her skin. *What if she was right and the attack wasn't random?*

"I saw the texts a few weekends ago when I stayed over. The three of us had decided to get sushi. But Brie was distracted. Kept disappearing into the bathroom. Dad didn't notice. I thought maybe she was touching up her makeup or whatever because, you know, she's Brie. We had to wait for her in the car."

Cora's eyes grew soft, remembering. "Once we got going, we were about a block from the house when Dad realized he forgot his wallet. So he turned the car around. I offered to run up and get it." She swallowed hard. "I wish he'd gone up himself. Like, maybe he would've found the phone instead of me? And they would've fought, but at least it would've been out in the open."

Julia's heart felt like a harshly squeezed sponge. "There's no changing the past."

"I know." But Cora's voice wavered. The words seemed no more of a comfort to her than they'd been to Julia over the years. "I saw Dad's wallet on the counter. I grabbed it—and then, on the dining room table, I noticed the phone." Her eyes slid back into focus, but she hesitated. She traced a fingertip along the table, as if composing a message she wasn't yet ready to speak aloud. When she met her mom's eyes, her expression pleaded. "I shouldn't have looked, but I was curious, you know?"

Julia felt a sudden pressure in her chest.

"You read her texts."

Cora offered a half nod. After what had happened between Julia and Eric, Cora was both slower to trust and fiercely loyal to those she let in.

"You sure?" Julia asked gently. It was possible Cora had jumped to conclusions about whatever she'd read.

Cora nodded again, more firmly this time, but when she adjusted her mask, her hand trembled. Her voice was flat as she recited, "*He'll get over it. The relationship is toxic.* And they talked about hooking up." She cast a tentative, sideways glance at Julia. "I'd left the front door open, so I didn't hear her come in."

Julia gasped. *Poor Cora.* "Brie?"

"Yeah. My guess is she'd realized she'd forgotten to stash the phone, because she was less than a minute behind me. She yelled, 'What the hell are you doing?' We hadn't really been getting along—she didn't really like sharing Dad's attention—but I'd never seen her that mad."

A dull anger flashed in Julia, but she squashed it. It didn't matter now.

Cora seemed not to notice. "But as mad as she was, she also looked kind of worried. I played it off, as if I'd just noticed the phone. As if I hadn't already read the texts. I was, like, 'I think one of your workers left his phone behind.'"

"You never talked about it with either of them after that?"

Cora shook her head but averted her gaze.

"You sure?"

Cora still wouldn't look at her. "I should've told Dad. I should've done *something.*"

"Stop." Julia moved closer to Cora, forced eye contact. "What would that have done? Now at least your dad has his memories—good memories—of Brie and their marriage."

"But if I'd told him, she wouldn't have been on campus yesterday."

"It's not your fault."

After a minute of silence, Julia gestured toward the gardening supplies on the worktable. "You still okay to do this?" She hoped Cora didn't catch the break in her voice.

When Cora nodded, Julia started dividing the soil into two new weatherproof pots. She pushed one toward Cora. They worked in silence. Cora did as she'd been taught, gently extracting the pitcher plant from its old pot and softly shaking the dirt off its roots. She picked loose the clods. Julia worked on her own pot, saying nothing, giving her daughter the space to talk, even as she thought, *What the hell were you doing, Brie?*

After a few minutes, Cora placed the plant back on the table next to its pot and looked up. "So I was thinking," she said tentatively. "If Brie was having an affair, maybe that's why she's dead."

Julia was suddenly glad that the mask covered half her face. "Are you talking karma, or are you saying you think she might've been a target?"

"Maybe both."

Julia's mouth went dry. Even if she was thinking the exact same thing, she couldn't have her daughter asking questions. What if they were still in danger? "Brie wasn't targeted any more than Bruce Murphy was. It could've just as easily been..." Julia stopped herself, a lump forming in her throat. *You. It could've been you.* Julia swallowed the lump, and the words. "It could've just as easily been someone else."

Cora fell silent and picked up the plant again, meticulously untangling the roots to separate out two plants from the one. Julia slipped on a pair of gardening gloves and started on the sundew, trying not to stare at her daughter—at that scuff on her eyebrow, and that bandage on her arm.

When the plant's roots were at last clean, Cora's eyes found Julia's again. "I was thinking of heading over to Dad's later." She handed one perfectly separated half to her mom.

Julia added it to the sundew she'd nestled in her pot. "I was going to grab my laptop from my office and talk to Mike later. Check on the greenhouse. I can drop you off then."

Cora hesitated, then handed over the other pitcher plant. "Actually, I was thinking of going by myself."

Julia patted it into the second pot with a little extra pressure. "Of course. I'll drop you off, and you can give him the plant."

Cora shook her head. "I'll just grab an Uber."

Julia's whole body tensed. She didn't want Cora alone with some stranger. Not yet.

Misting the sundew's leaves with distilled water, Julia reminded herself to take a deep breath. "I'm not sure that's a good idea."

"Why not?"

Julia put down the spray bottle. "They still haven't caught the guy, Cora."

"I doubt he's an Uber driver, Mom."

"Probably not, but even killers have day jobs."

Cora yanked off her mask and threw it on the table. "You're going to campus. You're actually *returning* to the place where Brie died. But I can't take an Uber for, like, the thousandth time?" Her face flushed. "That's so hypocritical."

Julia felt the heat rise in her cheeks and stripped off her own mask and gloves. "I'll drop you at your father's on the way to campus, Cora."

"It's not on the way."

"Okay. Then I'll drop you *not on the way*."

Cora hesitated, her chin tilting. "Maybe I should stay at Dad's for a couple of days. Make sure he's okay."

Though Julia had offered the same thing to Eric the day before, Cora's suggestion still stung. She forced a smile.

"Of course," she said. No trace of irritation remained in her. Anxiety left no room for it. How would she protect Cora if she went to Eric's?

Julia squeezed her eyes shut, clearing her thoughts as she'd learned to when she was fifteen.

Opening them again, she rounded the table and pulled Cora into a hug.

Cora stiffened before burying her head against Julia's shoulder. Though Cora made no noise, Julia felt her sobs in the slight heave of her chest. Her daughter's hair smelled vaguely sweet, maybe of coconut, but too faintly to identify for certain. Julia remembered when she'd smelled of powder and baby shampoo, and the whole of her body had fit against Julia's torso. Even then, Cora had struggled when Julia held her too tightly.

Cora pushed away, wiping her eyes with the back of her hand. "Were you smelling my hair?"

"Maybe."

"You're weird."

"Maybe."

Cora swiped at tears she had done her damnedest not to shed. "You'll be okay without me?"

Never. "Stay with your dad as long as you need to. But no Uber."

"Whatever."

With that, Cora headed back inside, leaving Julia alone in the garage, holding the final sundew.

CHAPTER 12

REN

Ren had a system.

She started by mining a target's medical history. Was he hypertensive? Diabetic? Was he being treated for cardiac irregularities? For one target with a heart condition, she'd used foxglove, which contained a toxin also found in the digitalis that kept him alive. Until it didn't. Years later, she still found satisfaction in the irony of that.

It was also a stroke of luck when a target was a heavy drinker. Those were the easiest jobs. Alcohol lowered inhibitions and magnified the effects of most toxins, including opiates. Its sedative effects made targets less likely to react when they started to feel sick.

Next Ren considered access. How close could she get to someone? As an attractive woman, she could sometimes approach the target directly. Make small talk. Lean in with a carefully hidden syringe or palmed vial.

But not every target was receptive to her advances. That was the professional hazard of killing really bad men. They knew they had it coming, so they watched for it.

There were other challenges too. Ren never used strychnine in public, for example. Too violent. And some toxins would be too suspicious, inviting postmortem testing Ren would rather avoid.

But sometimes, to make a point, Ren chose a plan that required more effort. Once she'd killed a smoker with nicotine-laced shaving cream. Easy to carry, and easily obtained. There were easier ways, but Ren thought it poetic given his propensity for putting out cigarettes on his girlfriend's arm.

For Karl Voss, death would come quickly and from oatmeal raisin cookies.

Ren held one up to admire her work. Lightly browned edges and just the right amount of golden raisins. The recipe had taken a while to perfect. She'd considered jimsonweed first, before deciding that death would come too slowly, and belladonna would be too bitter. She'd used the latter on occasion, but not alone, and always in small amounts of drink. Because of the taste, it was important that the toxin be consumed quickly. Before Ren had mastered the craft, she'd once baked a small tart out of the plant's berries—adding extra sugar and butter to offset the bitterness—and the target had taken much too long to die. His skin had reddened, and he'd started to hallucinate.

After much thought, she'd settled on barbados nut. She'd never worked with *Jatropha curcas* before; she'd read about it online a few months earlier, and she was eager to try it out. As a professional, she was always looking for ways to expand her craft.

Ren packed up the cookies and checked her watch. Plenty of time to get to the dog park before Voss arrived.

It was a two-hour drive from Ren's L.A. condo to the Bakersfield dog park near Voss's home. Though she and Nolan used to be willing to travel across the country for a job, for the past few years, they'd only worked within driving distance. Bakersfield was about her limit now, especially with her pregnancy-induced need to pee every couple of hours.

Once the baby came, their world would further constrict.

The afternoon sky was a familiar shade of brown. Nearby refineries belched smoke, which fused with the smell of fertilizer and car exhaust. Flanked on three sides by mountain ranges—the Sierra Nevada to the east, the California Coast Ranges to the west—the Central Valley was a bowl, smog trapped near the ground. With her pregnancy-heightened sense of smell, Ren fought a wave of nausea. She decided she wouldn't take any more jobs in the area until after the baby was born.

Even with the long drive, Ren pulled into the lot at the dog park right on schedule. As she got out of the car, she glanced at her watch: 11:45 a.m. She crossed the browning grass toward a bench that Voss favored, taking a seat and opening a novel on her lap: *The Lost Symbol,* by Dan Brown, Voss's favorite author.

At 11:50 a.m., Ren took a cookie from her pocket, tightened her ponytail, and waited.

At 11:54 a.m., Voss entered the park with his Labradoodle, Lucy. Voss sported a graying buzz cut and his usual short-sleeved button-up shirt and slacks, in khaki to better mask Lucy's fur.

Ren had chosen her own clothes just as thoughtfully. She wore wide-legged sweatpants and a hooded sweatshirt a size too large. At a distance, she would appear at least fifteen pounds heavier than she was, the musculature of her limbs hidden beneath the fleece. Underneath the sweatshirt, she wore a T-shirt, snug in the stomach but with a modest crew neck. It would reveal her pregnancy, but not her breasts. On a previous visit, she'd noticed Voss scowling at a woman in a jogging bra.

When Ren saw Voss, she unzipped her sweatshirt, lowered her head, and nibbled on the cookie. *Pretty good,* she decided, *if a touch sweet.* The extra brown sugar was necessary to mask the slight tang of the sedative. Of course, her cookie was a few ingredients short of the one hiding in her purse, which would have even more texture from the ground-up barbados nut seeds. With all this practice, she would be an expert baker by the time the baby was eating solid foods.

Ren waited a couple of beats before glancing up. On her other visits to the park, she'd avoided eye contact. Today she met Voss's eyes and, after a moment, added a hesitant wave.

At 11:58 a.m., Voss and Lucy headed toward her. Though there was an empty bench, he chose a spot next to her. Not too close, though.

He might've been a killer, but he probably didn't want to appear too forward.

He unleashed Lucy. There were no other dogs in the park, but that didn't stop her from racing from one end of the enclosure to the other. After a few laps, her tongue lolled from the side of her mouth.

Ren's gaze lighted on Lucy's coat. Her tight curls and muzzle were neatly trimmed, her tail clipped and feathered. If she were closer, Ren imagined, she might be able to catch the lingering scent of shampoo. If only Voss had taken as much care with the Shearwater workers as he did with his dog's grooming.

Ren nibbled on her cookie in exaggerated pleasure.

Voss licked his bottom lip. Oatmeal raisin cookies were his favorite, and she knew he preferred golden raisins. "I've seen you here before," he said. "But never with a dog."

The question was implied, so she laughed and tapped her book. "Dog parks are quieter than ones with playgrounds." She touched her stomach, just in case he hadn't noticed. "Guess I should get used to the noise, though."

Voss's cheeks were pink and clean-shaven. There were two small indentations at the bridge of his nose, an indication his reading glasses were too tight. He reminded Ren of an assistant manager at an office supply store, or maybe a cop from an old sitcom.

"You're pregnant. Congratulations."

"Thank you. You have kids?"

"A son."

She patted her stomach. "Mine's a boy too." She actually didn't know the tiny stranger's gender.

He gestured to the book. "That's a great one."

"I haven't been able to get into it, but I'm only about forty pages in."

"Give it time. It's a little long, but it's worth it, I promise."

When he wasn't dragging women to their deaths, Voss was friendly enough, so Ren welcomed the opportunity for a more leisurely kill. For a chance to get to know how this monster's mind worked.

But now Voss smiled at her.

It immediately made her suspicious.

Ren finished her cookie and brushed the crumbs from her hands. She reached into her purse and pulled out the plastic bag with the barbados nut cookie.

She offered it to him, but he shook his head. "I couldn't."

But his objection seemed half-hearted. *No, thank you* would've been a problem, but *I couldn't* merely meant he needed convincing.

On the lawn, Lucy was starting to tire, her laps growing shorter, lazier. "What's your dog's name?" Ren asked, chastising herself for not asking earlier. You never asked a child's name—that set off alarms—but you always asked about the pet.

"Lucy." Hearing her name, the Labradoodle moved closer, cocked her head, then dropped on a spot of brown grass about ten feet away.

Ren held up the plastic bag. "You sure? I've already had, like, five." She laughed again. Just an expectant mom with a ponytail and a sweet tooth. *No threat here.* "The baby's about to morph into one big cookie, so you'd actually be doing me a favor."

He waved away the cookie. "Oh, no, really." But he sounded less certain now.

"How about you buy it from me for, say, a nickel?" She watched his face for signs he found the request unusual. He should have. Ren usually had to root through the target's pockets when he was already incapacitated, though in the right setting, she might ask for change or take the smallest coin left as part of a tip. But she'd never asked a target to pay for his death before. Voss intrigued her. "I would've said a penny, but it's worth the extra four cents, trust me. I make a killer oatmeal raisin."

At 12:04 p.m., Voss reached into his pocket, pulled out a coin, and handed it to her. "How about a quarter, then?"

She traded him the baked good for the quarter, then offered a slight smile. "Pleasure doing business with you."

He was making this too easy. The hairs on her neck stood on end.

Voss shifted on the bench and checked his watch. He made no move to open the bag.

Ren tensed. If he'd declined the cookie, she could've pulled the syringe of curare from her purse. But that was risky. Voss was much larger than she was, and even if Lucy seemed exhausted and agreeable at the moment, the friendliest dog could go full Cujo if its owner was threatened.

"Come on, you can't keep me hanging," she nudged. "You've got to tell me if it's too sweet."

"No such thing." She knew this about him. Voss added two tablespoons of sugar to his coffee each morning. This thought made her second-guess herself. Should she have laced his box of sugar instead?

She shook off the doubt. Though Voss lived alone, his ex-wife might've dropped off their son unexpectedly. What if the boy wanted to sprinkle some sugar on his corn flakes?

For the same reason, Voss needed to eat the cookie. Ren couldn't risk him sharing it with someone else, or tossing it in the garbage where Lucy might find it. Voss wasn't getting off that bench until the coroner came for him.

Voss opened the bag and studied the treat. Ren unzipped the pocket in her purse that held the syringe. She didn't want to use it.

Eat the darn thing.

Voss picked up the cookie and sniffed it. "Are there nuts in this?" he said. "I have a walnut allergy."

He didn't. He just didn't like walnuts.

Ren fought the urge to stuff the cookie in his mouth. "Just steel-cut oats, raisins, brown sugar, eggs, cinnamon, vanilla. Butter." She moved her purse closer. "Probably too much of that too."

That did it. At 12:07 p.m., Voss finally took a tentative bite. "Hmm."

Was it too bitter? Too sweet, even for him?

She smiled in encouragement. *Don't disappoint the pregnant woman.*

Voss took another bite, larger this time. He chewed slowly—so slowly that Ren found herself grinding her teeth. Then, finally, he swallowed, the bit of poisoned cookie making a lump in his throat before disappearing on its way to his stomach.

He took two more quick bites, and the cookie was gone. Either he liked it, or he wanted to finish it so as not to be rude. Either way worked for Ren.

She checked the time on her phone, then faked a chill and zipped her sweatshirt. Her expanded stomach had done its job. Time to hide it again.

Alone, the barbados nut would take effect in about fifteen minutes, causing severe nausea and trouble breathing. But the sedative and second toxin would knock him out more quickly. Would Voss die because his lungs stopped working, or because he choked on his vomit?

The only thing she knew for certain was he would die within minutes. She didn't have much time. No longer worried about appearing odd, she asked, "What do you think it means to live a good life?"

He looked puzzled. "What?" When she repeated the question, he shrugged. "I don't know. I guess leaving this world a better place than you found it. Being kind." He grinned, but it was shaky. Was the poison already taking effect? Voss held up the now empty plastic bag. "Giving strangers cookies."

She stiffened. The sincerity in his voice offended her.

Voss blinked rapidly, then rubbed the indentations on the bridge of his nose. "I wish I'd been a better husband. I'm trying to be a better father." He took a deep breath, and his chest rattled. "How about you?"

She could tell he asked out of reflex, manners long ingrained taking over as his eyes started to go fuzzy.

"Listen, I think I'm going to go now." Voss started to stand, his legs unsteady, and Ren stopped him with a touch to his arm.

"You should sit. Why don't I call an ambulance?" She took out her phone.

"I don't have insurance. I lost my job recently."

Ren couldn't help herself. "Oh?"

Voss leaned back and closed his eyes. "Think maybe you should call an ambulance after all. Something's not right."

He still didn't suspect her. Why didn't he suspect her? They often did by this point. Even if it didn't matter what Voss thought. He was already dead.

Ren faked a 911 call, then asked, "Why did you lose your job?"

When Voss answered, he slurred, "Because my boss was an asshole."

She flinched at the obscenity but didn't call him on it. He released the plastic bag, and it fluttered to the ground. Ren picked it up and put it in her purse.

"I don't feel—"

Voss's eyes flickered, and he slumped forward. Ren reached over and positioned his unconscious body so it appeared that he was napping, not dying.

When Lucy trotted over to investigate, Ren grabbed her gently by the collar.

"Who's a good girl?" she cooed, scratching the Labradoodle behind the ear as she clipped the leash to the dog's collar. Lucy whimpered but leaned into the scratch. Ren had always been good with dogs.

After Ren wrapped the leash around one of the bench's legs, she gave it a quick tug. Satisfied her knot would hold, she double-checked that the collar was also properly buckled. She didn't want Lucy running into traffic.

By the time Lucy was secured—at precisely 12:14 p.m.—Voss had stopped breathing.

CHAPTER 13

JULIA

Though Anderson Hughes remained closed, Julia passed half a dozen staff members as she crossed the courtyard. They walked briskly, laptop cases tucked under arms, heads swiveling every few steps, eyes darting. An economics professor she knew casually tilted his chin in greeting, but no one paused for conversation. Julia saw it in their faces: the fear of lingering in open spaces, especially that one.

Julia glanced to her right, her eyes finding the spot where she and Cora had taken shelter behind the cart. The carts were all gone. She imagined Brie's blood was too. She headed in that direction.

She turned out to be wrong about the blood. A faint stain remained on the concrete.

Julia had told Cora she was coming to campus to retrieve her laptop, and she planned on doing that. But something else had also compelled her. Her instincts were tapping like a ball-peen hammer. The official story just didn't feel right.

Julia positioned herself where Brie had stood the day before. She closed her eyes, picturing the small wound in Brie's forehead. What was the caliber of the bullet? She squeezed her eyelids closed more tightly, straining to remember the details. Had there been an abrasion ring on Brie's forehead,

89

marking the bullet's entrance? She couldn't say. But before they'd taken away her body, Julia had glimpsed her from the back. The wound there had been larger, its edges rougher. Definitely the exit wound.

She opened her eyes to an overbright sun. At the edge of the courtyard, someone had propped a bouquet of white roses against the trunk of a eucalyptus. By the time classes started—still no word on when that might be—the roses would've shriveled. Would they be thrown away, or joined by tiny crosses and photos and new bouquets? How long would it take people to move on?

She squinted against the sun and turned as Brie had in her final moments. Julia studied the skyline with watering eyes, searching beyond the branches of the eucalyptus. Less than twenty-four hours earlier, a sniper had crouched on one of those rooftops. She was sure of it.

She stepped to the side to get a better view, then pulled her eyes away from the skyline to return to the spot where Brie had been killed.

She crouched, fingertips grazing the concrete. *Five rounds. Three dead.* The sun baked the back of her neck as she studied the ground. But it held no answers for her.

After several minutes, frustrated, Julia stood and glanced up again. At the moment the sniper had fired his first shot, Cora was standing to Brie's right. Though no one stood beside Julia now, she stretched out a hand at the memory, a reflexive act of protection. She imagined the air was cooler where Cora had been standing.

When Julia reached Wight Hall, she swiped her badge to gain access. It felt wrong to find the building locked in the middle of a weekday. It *was* wrong.

Inside Wight Hall, Julia's sneakers squeaked on the tile. Any other day, the sound would've been swallowed by a thousand others. Today the squeal of her soles echoed.

A week earlier, Julia had been finalizing her lesson plan. She'd started coming into her office a couple of hours each day to get used to being back on campus after the summer. She'd set up Blackboard sites, sent emails to her incoming students, updated her calendar. Her to-do list had been filled with projects and tasks that no longer seemed important.

Julia used a key to unlock her office, then another to open her desk drawer. When she pulled out the laptop, she sensed motion behind her. Then a voice, deep and friendly. "I've been worried about you."

Julia turned to find Mike Hanneman in the doorway. Mike's dark brown eyes were guarded, his grin a fraction of its usual wattage.

Seeing him, Julia felt some of the tension she'd been carrying uncoil. "Hey, Mike." She offered her own slight smile.

Mike had started his career as a reporter, and a good one—he had several awards to his name, including a Hillman Prize. Burned out, he'd returned to Columbia Journalism School for his PhD in communications. He now taught two classes—the Rise of Digital Culture, and Race and Media—both highly requested by Anderson Hughes students. Equally impressive was his ability to mix the perfect Bloody Mary. The secret, he'd told Julia, was the freshly grated horseradish.

She and Mike had been on one really bad date a few years earlier, soon after she'd graduated with her own PhD and taken the open job in the biology department. She'd talked too much about her ex-husband. He'd accidentally spilled a plate of spaghetti in her lap. They'd quickly decided it would be better to remain colleagues and, if they were lucky, friends. Julia had decided, anyway. Cora needed stability, and in Julia's experience, relationships rarely offered that.

"I thought about calling, but I figured you had enough to deal with," he said. "Where's the sidekick?"

Julia had dropped Cora at the curb outside Eric's house. Cora had refused her mom's offer to walk her to the door, so Julia had remained in the car, reluctantly watching her daughter leave her sight. She'd lifted her hand, ready to wave, but Cora never turned around. "She's with her dad."

Mike nodded, his expression tightening. To see him so serious seemed as wrong as the empty hallways.

"How's she doing?"

Julia slipped the laptop into its case, closed the desk drawer, and found Mike's eyes again. "She was shot."

Mike's face crumpled. "My God. You texted you were okay…I feel like an ass now."

"I didn't want to talk about it over text anyway." Actually, she didn't want to talk about it at all. But as usual with Mike, she found her shoulders relaxing a bit.

"But she's okay?"

"Physically, she insists she is. But with Brie's death—"

"Wait. What?"

While the media hadn't publicized Brie's identity yet, Julia had assumed the college rumor mill would have. "You didn't know Brie was killed?"

"Hell no. I'd only heard about that Murphy guy." His cheeks puffed as he exhaled. "I'm so sorry, Jules. How're *you* doing?"

It occurred to Julia that this was the first time since the shooting that she had been asked. She hadn't stopped to consider it much herself. She'd been more focused on Eric and Cora and their greater claims on the tragedy.

The question made her uncomfortable. "Mostly, I'm worried about Cora," she said. She didn't add Eric's name. Mike wasn't a fan.

To her surprise, Mike brought him up. "Eric must be devastated," he said.

"I don't know how to help him." She suddenly felt foolish for sending Cora with the plant. The gesture seemed hollow, and her daughter too far away. "I'm not sure it's my place to try."

"He's lucky to have you trying." Mike moved out of the doorway to stand in front of her. That close, he smelled of sandalwood and dryer sheets. "But Julia…what happened yesterday must've triggered you." He grimaced. "Poor choice of words."

She flinched but offered a small smile. "At least you don't have to make your living with them."

"Funny." But he didn't return her smile. "Seriously, Jules, how're *you* holding up?"

His concern almost broke her. "I'm managing."

"You don't need to *manage* when you're with me."

"I know."

"By now, I hope you do." He folded his arms across his chest. "I mean, we've been office neighbors for three full years. That means I know basically everything about you, right?"

Not everything. No one knew that. Sometimes she even lied about it to herself. "I doubt that."

"Is that a challenge?" Mike stroked the dark stubble on his chin. "Let's see. You love chicken, but you won't eat it on the bone."

She found her mood lightening in spite of herself. "Because it's gross."

"I know you donated five hundred dollars to the Police Canine Association after you watched *Turner & Hooch.*"

"A classic."

"Your favorite color is purple—"

"Because it's the best color."

"—but last year it was yellow, which is why your bathroom looks like the scene of a lemon turf war."

"That wouldn't happen. Lemons are a peaceful fruit."

Mike quirked a brow. "Are there fruits that *aren't* peaceful?"

"Pomegranates. Obviously."

"Obviously?"

"Have you ever seen a pomegranate in a fruit salad? No. Because they don't get along with the others."

He laughed. "You just don't like pomegranates. Or papaya, because it smells like feet."

"Ha!" Julia pointed a finger at him. "You got one wrong. Papaya *tastes* like feet."

He continued, snapping his fingers. "Oh—I also know you love corny jokes."

"Okay. There's a kernel of truth in that."

He groaned, but his grin widened. "You also never take the same way home twice in a row, and you named your daughter after a mysterious young woman you seem to have met after your parents died." He paused. "So, Jules, I just want to make sure you're okay."

Julia hadn't realized he knew quite so much. *Damn those Bloody Marys.*

"Were you on campus yesterday?" she asked finally.

"I was leaving my office when I heard the shots, though I didn't know that's what they were at first. When I figured out what it was, I called 911. Like everyone else, I guess." He looked at her. "Were you close to Brie? I mean, proximity-wise?"

"Yes." *But Cora was closer.* Julia couldn't say those last words aloud.

Even as she buried the thought, another wriggled toward consciousness. In her mind, she was back outside, again touching the concrete, staring across the wide-open courtyard. That makeshift memorial. *What was it that kept bothering her?*

"I'm so sorry, Jules. Whatever you need...," Mike was saying, his voice husky.

Coming back to the moment, she nodded in thanks and cleared her throat. "Have you heard anything about the investigation?"

"At least a dozen injured, but most of those were during the chaos after the shots. It's lucky more people weren't killed."

Lucky. "About that." She stopped, unsure if she should share her doubts with Mike. But if not with him, then with who? "Do you think it's strange that more people didn't die?"

"He might've missed some of his targets."

"You didn't see Brie." Julia jabbed a finger in her forehead. "The bullet entered here. Perfect shot. A sniper who can do that doesn't miss."

"You don't know that. Making that shot might've been as much chance as missing the others."

She wanted to believe him. If Brie's shooting was random, that meant Cora's was too. But still she asked, "Then why did he stop? A magazine can hold, what? Ten bullets? A hundred? Why only fire five?"

He reached out and rested his hand on hers. His skin felt warm, real. "Jules..."

Her throat constricted, and she swallowed hard at the memory she'd been repressing for years—so well that until yesterday she'd managed to barely think of it at all. But now, under Mike's worried eyes, she was just shy of fifteen again, stepping outside her parents' home to meet the police in the driveway, pointing, only pointing, at the house behind her.

They'd found her mom splayed on the lawn in the backyard near the dying palm, the one she'd constantly been trying to save. Whenever Julia thought of that day, that's what she saw first: her mother's nearly black blood beading on the dandelions, beneath a canopy of brown and brittle fronds.

With the memory, the idea that had been evading her coalesced into a cold lump in her gut. *The eucalyptus.*

"Have you heard anything about who else was wounded?"

Mike's forehead furrowed. "I saw a guy in the center of the courtyard who'd been shot in the leg. He looked to be in his fifties."

"With Cora, and Murphy and Brie, that's four rounds. Four of five." Julia couldn't keep her hands from beginning to shake.

"What are you getting at?"

"Near the center of the courtyard, two dead, two wounded. The unidentified student who died—the fifth bullet—might've been near us too." Outside, she'd had to step to the side to get a better view of the skyline. "But that angle wasn't optimal. The sniper's view would've been partially obstructed by the trees. Strange, if his targets were random."

Mike said nothing for a moment, then let out a sharp breath. "Regardless, the police will get there on their own. *If* it wasn't random."

"Cora was shot, Mike. I need to know." When he went silent again, she said, "Brie might've been cheating on Eric."

His brow creased. "Did Eric tell you that?"

"Cora. She found Brie's second phone."

"Damn. Poor Cora." He hesitated, and his expression darkened. Not anger exactly. Something else Julia couldn't quite identify. "Look, Jules, you're not being yourself. What matters right now is that you and Cora are safe. Let the police do the investigating."

Mike was right. What mattered was that Cora was alive.

But even as Julia tried to convince herself that she could let it go—that she could swallow this memory as she had so many others—all she could see was Cora's wound, which looked more and more like the one in her mother's chest twenty-three years before.

CHAPTER 14

REN

Ren hated the beach. It was loud, crowded, and the seabirds crapped everywhere. Then there was the sand. Had she worn a hermetically sealed suit, she wouldn't have been able to prevent the grains from caking her skin. But her father lived near Dockweiler State Beach in the Playa del Rey neighborhood, so that was where they met. *When* they met. It had been a couple of months since the last time. Before she found out she was pregnant.

After killing Voss, Ren had intended to return to the condo. Check in with Nolan. Going directly home was her routine after a job, and it's what Nolan, as her business partner, would expect. Ren texted Nolan to let him know she'd be late.

Anthony Petrovic approached with his hands in his pockets, his back stiff. Ren leaned in for an awkward hug that left them both uncomfortable.

Despite his rigid posture, his eyes warmed. "Great to see you."

She stepped back. "Yeah, it's been a while."

A plane departing nearby LAX roared overhead. That was the one thing Ren didn't mind about that particular beach. She enjoyed watching the planes come and go.

"I don't think you've ever visited without at least a day's notice," he said. "What's up, kiddo?"

A wind gust made Ren grateful she still wore a ponytail. She tucked some stray hair behind her ear and then stuffed her hands in her sweat-shirt pockets. She pulled the fleece away from her stomach to hide the baby bump.

"What was it like with that guy in Ventura?" she asked.

His face remained unreadable. "That was more than thirty years ago."

"And you have an excellent memory."

Her father started walking, and Ren followed. Though it was still a few hours before sunset, flames danced in many of the distant fire pits. She and her father avoided the people clustered around them. Same for the picnic benches.

"He wasn't innocent, that guy," her father said. "He may not have done what I thought he had, what my client thought he had, but he'd committed other crimes."

Ren knew the details well enough. It was one of her father's first kills, a man suspected in the stabbing death of his neighbor. Her father believed he'd gotten off on a technicality—until the neighbor's girlfriend was arrested. But by then, the man had been dead for two weeks.

That case was the reason her father insisted that her own research be thorough.

"I know that," she said. Even if the guy in Ventura hadn't killed his neighbor, the police had good reason to suspect him. He'd already served time for home invasion, and he was linked to a few thefts.

Ren took a step and grimaced when the sand breached her sneaker. "When did you realize it wasn't him?"

Her father pretended to consider the question, but she knew he'd committed that day's details to memory. After a moment, he said, "Right after I shot him."

The sand made it into Ren's sock, the grit scratching the soft skin below her ankle.

"How did you know?"

This time, he didn't hesitate. "He looked surprised. Guilty men know it's coming. Even if they don't know when, they aren't surprised by it." He paused to study her face. "Why are you asking?"

"The man I killed an hour ago had no idea I'd poisoned him." From her surveillance, she'd known it could be a fairly simple job. But in hindsight, had it been too easy? He'd taken the cookie, and he'd never left the bench, even when his eyes lost focus.

Voss had trusted her.

"That does sound like a problem," he said. "I assume you did your research." He knew not to make it a question but paused in case she wanted to correct him. When she didn't, he asked, "Any red flags?"

She stepped over a cigarette butt. "Other than the ease of it, nothing."

The targets came to her fully vetted by Nolan, but Ren studied them for weeks too. She'd seen Voss roll through red lights. Cut in lines. Walk through his neighbor's flower bed to save himself a few seconds. Voss had been the kind of guy who considered his own needs first, and everyone else's not at all.

Except for his dog. He'd always been kind to Lucy.

"You feel good about the kill?" her father asked.

She didn't hesitate. "Yes."

"So what do you do if you're second-guessing yourself?"

Again, she answered quickly. "More research."

"More research," he echoed.

They walked several steps in silence. A salty wind whipped Ren's ponytail, and when she tightened it, she felt sand on her scalp. Ahead of them, tiny pale seabirds skittered along the shoreline, stopping occasionally to peck at the ground. For worms? Insects? She shuddered.

"Nolan thinks I've gone soft," she said finally.

Her father stopped walking. "That's bullshit," he said, offended, as if Nolan's doubts reflected on him. "Why would he think that?"

Ren tugged on her sweatshirt. She wasn't sure he would approve of the baby. But she never lied to her father.

"I'm pregnant. And the target had a son."

The only reaction to her news was a slight gathering of his eyebrows. "But you killed him anyway," he pointed out.

"Yes."

"So what's Nolan's problem?" Ren's father exhaled deeply. "You should've killed him when I introduced you."

She half smiled. Despite his directive the day he'd ordered her to kill Nolan, her father had never intended she go through with it. It had been a test. Would it have been an ethical kill? And a lesson: *Be sure before you kill.*

A few hours before, Voss had deserved his fate. Ren was certain of it. Unfortunately, she was equally certain she didn't understand what had really motivated the hit.

"If I'd killed Nolan, you never would've worked with me again," she said.

"True. But did you have to marry him?"

"You like Nolan."

"Not if he's accusing my daughter of going soft." His gaze fell to her stomach. "Pregnant, huh?"

"Four months."

He nodded, but she couldn't quite tell if it was in approval. "Have you thought about taking time off?"

"I'm not going soft."

"Not saying you are." He tilted his chin toward her midsection. "*Shield the innocent,* remember? Nothing more innocent than a baby. And *defend the family.* That there's a two-for-one."

In an effort not to roll her eyes, she scanned the waterline. Near where the surf lapped the shore, a large shard of a beer bottle jutted from the damp sand. There were dangers everywhere, if you knew to look for them.

"I think Nolan sees the pregnancy as a liability. I can't make money if I'm breastfeeding." Which was ridiculous. She'd already bought a pump and several sets of bottles.

"Priorities."

"My priority is taking care of the baby. Which means working."

"Wouldn't be the worst idea to take some time off. You're more visible pregnant. More memorable too."

Ren was too busy thinking to be irritated. What if, postdelivery, she wore one of those fake stomachs? That would be all people noticed about her. The perfect disguise. And she could get one custom-made with a pocket to stash a syringe.

"People are also more trusting of pregnant women," she said.

Above them, another plane roared, its white composite skin splitting the sky. Ren imagined herself in one of its seats, her ears popping and her stomach surging. She thought of all the places she and Nolan had flown for work: Nampa, Idaho; Bisbee, Arizona; Green Bay, Wisconsin. That was before they'd commanded tens of thousands for a job. Before they'd met Baird.

Maybe her father was right about taking some time off. For a moment, she wished she were on that plane, elbow to elbow with the other passengers—the anonymous woman in seat 14A, who watched out the window as the plane steadied seven miles into the air, the world she'd left behind obscured by clouds.

She stared at the sky until the plane disappeared, hand pressed to her stomach.

"You should consider switching it up, at least," her father said, watching her.

She immediately understood what he was suggesting. "No," she said firmly. "No guns."

"Then maybe Nolan can do most of the jobs, at least for a while."

It wasn't that Ren hadn't considered the same thing, but she bristled. No one made career decisions for her. Not her father. Not her husband.

She changed the subject. "He did a job before telling me. Yesterday."

"Anderson Hughes?"

She wasn't surprised he'd made the connection. Though he'd retired a few years before, her father still knew people. "Yes."

"Did he say why he kept it from you?"

"He said there wasn't time. It was last-minute."

She didn't add that Murphy's death had been an accident. A mistake.

"A sniper attack with no planning?" His face still gave nothing away, but she sensed his concern.

"There was some planning. And he clearly got it right." *Except for Bruce Murphy.*

"Okay, then a minimum of planning."

Even though she'd been the one to bring it up and harbored her own doubts, she felt the sudden need to defend Nolan. "It was a regular client."

Instead of appeasing him, as she'd intended, the comment caused her father's face to darken. "You guys have regular clients?"

"Just one."

"That's dangerous."

"He has more to lose than we do."

"Exactly." Her father's eyes locked on hers. "This regular client doesn't know who you are, though? You've never met him in person?"

"I haven't." Not a lie exactly. Nolan had been the one to meet with Oliver Baird. "He pays well."

"It's *kill the guilty.* Not *kill to get rich.*"

Ren flashed to Nolan's face when she'd asked if the Anderson Hughes kills were ethical. He'd assured her they were—but first, he'd hesitated. "Those aren't mutually exclusive," she told her father. "Especially given our skill set."

"Still. Be careful with that one."

A woman jogged by holding the leash of a large mixed breed. It reminded Ren of Voss's dog. Ren wondered if someone had freed Lucy yet, or if she was still tethered to the bench where Voss lay dead.

"I'll be careful."

"You carrying?"

She grew suddenly aware of the holster tight on her ankle. Probably sand in there by now too. At least she had her curare-based sedative in the glove box.

"I'm carrying," she said.

His expression softened. Ren's father wasn't the sentimental type, but he reached over and squeezed her arm.

"Good. I wouldn't want you or my grandchild to end up dead." He reached into his pocket for his phone. "By the way, I found the woman in the photo you texted." He held up his phone so she could see the screen. Ren's breath caught in her throat.

It's her.

"She's an assistant professor of botany at Anderson Hughes. Julia Bennett."

Julia Bennett. A botany professor. That wasn't what she'd expected. An unexpected warmth filled Ren.

Only a mother, then, but she liked plants too.

CHAPTER 15

JULIA

Mike followed Julia to Encinitas in Brie's car. After they dropped off the Lexus and Julia returned him to his own truck on campus, she drove to another lot nearby and parked in her usual spot. She grabbed her laptop and got out of the car. Without Cora, there was only one place that might still feel like home, might offer her a chance to think through everything Mike had said. Julia walked briskly toward the familiar plexiglass panels of the Anderson Hughes Memorial Greenhouse. She fished in her purse for her keys. The greenhouse was divided into three biomes, separated by sliding doors. The desert biome was kept hot and arid for the prickly pear, ice plants, and barrel cactus that grew there. The tropical biome, with its palms and orchids, featured a sawtooth roof that allowed venting of the warm, swampy air. And then there was the largest of the biomes, the one that housed plants grown in more temperate climates.

The kinds of plants Julia's mom had grown.

Julia could still see the small plastic shovel her mom had given her the day she'd asked Julia to help plant a flat of wildflowers. How old had she been? Five? Six? What kind of flowers had they been? Julia couldn't remember those details, but she could feel the warmth of the soil sifting through her fingers, and she could smell her mom's freshly bleached gardening apron.

Then, just as vividly, she felt the stir of the air caused by the old fan, saw an open back door that both repulsed and compelled her. And on the other side of the door, in the yard—

Laptop tucked under her arm, Julia fumbled her keys, dropping them on the gravel.

Get it together, Julia.

She picked up her keys and steadied her hands to open the padlock.

When Julia entered the temperate biome, she found the cat asleep on a bag of potting soil.

Cora had named the notch-eared tabby Cilantro. The cat had unofficially taken up residence in the greenhouse a year before, squeezing her way in through cracked doors and open windows, drawn by mice fattened on stolen acorns and sunflower seeds.

Julia put her laptop down and returned her keys to her purse, reaching inside for the small plastic bag she'd stashed there earlier. Recognizing the movement, the tabby stretched, yawned, and arched her back before sauntering across the room. She stopped at Julia's feet and blinked expectantly—Cilantro would never debase herself by meowing—and Julia shook a few treats into her palm. Cilantro allowed Julia to stroke her head with her free hand as she gobbled up the treats. Then, done, she offered one quick lick of Julia's palm and stalked back to her bag of potting soil.

Julia refilled the cat's water bowl, checked the mousetraps—all empty— and set up her laptop on one of the worktables near the marigolds and zinnias. She grabbed a stool from the utility room, then logged on, intending to record data on the nearby plants, an activity that always soothed her. How tall were they now? How many leaves? And how many plants had produced flower buds? She'd share these early charts with her incoming fall class, who'd help her monitor over the coming months.

Her thoughts drifted to her students. How were they coping? How many would return to campus, and how many would decide to take the semester off? She thought of Emily Murphy and the unidentified student who'd died. Other students were likely among the injured. And even those who weren't hurt, or who hadn't lost someone, would forever be marked by the violence.

She backed out of her spreadsheet and started googling. Had any new information been released? Had she missed any details in the haze of last night? She knew it was inevitable that she would begin her grim routine— she couldn't help it—and twenty minutes later, she was clicking on the link for an old story about an attack in Toledo, Ohio.

Scrolling through the comments section, she froze, stopped by a simple sentence posted on the Mother's Day following the attack.

I'll never stop missing you, Mom.

Julia fought for breath. Though insignificant to her investigation, the comment made it all too much. The shooting the day before. Bandaging her daughter's wound. Talking with Mike. *Brie.* The weight of it all grew suddenly too heavy and, finally alone, finally somewhere she could let her guard down, the door she'd kept closed for more than twenty years blew open. While the world inside the greenhouse blurred, the vision out that back door, of dark blood on the green grass, opened as vividly as it had the day she'd met the police on the drive.

It'd been the week of Julia's fifteenth birthday. And it had been because a man had dumped a body in the lake near the Bell house. Or what passed for a lake, anyway. Julia had always thought that was too fancy a word for it, given its small size and general stink. In the summer, the lake retreated from its banks, leaving behind skid marks of algae and the reek of rotting carp, though even in the winter, it maintained an oily and fetid sheen.

In Julia's opinion, "house" might've been too grand a term too. Her family lived in a mobile home. Not a manufactured home either, but a trailer that could be hooked up to a truck and hauled away in the middle of the night if a family got too far behind on space rent. The Bells were always a few weeks away from one of those midnight escapes, though her father would've had to borrow a truck to tow the trailer. But at least they had a yard. Julia's mom, Serena, loved that tiny patch of grass and the small garden, tending both with as much care as if they were the greens at Pebble Beach.

The day the man dumped the body, the weather was unremarkable. Temperatures hovered around seventy with a muted sun and the faintest of breezes. But Serena Bell liked a cool house, so she'd set up an oscillating fan by the kitchen window.

The fight between Julia's parents started earlier than usual, and it had a scalpel's edge to it she'd never heard before—the words sharper, the wounds deeper. It began as an argument over the cable bill and became one about the electricity payment that had bounced. Her parents' fights were always about money. But that day, the fight turned to how her dad had failed to provide for his family, how her mom had failed as a wife. A thousand synonyms for inadequacy aimed with pointed precision. When Vince and Serena Bell fought, it was always better to be somewhere else, but that morning Julia's urge to flee vibrated beneath her skin. She left without grabbing her wallet, an oversight she would later regret.

Julia decided the somewhere else she needed to be that day was the bookstore. She passed the fan on her way out. She considered turning it off. Too close to the window, the curtains might get tangled in the blades.

She moved the fan farther from the window but left it oscillating, then slipped out of the house.

At the mobile home park's entrance, Julia was nearly hit by a man in a battered sedan headed toward the lake. She didn't make note of his license plate. At that point, she had no reason to know the driver's name was Walter Brooks, or suspect he'd stashed his cousin's body in the trunk.

At the bookstore, Julia selected a novel and found a quiet spot to read. She managed only one chapter before an employee started looking at her sideways. Reaching for her wallet, Julia realized she'd forgotten it at home. She had no money to buy the book.

The walk home took twelve minutes. Later, she learned that had it taken eight, she likely would've encountered Walter Brooks in his battered sedan again, this time on his way out. Had her walk taken sixteen minutes, the police would've already arrived.

If Julia had read another chapter, or lingered at the register with cash in hand, the police would've found her mom's body instead.

The man who killed Serena Bell was an addict. In hindsight, Julia shouldn't have been surprised. Who else but a dangerously high man with compromised reasoning skills would've chosen a crap lake near a mobile home park as his dumping ground instead of the nearby reservoir or open desert?

According to his confession a few days later, Walter Brooks hadn't planned on killing Serena Bell. After he'd dumped his cousin's body, he'd turned to leave. But then he noticed someone peering at him through the curtains.

Of course, the fluttering hadn't been caused by a person at all. It had been caused by the oscillating fan.

When Walter Brooks came to the front door, Julia's mom answered, because she always did that kind of thing—answered a door without asking who was on the other side.

Julia's dad, Vince, was home too, though the stranger claimed he'd never known that.

The man asked Julia's mom why the fuck she'd been staring at him. What the fuck had she seen? Before her puzzled expression had fully formed, he'd pulled a gun.

That's what Walter Brooks told the police, anyway. There weren't any witnesses left to corroborate his story.

The gun was aimed with drug-jittered hands, the bullet penetrating inches from Serena Bell's heart. Unlucky for her, as it turned out, since it shredded a major vessel, allowing her only the seconds she needed to stumble outside through the back door—away from Brooks, perched in the front—and onto her prized lawn. There she collapsed.

Later, the police would tell Julia her mom hadn't suffered. Death had been quick. Even in her grief, she'd recognized the lie. It was forty-three feet from the entryway to that patch of grass.

Julia had found her mom haloed by her own dark blood, staining the stray dandelions she hadn't yet had time to weed. Julia dropped to the ground at her side. Then she plucked the offending dandelions, careless of her mother's blood. They were still crushed in her fists when the police arrived.

Later, she'd learn that a neighbor had reported the Bells' fight, but priorities being what they were, it had taken thirty-seven minutes for the police to respond.

They'd only taken things seriously when another neighbor called to report a suspicious vehicle down by the lake.

A few days later, Walter Brooks was arrested on a minor drug charge. When the plates on his sedan matched the alert, he ended up confessing to the murder of Serena Bell.

Before that, everyone believed Vince Bell had killed his wife. Including Julia. Shootings were rarely random, the Bells had been fighting, and wasn't it often the husband?

The crunch of gravel snapped Julia from the past. She pricked up her ears. Had the sound come from outside? Inside? She listened for several seconds but heard nothing else. Her gaze darted to Cilantro to see if she'd heard it too, but the cat still dozed on the bag of soil.

Thinking of the padlock she'd left unbolted, she felt vulnerable. *Even here.*

Julia slid from the stool to stand on the plank floor that surrounded the worktable. She took a few tentative steps, crunching back onto the gravel, and looked around, suddenly aware of the room's clutter, and how many objects obstructed her view. Overhead, mesh netting had been draped for shade. A large bin for organic waste blocked one corner. Dark dripwalls covered another. There were shelves of pots. Tables piled with jars of French beans and sunflower seeds. A cluster of ginkgo trees. So many shadowed spaces. So many places to hide.

Julia inhaled deeply and drew up her shoulders so she stood taller.

I'm just jumpy because of the shooting, and because I let myself remember, she told herself. *That's all this is.*

But the attempt felt hollow. She'd learned it over and over: the mistake wasn't in listening to her instincts. The mistake was in thinking she could ever be safe.

Julia sharpened her focus. Took in the scent of flowers and damp earth. Listened to the quiet dripping of the irrigation system and Cilantro snoring softly. Scanned the plastic panels—

The shadows shifted along one wall. Julia took a quick step back, smacking her thigh hard against a large basin set up for a water fern experiment. A small heat lamp came loose, tumbling in. Ripples formed in the murky water. She unplugged it but, distracted, left it submerged.

Heart thudding, Julia crossed to a rack of gardening supplies and pulled free a trowel. As she moved, she kept her attention on the wall, but nothing more shifted. She squinted. Did the patch of plexiglass that had drawn her attention seem lighted now?

Screw this.

Before she could change her mind, Julia fast-walked across the room and slid open the door, trowel slick in her hand.

No one waited for her. The air outside was still. She moved to get a better view of the parking lot, but the only car there was her own Honda Civic.

Julia's gaze fell to the gravel walkway, but there was nothing to see but her own indentations in the tiny bits of stone.

CHAPTER 16

REN

Ren wondered if the tiny stranger would like a cat. Were cats acceptable pets for babies? She'd read in her pregnancy book that she should avoid cleaning a litter box for the next five months or so, but she didn't remember reading anything about whether cats and small children got along. She made a note to look into that.

Ren had never considered getting a pet before. In her profession, she couldn't very well hire a pet sitter, but after seeing Julia with the tabby, Ren was starting to reconsider. If that creature could live alone in a greenhouse, surely hers could stay untended overnight if she and Nolan were called away on a job?

She had to admit, she'd been charmed by both the cat and Julia—and was glad she'd taken time to follow up on Julia's identification.

As she neared home, the sun glinted off the high-rises, casting them in copper light. Soon the sky would become the lavender blue of the toxic larkspur. Ren tapped the phone button on her steering wheel.

"Call Nolan on mobile."

While she waited for him to answer, Ren shifted in her seat. Sand still scratched at her skin, made more sensitive by hormones. She couldn't wait to get home and strip off her clothes, and the holster, which was cutting into her swollen ankle. She also needed to pee, especially after all that time spent watching Julia.

Nolan's voice came to her through the speakers: "Hey, love. Your project go okay?"

He meant Voss. There was an urgency in the question that caught her off guard. "Finished in record time. Why?"

"No reason." But he sounded…disappointed?

She almost pushed him on it but decided it could wait until she got home. There might be a reason he didn't want to discuss it on the phone.

"I'm five minutes out," she said. "Have you eaten?"

"I picked up some sushi earlier. It's in the fridge."

"I can't—"

"I know. No raw fish for you or the little guy. I got you some cucumber-avocado rolls and veggie tempura."

She could hear the smile in his voice, but he seemed distracted. "Everything okay?"

He hesitated. Then: "I'm not sure."

Ren stopped too quickly at a red light, and the seat belt strangled her bladder. "What's going on?"

He released his breath in an extended hiss. It was the sound some targets made when emptying their lungs for the final time. "We received only one of the expected installments." His voice lowered into a coarse whisper. "We're short fifty grand. If everything went okay with your job, then that means we're still owed the second payment for yesterday."

The stoplight turned green, and she eased through the intersection.

If someone delayed payment, that meant they weren't too worried about the consequences. Shortly after she and Nolan had married, a client hadn't paid on time, using the money to finance a trip to Sicily instead. A couple of days later, he'd collapsed face-first into his plate of caponata. Ren wouldn't have killed him just for skipping out on payment, of course, but she'd also learned that the client had really ordered the hit to get his girlfriend's husband out of the way. She never allowed that kind of oversight again, although Ren remembered the trip to Italy fondly. She and Nolan had also managed to squeeze in a visit to the Capuchin Catacombs of Palermo to see its rows of mummified dead. An impromptu honeymoon.

Ren shook off the nostalgia, refocusing on the problem at hand. There were only three reasons a client like Baird would withhold payment. He didn't have the money. He was trying to cheat them. Or they had screwed up the job. With Baird, only one of those reasons made sense.

Baird wasn't happy with them.

Ren bit at her cuticles, grimacing when her teeth crunched sand. "You should check in with the client. Get more details about the job, and his expectations."

"Already set up a meeting."

She approached the gate to the residents' parking garage. Her car triggered the sensors, and the gate slid open. She still relished this convenience. It would certainly make things easier when there was a little human screaming in the back seat, and the condo's location meant a shorter commute to day care than from the old place, although she had to admit that most days she still missed her garden. "When?"

"First thing tomorrow. Client just got back in town, and he has some free time in the morning. I thought it best if we talk face-to-face."

Ren pulled into her reserved spot, switched the call from Bluetooth to her handset, then killed the engine.

"We'll talk more when I get inside."

"I'm running an errand, but I'll see you later tonight. Eat without me."

"Did you remember the wasabi?"

"Left it on the table next to the Tums."

Ren disconnected, stowed her phone, and got out of the car.

Though the overhead LEDs were bright, the thick concrete posts and rows of vehicles threw deep shadows. Ren took several steps and then froze, uneasy. She held her breath and pricked her ears. The garage appeared empty, but her instincts screamed.

And her instincts were even more reliable than ricin.

Ren released her breath and took a step back toward her car, tensing to run. Before she could, two men stepped from behind a post less than ten feet away. One was ruddy-faced and thick-necked, the other wiry with eyes like black marbles. But both were clean-shaven and in expensive suits. Both had weapons they hadn't yet drawn.

She'd never seen them before but she immediately recognized them for who they were. Baird's men.

She hesitated. Their weapons remained holstered. Should she see what message they had for her? That would be the civil thing to do.

But her instincts continued to shriek, and sometimes being polite got a person killed.

Ren knew she wouldn't make it back into her car. She bent at the waist toward her ankle holster, but her reflexes were compromised, and with their long strides, the men covered the distance in the span of a few heartbeats. As her fingertips grazed her gun, the man with the marble eyes grabbed her arm and jerked her upright.

"We're not here to hurt you," he said.

She arched an eyebrow and shot a glance at her throbbing arm.

The ruddy-faced man grabbed her other arm, his grip equally tight. "Mr. Baird just wants to talk."

In an attempt to steer her toward their Buick, the man's hand slid to her stomach.

Ren felt it immediately, the familiar seizing in her chest. It grew harder to breathe, the air abruptly heavy and hot. The skin between her shoulder blades burned. Her cheeks flamed. Her eyes narrowed. She didn't get angry often, but when she did, it swallowed her.

Ren stared at the palm pressed against her stomach. She spoke slowly through clenched teeth. "Remove. Your. Hand."

"Can't do that." He pressed harder. A grin spread across his florid face, and Ren fervently wished she'd had a syringe of strychnine in her pocket.

CHAPTER 17

JULIA

Still reluctant to return home, Julia took the long route, stopping at a random deli and unwrapping her sandwich in the car. For the second day in a row, she ate dinner in the driver's seat. It was probably time to Scotchgard the upholstery.

By the time she put her key in her front door, the setting sun and lingering haze had painted the sky a brilliant orange. She carefully locked the door behind her and closed the living room blinds. She left the lights off. Better to stay hidden in the dark.

As deepening shadows hid the empty corners of the room, she felt her daughter's absence acutely. Only last week, with Cora poised to move into the dorms, Julia had struggled with the first waves of loneliness, but her happiness had outweighed any melancholy.

But there was no joy in this transition. Only unspeakable loss, and nearly debilitating worry.

Julia settled on the sofa and dialed her daughter's number. It went to voicemail.

"Hey, Cora. It's Mom." As if her daughter had already forgotten her. "Just calling to see how you're doing. To see how your dad is doing too." She waited a couple of breaths, but it wasn't as if Cora would pick up mid-message. "I also wanted to tell you that I love you. Very much. And call me. I'm worried about you."

The last part came out more urgent than she intended. Julia tried to think of something she could say to lighten the mood—one of her usual corny puns, or something about how they would get through this crisis together. But her mood was too dark, and she ended the call with her fears hanging between them.

Needing distraction, she grabbed the remote. A baking show, maybe? Another episode of that docuseries on marine mammals?

She switched on cable news instead. She caught it mid-commercial, but when the show returned, a banner popped on the screen in all caps: TERROR ON CAMPUS. The anchor provided an update—the missing fifth bullet had been found in the trunk of a eucalyptus. A sudden foreboding caused Julia's heartbeat to grow heavy. *The fifth bullet had lodged in a tree?* But before she could think too long on that, a warning about graphic content flashed, and video captured on cell phones started to play.

Taken from different angles, some snippets were only a few seconds long, while others lasted a full minute. The footage was spliced together in a montage that the banner got exactly right: it was terrifying. In the moments following the shooting, Julia had focused solely on her daughter. Many details had escaped her. Now, though, she could freeze time with a click of the remote. See now what she hadn't then.

Emily Murphy appeared on the screen. Julia turned up the volume.

"I heard the gunshots." Emily blinked hard. Took a shuddering breath. "I thought someone had dropped a suitcase or whatever. But then I looked over and saw that this girl near me wasn't breathing, and my dad…" She had to stop again, her voice thick with emotion. She wiped her eyes. "They weren't moving, and there was all this blood, and I realized someone was shooting at us."

Julia muted the sound and rubbed at her own wet eyes. She took a breath and forced herself to watch. When a woman with a messy bun appeared on the screen, Julia hit the pause button. She vaguely remembered her, only a few spots ahead of them in line.

Julia hit play again. The woman smiled broadly and held her phone so that she and the young man next to her were both in the frame. Mom and son, Julia guessed.

The woman started to lower the phone. Julia inhaled sharply and paused the video again. In that frozen moment, she could see her entire family. Brie stunning even in grainy profile, flanked by Eric and Cora. Julia could just make out the man in the plaid shirt and his daughter, Emily, with her strawberry blonde braid.

Julia wrinkled her brow. Where was she? Then she remembered: she'd turned away, intending to return to the library to retrieve Cora's phone. Which meant—

Julia held her breath, suddenly reluctant to restart the video. This was the moment before Brie was killed. Before Cora was shot.

The last moment when they'd all believed it was a day to celebrate.

Julia went back a couple of frames, to when the mom who held the phone was still beaming.

I should stop it here. Pretend the next part didn't happen.

But she couldn't turn away. She watched in real time. Heard the *pop pop pop* of gunfire. Saw herself turn and dive toward Cora, pulling her onto the concrete. They both hit the ground hard.

On the screen, Brie collapsed. Despite the warning about graphic imagery, the video was blurred to camouflage the worst of it.

Julia rewound again. She played the video in slow motion, a tragedy that had taken only seconds unfolding one frame at a time.

Slowly, the smiling mom stepped aside. Brie's head turned. Did she sense something? Hear something? There was expectation in her craning neck.

Julia decided she was reading too much into it. In real time, the gesture had taken a fraction of a second.

Next to Brie, Eric stepped away. Brie shifted again, her attention back on Eric. Sensing his sudden distance?

Brie offered Cora a one-armed hug, as Julia turned her back on her family.

The day before, Julia hadn't seen what happened next, so now she leaned in until she was within a foot of the TV. Bruce Murphy pushed into the frame, crowding her daughter until she took one step to the side. He opened his mouth. Intending to apologize? Julia couldn't say for sure, because he'd picked the exact wrong moment to bump into Cora.

Standing in the spot previously occupied by her daughter, the man took a bullet to the stomach.

A blink later, a bullet grazed Cora's arm, but only because by then, Julia had already grabbed her, and they were falling.

Heart thundering, Julia leaned back, away from the horrible images.

In the video, she and Cora continued their slow-motion descent, while Brie collapsed beside them.

Wait.

Julia paused the screen again, fighting a wave of panic. There was no way these shots were random.

A new theory slipped into her head, and Julia's hand began shaking in a way it hadn't in more than two decades. She nearly dropped the remote, the thought dark and rotten: a heartbeat before, Cora had been standing where Murphy had been hit. If he hadn't crowded her, the bullet likely would've drilled into Cora's chest.

She rewound and watched again. The events unfolded the same way, frame by frame, until her heart seized.

There. Cora's chest. A blink later, Murphy's stomach.

But it was watching the second shot in slow motion that nearly drove Julia to her knees. Again, Cora moved, this time propelled downward by Julia. And so the bullet grazed Cora's arm.

For a second time, just missing her chest.

In the video, Cora's sleeve was immediately blackened by blood. She lay on the ground, limp, before Julia dragged her behind the cart and out of view.

The third shot caught Brie. But Julia was still fixated on that second shot. Her focus sharpened as she leaned in farther, only inches away now, and replayed it all again. The sniper shot Bruce Murphy. Fired again.

What if that first shot was actually a miss?

What if it was only after the sniper thought Cora was dead that he moved on to Brie?

What if the third fatality hadn't been confirmed by media because there *wasn't* a third fatality?

Julia had believed the death of the unidentified student had been caused by the fifth bullet. The bullet she now knew had hit a tree.

Emily's voice buzzed in her head: *I looked over and saw that this girl near me wasn't breathing…there was all this blood…*

Julia wanted so badly to believe it was a random attack. Maybe the sniper hated pretty brunettes. Maybe he'd been recently dumped by a woman with brown hair, and that had driven him to that roof. That had to be it, because even if Brie had her enemies, no one would want to hurt Cora.

Unless…

Julia tried to ignore the thought, but it insisted. Only two things connected Cora and Brie: Eric, and Cora's knowledge of Brie's affair.

Since Cora had told her about the texts, Julia had pushed back against the emotions that fought to surface. The anger that Brie had put Cora in that position. Worry for Eric. And, if Julia was being honest, a twinge of satisfaction that her serially cheating ex-husband might finally understand what he'd once done to her, and to their daughter. It all seemed petty— unimportant—and best left buried. But now the revelation of Brie's affair carried more weight.

What if it was the reason someone had tried to kill Cora?

But that was crazy. Who'd kill a child to cover up something like an affair? Affairs happened every day. After thirteen years with Eric, she should know.

Julia stabbed the remote and restarted the news coverage. She fast-forwarded through the commercials, then clicked a few more times until she caught up with live TV.

Apparently, Brie's family had finally been notified of her death, because her face filled the screen. Julia felt a pain, low and deep, as Brie's usual glow stretched across the screen. The photo had been taken at her wedding to Eric. While Julia hadn't been there, the white dress gave it away. Then there was the caption: ANDERSON HUGHES VICTIM IDENTIFIED AS NEWLYWED BRIE BENNETT.

Another photo faded over the first. Brie again, smiling harder in this one. This had been taken at a formal event of some kind. Another fancy dress, this one gray and beaded. Accepting an award or bestowing it? Julia couldn't tell. The third photo appeared to be a vacation shot, someplace sunny and generic. Julia couldn't guess the location. It wasn't as if she and Brie swapped vacation stories. It was challenge enough to swap civil hellos. Brie had never liked the idea that Eric once loved someone else. Was that why she had cheated? To have something of her own to level the playing field? Or had she truly meant to leave Eric?

On the TV, the news anchor was again detailing the shooting with unfettered zeal. How long before interest cooled? How long before Brie's death would be relegated to the news ticker at the bottom of the screen? Julia gave it three days, tops. Or at least she desperately hoped. She needed the sniper to believe he'd fatally shot Cora. The story had to fade before Cora was identified too—as among the injured, not the dead.

The caption changed, and Julia froze.

What the hell?

Staring at the screen, everything Julia knew turned upside down.

This news story wouldn't be going away in three days after all.

CHAPTER 18

REN

Oliver Baird lived on a sprawling estate off Benedict Canyon in Beverly Hills, masked by a thicket of old sycamores and tucked behind a ten-foot security gate. As the Buick carrying Ren approached, the burnished doors parted with deliberate leisure. Visitors should be willing to wait for Oliver Baird.

On the other side of the gate, the Buick stopped at the small guard shack. A formality, really. With sensors installed along the quarter-mile approach and mounted cameras complete with facial recognition technology, the guard had long known they were coming. After checking in, they followed a winding cobblestone driveway to the main house.

During the drive from the parking garage to Baird's estate, Ren had made the ruddy-faced kidnapper stop at a gas station so she could use the restroom. Of course he'd already taken her gun. But she needed to be clearheaded, since her wits were all that was left of her. Bladder empty, she was finally able to focus on her deep breathing.

If Baird made a move, could she pull off a fatal jab to the temple? Or a blow to the Adam's apple? If she could find the right weapon—a letter opener, a pair of scissors—she could puncture a trachea.

No, she decided. With his goons keeping watch, that was unlikely.

So she practiced her breathing and surveyed the grounds, keeping an eye out for exit routes and weaknesses, but finding none. The large house up ahead drew near.

The night before, when Ren had again researched Baird, she'd come across photos of this house. In recent years, the estate had swallowed the smaller properties that once flanked it, allowing Baird a second guesthouse, a tennis court, and a nine-hole golf course. But the showpiece remained the original Georgian mansion at the end of the driveway. Its front doors were polished wood inlaid with wrought iron and thick glass. As imposing as the security gate.

Ren was dragged out of the car, and before anyone could knock, the heavy doors opened. A woman in navy slacks and a simple white blouse greeted Ren and the two thugs. As they followed her, Ren noted that the woman's attire was the only simple thing in the entry. Paintings hung in carefully lit gilded frames. Muted hillsides, domed buildings, and serious people with pale faces. Though the paintings left Ren cold, she recognized their expense. The stone floors too were a little stark for Ren's taste.

But the staircase—that impressed her. The balusters were wrought iron, the handrail the same polished wood as the front doors, and the carpet runner plush. Long and curving, the staircase must've taken a full minute to climb. Above it hung a cut glass chandelier the size of Ren's Prius, and probably almost as heavy.

At the top of the stairs, an older woman appeared—black dress worn with bare feet, silver hair secured in a severe bun, sharp cheekbones below hollow, watchful eyes. Baird's wife, Lydia. When their gazes locked, Ren noticed a fuzziness she hadn't at first. Whether it was caused by grief or medication, Ren wasn't close enough to gauge, but she suspected it was a combination of both. A moment later, the older woman broke eye contact, spun on her heels, and disappeared.

Next to Ren, the woman in the white blouse cleared her throat. When Ren looked at her, she motioned to Ren's sweatshirt. "May I take your jacket?"

Ren became aware again of the sand that scratched her skin. Normally, she would've been eager to be rid of it, but it camouflaged her expanding stomach, and Baird apparently liked a cold house. Though it was already night, she guessed the thermostat was set to the low sixties. Soon it would be impossible for her to hide her pregnancy, but for the moment, she intended to control that information.

"No, thank you," Ren said. "I won't be staying long."

She shot a pointed glance at Baird's goons.

The woman offered a friendly nod, then led Ren to a room that might've been a den or a library or an office. There was space enough for it to be all three. The room was huge. Bigger than her condo, certainly.

When Ren entered, the two goons remained outside, flanking the door. Perhaps the jab to the temple was an option after all.

Oliver Baird sat behind a desk, but when he saw her, he stood. His beard was trimmed close to his face, a shadow of silver and black. He took equal care with his nails, manicured and buffed to a glossy sheen, and with his sport coat, its lines pressed knife-sharp.

Ren's body tensed. She had never met a client before, and she felt vulnerable. Ren hated feeling vulnerable, even more than she hated when people cursed. She stood taller, sucking in her baby bump.

Baird moved toward a leather chair near the fireplace and motioned to one of two much smaller armchairs opposite him. They all looked old and expensive.

"Have a seat," he said.

Baird had been born in Aberdeen, Scotland, the son of a textile worker and a teacher, but if Ren hadn't done her research, she would've missed the slight brogue.

She remained standing. As she always did when entering an unfamiliar room, Ren looked around. She wasted little attention on the bookshelves and open areas, concerning herself instead with the furniture-blocked nooks and the shadowed corners. Places where threats might wait. By the time she finished her scan, the woman was gone and the door closed.

"Why am I here?"

"Please. Sit."

Ren finally sat, and he did the same. She shifted to get comfortable in the armchair. The bare wood was hard, the seat pan too long. She had to choose between back support and having her feet planted on the floor. She inched forward. She couldn't have her legs dangling like a toddler's.

Ren considered whether she should ask about the missing payment, but instinct kept her silent.

Baird gestured to a nearby table, which held a tray with a pitcher and several glasses.

"Water?" he asked.

As someone who poisoned people for a living, she declined.

"My wife and I just got back to town this evening. I assume you've been following the Anderson Hughes shootings?"

Ren kept her expression neutral even as she grew more annoyed. "Yes."

"Then you've heard they've identified a second victim?"

Ren shook her head. "I've been busy."

"Ah, yes. Voss. I suppose I should ask how that went, but frankly, at this moment I don't give a fuck." He leaned back in his more comfortable chair and studied her. She watched him just as intently. "My daughter is dead."

Her eyes snapped wide and her body went rigid. "Your daughter?"

"At the college. She was shot."

A sudden and bone-deep chill raised the hairs on her arms. Nolan had killed Oliver Baird's *daughter*? Baird wasn't the client?

Nolan had lied to her.

Ren thought of the tiny stranger, and her stomach fluttered. She thought about how the goon had groped her stomach. Surely he'd known that the bump at her midsection was more than bloat. Did Baird know too?

"I'm comforted by your expression of surprise. It feels nearly authentic." The brogue slipped into his voice more noticeably, his vowels hardening, and she read anger in the slight clenching of his jaw.

It wasn't surprise on her face. It was shock. Inside her, every nerve sparked. Nolan had *lied*. She willed herself into stillness as her skin tingled.

She knew she wouldn't be able to pull off sympathy so she aimed to keep her voice neutral. "I'm sorry for your loss."

He nodded in acceptance of her condolences. She watched him for signs that he too was sorry, but though he seethed, she saw no grief in him.

"Don't worry," he said. "I know it wasn't you. If a toxin had been found in Brie's body—say, arsenic—then we would be having a very different discussion."

"Arsenic's a toxicant."

"Excuse me?"

"Toxins are poisons created by biological systems. Arsenic is a toxicant. Besides, I wouldn't use arsenic."

"Why not?"

"Because we're not living in the Victorian era."

He blinked several times in quick succession. "You're an odd one, aren't you?"

Her feet tensed in her sandy sneakers, the urge to run as powerful as the urge to kick him.

"But you're smart, and you don't lie, so I trust you'll answer this question truthfully: did Nolan kill my daughter?" Baird asked the question casually, the same way he might inquire about the weather.

Ren aimed to keep her tone just as casual. "Why would you ask that?" A second later, she realized what she should've said: *No. Nolan had nothing to do with that.* But Baird was right. She preferred a misdirect to an outright lie.

"It's an obvious question, given your husband's particular talents." He leaned forward, resting his elbows on his knees and steepling his fingers. "Though it doesn't make sense, considering our business relationship."

"I agree. It doesn't."

"It's curious, though, that he wanted to meet tomorrow to discuss a missing payment."

She strained to keep her expression neutral. "That was about Voss." An inexpert liar, she felt her jaw pulse.

"That payment was transferred this afternoon."

"It was probably a glitch with our account. I'll let him know the money's there."

"I'm relieved to know Nolan wasn't involved." Baird's eyes narrowed almost imperceptibly. "Still, how many snipers do you think could've made that shot?"

"Not many. Then again, who's to say the shooting was a professional hit? Maybe the sniper just got lucky."

Inwardly, she cringed at the phrasing—the implication that luck had a role in his daughter's killing—but Baird seemed unbothered by the slip. "That might be, but why don't you ask around anyway? You have connections, and I would very much like to know who shot my daughter."

Baird had connections too. Likely more than she did. If Baird got confirmation that Nolan was involved, he would have them both killed. Even harboring a strong suspicion might be cause enough. Ren fought the urge to touch her stomach, her back painfully rigid as she perched on the edge of her armchair.

"Anything we can do to help."

Baird unlaced his fingers and leaned back again. He appeared relaxed. Ren knew better.

"Can I be honest here?" The accent grew thicker, and his nostrils flared. His irritation was surfacing, like a wasp emerging from its cocoon. Ready to sting.

"Always."

"I have some reservations about our business relationship."

To her left, the doors to the office slid open. Baird's guards loomed on the threshold with their arms at their sides.

Baird's half smile was icy, his gaze predatory. "Don't mind them. We're just talking here."

She knew better. Baird might not move against her now—she still couldn't get a read on that—but he was making a point.

Keeping her eyes on Baird, Ren ran through the possible exits. She couldn't go through Baird's guards, and the windows were closed. Even if they were unlocked, if she had to escape quickly, there would be no time to open them. And there would be no jumping through. It took a great deal of pressure to shatter a window, and if the impact alone didn't leave her battered, the broken glass would. On a previous job, a target in the throes of dying had attempted to escape just like that, only managing to slice his carotid in the process. And Baird's windows were likely reinforced.

Her only choice would be to grab Baird by the throat, shatter the water pitcher, and negotiate her way out by holding a shard to his neck. But even if she made it out of the room, she would be dead within the week. There were others as skilled as she was who were willing to take Baird's money.

Calmly, Ren prodded. "You were saying you have reservations?"

"I think you and I are alike in some ways. We're planners. But you're pragmatic too. You think before you act." He paused, his eyes glittering. She sensed that even if Baird hadn't had his daughter killed, he was a man capable of it. "Does Nolan?"

Her whole body went rigid. Suddenly, holding a shard to his neck seemed like an excellent idea. "We both understand the need for caution."

"Perhaps. But you understand my concerns, especially given that that really was one hell of a shot. I'll feel a lot better if you get me a name." His eyes grew cold. "I'm sure you'll feel better too."

She matched his icy stare with one of her own. She needed to buy time. "I'll have a name for you by next week."

"Make it sooner than that," he said. "And Ren? Look into this yourself. Don't involve Nolan."

A little hard to keep him out of it. "If that's what you want."

"It is." He paused. "And I hope you figure out that *glitch* with your bank account." Baird let the words hang between them for several seconds, then he waved his hand, dismissing her. "My men will drive you home." She made it to the door before he called after her. "Oh, Ren?"

When she turned, his eyes were half-hooded but sharp. "I almost forgot. Congratulations on your little one. I trust it won't interfere with the work."

*   *   *

Once she was outside, Ren paused to look back at the Baird mansion, with its rigid symmetry and the hard lines of its pale brick exterior. Four chimneys meticulously aligned. Two identical rows of double-hung windows with decorative grids flanking the entrance. The exterior lights casting a harsh glow. An unforgiving home for an unforgiving man.

All those windows gave Ren the impression she was being watched. More than a dozen cold and unblinking eyes. The exterior lights glinted off the glass. Ren was glad. If not for that, she might not have noticed that the last upstairs window on the right was open.

Ren *was* being watched.

A wraith in black with silver hair floated behind the screen, haloed in light. Ren moved to stand beneath the window, staring up at Lydia Baird. A current passed between them, mother to mother. Ren was suddenly ashamed of the swell of her stomach. It seemed an offense to this woman, whose daughter had just been killed by the man who'd fathered Ren's own child.

Ren wondered if the older woman would call out to her. Half expected it. But Lydia Baird stood in silence for another minute before stepping back into the shadows.

The ruddy guard reached for her, to hurry her along to the car, but dropped his arm when he saw her expression. She glanced from his eyes to his Adam's apple and back again.

"Touch me again and I'll kill you," she said coolly, before lowering herself into the Buick's back seat.

CHAPTER 19

JULIA

Julia had turned off the TV but continued to stare at the blank screen. Brie had rarely mentioned her family, but Julia had picked up a few details. She knew Brie's estrangement predated her relationship with Eric, and that before they'd married, Brie had gone by her mom's maiden name. She'd said this was because her dad was more of a prick than her mom. Julia had intuited this was a high bar to clear in her family.

Now Julia wondered if Brie also sought the anonymity in her mom's maiden name. Scrutiny was much gentler for a Cunningham than it was for a Baird.

That made Julia think of her own cursory searches online. When she'd first found out about Eric's new wife, she'd downed several glasses of pinot while she drunk-googled "Brie Bennett" and "Brie Cunningham." But Brie had been thorough in reinventing herself. Julia found just the usual stuff: filtered photos of artfully foamed lattes and warm-weather vacations, a LinkedIn profile that hadn't been updated in years, and a beauty blog she'd started in college.

The decision not to dig deeper now felt reckless. She should've hired a private detective. Asked more questions. Brie had been an important part of Cora's life, and Julia should've known more about her.

Thinking of Cora brought back those slightly blurred video frames. Her daughter had been spared only by inches. She'd been lucky, but luck could be fickle—and brutal. Especially now that Brie's death would keep the shooting in the headlines.

Julia had just grabbed her keys, intending to drive by Eric's to check on Cora, when her phone rang. Cora finally calling back. Julia jabbed the screen hard enough that her finger tingled.

"How are you?"

"You can stop asking that, Mom."

Her words came as clearly as if only a few feet separated them, but never had her daughter seemed so far away. Julia's hand clenched around the keys, the metal teeth digging into her palm.

"You're coming home," she said. She picked up her purse. Opened the front door. "I'm on my way to your dad's house now."

She waited for Cora to resurrect familiar arguments. To argue that she was an adult. Capable of making her own choices. To remind Julia that Eric was her father, and equally capable of ordering takeout Thai. Beneath the protests would be an unspoken truth. In that moment, Eric and their daughter were connected by their trauma, which was far different from her own. Not just because they had experienced a greater loss, but because they'd never before experienced true violence. They'd only just learned, on a visceral level, how deeply fucked up the world could be.

When no response came, Julia gripped the phone more tightly. "What's wrong?"

She hoped for one of her daughter's usual answers: *Nothing. I'm fine. Stop asking that.*

Instead, Cora let out a long, shaky breath. "You can't come to Dad's."

Julia's stomach knotted. "Why not?"

"I'm not at Dad's."

"What do you mean you're—"

"That's why I called." Cora's voice cracked. "It's about Dad."

*   *   *

The hotel in San Clemente was what Julia had expected: palm trees, pale walls, tile roof. A mid-tier establishment well maintained. But she wasn't looking for the hotel. She was looking for the attached bar, which emanated the buzz of an energetic crowd out to her on the sidewalk.

Julia hadn't been in a crowd since the shooting—and honestly, she'd never been a fan of crowds before that—and if anyone else had asked her to come, she would've told them how easy it was to install a ride-share app. But Cora had been the one to ask.

Her whole body clenched at the sound of the patrons shouting inside, laughing and clinking glasses. Many of them were drunk.

She scowled at her own hesitation and pushed her way inside. There a colorful array of surfboards was mounted overhead. A few of the patrons wore button-up shirts with slacks or halter dresses, but most of the clientele looked as if they'd just stumbled in off the beach. Flip-flops. Shorts. T-shirts that showed tanned arms, and tank tops that bared sunburned shoulders. On a corner stage, a young man with long red hair tuned his guitar while a few patrons sat at tables nearby, but most of the action was centered around the large curved bar in the middle of the room. Scores of people gathered there, with dozens more spilling out onto the patio. She envied their joy.

Julia scanned the room for Eric. She found him seated at a table in the back. The bar featured dozens of craft beers and brands of tequila. Judging by the way Eric listed in his chair, he'd sampled many.

Watching him, she wished for the ease of those early days. She and Eric had met when they'd both joined a philosophy study group at San Diego State. A week later, Eric dropped the class, though Julia didn't find that out until she asked him what grade he'd received on his midterm.

Oh, I'm not in the class anymore, he'd said casually.

Confused, she'd asked him why he remained in the group.

He answered by asking her on a date. A picnic. He'd splurged on expensive cheese, but it had spoiled when he forgot it in his car overnight. So they ate spray cheese with their fancy water crackers, and shared a bottle of sparkling cider since they were both too young for champagne.

A bug had landed in Julia's glass, and Eric was so nervous he spilled cider on the blanket. Midway through the date, the sting of sunburn bloomed on her neck. The grass left a rash on his ankles. But they stayed until dark, neither wanting the date to end.

Eventually, the relationship soured, more slowly than it started. So slowly, they failed to notice for a while. Still, it was that awkward boy Julia thought of, with his borrowed picnic basket and can of spray cheese. Now old enough to drink and taking full advantage of that fact.

The wall of patrons surged around her, offering a sweaty and unwanted embrace as she made her way to Eric's table.

When he looked up, his eyes were rheumy and swollen. "Why're you here, Julia?"

She exaggerated her wince at his flammable breath. "Good thing this place doesn't have candles."

He shrugged, the simple movement making him list in his chair again. "I've had a few."

Gallons? "I'm here because Cora called. From Evie's." She emphasized the last two words.

Even drunk, he noticed the slight chill. "You don't like Evie?"

"Evie's great."

"Then I don't understand." He picked up a nearly empty mug from the table and swallowed the last few drops. There was still condensation on the glass. It hadn't had time to warm.

"Just saying it'd be good to know where my daughter is."

"*Your* daughter?"

Old habits. "Our daughter."

When he waved his hand, he bobbled. "She's with a friend, that's all. And Evie's mom is there." He blinked, longer than usual, and Julia wondered how close he was to passing out.

"Cora's fine. She'll be back home soon. Unlike my wife."

"Eric—"

He cut her off. "Cora's not you, Julia. She has two parents to keep her safe."

She recoiled, even though she understood that Eric's lashing out wasn't about her. Eager for a break from his grief, he'd chosen anger instead.

Despite knowing this, Julia felt her chest tighten, and she had to look away.

"You need to let her go," Eric slurred. "She's eighteen, not eight."

"I'm aware." *Unlike you, I've been at every birthday.* "Anyway, Cora thought you might need a ride."

Eric swallowed hard, as if working to keep his beer down. "I'm good."

"What are you doing, Eric?"

He looked around, probably for someone to bring him another drink. Then his attention landed on Julia again. "She came here with him." His voice was thick.

So Eric had known about the affair. Still, she asked, "Who?"

"The man she was screwing."

"You have proof?" she asked. What she really wanted to ask was *Do you know who he is?*

"I went through her credit card charges."

She laughed harshly—*Really, Eric? You want to talk about this with me?*—but managed to keep her tone flat. "That's all you got?"

"It was a prepaid credit card. One of those that doesn't have to be linked to a bank account." He hunched over his empty beer mug and inhaled, as if not wanting to waste even the fumes. "She used it at this bar."

"Why are you torturing yourself with this? It doesn't..." Her voice trailed.

"It doesn't matter?"

"Actually, I was going to say it doesn't change things."

He twisted the mug in his hands. "I've known about the card for a couple of weeks." He stopped twisting the mug, noticing a server. He pointed to his empty mug. Then he focused on Julia again. "I was putting away a basket of Brie's clothes, and I found the card in a drawer, wrapped in one of her T-shirts." Between his slurring and the crowd, Julia had to lean in to hear. "I told myself I was doing something nice, helping with her laundry, but I knew she was cheating. I was looking for proof. I can admit that."

Julia hesitated, considering whether to tell Eric about the texts, the second phone. Then her gaze fell again on his swollen eyes, and she decided against it.

"Let me drive you home," she said at last.

The server arrived with a fresh mug, and Eric tossed a twenty on the table, waving off the change. Once she'd gone, Eric took a couple of long drinks.

"Karma." He wiped his mouth with the back of his hand. "That's how you caught me too. The credit card charge for that dress I bought that woman."

The damn dress. Julia wondered if he had said "that woman" because he no longer remembered her name.

To celebrate three months of togetherness, Eric had bought *that woman* an Armani jersey dress. Or, rather, he and Julia had bought the dress, since it was charged on their joint credit card.

Julia swallowed a pebble-sized lump that always came with that particular memory, though time had eroded the original anger into a passing irritation. "Brie could've been meeting a friend."

"I called all her friends."

"It could've been a new friend."

When Eric lifted his mug it wobbled in his hand. "Yeah. That's what I'm thinking too."

"A new *platonic* friend."

"Then why come all the way to San Clemente?" He broke eye contact, his eyes darting around the room.

He looked so lost, and she felt an unexpected wave of sadness. She understood what it felt like to have your world knocked off its axis. What surprised her was how much she wanted to balance it again for him. "Maybe the friend lives here."

"No. She was hiding it. It's what I would do." He paused. "It's what I did."

"I don't know. I heard the poke bowls here are pretty good."

"If she came here for a poke bowl, then why would she need to reserve a hotel room?"

Before Julia could digest that one, Eric wagged his finger, his gaze settling on some distant distraction. When she turned, she saw that he was pointing at a large man a few tables away. "That guy's been staring at me for the past ten minutes."

The man was definitely staring. Julia scanned the room. Several others threw glances their way too, though they looked away when her gaze met theirs—except for the large man at the table, and another man closer to the door. This second man was lean and angular, and unlike the other curious patrons, he seemed to be watching her. Not Eric.

A moment later, his attention shifted too, so abruptly she wondered if she'd just imagined it.

Julia shifted to block Eric's view of the rest of the bar and crossed her arms. "Don't."

He stood, unsteady. "What if it's him?"

"It's not him." She stood too.

He pushed past her, moving with impressive speed considering moments before he'd struggled to remain upright.

A few feet from the man's table, Eric shouted, "What're you staring at, asshole?"

Julia strained not to roll her eyes. She quickly moved between them. But despite the insult, the larger man remained seated. "Sorry if I was staring. And sorry about your wife, man."

Her gaze fell to the table, where the man's phone rested faceup. He'd been streaming coverage of the Anderson Hughes shooting.

Eric didn't notice. His shoulders tightened, his fist clenched, and Julia exhaled in exasperation.

"So you admit you were screwing her."

The man's brow wrinkled in obvious confusion. "I only know you from what I saw—"

Julia noticed the tension in Eric's shoulder the instant before he threw the punch, slow and sloppy but headed at the other man with enough power to make the stranger's face darken. But before Eric's punch could land, Julia swept his leg out from under him. He landed on his backside.

Better the floor than on the other guy's fist.

For a moment, Eric looked confused, but then he glared up at her. "What the—?"

"Are you done being stupid?" A rhetorical question. Eric had never been able to separate drunk from stupid. Julia held out a hand. "Now let's get you home."

He slapped her arm away. He reached for a nearby chair for support, but when he pulled himself to standing, his weight tipped the empty seat. He stumbled and grabbed the table, but he put too much pressure there too, and it tilted. Wineglasses, beer bottles, and an array of half-eaten appetizers began a slow-motion landslide that Julia could've easily stopped—if not for Eric's clumsy step, his foot sliding out from under him at the same moment. This time, she saw, he wouldn't fall on his backside. He'd staggered too close to the wall, the back of his head within inches of it.

Shit.

Julia's hand shot out, and she grabbed Eric by the arm just before his skull made contact—which allowed the avalanche of glass and food and garbage to tumble to the floor. A bottle hit Julia's knee hard, beer splashing her pants, before it and everything else landed in a messy clump, half on the floor, half on her sneakers.

Eric rubbed his arm. "That hurt," he slurred. "Better not leave a bruise."

She kicked a pile of rice and bits of avocado off her toe. *For Cora,* she reminded herself again.

Julia glanced toward the open door, planning their exit, and caught the eyes of the angular man with the sharp jaw again. He'd since stepped just outside the entrance, and if the moon hadn't been so bright, and if her nerves hadn't been so frayed, she wouldn't have noticed him at all.

She pretended that she didn't, forcing the knots in her shoulders to uncoil and her eyes to go soft. Over the years, she'd grown expert at pretending. But when Julia turned away, she still felt the heat of his attention on her.

CHAPTER 20

REN

The condo was dark. Apparently, Nolan was still running errands. Ren took out her phone to text him that she was home but realized he thought she'd returned hours earlier. So instead she texted, Home soon?

He responded quickly: By 11. Then a second text: Everything ok?

She thought, *Not at all. Baird thinks you might've killed his daughter.* But that argument would wait. She typed Talk later.

Ren put the phone down on the kitchen counter, crossed to the refrigerator, and inhaled the vegetable rolls Nolan had left for her. Extra wasabi. After chewing a couple of Tums, she picked up her phone and took it to her favorite chair in the living room. She pictured the notch-eared tabby curled up on her lap, and remembered the way it had nuzzled Julia's palm. Should Ren return to campus for it? Nolan could clean the litter box until after the baby was born, and they could buy one of those carpeted climbing structures to keep it occupied. They'd have to hide it in their bedroom, of course, since she wouldn't want something like that in her living room, and the office would soon be a nursery.

In her browser, she typed,

Trendy cat towers

Are cats good for babies?

How to keep cat from scratching baby

Best names for cats

She stopped herself. What if the tiny stranger turned out to be allergic? And what if the cat's absence upset Julia?

Ren leaned against the chair's sculpted backrest, pulling up her feet so she sat cross-legged, and shifted focus to searching for news on the dog park death. There were few details. Karl Voss had died in obscurity.

Next she looked into Brie Bennett, but there wasn't much there either, and certainly nothing suspicious. But researching Brie led Ren back to the former Mrs. Bennett—Julia.

Since Nolan still wasn't home, Ren plugged Julia's name into her browser. There was a headshot posted on the Anderson Hughes faculty page. A group photo at a Walk for Animals event. And, eventually, an older photo attached to a near-ancient article about a man named Walter Brooks, who'd shot and killed Julia's parents.

How sad. Ren felt a pang of guilt that she'd considered taking the greenhouse cat. *Unless they'd deserved it.*

She clicked on the newer photos and downloaded each of them to her phone. She stashed them with the others in a folder slugged "Her."

Ren had lost fifteen minutes before, reluctantly, she signed off and moved on to the next item on her to-do list. Finding a phone number for Lydia Baird.

It took some effort. People as wealthy as the Bairds tended to safeguard their privacy, as evidenced by Brie Bennett's carefully curated social media. She checked the time. Nine fifteen. Not too late. She punched in the number.

Given the circumstances—Brie's recent death, the fact that Ren's number would be unlisted—she half expected the call to roll into voicemail. Instead, it was answered on the second ring.

For a few heartbeats, Ren heard nothing but a few ragged breaths. Then Lydia Baird's voice came, slow but knife-sharp. "You're her, aren't you? The woman I saw earlier, who sometimes cleans up messes for my husband?"

It had been a mistake to think Lydia wouldn't know her number. Lydia had probably done her own research into the strange woman who'd shown up at her home to discuss her daughter's death. Ren placed her left palm on her stomach.

"Yes."

"I heard you earlier. Oliver asked you to find out who killed Brie." Each word seemed to take great effort. "Do you have a name?"

"Not yet." The lie was necessary but bitter nonetheless.

"Then why are you calling?"

Ren didn't know enough about the other woman to fake small talk. Better to be blunt. "Can you think of anyone who disliked your daughter?"

"Disliked?" Ren imagined the other woman's scowl. "You mean hated her enough to put her down like a sick animal? Of course some people *disliked* Brie. She was beautiful and rich, and highly aware of both of those things. As she should've been. Brie was special."

Ren rubbed her fingertips over her belly and chose her words carefully. "Other than envy, any other reason someone might've wanted to hurt Brie?"

For several moments, the silence swelled. Was Lydia's hesitation caused by indignation—or guilt? When she spoke, her voice was deeper. "If we knew who was to blame, my husband wouldn't need you, would he?"

Ren picked up on the threat. "What about her husband? Did they get along?"

The other woman sighed, obviously tiring of the conversation. "As well as a married couple can, I suppose. There are always compromises."

"What kind of compromises?"

Lydia released a slow, rattling breath, and this time, Ren recognized the grief in it. Perhaps it wasn't the conversation that left the other woman weary, but rather the chore of existing in a world that no longer included her daughter. "Eric was having an affair, or at least that's what my daughter believed."

That didn't seem like a *compromise* to Ren. That sounded like a reason to serve Eric Bennett a mug of belladonna tea.

"But I suspect Brie might've been having her own."

This surprised Ren. "With who?"

"I have no idea. Brie was like Oliver in that way—she liked her secrets." Lydia's voice hardened. "Look, dear, my husband didn't hire you to investigate my daughter. Why don't you focus your attention on what happened to her?"

It was clear that she intended the comment as a dismissal, but Ren pretended not to notice. Nolan had been sure he'd been hired by Baird. If he hadn't been, there was one more question she needed to ask.

"How careful is your husband with his passwords?"

The other woman hesitated again, and Ren wondered if she intended to answer at all. Then she laughed once, quick and harsh. "He's Oliver Baird," she said. "My husband's a very wealthy man, and this house is a fortress." But after a beat came "The problem is that when people consider themselves untouchable, they can be arrogant. And careless."

Her voice grew wearier, and Ren could picture her as she'd been earlier: the woman with hollow eyes who'd faded into shadow.

"I won't tell Oliver you called, because I don't think he would appreciate the intrusion. But if my husband's right and your husband had something to do with what happened to Brie…" Her already brittle voice cracked. "Oliver's not a patient man, but he has his businesses and his charities to distract him. With Brie gone, I have no such distractions." She went quiet for several seconds before releasing a hiss-like breath. "Now do what my husband asked. Find out who killed my daughter."

After the other woman disconnected, Ren realized she'd used that last phrase throughout their conversation—*my daughter*, never *our daughter*, as if in death, Brie belonged exclusively to her mother, the pain too precious to be shared. While Oliver Baird had taken their daughter's death as a personal affront, Lydia Baird burned with her grief. This made the woman as dangerous as her husband.

CHAPTER 21

JULIA

By the time Eric and Julia reached Encinitas, Julia had convinced herself to forget about the man at the bar. It wasn't that she didn't trust her instincts—the guy was definitely a predator. But it was a Friday night, and some men used the excuse of too many beers to do horrible things.

Eric had managed not to vomit in Julia's car, and by the time she pulled into his driveway, he'd sobered up enough to navigate his front steps without her help. His only goodbye was a slammed door. Ego obviously still bruised.

You're welcome.

Noticing how the fuel gauge needle hovered near empty, Julia headed to the nearest gas station. While her tank filled, she called Cora and told her that her dad was safely at home.

"How's the arm?" she asked.

"It fell off."

"Funny."

"It's okay, Mom. I grew a new one. Apparently, I'm able to regenerate limbs like a sea star."

Cora often used humor to deflect, and Julia caught an undercurrent in her daughter's voice.

Julia wanted to ask if she'd taken her ibuprofen and if she'd been tending the wound, but Cora was already on edge. "What about the rest of you?"

Cora grunted something that sounded like "Fine."

Tank now full, Julia replaced the nozzle in its holder and screwed on the gas cap. She got in the car. "I thought I'd stop by."

"You don't need to do that."

"I kind of do. I need to see that sea star arm of yours for myself."

"Whatever. But I'm not coming home. Evie needs me."

Julia understood what Cora left unsaid: she needed Evie just as much.

"Evie can stay with us."

"We're fine here. Her mom's in the next room." She paused, and when she spoke again, her voice sounded less confident. "But, you know, if you want to get me tomorrow, that'd be cool."

Tomorrow seemed impossibly far away. Julia buckled her seat belt and started the car, connecting the call to Bluetooth. "Did you know Brie's dad was Oliver Baird?"

"Yeah."

"You never mentioned it."

"Like you would've wanted to know that Dad's new wife was rich. She also went to Pilates three times a week and never had a cavity."

At the gas station's exit, Julia looked to the right. A dark sedan was parked down the street. It lingered in the shadows between two streetlights.

Had she seen the car before? Outside the bar in San Clemente? In Eric's neighborhood? She'd been so focused on Eric not throwing up in her front seat that she couldn't be sure.

"Mom?" Cora sounded worried, as if she'd been talking and Julia had missed it.

"Sorry. I zoned out for a second there."

Julia shook off the questions even as the skin on the back of her neck prickled. She pulled onto Encinitas Boulevard toward I-5 North and Evie's apartment in Oceanside. She checked her rearview mirror. The dark sedan remained parked.

"I was asking if you'd seen the video on the news?"

The horrifying images flashed in her brain. "I did."

"It was weird, seeing it like that. When it was happening, I didn't realize…" She took a breath. Let it out. "I didn't realize how close I was to getting hurt worse."

"What matters is you *weren't* hurt worse."

"Watching the video, though…I didn't actually see it when Brie was shot, and I know they blurred it, but that video…" Her voice trailed.

Julia's chest swelled, tension settling in her jaw. Her usually fearless daughter was afraid.

She turned the corner and took one last glance behind her—just in time to see the dark sedan coast away from the curb.

"Maybe you shouldn't watch the news for a while. And don't talk to anyone, okay? Like if anyone from the media calls, or even your friends. Keep a low profile."

Even though Cora stayed silent, Julia could picture her nod through the phone.

Julia thought again of the man at the bar. "Do you know anything about the guy Brie was seeing?"

"Why?"

Wondering if he might drive a dark sedan.

"Just curious."

"I only saw those few texts."

The words came quickly, as if she wanted to be done with the conversation, and Julia's instincts pinged.

"And you're sure you never said anything to Brie or your dad?"

Cora went silent, just as she had that morning when Julia had asked the same question.

Julia put on her blinker and eased into the left lane. Half a block back, the sedan did the same. It didn't signal. She strained her eyes, but even with the glow of the city and a dozen headlights, she couldn't see the driver. She eased off the gas, coaxing the sedan closer.

Instead, a truck merged into the lane behind her.

She told herself she was being dramatic. They weren't alone on this road. Far from it. It might not even be the same sedan she was now certain she'd seen earlier in San Clemente, as she'd helped Eric stumble to her car.

But she'd long ago learned to pay attention to details. The headlights were the same shape: round bulbs framed by twin boomerang-shaped accents, slanted like the eyes of a B-movie alien.

The longer Julia considered it, the more certain she grew. She was being followed. Blood thrummed in her ears.

"You need to tell me everything," she said to Cora, eyes locked on her rearview.

Cora harrumphed. "Like you've always been so honest." She sounded more sad than angry, and the words stung.

Julia flicked her tongue across her lower lip, which had gone dry. "Cora." Her tone a warning.

"It was nothing."

"I need to know."

Cora sighed, and when she spoke again, she sounded tired. "When I played it off like I thought it was the worker's phone, at first I thought she bought it. But then her eyes got all squinty, and I could tell she knew I was lying. I mean, I'm not stupid. Why would she have gotten so upset if it belonged to someone else?" Cora paused. "So, she slapped me."

Instantly, Julia forgot about her tail. A dull anger gathered inside her chest that she didn't know what to do with. She couldn't direct it at a dead woman. So she turned it inward. If she'd been more open with Cora, maybe—

A horn blared. Julia jerked the steering wheel to bring her car back into its lane.

"She slapped you." Julia's voice was icy as she crossed under the overpass. She considered merging quickly to the right without signaling. Taking I-5

South instead. The dark sedan might follow, or it might not. But either way, the driver would suspect she'd picked up on the tail. She wanted him to believe he remained anonymous. For now.

"It was no big deal, Mom." Slipping into the familiar role as peace-maker. Wanting everyone to get along, even now that Brie was dead. "The rest of the night, she wouldn't let me out of her sight. Probably waiting for me to say something, either to her or to Dad. Later, she even tried to get me alone. Asked if I could help scoop ice cream. I mean, Brie eating ice cream? Like that's not a huge red flag."

Julia gripped the wheel so she didn't drift out of her lane again, and somehow she managed to keep her speed steady as she climbed the on-ramp.

Julia opened her mouth to ask, *Why didn't you tell me? Why didn't you tell your dad?* But she knew. Eric had been absent from Cora's life for years after the divorce. Cora had probably worried that he wouldn't believe her. That he might leave again. The lump in Julia's chest grew colder. "Oh, Cora."

"It's why she bought me that cell phone."

So the phone had been a bribe? What else had she missed?

Julia pulled into the far-right lane, keeping her head still as her gaze darted from her rearview mirror to the highway in front of her and back again. On the side of the road, she caught glimpses of concrete barricades, construction equipment, and palm trees with fronds painted black by the night. But the cars that traveled the road behind her were without color or shape, each reduced to a pair of glowing orbs.

A sign flashed her speed and a warning: SLOW DOWN.

The traffic was light but steady, with most cars cruising at around eighty miles an hour. Julia slowed to the posted limit, weeding out the more impatient drivers, who swerved their vehicles around hers. She glanced in the rearview mirror and again caught sight of the alien-like headlights.

Julia put on her blinker and took the exit toward South Carlsbad State Beach. The other vehicles kept to the highway, but the dark sedan peeled off, following her. She dropped her speed further.

Could it be a cop? The police drove dark sedans too, though she couldn't recall ever seeing one with those distinctive headlights.

Her gut told her it wasn't a cop.

"You never saw that phone of Brie's again?"

"What's going on, Mom?"

The alien lights grew closer. "Nothing's going on."

At the stoplight, Julia turned left, willing her hands to relax on the wheel. They remained rigid. She glanced in the rearview mirror again. The dark sedan turned too.

"You think the guy she was hooking up with might've shot her?" Cora asked.

"Of course not," Julia said too quickly.

Cora sensed the lie. "Okay." Her voice was suddenly guarded.

Ahead, Julia spotted a McDonald's. She turned right onto the side road, toward the fast-food restaurant. The dark sedan remained behind her. She edged into the left lane. At a break in the concrete median, she jerked the wheel into a U-turn. Drifted into the left lane. There was a moment when the two cars passed each other and Julia's headlights caught the front of the sedan. Her gaze dropped toward the bumper, looking for the license plate. It had none. Either stolen or removed. She pulled her gaze to the driver's face, but it was too late. He'd already passed.

"Look, Cora, if you're really sure you're okay, I'll wait until the morning to come by." The tension had climbed up her arms and nested at the base of her neck. As much as she wanted to see Cora, Julia couldn't go to Evie's apartment. She couldn't risk leading the dark sedan to her daughter.

"Sure. Whatever."

"I'll see you in the morning. I'll bring pastries."

But Cora had already disconnected.

With her daughter's voice suddenly gone, it felt as if all the air had been sucked from the car's interior. Julia switched on the fan and positioned the vent so it blew cool air on her face. At the light, she turned left and took the on-ramp onto I-5, headed south this time. The sedan reappeared in her wake. A cold weight settled in her stomach.

She waited for the cars to her left to clear and then stomped on the gas. In seconds, the dark sedan was less than a few car lengths behind her. Her gaze darted to her speedometer. They were both pushing ninety-five.

She knew she couldn't outrun him. She just needed to be sure.

Heart thumping, Julia wrenched the steering wheel, pulling her car farther to the left. The road was rougher here, her tires vibrating at the high speed. The sedan cut behind her. Nearby, brakes screamed and a horn bleated.

Julia's foot relaxed on the gas. Time to call the police.

As if intuiting her intentions, the dark sedan abruptly slowed and switched lanes, pulling right. At the next off-ramp, it banked another hard right, soon lost to the steady flow of exiting cars.

CHAPTER 22

REN

When Nolan came home, Ren was still sitting in her chair, though she'd switched to researching on her laptop instead of her phone, and she'd put on her computer glasses. The TV played in the background, volume turned to whisper level.

Nolan took off his shoes and turned toward the TV, staring at the screen with arms crossed. Photos of the dead woman flashed. Ren slipped off her glasses and turned her attention to the screen too. Everything about Brie Bennett had a luster to it. The warm brown hair expertly messy in every photo. The wide bleached smile. The blue eyes that might've seemed icy if not paired with those teeth.

She was also newly married. There were at least a dozen photos of her in a satin, side-slit dress that would've looked equally appropriate at a formal cocktail party. Nolan had picked the wrong woman to kill.

Ren grabbed the remote and turned off the TV. If she'd been less in control of her anger, she might've thrown the remote against the wall. It would've been satisfying to see it shatter. But anger wasn't good for the baby. She placed the remote carefully on the table, then set her laptop and glasses next to it.

"A couple of Baird's thugs were in our parking garage. Waiting to escort me to his estate," she said.

Nolan crossed to her and grabbed her hand. "You're not hurt?"

"I can take care of myself." She pulled back. "He just wanted to talk." *And threaten our family.*

She studied her husband's face: jaw tight, eyes strained. With its complexity of muscle groups, the face was capable of thousands of unique expressions, but Ren had no problem reading her husband. He was nervous. He started rubbing the wrist he'd broken while training at Fort Benning.

"Baird wanted to discuss his daughter's death?"

"He's suspicious. He wants me to find out who killed her."

"I should talk to him. Convince him we had nothing to do with it."

"That's not the best idea. He already thinks you're involved."

"Then I definitely need to talk to him. Tell him—"

She cut him off. "He asked that I keep you out of it." Though, really, Baird wasn't the type to *ask*. He'd demanded.

"He doesn't trust me." Nolan looked as though he'd been slapped.

"Do you blame him? You did kill his daughter."

"For all he knows, it could've been random."

She bit back a surge of anger. Nolan should've involved her from the beginning.

"Random. Was Bruce Murphy *random*?"

Nolan's wrist grew red where he rubbed. "That was an accident."

"You mean a mistake. Like lying to me about Baird being the client."

Nolan sighed in exasperation. "I was sure he *was* the client. What else did you tell him?"

Ren ran through the relaxation techniques she'd learned from her pregnancy book. *Take a deep breath and release it slowly. Close your eyes. Clench your jaw.* She had the last one down, at least.

"I told him I would look into it."

Nolan had told her that Brie was targeted because she'd killed someone. Who had she killed? And, more importantly, who had that person left behind? That's who they needed to be looking for.

"We need to know more about Brie Bennett if we're going to figure out who would want her dead," she said finally.

"As soon as I heard about that"—Nolan gestured toward the TV—"and realized who she was, I started looking into her."

Ren stood and moved in front of him, forcing his eyes to focus on hers. "What do you mean *started* looking into her?"

"You know what I mean. Of course I looked into her before the job. But there's a difference between killing newlywed Brie Bennett and killing Baird's daughter."

Ren gestured toward her laptop. "I've been looking into her too." She didn't mention her searches on Julia. She didn't want him to think her sentimental.

"So you know," Nolan said. "There's nothing online to suggest who she might've killed. No boyfriends or college roommates who went to the Bahamas and never returned. Not so much as a car accident or suspicious fire."

Ren knew that even if there had been an accident, Baird could've covered it up—just like he'd done at the Shearwater.

"I think he paid someone to scrub her online presence, maybe to protect her," Ren said. *Or himself.*

"Nothing on social media either."

She stared hard, taking in his pressed lips and slight pallor. Was he nervous because Baird might have them killed? Or was he keeping something from her? Nolan had always been her blind spot, but she felt the tingle of instinct. "So there's nothing on who she might've killed. What about the person who hired you?"

"The anonymity is what protects us. Other than Baird, I've never met any of our clients."

She crossed her arms but stayed silent. For the baby, she decided not to resurrect old arguments, even as her temples throbbed. As a repeat client, Baird understood that she and Nolan might eventually notice a pattern to the kills—connect them to one client, and then to him—so after their third job for him, he'd summoned Nolan for a face-to-face meeting.

Mutually assured destruction and all that. At least Nolan had gotten the respect of a phone call, and not two goons in a parking garage.

"If we don't give Baird a name, he'll kill us," Ren said matter-of-factly.

Nolan hesitated, as if making a decision. Then he walked out of the room, returning a minute later with a small kraft paper mailer.

"I usually destroy these after the job's done. Like you with your maps. But since we haven't received that second payment…" His voice trailed off and he held out the envelope.

She took it. She rubbed her fingers over the light brown paper, feeling the hard squares contained inside. She knew what they were. The Polaroids. He'd mentioned them to her before, but she'd never seen any.

She sat in the chair, reached for her glasses, and unclasped the envelope. As expected, it held a small stack of photos—shots of the conversation between Nolan and the client, each photo numbered in red Sharpie. Even with glasses, she squinted as she read the first one.

I've got another job for you.

When?

Soon.

Details?

To come.

Ok. Deposit in usual account?

This one's sensitive. Has to be cash.

Pick up?

No. I'll text with a drop location.

"Messages are end-to-end encrypted, set to self-destruct, and can't be forwarded." Nolan sat across from her. "Screenshots are disabled too. But those—" He pointed to the photos. "It's helpful to have an insurance policy. You know, if something goes wrong."

Ren understood that was the reason she'd never seen the other photos. She'd never needed to.

She flipped to the second Polaroid. This one with the screen of a phone instead of a computer. An address. Nothing more.

"The first payment was there just as he said it would be, along with details about the targets," Nolan said. "A photo of the woman and the girl."

"You still have those?"

He gestured toward the photos again. "These, I could explain away. Photos of the victims? Details of where they would be on the day they died?" He shook his head. "I memorized them, and then I destroyed them."

Before flipping to the third Polaroid, Ren held his gaze for a few seconds to let him know she wasn't sure she believed him. More texts.

12:30 p.m. tomorrow.

That's soon.

It has to happen then. You got the cash and the photos?

Yes.

Second payment when I get confirmation.

Ren set the photos in a row in her lap, studying them. "I'm guessing you've destroyed the phone too?" Her voice was cool, and maybe a touch sarcastic.

"Yes." He reached across and tapped the first photo. "Like I said, I assumed it was Baird, because this is the messaging platform we always use. Exclusively. I use a different one with other clients, and whoever signed on would've had to know Baird's username and mine in order to initiate contact."

That might not mean much. Lydia Baird had confirmed that her husband was careless with his passwords.

"And after initial contact you switch to burners."

"Yes." Grooves cut into his forehead—his thinking face. "You sure Baird wasn't fucking with you? If his daughter did something he considered evil, I could see him paying to take her out, especially if it might reflect poorly on him."

She frowned. "We don't kill to protect a client's image."

He held up his hands, palms out. "Come on, Ren. You know what I mean. Baird's a zealot, maybe even an asshole, but our goals are aligned, aren't they? And his contracts have been lucrative over the years."

While Ren knew she often misread the subtext of conversations, she was an expert at body language. Did the way a target touched his waistband indicate his pants were slipping, or that he'd hidden a weapon there? Did the way his knees jerked mean he was getting ready to run? What about the tension in his shoulders? There were a thousand different twitches and spasms and tightening muscles that she'd cataloged. Poisoning was as much art as science, one she'd spent years studying, as a woman often alone with men twice her size.

Because of this, Ren knew: there was no way Baird was involved in his daughter's death. His body language had been honest.

"Those are all you got?" she asked, gesturing toward the Polaroids.

He nodded once, his lips compressed so tightly they nearly disappeared. Fatigue had deepened the creases around his eyes.

"There's something else. I know why we didn't get the second payment." He released a hard breath. "It's the girl. The second target. She's not dead."

Ren inhaled sharply but said nothing. She didn't trust herself to speak. She took off her glasses again and carefully returned them to their case.

She set the case down next to the Polaroids. Then she stood, drawing her spine into a rigid line, waiting for him to continue.

"There's a recent photo of the girl on social media, and it's starting to circulate. Apparently, the report of her death on social media was based on a misunderstanding."

Misunderstanding. Another word for "mistake." Her body stiffened, every muscle taut. "You said the girl was dead."

"I took two shots, and the second one got her. I'm certain."

Nolan could make that shot from a mile away. But this time he'd missed.

"And then that woman dragged her body away. She didn't move after that…" As his voice trailed, his eyes lost focus. "After seeing that photo online, I tried to find her. That's where I've been. I tracked down her father—Brie Bennett's husband—hoping he'd lead me to her."

She held up a hand to stop him. "So the girl is the victim's stepdaughter?"

His jaw clenched, and he stayed silent for several seconds. "They're *targets*. Not *victims*."

"Answer the question."

"I told you they were related."

Her own muscles tightened further, nearly snapping. "When you were following the father, I take it you didn't find the girl?"

He hesitated, drawing away. Only a few inches, but Ren noticed. He offered a slight shake of the head. "Whoever hired me must've heard the girl's still alive too. We need to finish the job."

"Not until we know who's behind it."

Nolan's eyes hardened. "We should talk to your dad. In person."

The *in person* part went without saying. It was too delicate a conversation to have any other way. But Ren was reluctant to bring her father into it any more than she already had.

"We can figure this out without his help," she said.

"He has contacts we don't, Ren. He has more experience than we do."

"He's retired."

Fatigue shadowed the skin beneath his eyes. "You want to protect him.

I understand. He's my family too." He touched her stomach. "Which is why I know he'd want to help."

Ren paused, considering, before offering a half nod and moving away from his hand. "I'll set something up."

She tried not to dwell on what might have to come next.

CHAPTER 23

JULIA

From her car, Julia dialed Officer Sandra Lee, updating her about the wolfish man at the bar and the odd behavior of the dark sedan. Lee was attentive, but the call failed to soothe Julia's frayed nerves. There seemed to be no other helpful news. After disconnecting, she drove aimlessly for more than an hour, attention darting frequently to her rearview mirror. Only when Julia was convinced that no one followed did she drive to Oceanside. She needed to know Cora was safe. Twenty-three years earlier, Julia had arrived home too late. She wouldn't allow that to happen again.

Despite the late hour, the lights remained on in the Fourniers' apartment. Julia parked along the curb next to a sign warning of street sweeping the next morning.

Screw your street sweeping.

Julia killed the engine and watched the upstairs window, its sheer curtains drawn.

She took out her phone and started typing into the browser, intending to revisit the familiar list of shootings as she had dozens of times over the years, counting on each like a talisman. But she managed only a few letters before her fingers froze. She couldn't look at another photo of a devastated parent. Couldn't read another quote about hopes and prayers.

In the greenhouse, the past Julia had fought to keep at bay for decades had settled in her gut like a stone. She couldn't deny those memories were a part of her too. Now they crowded in alongside her in the Civic, begging for her attention. Her blood throbbed in her ears, and her body twitched. Her knuckles blanched as her grip on the phone tightened. She couldn't just sit in the car and wait for morning.

But waiting, and watching, was all she could think to do, so her gaze flashed again to the window, hoping for a glimpse of her daughter. And indeed, someone stood behind the curtains now, their shape reduced to a gauzy shadow, edges blurred. Still, Julia recognized Cora's familiar movements. Julia could picture her, wearing her favorite pajama shorts and oversized T-shirt with the rabid bunny, washed so often the red had faded to a ghostly pink. When Cora was anxious, she would ball her hands around the shirt and tug, so that over the years its hem had stretched to near transparency. Julia pictured her daughter like that now, hands balled in her shirt, her face the same as it had been earlier that day—pale and pained and lost.

Julia wouldn't be one of the parents in those photos. In the morning, she would call Mike. There were other searches she hadn't yet tried. Without answers, her daughter would never be safe.

A few minutes later, Cora moved away from the window, but Julia continued to watch until the apartment blinked into total darkness.

Julia left before the street sweeper came after all. While her daughter slept, she found a bakery advertising PASTRY CAKES COFFEE in its window. In case that wasn't enough, there was also a sandwich board that promised, in bold cursive, the best lattes, according to Thrillist. Starving, Julia needed only the OPEN sign to be lured inside.

The bakery smelled of coffee and baking bread. Julia ordered one of their famous lattes and too many pastries: cranberry-orange scones, churro croissants, and éclairs filled with vanilla crème.

After she got her overloaded box and coffee, Julia went outside, choosing a round table beneath a blue umbrella. It shaded all but a sliver of her right arm. She adjusted the chair to bring the arm into shadow. As she sat in front of the bakery, she watched the street for dark sedans, and the storefronts for possible stalkers.

Satisfied that she was alone, Julia took out her phone and scrolled through her contacts. Though she'd never called Rebecca Fournier, Julia knew she had the number. Somewhere. Was it under her first name? Last name? She checked both *R* and *F* before finally finding it under *E. Evie's mom.* Of course. Julia composed a quick text and hit send: How are the girls?

The answer appeared within seconds. Hanging in there.

I was hoping you could look out for Cora until I can get there to pick her up.

Julia had met Evie's mother only once—at Cora's graduation—and though they'd exchanged phone numbers with vague plans to grab coffee, neither had reached out. But now there was no hesitation. You don't even need to ask. The bubbles danced for a few seconds before a new message popped on the screen. Glad the girls have each other.

Blood thrumming in her ears, Julia sent another text, this time to Cora—Call me when you're up—before punching in Mike's number. When he answered, she skipped the small talk. "Remember that story you wrote about the activists?"

"Good morning." Mike sounded amused. "So nice to hear from you. How're things?"

Impatient, she took a sip of her latte, scalding her tongue. She grimaced and put the cup down. "Yeah, good morning." Her tongue felt fuzzy. "We should get together for Bloody Marys soon and talk about what a wonderful guy you are. How helpful you are to your friends. And colleagues. So: remember that article?"

He was silent for a few seconds. "You're going to need to be more specific. We live in Southern California. I covered a lot of protests."

"The one that won that award."

"Well, not to brag…"

She heard the grin in his voice. Normally, she would've smiled in response. Today she didn't have time. "I know. You won a lot of awards, though not nearly as many as you deserved, being the brilliant writer that you are."

"That's a very kind and spontaneous comment." Then his voice lowered, growing more serious. "Are you talking about the protests surrounding the Libyan journalist?"

"That's the one."

"While I applaud your interest in world politics, I wrote that story nearly a decade ago. Why the interest now?"

Julia tried another sip of coffee, eager for the caffeine. "In that story, you mentioned how dissidents and journalists use the dark web to avoid government censorship."

"Sure. Everyone does, these days. Even the BBC."

"Could you show me how to use it?"

"The dark web?" He paused. "Planning on overthrowing the government?" While he kept his tone light, she heard the concern.

"I've been thinking about the shooting."

"Of course." He sounded suddenly guarded.

"What if the guy Brie was seeing killed her?"

"And I've been thinking the police are already investigating this."

She sighed, rubbing her temple. "Come on, Mike. I'm not planning to buy a fake badge and go door-to-door. You said the dark web is anonymous."

"Yes," he said begrudgingly.

"It's encrypted, and there's no way anyone can trace my name or location?"

"It's not that simple."

She couldn't hold back her exasperation. "Then tell me. That's why I called you."

Mike went silent. When he spoke again, his voice was as serious as she'd ever heard it. "You remember that Libyan journalist was killed, right? And that during my research, I met this activist. An earnest and funny young man born in Libya but raised here. UC Irvine student named Kamal. Collected old records. Dylan. Led Zeppelin. The Who." That reminded Julia of Cora, who'd taught herself to play "Stairway to Heaven" on the guitar at thirteen.

"He was all over the dark web. Until he once mentioned a coffee shop near his house. Kamal didn't name the place. Just a distinctive drink they served. But that was enough for him to be tracked."

This was a cautionary tale, and those never had happy endings. "What happened?"

"They doxxed him. Posted his banking information online. Sent a compromising photo to all his contacts. It wasn't him—it was Photoshopped—but it didn't matter. Enough people believed it was, and quite a few of his *friends* forwarded it."

Julia felt the sun sneak back over her arm. She left it to bake. She welcomed the pain. Better than the cold that had settled in her bones.

"After that, he dropped out of college. Then, a few weeks later, someone waited outside Kamal's apartment and beat him nearly to death."

Julia pushed away her latte, having lost the stomach for it. "That's horrible. Was he okay?"

"He's not okay, but he survived." The way Mike put it in the present tense made Julia think he still checked up on the kid. Though ten years later, he wouldn't be a kid anymore. "That's the case that made me decide to stop being a reporter. I didn't have it in me anymore."

"I'm sorry," she said. She let the moment stretch, because both of them seemed to need the silence. "I wouldn't make a mistake like that, Mike."

"People rarely intend to make mistakes."

"You can help me. Make sure I'm as careful as I need to be."

She sensed him wavering. "What are you hoping to find?"

"Would it be naive to say answers?" *About a man who might've targeted Cora too.*

Mike's breathing became loud enough for her to hear it clearly through the phone. "You're never naive, Jules. Just stubborn."

"So you know I'm doing this." Julia told him about the video, and her growing theory, even as it left her momentarily unable to breathe.

"If she hadn't moved…"

"But she did. She's okay." Mike's voice held an urgency that nearly broke her. "The worst didn't happen."

"That's the thing," Julia said. "It's like with Kamal. Cora survived, but she's not okay, and what if he really did mean to kill her?" Julia paused to steady herself. "You get me there, and I can just browse. I don't need to interact with anyone."

He grunted, but she knew she had him.

Julia also knew what Mike was leaving unsaid: if she was careless, getting doxxed wasn't the worst that could happen.

CHAPTER 24

REN

Anthony Petrovic lived on the west side of Los Angeles in a 1940s two-bedroom bungalow, painted an unremarkable gray with simple white trim and a dark blue door. There were no potted flowers on the small porch. No mat that said WELCOME by the door. Ren's father saw no reason to encourage visitors.

When Ren and Nolan pulled up to the curb, he was waiting for them at the door, arms crossed.

As Ren opened the gate to start up the small walkway, her eyes flashed to the paper bag Nolan carried, and her brow tightened. Earlier when she'd asked about it, he'd refused to tell her what was inside.

When Nolan caught her look, he leaned in and, with a half smile, whispered, "You hate surprises, don't you?" His breath was hot on her neck, and her skin tingled.

She scowled and kept walking. When they reached the porch, her father's expression grew even more guarded.

"Twice in two days." The weight of his attention shifted to Nolan. "I'm guessing this case is more screwed up than Ren thought."

Beside her, Nolan stiffened, his hands tightening on the handles of the bag, but he kept his face neutral. "Afraid it is," he said.

Ren's father glanced at the bag but didn't ask about it. Less curious than she was, apparently. He stepped aside and gestured them into his home. Inside, a gray sofa and dark wood furniture dominated the living room. The walls were bare and painted a stark white. The only personal touches were the books stuffed on a shelf—Tom Clancy, legal nonfiction, weapons manuals, and a dog-eared copy of *The Power of Ethics: How to Make Good Choices in a Complicated World*—and, on a side table, two small framed photos. One was of Ren and Nolan the day they married, the other Ren as a child with her father, him with a Glock and her with a lightweight Ruger. These books and photos, along with the weapons in his bedroom closet, would be the only objects he would grab if he had to leave in a hurry. Ren knew this from experience.

Her father motioned them toward the sofa, then settled himself in a blue-and-gray-striped armchair. "So what's going on?"

Ren let Nolan explain the situation. The shooting. The girl who was supposed to be dead but wasn't. Baird's request for a name. Nolan and her father had always possessed an easy rapport, but when Nolan reached the part where Baird had expressed reservations about their business relationship, her father tensed. His lips compressed into a thin line, and for several seconds that felt much longer, no one spoke.

Then her father sighed deeply. "I warned you, Ren. Working with a client more than once is foolish."

Ren's hands knotted on her lap. Nolan noticed. He reached into the bag and brought out a decanter filled with an amber liquid. He set it on the coffee table and twisted the bottle so the label faced her father. The older man nodded in approval.

"Single malt. Aged thirty-three years."

"Distilled the year Ren was born."

Nolan pulled the stopper out of the bottle, then put his hand back in the bag to retrieve three glasses. One was engraved. He pushed this glass across the table. Her father's face softened as he reached out to touch the word cut in the heavy crystal: GRANDFATHER.

Nolan poured a finger's width in each of the three glasses. Ren knew her pour was symbolic. They were in this together, even if one of them couldn't drink because she was incubating a human.

Nolan pulled his own glass closer but left it on the table, allowing the whiskey to breathe. "I know it's probably too early in the day for this, but who knows when we'll have another chance."

Her father picked up his glass and rested it on his thigh. "A payoff to help get you out of this mess."

Nolan shook his head. "A celebration, and a promise that I'll always do what's right by your daughter, and your grandchild. Which is why we're here."

"Like I said."

Impatient, Ren leaned forward. "Have you heard any rumors about who might've hired Nolan?"

Her father swirled his whiskey and brought it to his nose. He closed his eyes and sniffed. When he opened his eyes again, his gaze settled on Nolan.

"Remember that case the three of us worked in Seattle?"

"The human traffickers. Sure."

"The women in that hotel room. Girls, really. None older than twenty."

Ren had suggested strychnine for that one—she wanted to see the hotel clerk and his two associates suffer—but her father had insisted he and Nolan take the lead. Three gun deaths would make sense to the police, given the nature of the men's business. Her father had tasked her with keeping watch. *Keeping watch,* as if she were twelve years old again.

Ren hadn't done as she was told. While her father and Nolan dispatched two of the men, she'd found the clerk alone in his office and injected him.

Her father's eyes wrinkled at the corners as he nearly smiled. "You wanted him to know it was coming."

"It worked out, didn't it?"

His expression grew serious again. "I wouldn't say that."

Ren fought the urge to roll her eyes. "A scratch. A cat would've done more damage."

She thought of Julia's tabby, but shook it off. This wasn't the time.

"Nolan had to stitch you up."

The desire to roll her eyes grew stronger. "Two stitches, Dad. So quick, I barely felt the needle."

Her father stared at Nolan. "You took good care of my daughter that day." His voice was gruff. He cleared his throat and drained half of his whiskey. He cradled the glass in his hands. "Have you considered Eric Bennett?"

Nolan took a drink, then held his glass in the same way. Ren recognized what he was doing: Mirroring her father. Showing deference. "You think he did it?"

Her father lifted one shoulder in a quick shrug. "I've heard some talk about a large bank withdrawal." Ren knew that meant he'd already been asking around. *Defend the family.* "He's worth a look, at least."

Nolan leaned forward, meeting her father's unrelenting gaze. "As the son-in-law, he would've had access to Baird's estate. And he would know that the girl is still alive, which would explain why he withheld payment."

Ren supposed the theory made some sense—except for one crucial detail. "We're back to the same question we had about Baird: why would a man kill his own daughter?"

Without looking away from Nolan, her father said, "What about that guy in Vancouver?"

She remembered the news story. A year earlier, a man had pushed his son off a cliff while they were hiking in the Pacific Rim National Park Reserve. A gambler with lousy luck, he'd wanted access to his son's trust.

Nolan tore his attention away from her father. "Bennett has two beneficiaries, right? His wife and his daughter. What if, like that guy in Vancouver, he needed money, or wanted to keep a family windfall to himself?"

Ren rested her hand on her stomach, forehead tightening. Her gaze moved from Nolan to her father, and back again. "Seems a stretch."

"Okay, what about that woman who drove her kids into a lake?" Nolan asked. "Or the man who killed his toddler to keep his ex-wife from getting custody? We might never know why I was hired, but unless you have another idea…"

His voice trailed off as he watched her. Waiting for some sign he'd convinced her?

Ren rolled the idea of Eric Bennett around in her head, the possibility tenuous at first but growing more solid the longer she considered it. Since Baird was careless with his passwords, it could've been anyone who'd been in his home. Still, Eric Bennett would've had greater access. Ren's skin warmed. True, the motive was shaky, but she'd witnessed enough evil to know it was often hidden. The youth minister. The high school English teacher. The guy who sold you lottery tickets at the mini-mart.

That clerk who'd kept six malnourished and bruised girls sedated in a Seattle hotel room. Who had three adult children of his own, two of them daughters.

"I could do some surveillance," she said.

Nolan took her hand and squeezed. "He feels right, Ren. He'd be perfect."

Her father's eyes narrowed to slits. "What do you mean by that: *He'd be perfect?*"

"He makes sense as the person who hired me."

Her father's expression grew guarded again. "I hope that's what you meant, Nolan." His tone cooled. "I hope you didn't mean he'd be a perfect person to set up for this. Because that's not how we do things in this family."

Ren watched Nolan's face for a reaction to the rebuke, but if he took offense, he gave no sign. "*Shield the innocent.* I know."

Her father relaxed and picked up his whiskey. He tilted it toward Nolan in a solo toast. "You're going to be a great father," he said. He let the rest of the amber liquid flow down his throat and smiled. "And if you don't do right by my grandchild, I still have my guns."

CHAPTER 25

JULIA

Mike sat next to Julia at her kitchen table, their chairs pushed close enough that they could both read the screen of her laptop. Mike took the last bite of his scone before wiping his fingers with a napkin. Julia had dropped off the box of pastries at Evie's apartment on the way back to her house, but she'd saved Mike a couple of the cranberry-orange scones. His favorite.

Despite the infusion of sugary carbs, Mike wore a pained expression as Julia carefully typed in the URL he had given her.

"You're the smartest person I know," he said.

Julia continued to tap the keyboard. "Don't let anyone in the physics department hear you say that."

"Damn funny too."

"I'm working on a set." She pointed to the scrap of paper where he'd scribbled the Web address, a random series of numbers and letters. "Is that an *O* or a zero?"

"Zero."

She typed in the digit and then glanced sideways at him. "Go on." She waved her hand. "I believe you were complimenting me, and you hadn't yet made it to my ability to quote classic sitcoms."

"That's covered by the part about you being smart. You're also thoughtful and tenacious."

She squinted at the paper and then typed in a few more digits. "You mean stubborn."

"Maybe." His pained expression deepened. "But Julia—you can't type worth shit."

Unfazed, Julia held the scrap of paper next to the URL she'd typed. They matched. "You told me to be careful."

"*Careful.* Not *glacial.*"

Julia hit enter, bringing up a black screen with strings of white and red lettering. "We're in. I think?"

His forehead wrinkled as he leaned in to study the screen. "Appears that way," he said cautiously.

She turned to him. "I thought you knew this stuff."

"I'm a former journalist. I know enough to write a story, but not enough to sell cryptocurrency." He paused. "But it looks right."

"Better be, or we might get voxxed."

"Doxxed."

She grinned. "Just messing with you." Her grin faded as she read the rows of text. "So, where do we find people talking about the Anderson Hughes shooting?"

He gestured to the laptop. "Do you mind?"

She held up her palms. "Go for it."

He scooted the laptop closer to him and started scrolling. Julia leaned in, and in the same instant, Mike did too. Their faces hovered inches apart, two pairs of eyes fixed on the screen, and she felt the sudden warmth of him. Julia held the position for a moment before leaning back again.

On the screen, threads on gardening, books, and video games shared space with ones on masturbation, insurance fraud, and recreational drugs. There was also a discussion slugged "Animal friends." Julia hoped it was a forum for pet photos.

Another thread caught her eye, and she pointed to the screen. "Melissophilia?"

"A fetish thread."

"People have fetishes involving women named Melissa?"

"Probably. But melissophilia is the term for those who get aroused by stinging insects."

Her nose scrunched. "That's a thing?"

"And that's not the worst of it." Mike stopped scrolling. "Found it."

The Anderson Hughes thread began with a discussion about guns.

Anonymous: everyone knows it's the shooter not the gun

Anonymous: Bullshit. Gun matters especially with a shot like that.

Anonymous: wouldnt have to be very good if he had a decent scope maybe he was close too

Anonymous: I've seen the area. Only place he could've had that shot was at least a mile away.

A third person joined the conversation.

Anonymous: Come on. There are buildings taller than that right on campus.

Anonymous: Not with a decent view.

Then a fourth.

Anonymous: heard it was an M24 so military?

Anonymous: Wouldn't have to be military. Any deer hunter could've made that shot.

Anonymous: Bolt action or semi-auto?

Anonymous: Bolt action. You can get lower to the ground.

Anonymous: I vote semi-auto heavier bullets too because of wind

Anonymous: not much wind thursday

Anonymous: Enough to send a shot off course if you didn't know what you were doing.

Anonymous: as warm as it was there prob wasn't much drag either

Midway through the thread, someone posted a link to the cell phone video. Julia's heart thrashed in her chest like a startled bird. The memory played, unbidden. Cora stepping aside a fraction of a second before the first bullet struck. The second grazing her arm.

The third killing Brie.

Julia took a long breath and blinked to refocus.

Though Mike had control of the keyboard, he turned to her and said, "Don't click on anything unless you trust the link. And in here, you never trust the link."

Julia had no intention of watching that video again. "Don't click," she said, her mouth dry. "Got it."

Mike continued scrolling slowly, both of them reading and Julia jotting notes. Most of it was speculation, but she filled pages anyway. If the police ever searched her home, they'd have a field day with this notebook.

A few minutes later, Mike slowed his scrolling when the discussion turned to motive.

Anonymous: think it was random like the cops say?

Anonymous: Makes sense. Sniper attack is a risky way to kill someone.

Anonymous: I don't think it was random. Brie Bennett wasn't even her real name. It was Melody Weaver.

Julia frowned. *What the hell?* A flurry of responses popped onto the screen.

Anonymous: u mean the little bitch killed while camping w/her parents?

Anonymous: Wasn't that a cult thing?

Anonymous: I heard she was sacrificed to the space-traveling lizard men who rule our planet.

Anonymous: It wasn't lizard people. It was the Bairds. They were having some kind of sex party and their daughter walked in on it. So the mom killed her to keep her quiet. Then they stole Melody and pretended she was their daughter.

Julia rolled her eyes. "The conspiracy theories have started." Beside her, Mike scowled, and she nudged him with her shoulder. "What?"

He rubbed his forehead, as if releasing tension. "This isn't good."

"What do you mean?"

"There's some creepy stuff on these sites—"

"Obviously."

"—and as horrible as the Anderson Hughes shooting was, there were over six hundred mass shootings in the U.S. last year."

Julia nodded. She knew the number.

Mike continued. "True, there are some zealots who follow this type of violence…" She felt the heat rise in her cheeks, and his gaze softened. "I'm not talking about the average person, who's outraged. Horrified. The people I'm talking about—they get off on it."

Julia felt suddenly queasy, and angry.

"But like I was saying: even with Baird's high profile, most of these trolls will move on quickly."

"Which keeps Cora safe."

"Exactly. But if a conspiracy gains traction, the masses online might become more…engaged."

She understood then: if the story gained traction, it grew more likely that Cora's survival would become bigger news too. Mike was right: this wasn't good.

Julia turned her attention back to the computer, hoping interest had waned, but new comments flooded the screen.

Anonymous: Baird's hotels are a front for traffickers.

Anonymous: the rich always get away with shit

Anonymous: sex club photos here (link)

Anonymous: Traffickers killed his daughter because he screwed up a job and a girl died before she could be delivered.

Anonymous: thats prob why the bitch was killed in public to make a point

There were dozens more like that. And then a new one flashed. Julia's blood boiled.

She reached toward the keyboard, but Mike rested his hand on her wrist. "Don't."

"They can't say that."

"Like I said, there are worse things on here."

Julia read the words again.

Anonymous: I heard the new husband had a friend do it.

"We're here to listen," Mike reminded her.

"But we can't just let that go unchallenged." Julia had been so consumed by her need to keep Cora safe that this new threat threw her off-balance: was Eric at risk too? How had she missed that? "He didn't do it. We need to…" She stopped, her mouth dry, tongue tacky.

"What?"

"I don't know. Defend him."

Mike leaned back in his chair and folded his arms across his chest. "Tell me what you'd say."

"I would tell them they're dumbasses, obviously."

"They would rip you to shreds."

She stared at him defiantly. "You don't think I can handle a couple of trolls?"

He grinned in that lopsided way, though now it held more than a hint of sadness. "Actually, I think it would be entertaining as hell watching you eviscerate them. But other than that, how would it help?"

In the time they'd been debating, a spate of new comments had populated the screen. Julia leaned back in.

Anonymous: really?

Anonymous: Who has friends like that?

Anonymous: Don't WE have friends like that?

Anonymous: Anyone else hear it might be the husband?

As Julia had feared, the trolls started piling on.

Anonymous: It's definitely the husband. Gotta be.

Anonymous: What do you know about him?

Anonymous: some finance douche lives in encinitas

Just like that, Eric's occupation and where he lived were out there. Anxious, but still she kept reading.

Anonymous: Must be rich.

Anonymous: not as rich as her

Anonymous: She's not rich anymore. Just dead.

Anonymous: Rich people don't like to share their money.

Anonymous: So motive?

Anonymous: what the fuck do you think?

Anonymous: How much would it take for you to kill your wife?

Anonymous: I don't know? A hundred bucks?

Anonymous: a lot less than that bitch had thats for sure

CHAPTER 26

REN

After talking with her father, Ren dropped Nolan at the condo, intending to check in at the gym before heading to Encinitas. Instead, she found herself on the I-110 headed toward Pasadena. Once she found a spot near a strip mall downtown, she took out her phone, navigated back to the dark web, and checked in on their earlier handiwork.

Ren scrolled through the feeding frenzy her post had ignited.

Anonymous: Anyone else hear it might be the husband?

Anonymous: It's definitely the husband. Gotta be.

Satisfied, Ren tucked away her phone and got out of her car.

Ren had of course destroyed her kill map for Karl Voss, but she didn't need it to locate his ex-wife, who, fortunately, lived in Pasadena and not Bakersfield. Ren's bladder wasn't up to another long drive. She had memorized Clarissa Voss's routines, and Saturdays were reserved for their son K.J.'s judo class.

Ren decided the martial arts studio wasn't an option. The small cinder

block building would be filled with about a dozen parents and staff members. They would immediately identify her as an outsider.

But the fifteen-minute window after class was possible. That was when Clarissa would take K.J. for a treat, usually frozen yogurt in the same strip mall as the studio. K.J. liked vanilla-chocolate swirl topped with gummy worms and crushed Oreos. They always ordered it to go. Not ideal, but Ren could make it work.

Arranging to bump into Clarissa and K.J. was risky, but Ren needed to know she'd done right by poisoning Voss.

As soon as she'd walked into Baird's office, Ren had recognized him as a predator. The dry-eyed stare. The shifting brogue meant to charm. The way he'd subtly threatened the child she was carrying after so recently losing his own. What had Nolan been thinking to ever trust Baird?

Ren walked slowly to the yogurt shop. When she saw Clarissa and her son leave the studio, Ren sped up. As always, her timing was spot-on. Clarissa held the door for her.

Creatures of habit.

Clarissa Voss was a broad-faced woman with curly blond hair she'd tamed into a ponytail. A smattering of freckles crossed the bridge of her snub nose. Ren thanked her and offered a slight smile. Then she tilted her head, feigning puzzlement. "Wait. Do I know you?"

She studied Ren's face, her confusion genuine. "I don't think so."

Ren slipped on what she hoped passed for an apologetic look. "I'm usually here with my daughter, Maddy. That might be it?"

From her surveillance, Ren knew that Clarissa was rarely impolite. The other woman hesitated, then said, "Maybe."

"Sorry. It's just that you look so familiar." Ren started to move away, then stopped, pivoted, and snapped her fingers. "The Shearwater."

Clarissa's mouth pursed and she glanced down at her son. "Why don't you get started on your yogurt?" After K.J. headed toward the counter, Clarissa's eyes narrowed to slits. "What about the Shearwater?"

Ren took a small step back. Not too close. She wanted to put the former Mrs. Voss at ease. "I worked with your husband, Karl, briefly." She watched the woman's face for signs of suspicion, but she seemed to be buying the lie. "It's been a while, I know, but I'm sure that's it. He had this photo of you and your son on his desk." Ren laughed, but it came out a little sharp. She needed to work on that. "Though I can't say I would've recognized your son if he hadn't been with you. He's twice as tall now."

Clarissa's face relaxed a little, though her eyes remained hooded. "Yeah, that was probably an old picture."

Did the ex-wife know Voss was dead? It had been a full day since Ren had left him on that park bench, but if Clarissa knew, would she still be here? Ren was pretty sure that if K.J. knew he would never see his dad again, he wouldn't be scooping crushed cookies onto a cup of frozen yogurt with quite so much gusto.

Ren felt a sharp pang she passed off as a cramp.

"This might be inappropriate," Ren said, dropping her voice, "but do you have a current work phone for Karl? I'm looking for a new job, and I'd love to add him to my references."

Clarissa snorted. "We're divorced. And trust me, you don't want to use Karl as a reference."

So that answered Ren's earlier question: Clarissa didn't know.

"Oh, I'm so sorry. I heard he left the Shearwater, but I hadn't heard, you know, that your marriage had ended." Ren faked another awkward laugh. Better this time. "Trust me, I get it. Maddy's dad—he's a real jerk." She whispered the last part, making a show of looking around to verify that little ears weren't listening.

She waited for the other woman's reaction. Clarissa seemed to be considering how much to share with this stranger. Experience had taught Ren not to push. Made uncomfortable, one of her targets had once tried to stab her in the eye with a ballpoint pen.

Clarissa leaned in. "Hate to burst your bubble, since you seem to have a good relationship with Karl, but my ex is a *jerk* too."

The way she said the word suggested she would've preferred a stronger one. Ren respected her discretion.

Ren had been keeping tabs on K.J. out of the corner of her eye, and across the room, she saw him drop a pile of gummy worms onto his yogurt. That meant he was done creating his masterpiece. Sure enough, the boy turned to start the short walk back.

Ren swallowed her disappointment. Apparently, there would be nothing real learned from Clarissa Voss.

"Well, it was nice meeting you, at least," Ren said. "Guess I won't be asking you to tell Karl hello for me."

Clarissa smiled. "Probably not the best idea."

K.J. at her side now, the other woman took a step, then, as if remembering something, turned back toward Ren. "Have you tried calling the other Baird properties? For a job?" When Ren shook her head, Clarissa added, "Karl managed a few different places besides the Shearwater, at least until he was fired. Paid pretty well. It might be worth checking them out."

Ren knew better than to assume, so she asked, "Were these all-night shifts?"

Clarissa nodded. "I'm sure they have day shifts too, but Karl got more money for working nights, and traffic was better. Made it easier for him to juggle a few hotels. Good money, even if he did put in twelve-hour shifts. Not sure if you're up for those kinds of hours, with a kid and all." For a moment, Ren thought she meant the tiny stranger, but then she remembered her fictitious daughter, Maddy. Clarissa gestured to her son. "Anyway. Don't want the yogurt to melt. Good luck with the job hunt."

After Clarissa and K.J. left the shop, Ren paid cash for a small strawberry yogurt she didn't want, and, once out of sight, she threw it in the trash. The thought of eating anything roiled her stomach.

On the walk back to her car, Ren couldn't stop thinking about the Anderson Hughes shooting, or how Nolan had said Karl Voss was lazy, a man who'd lock workers in so he could hook up with a girlfriend.

Yet apparently, Voss had been putting in twelve-hour shifts juggling multiple properties. When did he have time for an on-the-clock affair?

There was a chance Clarissa had gotten it wrong, and that Voss was spending the time he was supposed to be working cheating on her instead. But Clarissa didn't seem the type to cover for her ex-husband.

So had Baird lied to Nolan, or had Nolan lied to her?

Besides, if Voss was managing several of Baird's properties, what were the chances the billionaire didn't know what his night manager was doing? According to Nolan, Voss told the cleaning crew he was only following Baird's orders. What if he had been?

Having now met both men, Ren knew which one she thought was more likely to lock employees inside. And it wasn't the man she'd poisoned in the dog park.

CHAPTER 27

JULIA

After Mike finally left, making Julia promise to check in later, she texted Eric: ok if I come over?

He responded within minutes: sure

While Julia was growing increasingly worried about Eric after seeing the talk online, she was also growing worried about how she'd bring it up. The last time she and Eric talked, she'd tripped him in a restaurant.

Maybe a different approach this time.

Julia checked in with Evie's mom by text before calling Cora to say she would be picking her up soon. She didn't tell Cora she was headed to Encinitas first. Cora would've insisted on coming, and this wasn't a conversation Julia wanted to have with their daughter in the room.

On her way, Julia stopped at the grocery store to pick up some seeded sourdough, a bottle of distilled water for the newly potted plant, and a large can of Eric's favorite lentil soup. Good hangover food. And a peace offering.

At Eric's house, she'd made it up the short walkway before she froze. The front door was already ajar. This was a habit of her ex-husband's—leaving doors open if he was running to his car or taking out the trash. But open doors set Julia on edge. Why make it easy for people to harm you?

Cautiously, she approached. Though the door was open, she knocked. When no one responded, she jabbed the doorbell twice, then took out her phone and entered quietly.

Seeing nothing amiss, she closed the door behind her, then set her grocery bag on the kitchen counter. For several seconds, she listened, but she heard only the soft ticking of the refrigerator. She called out Eric's name. Then a loud thumping erupted from the back of the house.

Eric shouted a curse, then called out, "In here."

Finally releasing her breath, Julia followed Eric's voice to the master bedroom. She hesitated in the doorway. The floor was a tangle of clothes and hangers. Drawers had been ripped from dressers and dumped onto the floor. Mounds of shoes reached knee level.

"What's going on, Eric?" she asked softly.

He emptied a laundry hamper on the bed and tossed it aside. It landed near Julia's feet, nearly clipping her leg.

Eric was rubbing his eyes so hard she worried he might break skin. He wore the past two days as thick stubble along his jaw and bruise-like smudges beneath his eyes. His T-shirt and jeans were the ones he'd been wearing the night before.

He burrowed into the pile. "It's not here," he said, voice and expression frantic.

"What's not there?"

"Brie's favorite blouse." He looked up, the sclera of his eyes more pink than white. Had he slept at all? "She would want to be…" His voice caught. After a moment, he tried again. "She would want to wear that for the funeral." He choked on the last two words.

Julia knew it wasn't about the shirt. "Let me help. What color is it?"

"Blue."

"Long sleeved, or short?"

"Long." His brow knitted. "No, short." He pointed to his elbow. "It hits her here." Obviously frustrated, he started throwing the clothes on the floor, one piece at a time.

"Blue shirt. Got it." Julia knelt and started in on the piles. After a minute, she found a blue shirt with three-quarter-length sleeves. She held it up. "This one?"

He shook his head impatiently. "I've already checked there."

"Did you check the washer and dryer?"

Immediately, his shoulders slumped. "I didn't think..." His voice trailed off, as if overlooking that was an unimaginable failure. She reached out and rested her hand on his shoulder for a moment before standing.

"I'll check." She grabbed the hamper on the way out of the room. In the dryer, she found a small load of laundry. Among the delicates was a teal blouse with three-quarter sleeves. She loaded it and the other clothes into the basket and returned to the master bedroom.

She pulled out the shirt, creased from its time forgotten in the dryer. "Is this it?"

Eric crossed the room, somehow without tripping, and grabbed the shirt from her hands. He pulled it to his face and inhaled sharply. He closed his eyes, as though remembering a scent that had been washed away. He brushed his fingertips over the wrinkled fabric. "It's ruined now."

Julia grabbed his hand, clammy and cold, and took the shirt back. She smoothed out the creases as best she could and put the shirt on a hanger. "We can iron it." With her back turned to him, she said, gently, "Eric...I was online today and saw some comments suggesting the shooting...might not have been random." She saw no need to mention where she'd seen the comments, or what they'd written about him.

"No one would want to hurt Brie." But his voice wavered, and he didn't sound as convinced as he'd sounded two days before.

When she turned to face him, she saw that he'd picked up another of Brie's blouses. He sat on the bed, holding the blouse to his chest, eyes half-closed.

Julia sat beside him. "What about the boyfriend?"

Eric exhaled sharply but it took him a moment to answer. "I was wrong last night. There's no use in talking about it." His voice hitched. "She's dead. Like you said, nothing changes that."

Julia thought of the video, and how Brie had scanned the crowd. "If she was seeing someone, any chance they were on campus that day?"

"I don't know." The fissures in his forehead deepened, even as his attention seemed to shift. "You want to hear something pathetic? I would've stayed. As long as she would have me." He kneaded Brie's blouse, balling it up in his fists.

"That's not pathetic. You loved her." *More, it seems, than you ever loved me.*

His chest heaved, as if even breathing was an effort, and he released the blouse onto his lap. He nodded.

"What about her father? Did they have a good relationship?"

He attempted a shrug. "They'd been estranged for years, but they reconciled shortly after the wedding. Nothing like finding out your daughter's gone and gotten married to make you sentimental." His face grew pinched. "But I think they might've had another falling-out."

"What makes you think that?"

"On Tuesday, she went to visit him, and when she got home, she was in a terrible mood. Wouldn't talk about it. Didn't leave the house for two days. I had to convince her to come to Cora's move-in day." His eyes softened and he blinked hard. "I wish I hadn't tried so hard to get her there."

"It's not your fault," Julia said, even as she thought, *Things* had *been tense between Brie and Eric.* And he'd convinced her to go to Anderson Hughes. If the police found out about either of those things, it wouldn't look good for him.

Eric seemed unaware of the implications of what he'd just said. "A few months ago, we were planning a belated honeymoon. To celebrate after…well, I haven't even told you yet, but I just started a new job. It was supposed to mean better things for us. Instead, she's…"

He swallowed, and Julia felt a lump rising in her own throat.

"I brought you some soup." She rose and was heading toward the kitchen when there was a sharp rapping on the front door. Three quick knocks. Eric picked up the blouse from his lap, carefully folded it, and set it on the bed beside him. He planted both palms on the mattress to steady himself, but even then he nearly toppled as he stood.

As she followed Eric to the living room, Julia checked her phone. She wasn't going to get more out of him now, and at least he was safe for the moment. She wanted to get back on the road. On her way to Cora.

But when Eric answered the door, Julia immediately recognized the man on the porch. Or, rather, she recognized his type. Sharp-eyed. Graying hair. Expression both pleasant and wary. Her impression was confirmed when the man pulled out his badge.

"Detective Hoffman," he said. "You have a moment to talk?"

CHAPTER 28

REN

When Ren walked into Anthony's Gym, Darien was helping an attractive woman with short blue-streaked hair figure out the cable tower. He tilted his chin in greeting, then returned his attention to the woman, who was obviously more interested in Darien than in the machine.

Ren retreated into her office, closing the door behind her, and unlocked the largest desk drawer, taking out the mason jar of coins. She set it on the desk and fired up the computer.

After navigating to the encrypted browser, Ren unscrewed the mason jar's lid and dumped the coins on the desktop. With the tip of her index finger, she slid them one at a time across the wooden surface, creating a line sorted by value. She started with the five quarters. On the last one, her finger froze. She reached into her pocket and pulled out the quarter she'd been carrying since Friday. Voss's quarter. She noted the year—2016—and made space for it in the line.

Next she lined up the single dime, six nickels, and eleven pennies. Lately, it had been harder to come by the coins she needed for her collection, and several times she'd resorted to checking a target's cupholder or junk drawer. Still, though her habit occasionally proved inconvenient, she couldn't very well keep a jar of debit cards.

When Ren was done sorting the coins, she felt calmer, studying the tidy rows of silver and copper, each inscribed with a year she'd worked to memorize. She didn't need to count them, but she did. It was part of the ritual.

Twenty-four dead. And that didn't include Nolan's solo jobs.

She picked up one of the pennies. They were the easiest to collect. Targets surrendered them freely, as if eager to be rid of them. Yet they were the most memorable; some of the pennies in her collection were a dull brown, others a bright copper, one a crusted green.

It was the shiniest of the pennies she held in her palm now, the copper-plated zinc, newly minted when she'd taken it a few years before. It had once belonged to a con man she'd poisoned with rosary pea, a small plant with pale violet flowers, slender stems, and glossy seeds that reminded Ren of ladybugs. A single chewed seed could kill a person, but her target had cut his finger the day before, so it had been easier to sprinkle a little rosary pea dust on the wound.

Ren placed the penny back in line and started brushing her fingertips across each of the others in turn, remembering.

The 1993 penny had been taken from a man who'd overdosed on morphine, the drug's effects hastened by the cheap vodka he'd been drinking. He'd stopped breathing within minutes—just like the woman he'd strangled in Austin, Texas.

The 2018 penny had been an oleander death. The 2019 penny, foxglove. The 1988 penny had been hemlock, but he'd lingered so she'd needed her gun to finish him. She didn't like to think about that.

Since Ren had started collecting more than a decade earlier, she couldn't see a penny without thinking of the dead.

Ren dropped each of the pennies into the mason jar. When she was done, she turned her attention to the other coins. She picked up one of the quarters. Nineteen eighty-five. Rubbed it between her right index finger and thumb. The quarter had been the first coin in her collection. The man she'd shot the night she'd met Nolan. When the target had fallen, the quarter had slipped from his pocket and rolled a few inches, hitting her boot. Reflexively, she'd picked it up, rubbing it as she did now. She hadn't planned to take a trophy. She wasn't that kind of killer. But she had dropped the quarter in her pocket and carried it with her for a week. Not as a prize, but as a reminder.

When Ren dropped the quarter in the mason jar, it clinked against the glass.

She went through the rest of the quarters in turn, saving for last the one from 2002. It had belonged to the only woman she'd ever killed, one of the few times she'd needed to administer a second injection. The atropine found in belladonna was a wonderful poison. It broke down rapidly and was difficult to trace. Even the telltale dilation in the eyes mimicked what happened naturally after death. But atropine was also used as an antidote for other poisons. No use bringing someone close to death, only to offer them the antidote in the same dose. The target in that first belladonna poisoning had been implicated in the death of her teen son, whose body had been found in their crawl space, so Ren hadn't minded the woman's extended suffering. She dropped the quarter in the jar and wiped her fingers on her pants.

Ren moved on to the lone dime. Though she knew she was imagining it, this coin felt colder than the others. It came from the first job they'd done for Baird, three years before. Jim Usoro. Usoro abused his wife. His stepson. His sixteen-year-old girlfriend. Ren had followed the man for two weeks before slipping some strychnine salt into his wine. It had been a violent death. Usoro's face had reddened and contorted. His eyes had bulged. Though spasming violently, he remained conscious for the hour it took for him to die, face fixed in a rigid grin. Ren had felt a hint of guilt until she'd seen the photo of his stepson in his soccer uniform on the mantel. The boy no longer played soccer, owing to the broken leg that never healed quite right.

After dropping Usoro's dime into the jar, Ren broke with tradition to type his name into the search engine. When she switched from Jim to James, the number of hits doubled. Because of his relatively unusual last name, it was easy for Ren to identify which of the James Usoros was the man she'd poisoned. She navigated to his social media, where responses to his death were more a trickle than an outpouring. But one in particular stood out.

Jim's timing always sucked. Two weeks later and his wife would've been rich.

Ren furrowed her brow. Intriguing.

Next she typed in two names: James Usoro and Oliver Baird. The results were scarce, and all referenced the same article from *Forbes.* According to the article, before Usoro died, he and Baird had been negotiating a minor real estate deal. Minor by Baird's standards, anyway. The billionaire probably spent more each week on his security detail. But for someone like Usoro, the deal might have been life-changing.

As Ren scanned the article, though, she realized the deal had fallen apart a month before Usoro's death. There would've been no getting rich for his widow.

Unless.

What if there was something she wasn't seeing? She read the article a second time, but there were too few details to reach a conclusion. And the most reasonable explanation remained the narrative Nolan had sold her back then: Usoro had come to Baird's attention through a minor business transaction, and when Baird found out what kind of man Usoro was, he scuttled the deal.

A simple and straightforward story. Made sense then. Made sense now. Yet Ren found herself wondering how Usoro would have taken the news of the failure. He couldn't have been happy. Did he try to force Baird back to the table? Had there been a signed contract?

Ren could see that annoying Baird. But she still couldn't see him hiring an assassin over what would have been, at most, an inconvenience. Baird had a team of lawyers on retainer who would've fought any resulting legal battles, and besides, there was no mention of any lawsuit in the article. But her intuition pinged—because she knew that even if Baird wouldn't kill over an inconvenience, he might kill over a threat.

Using one of her fake social media accounts, Ren sent three friend requests: to Usoro's widow, to his former girlfriend, and to the man who had posted the comment. Then she continued dropping the coins into the mason jar, one by one, pausing with every drop to research each of Baird's targets but finding nothing else.

Ren was catching up on the posts about Eric Bennett when someone knocked on her office door.

It had to be Darien. Who else?

"Come in," she said as she minimized her browser window.

Her manager bustled in and dropped onto the small sofa that had been there nearly as long as the gym itself. Decades of sweat had worn the nubs off the once-textured fabric, and stains darkened the backrest, but Ren saw no reason to replace it. She never sat there herself, and Darien didn't seem to mind. In fact, Darien practically snuggled into the sofa, stretching his arms across the backrest. The shape he made matched up with the stains.

"Figured I should check in since it's been a couple of days," he said, tugging his Pomeranian-mangled ear as he sometimes did. "Expected to see you Friday."

She thought of Voss, and the doubts returned. What if she had indeed killed the wrong man?

"I was baking," she said.

"Didn't know you liked to bake."

"Sometimes."

"What did you bake?"

She only hesitated slightly. "Oatmeal raisin cookies."

He grimaced. "An inferior baked good. With nuts?"

"The nuts were the point." She swiveled so she more directly faced him. "I saw you helping that member. Very personalized service."

"I should probably get employee of the month." He motioned to the coin jar. "You know parking meters take credit cards, right?"

She returned the jar to the drawer but didn't lock it. She couldn't have him guessing how important it was to her.

"I had a cousin who was a numismatist," he said. "She kept her collection in these tiny plastic sleeves so the coins wouldn't get scratched."

Darien and his relatives again.

"That wasn't a collection," she lied.

"Well, if you find any you think might be valuable, hit me up and I can run it by her."

"I'll think about it."

Ren hated small talk, especially now. She wanted to check the status of her friend requests. See if there had been any more posts about Eric Bennett. Find his address so she could drive by his house. She forced a small smile. "How's it been around here?"

"A little slower than usual. I think people are spooked by that Anderson Hughes shit."

Suddenly, Darien had her full attention. She stilled, and she willed the tension from her face. No one gave a neutral face better than her. "Are members talking?"

He shrugged with one shoulder, arms still draped on the backrest. "I mean, a rich kids' college gets shot up only a couple of hours away. Of course people are curious." Seemingly becoming more interested, he leaned forward. "Steph said she heard the husband did it." He tugged his ear again. "Makes sense, right? Steph's the member that, ah, needed some help."

"Naturally." So the rumor she'd started that morning had already spread. Unless Steph frequented the dark web? If the rumor was spreading this quickly, she wouldn't need to go to Baird with the name. He would hear it on his own.

But there were also risks to it spreading so swiftly.

Darien was still talking. "The *real* question is who the husband hired to kill her."

There was nothing unusual in the way he said it, but Ren's pulse jumped. Yes, there was that.

Darien furrowed his brow. "Everything okay, boss?" he asked finally. "You seem distracted."

So maybe her mask had slipped a little after all. She went with the easy lie. "Morning sickness."

He nodded. "Heard that can be brutal. You should drink plenty of water and avoid spicy foods."

Pulse still racing, she cocked her head. "I didn't know you were an expert on morning sickness."

"Guess it's like your baking," he said dryly. "We're both full of surprises."

CHAPTER 29

JULIA

Detective Hoffman's slight smile cut deep grooves in his cheeks, his dark but silvering stubble suggesting he'd put in a couple of long shifts. His face was narrow and while his hairline receded, the hair that remained was thick, and his mustache was carefully trimmed.

"I was hoping to speak with you again, Mr. Bennett." He managed to sound both friendly and somber, but Julia noticed Eric's shoulders tighten. "Just a few follow-up questions. Mind stepping outside?"

Eric stepped onto the porch, and Hoffman's gaze shot from Eric to Julia. He squinted behind his glasses, the frames rounded, the lenses lightly tinted in the sun. "And you must be Julia Bennett."

Her spine stiffened. Of course he knew her name. What else did he know? Julia could suddenly smell the fetid lake near her childhood home and the tang of blood. She fought her fingers, which moved to clench around an imaginary dandelion.

"Since you're here, I'd like to talk to you too. It shouldn't take long."

The silence stretched, and Julia realized the detective was awaiting her confirmation.

"Of course," she said, stomach knotting. She fought to keep from looking at Eric. While she wanted answers too, she worried that the ones the detective sought might be ones she desperately wanted buried.

Hoffman's smile deepened, though still not enough to expose any teeth. "Would you mind waiting in here for a few minutes while I talk to Mr. Bennett?"

She nodded again, thinking of the dark web posts.

Anyone else hear it might be the husband?

It makes sense.

It's definitely the husband. Gotta be.

Hoffman and Eric stepped away from the door but left it open. Wordlessly, Julia crossed the living room to water the new pitcher plant and sundew, which Cora had named Anya, and then retreated into the back of the house.

The spare bedroom was darker than the living room had been, the blackout blinds still drawn. The room was too warm, and Julia caught a faint citrus scent with a hint of spice. Cinnamon, maybe? Or clove.

She kept the door open, using the dim light behind her to cross the space. When she reached the far side of the room, she opened the blinds and cracked the window. The slight breeze carried with it a hint of ocean. She closed her eyes, letting the air gently scrub the heat from her cheeks. Reluctantly, she thought of Eric's questions that first day.

Did they ask about me? They always ask about the husband, don't they?

Julia opened her eyes, and looked around the room. The bed was hastily made, the green comforter more lumps than smoothed edges. On the nightstand sat a nearly full mug of tea, the string from the tea bag trailing onto the tabletop. This was the room Cora used when she stayed over, and when she looked around, Julia found other traces of her daughter. A pair of sneakers half-hidden beneath the bed. Her Burt's Bees lip balm on the dresser. Without reading the label, Julia knew it would be vanilla bean.

Julia sat on the corner of the bed and texted Cora a cat meme. Breathing in the lingering scent of her daughter's life, she waited for a reply that didn't come. When she could no longer detect any trace of Cora in the air, she returned to the front of the house to wait.

*   *   *

Twenty minutes later, Eric came back inside, and Detective Hoffman motioned for Julia to join him on the porch instead. His eyes landed on her hands before he found her eyes. He moved to place both the open door and Julia in his line of sight.

His expression remained as guarded as his movements. "I appreciate you sticking around to talk to me," he said, raising his notepad and pen.

"Happy to help if I can."

"I've seen the video from the shooting. You took cover pretty quickly."

"You hear gunfire, that's what you do."

"Most people don't recognize gunfire for what it is, not in a setting like that. But you—impressive how fast you moved." He didn't seem impressed. He seemed suspicious. "As far as I can tell, you were first on the ground."

"Someone has to be first."

"You have training with guns?"

"No. I tried, but…" *Experience, but not training.*

"Just great reflexes, then." The corner of his mouth twitched as if he might smile again, but his face remained passive. "You also stepped away right before Mrs. Bennett was shot. The interview notes mentioned you were leaving to retrieve your daughter's phone?"

"Yes."

"Did you ever find it?"

She strained to follow the logic of his questioning. "I did. Later. In the library."

"A witness also mentioned you crawled back out to save a girl. After the shooting began, I mean. What made you decide to do that?"

She couldn't help it: she squirmed. She'd already answered that. Were they trying to catch her in a lie? "It wasn't a decision. I reacted."

"I understand. Just like when you took cover." He looked down at his notepad, adjusted his glasses, then locked eyes with her again. "Your parents were killed when you were fourteen."

Her mouth went dry. So he'd done his research. "A couple of days before I turned fifteen, yes."

She squared her shoulders, bracing for his next question, but instead his eyes softened.

"This must be especially hard on you, to go through something like this again."

There was no question in there so she said nothing.

He dropped his hands, holding the pad and pen clasped at his waist, giving the impression the interview was paused. Julia knew better.

"Think that's part of why you reacted when you heard the gunfire?" he asked innocently.

Julia opened her mouth to answer that, naturally, the murder had made her cautious. More wary of guns, strangers, and unlocked doors.

But for some reason, the half-truth wouldn't come. That violence wasn't the reason she was so jumpy. She owed her heightened reflexes to all that happened next.

Without a family member to take custody of her, Julia was named a ward of the state. Foster care. That meant a twin bed in a nicer home than she'd lived in before, which she immediately hated because her parents weren't sleeping in the next room.

At the time they died, Serena and Vince Bell had no real assets. Most of their furniture had been purchased secondhand, and the cash in their checking account wouldn't have covered a venti latte at Starbucks. So Julia arrived in foster care with only her grief and a backpack.

She left the same way. The phantom weight of that battered backpack lodged between her shoulder blades.

"I was homeless for a while." It was strange, finally saying it out loud.

Hoffman had to have known already, if not from social service records then from the police reports filed that last night on the streets. Julia respected that he didn't pretend the information was news. Instead, he nodded once in acknowledgment.

"Can't imagine that was easy. I've seen what can happen to young women in that situation."

Julia had too. Far too often. On the streets, being an attractive young woman sometimes brought offers of food, a tent to share, drugs. But not all were made out of kindness. What Julia remembered most from those days was the fear. The sense of always being on edge. During that time, Julia had scratched at her wrists until welts appeared, then worried they would become infected because she had no way to clean them. She knew now that she'd been punishing herself. Then, she'd only known she had to survive.

"There was someone who was kind to me." *Kinder than I probably deserved.*

Hoffman raised his notepad, all business again.

"I heard you called in a tip that Mrs. Bennett might've been having an affair." When she nodded, he asked, "What do you know about that?"

"Just what I told Officer Lee on the phone." She recapped the details: the prepaid credit card, the charges to the hotel.

"Anything else?"

Julia hesitated. Then that horrible video flashed through her mind again, and she said, "Cora mentioned that Brie might have a second phone."

His gaze sharpened. "What makes her think that?"

She thought, *She saw texts that mentioned Brie was leaving Eric.* But she couldn't say that. Not with the target already on Eric. "She saw it on the dining room table."

Hoffman did some more scribbling and then stared at her again, unblinking. "Looks like the Bennetts have recently done some remodeling in the kitchen. Know anything about that?"

What did the remodel have to do with anything? "I'm the ex-wife, not the contractor."

"Know who the contractor is?"

She shook her head.

"Can you tell me about your routine in the days leading up to the shootings?"

Dark blood on green grass. Dark blood on chipped tile. But those weren't the shootings he was asking about, so she shook her head to clear it.

"Why do you ask?"

"Just trying to establish Brie Bennett's routine in the days before she was killed. It helps to look at the people in her life."

"I wouldn't exactly say I'm *in her life*."

"You share parenting duties."

Did we? Brie had slapped Cora, and her daughter had kept it from her. Julia's jaw tensed, and she hoped Hoffman didn't notice.

"Before Thursday, we hadn't spoken in weeks."

"Two weeks, right? Let's go back to that last time you and Mrs. Bennett spoke. How'd that go?"

"How it always went. She came with Eric to pick up Cora. We were civil."

"Where were you Tuesday night?"

Tuesday night? "Cora and I went shopping for plastic bins, for her dorm, then we got Thai food." Cora had picked yellow curry, medium heat. Julia had gone with the pad Thai. "What does what we did Tuesday night have to do with the shooting? I'm sure you've seen the cell phone video they've been showing on the news." Heat rose in her cheeks. "My daughter was shot. Nearly killed. Why aren't you looking into that?"

He scribbled in his notepad. "Who says we aren't?"

Her whole body stiffened. "And?"

"It's still early days, but as soon as we get any solid information, we'll let you know." Hoffman handed her his card, then slipped his notepad into his pocket. "I appreciate your time."

As Hoffman walked to his car, Julia slowly unclenched her fists. *Still early days.* As if that wasn't the precursor to a parent being told "Too late."

She returned inside to find Eric pacing. He looked up, eyes wide, face haggard.

When he spoke, his voice rasped. "I think I screwed up."

CHAPTER 30

REN

Even on a Saturday afternoon, the I-405 South slowed to a creep just north of Encinitas. On the hillside to the left, palm trees loomed over the rooftops of barely visible houses. To the right, orange construction netting cordoned off a stretch of hard-packed dirt that bristled with weeds. The sky above was pale and cloudless.

Though there was no other route that would've taken Ren where she needed to go, she glanced at the traffic app on her phone. One report attributed the slowdown to an animal in the road. Another blamed a minor collision. But when the traffic cleared a mile shy of her exit, she saw nothing out of place. Just the blur of vehicles on an open highway.

A few minutes after the traffic cleared, Ren pulled onto Encinitas Boulevard, passing more orange netting and work signs as she headed toward the subdivision near Moonlight Beach. She found a spot a discreet distance from Eric Bennett's town house and parked. Bennett's dark blue Mercedes was at the curb in front of his house. His blinds were drawn. His front door was closed.

Ren thought of the vial she'd moved from her pocket to the glove box. Still unsure what to do, she turned off her car and picked up her phone.

She used the Onion Browser and navigated to the fake social media account to check her friend requests.

Interesting.

While Jim Usoro's widow and girlfriend hadn't responded, his friend Scott had accepted. Probably had something to do with the fake profile picture of "Sara," a pretty blonde who was into golden retrievers, matcha lattes, and the San Diego Padres.

Ren picked at her cuticles as she thought of Usoro's history, and how he'd abused his wife and stepson. What kind of a person was Scott to be friends with someone like that?

Unless that story about the abuse had been fed to them by Baird.

With the engine off, the heat inside the car spiked. Ren cracked the window. Still warm, but in the slight shade of a palm, at least she could breathe.

With one sweaty hand holding her phone, she used the index finger on the other to scroll through old posts. She found the comment from Scott that had first intrigued her: *Jim's timing always sucked. Two weeks later and his wife would've been rich.*

Ren continued scraping her cuticles, glancing from her phone to Bennett's door and back again. She squinted at the screen, wishing she had her glasses.

How to play this?

It would be stupid to respond to Scott's original comment directly. While any contact posed a risk, posting on a years-old thread was especially dangerous. Any comment she made would cause a flurry of alerts to be sent to anyone following that thread, and even though she used an encrypted browser, it would be unwise to engage with strangers in such a public way.

The only option was to direct message. Ren was confident she knew enough about Usoro to convince Scott she was a friend of a friend.

As "Sara," Ren typed, I know it's been a while but I just heard about Jim. So horrible!!!

She cringed at the multiple exclamation points and the string of broken heart and crying face emojis she tacked on next. Not at all Ren's style, but it seemed fitting for a woman whose favorite color was listed as flamingo pink.

The reply came instantly: Yeah, it's crazy. How did you know Jim?

I worked with him briefly, right before that whole Baird mess.

The comment was meant to get Scott talking about Baird, but it backfired. You worked at Howell and Hannigan too? What department?

Was he suspicious? Or just hoping to connect with the pretty blonde in the photo? Ren used the collar of her shirt to wipe sweat from her face. When she brought her hand down, she noticed a tiny bead of blood on her thumbnail. The skin below her cuticles was an angry red.

Ren wiped off the blood and typed, Commercial sales. I was an admin for like a minute before quitting. Jenkins was a jerk. Cal Jenkins, junior partner. She didn't know for certain Jenkins was a jerk, but he had been married three times so at least two women out there probably thought he was. Jim was cool though. Wish I would've kept in touch. She followed that with a pair of angel emojis and praying hands.

Jim could be a dick too. Laughing face emoji.

Apparently, her earlier instincts had been right: Usoro wasn't missed much.

After responding to Scott's laughing face emoji with three of her own, Ren decided on the direct approach: Saw your comment about how Jim's timing sucked. What happened to his wife? She always seemed nice.

Never liked his wife much myself. If she hadn't smelled money coming, she would've left him long before he died.

Money? Thought the Baird deal was already dead by then?

The deal sure. But he was still going to make that asshole pay.

She cringed—expletives were just lazy language—then considered what Scott had said. How did Usoro intend Baird to pay? Maybe he'd planned to sue, but she still couldn't imagine Baird's lawyers leaving any loopholes in a contract. And even if they had, Usoro wouldn't have had the money to take on the billionaire's legal team.

Ren glanced again at Bennett's door—still closed—then back at her phone. She typed, Think Baird would've settled?

Settled? Confused face.

Ren cocked her head as she studied the screen. Thought you said he was suing Baird?

More laughing emojis. Can you imagine Jim taking on Baird in court? No way that would've worked out.

So how was Jim getting his big payday?

Bubbles popped on the screen as Scott composed his next message. Five seconds. Ten. Ren risked another glance at Bennett's door. It remained shut, but someone had opened the blinds. She squinted, but she couldn't see inside. She opened the glove box and pulled out her binoculars, careful not to break the tiny glass vial next to them.

Settling the binoculars in her lap, Ren returned her attention to her phone. Scott had replied. He wasn't suing Baird. He was blackmailing him.

Ren bit at the raw skin on her thumb. The gentle pain grounded her. That's ballsy. About what?

Hey, it worked. Baird said he'd pay.

He'd ignored the second part of her reply. Jim died before he could collect?

Yeah, poor guy. Should've laid off the supplements.

That had been Ren's way in: she slipped a fatal dose of strychnine into his wine, then mixed a smaller amount of the white powder into Usoro's package of black ginger and red ginseng.

She'd been proud of that one; the powdered poison came from the seeds of the *Strychnos nux-vomica,* also known as *Semen strychnos.* Semen was Latin for seed, of course, but also an appropriate name given that the supplements Usoro had taken had been for improved sexual vigor and longevity.

Ren played dumb. Supplements?

He got this boner powder from an herbalist and they found strychnine in it. At least that's the story.

Sweat dripped into Ren's eyes. She blinked to stop the stinging. When she'd left Usoro's place, she'd taken the half-empty bottle of wine and the tainted glass. Could she have left some other evidence behind?

It was still too darn hot. Ren started the car, rolled down the window a few more inches, then killed the engine. If Nolan was driving, he would've let the engine idle to keep the air-conditioning on. He didn't care as much about his carbon footprint as she did.

She encouraged, Oh my god.

Scott typed, That's some nasty shit is all.

Ren knew it was. Strychnine caused a particularly painful death. That was the reason she'd chosen it for a man who twice put his wife in the hospital and left his underage girlfriend blind in one eye.

Scott typed, You'd think he would've called 911.

He might have if Ren hadn't hidden his phone. She took a deep pull of overheated air, then asked again. Yeah not very smart. So how was Jim blackmailing Baird?

She had to wait several beats for the reply: Why so interested?

Shoot. Just curious.

Jim was curious too. See how that worked out for him.

She sent him praying hands. Yeah poor Jim. Trying to get him on her side again. Or was he threatening her too? It was kinda stupid to try to get one over on Baird.

That was Jim. Always looking to make the easy buck.

She tried again. So what did he think he had?

The answer came slowly. Something to do with one of his hotels I think.

Ren immediately thought of the Shearwater, and of Karl Voss. But the Usoro job had been ordered years before. It further solidified her suspicion that Baird wasn't a righteous man.

Ren could still picture the way Usoro had died: seizing, twitching, frothing at the mouth. Inside her, she felt a quickening. She laid her palm on her stomach. Which hotel?

Immediately, she recognized it had been rash to ask so directly. Scott went silent. No bubbles this time. The heat in the car surged, her jaw ached, and she wiped it free of sweat with the back of her hand. She waited, impatient, but no response came.

A minute later, the green bubble next to Scott's name blinked off. He was no longer active.

Ren waited, studying Eric Bennett's front door and cursing her misstep. She fought the urge to delete Sara's profile. That would've been compounding one foolish action with another. Sara couldn't disappear too quickly.

Bennett's front door swung open and a woman stepped onto the porch, her back to Ren.

Ren pulled the binoculars from her lap and squinted into them. The woman started to turn, and even before her profile grew visible, Ren sucked in a sharp breath. All thoughts of Usoro and Baird and the fetid heat vanished in a blink.

Julia.

Ren's car was partially obscured by the trunk of the large palm, so she leaned forward, hands tight on the binoculars. Eric Bennett came onto the porch then too, but though it was him Ren had come to surveil, her focus remained on Julia.

The other woman's highlighted hair fell just below her shoulders. Unstyled but well cut. Ren guessed Julia was about five seven, five eight. She had an average build leaning toward active. Ren knew she loved plants, but did she have other hobbies too? Did she surf? Bike? She didn't strike Ren as the yoga type. Too much tension in her shoulders.

Another way they were alike.

Ren was mid-smile when Eric's hand shot out and latched on to Julia's arm, and Ren's expression froze.

He really shouldn't touch her like that.

Ren picked at her cuticles as she stared at the fingers wrapped above Julia's wrist.

CHAPTER 31

JULIA

Eric held tightly to Julia's wrist. "Wait."

She arched an eyebrow and stared down at his hand. He released her.

"Why should I? You're not answering my questions."

His mouth tightened. "I don't need another interrogation."

Julia tried to soften her expression, but they'd been talking in circles for more than thirty minutes. Ever since Eric had blurted, *I think I screwed up.* But since then, he'd evaded giving any explanation.

Julia was exhausted.

"I need to pick up our daughter."

When she turned to go, Eric's hand shot out again, but seeing her expression, he stopped just short of renewed contact. "Did Hoffman ask you what you were doing Tuesday night?"

All impatience drained from her in an instant. "Yes." She studied his face, which was paper pale and beaded with sweat. Was it more than grief she saw there?

He began pacing. The porch was tight, so he managed only a few steps in each direction.

"Did something happen Tuesday night?" she nudged.

Eric's body jerked as he continued pacing. She thought of a caged predator, and the comparison didn't favor him. If he'd behaved like this in front of Hoffman, then he really *had* screwed up.

He stopped and looked at her. "I lied."

She backed off the shaded porch and into the sun, pausing on the second step, and waited for him to explain.

"I told you that Brie wouldn't leave the house until move-in day. That wasn't entirely true. She was so upset after her visit with her father that I suggested we get takeout from this Asian fusion place she loves. She wanted me to pick it up. It's not far. Only a few blocks. But I thought it would do her good to get out, and honestly? As upset as she was, I was afraid to leave her alone." His pupils were dilated. The caged predator now cornered. And since when was Brie someone who couldn't be left alone? "So I convinced her to go with me, which turned out to be a bad idea. In the car, we started arguing, and by the time we got to the register at the restaurant, it had become a full-on fight."

She thought again of how Brie had slapped Cora, and she tensed. "About what?"

"It doesn't matter."

"It must matter if Hoffman's asking about it." Her tone was icier than she'd intended.

Eric's face contorted in obvious frustration. "It wasn't the subject of the fight that attracted Hoffman's interest so much as…that it got messy."

"How messy?"

"Very. Brie threw her container of peanut noodle salad at me."

Julia crossed her arms. "So Brie had a temper."

"It's not that. It's just…she could be impulsive."

Buying a pair of shoes full price was impulsive. But striking Cora? Throwing food? That felt like rage.

Now that he was no longer pacing, Eric channeled the nervous energy into his hands, clenching and unclenching them at his sides. "It was my fault. I saw how dark her mood was, but still I pushed. I wanted to fix it. I should've left it alone."

This was a habit of Eric's she knew well. When he and Julia were married, he'd done the same thing, offering advice at moments when all she'd wanted was comfort.

"Needless to say, we left immediately, but Brie's face is all over the news, and someone reached out to the police. Told them about the fight. That's why Hoffman asked about Tuesday night." Eric raked his hair with fingers that still twitched. "Of course I didn't know that at first, because he asked about other days too. Casually, as if he was just re-creating a timeline of events. So when he got to Tuesday, I was worried about how it would look if I told him the truth. So I told him I grabbed dinner with Cora."

Julia suddenly understood: when Hoffman had asked her the same question, he hadn't been confirming her whereabouts. He'd been confirming Cora's—and Julia had proven that Eric had lied.

"But you eventually came clean?"

He stopped twitching and stared at her. "No. When he eventually confronted me, I told him the tipster was wrong. It wasn't me and Brie. That it couldn't have been because I was with Cora."

She exhaled in frustration. "Eric."

"I know. But it's not like whoever reported it heard anything important."

"You still shouldn't have lied to the police."

Because you've always been so honest with the police, Julia?

She shook off the thought.

"You don't understand." He sounded impatient. "I couldn't tell Hoffman the reason for the fight. It would've complicated things."

"Tell *me* then. Maybe I can help."

He shook his head. "It doesn't matter why Brie and I argued, because it wasn't about that anyway. She was upset after she saw her father, so she picked a fight over something stupid." He waved his hand dismissively.

It bothered Julia that he was being so evasive, especially after making Cora his alibi. "I'm your ex-wife. I don't expect you to tell me everything, or much of anything, really. Only the stuff that affects our daughter. And this affects her, Eric."

"You're more than my ex-wife. You're Cora's mom." He sounded weary, and his brow furrowed. When he spoke again, he looked away. "Fine. *That's* what we fought about. She wanted me to stop seeing you. Thought you still had feelings for me."

"That's ridiculous." And it was. Julia cared about Eric. And since he'd moved to Encinitas, she'd been surprised to feel like friends again. At drop-off, they sometimes shared a coffee or a brief conversation, but Julia hadn't felt a spark for Eric in a long time. Before Brie. Even, if she was honest, before the divorce.

"Brie's always been the jealous type." He paused. "I think Brie was feeling a little excluded because of all the excitement around Cora starting college."

Julia wondered if this was why Brie had cheated. Was she punishing Eric?

"Brie wouldn't relax, even after I assured her you'd be okay with her joining us."

Julia hadn't been, but that earlier hesitation felt petty now. Judging by the darkening of Eric's expression, he had regrets of his own. After all, he'd been the one who'd convinced Brie to go.

"Hoffman's not going to like that you lied."

Another long silence. "Hoffman also didn't like that there was money missing from my savings account." Before she could ask him what he meant by "missing," he continued. "We paid the contractor in cash for part of the work on the kitchen. The contractor knew a great tile guy, but the guy would only do the work off the books."

"How much money are we talking?"

"A hundred thousand."

Julia whistled. "That's some expensive tile work."

"It included the cost of the countertops. Calacatta marble. Apparently, it can only be found in one quarry in Italy, or at least that's what the guy told us." He sighed. "I hate those fucking countertops."

One of Hoffman's questions came back to Julia: *Looks like the Bennetts have recently done some remodeling in the kitchen. Know anything about that?*

She could guess what the detective had been thinking. People online were sharing rumors that Eric had paid someone to kill his wife, and he and Brie had fought, right after a hundred thousand dollars disappeared from his account.

A chill pricked at her spine. Julia had mastered suppressing thoughts she didn't want to face, but her carefully constructed barriers were weakening. Maybe the detective was right to be suspicious.

"You believe me, don't you?" he asked.

She wanted to reassure Eric that she did, but the past—her past—prevented such blind trust. Eric had misled the police. What would keep him from doing the same with her?

"Julia?" His tone was imploring, but angry too. When he took a step forward, she involuntarily took one backward.

"I know you wouldn't hurt Cora."

He looked confused. "My God. Why would you even say that?"

"Because whoever shot Brie also shot Cora."

His face clouded, and for a moment, she wondered: *Was that guilt I saw there?*

No, she decided, pulling those barriers back into place. What she saw on his face she felt on her own. Terror for the safety of their daughter.

"It doesn't matter if I believe you, Eric. It matters if the police do."

Her phone vibrated in her pocket, and she pulled it out.

"Sorry," she said, gesturing to her phone. "It might be Cora."

She checked the notifications. Not Cora. Mike. You up for schnitzel?

The German place they went to was in Long Beach, a ninety-minute drive from Encinitas. Pretty far to go for schnitzel.

There's also beer.

I have to pick up Cora.

I know it's far but there's something I need to talk to you about.

Mike wouldn't have insisted if it wasn't important, but nothing in that moment—in *any* moment—was more important than Cora.

Sorry. Can't.

The bubbles danced for a moment. Then: See your daughter first. I'll wait. But please come.

If it had been anyone else, she would've ignored the text and silenced her phone. *Is this something Cora can hear?*

The response came quickly. *Probably better if she didn't.*

Julia returned her focus to Eric. "I have to go."

"Everything okay with Cora?"

"It's something else."

She took several steps toward her car before turning to face him again. Behind the shadowed eyes and pinched expression, beneath the graying stubble that grew in patches, the Eric she'd loved was still there: the young man who had courted her with spray cheese. The dad who'd been terrified to hold his newborn daughter for fear he'd fumble her. The new husband who'd told jokes so badly they'd made Julia laugh until her sides cramped.

She felt an unexpected swell of tenderness. "You should get a lawyer. Ask your family to come sooner."

Standing on the porch, Eric fidgeted, looking so lost that she almost reached out to him. But there was also a trace of anger in his expression. Eric's life had been gentler than Julia's. He was blindsided now to learn it could also be cruel.

Julia softened. "You should have someone here, and it shouldn't be me."

And it can't be Cora. Not until I know she's safe.

But she kept the last part to herself. Eric didn't look as though he could handle hearing that.

CHAPTER 32

REN

R en studied Julia Bennett. The way her eyebrows lifted. The surprising way she leaned in when her ex-husband grew agitated.

Despite how he'd grabbed her arm, she seemed to care about him.

Strange.

Many of the potential clients who approached Ren or Nolan sought to have a lover—past or present—killed. Not just killed. They wanted them to suffer. Ren never accepted that kind of job, of course, but she understood the desire. When Julia pulled away from the curb, Ren pressed the brake pedal and reached for the car's automatic start button. But she hesitated before pushing it. She really should continue to keep an eye on Eric. But with his stubbled jaw, weary eyes, and wrinkled shirt, he was in no shape to go out. Ren started the car.

Almost immediately, Julia surprised her. On the way out of Encinitas, Ren expected her to turn right onto I-5 toward her home in Kearny Mesa. Instead, Julia headed north.

One hand on the wheel, Ren scraped the cuticle on her thumb with her fingernail. *Where are you going, Julia?*

Ren kept her foot light on the gas, her nondescript hybrid blending with the countless others like it. Occasionally, the traffic would swallow Julia's white Civic, but it always spit out the car a moment later. It was probably good that Ren was forced to focus on that flash of white. It kept her from looking too closely at why she was tailing Julia.

Half an hour in, Julia exited without using her blinker. Ren dropped back, worried Julia had noticed her. She waited for that burst of speed that often came when a driver suspected a tail. But Julia maintained a steady pace. Ren followed her onto the off-ramp but slowed, allowing the gap between them to grow.

Three and a half minutes later, Julia turned onto a palm-lined street. Traffic thinned. Ren didn't follow. She couldn't chance Julia spotting her. But she did risk a quick sideways glance as she passed and saw that Julia had slowed. Looking for a parking spot?

Ren kept her speed at precisely three miles below the limit, careful that her eagerness didn't make her foot heavier on the gas. She took her next right. Then another. Then a third. She coasted onto the same street Julia had earlier, approaching from the opposite direction.

Down the block, Julia was climbing out of her car. There were no legal spots, so Ren pulled over and parked in a red zone. Risky, maybe, but she could move once Julia was out of sight. First she needed to know where Julia was going. Who did she know in Oceanside?

Julia approached an older three-story apartment building—boxy, stuccoed, and in need of a pressure washing. She paused on the sidewalk, and Ren glanced in her rearview mirror. No parking enforcement. When she looked forward again, a girl was walking toward Julia. Ren slouched in her seat and pulled out the Steiner binoculars. She studied the girl. Short brown hair. Pale skin. Eyes swollen and pink-rimmed.

Julia's daughter. Which would make her Nolan's second intended victim. And his first failed one.

Ren's gaze fell to the girl's arm, and the large bandage wrapped around it. The girl stopped short of her mother, but Julia reached out. She embraced her daughter fiercely, but with an obvious awareness of that bandage and the wound beneath it. The wound caused by Nolan's bullet.

Julia seemed like a good mother. The kind of mother Ren sometimes wished she'd had. The kind of mother she hoped to be.

Ren put away the binoculars, suddenly uncomfortable.

Julia stayed inside the apartment for an hour. By then, Ren needed to urinate, badly. She had been considering abandoning her watch to find a gas station when Julia emerged, alone.

Ren decided against the gas station. She couldn't risk losing Julia. Back on the highway, Ren picked at her cuticles and cursed her thimble-sized bladder until, finally, the white compact exited the I-405 at Atlantic Avenue, drove several minutes, then parked on the street in front of a restaurant that advertised beer and German food. Ren found a spot a block away.

It seemed too far to drive for takeout, but Ren watched from her car to make sure Julia intended to stay. When the other woman remained inside, Ren retrieved the tiny glass vial from the glove box and slipped it into her pocket, then headed toward the restaurant.

The building's blue-trimmed exterior was simple and modern. Succulents sprouted from the planter box that partitioned off an area for outdoor dining. Ren passed the patio, stopping on the restaurant's threshold to peer through the open door. Not too busy for a Saturday evening. There were still a few empty tables.

While Ren knew she shouldn't approach Julia—a risk taken for no real gain—she was nonetheless drawn inside. There sports jerseys hung above the front door, the requisite TV mounted on the wall nearby. Overhead, exposed ducts and hanging copper light fixtures were mixed with the occasional set of fluorescent bulbs and a chandelier of antlers. The Verve's "Bitter Sweet Symphony" played through speakers, but not loud enough to be obnoxious. She appreciated that.

After using the restroom, Ren checked her watch: 7:12 p.m. She scanned the restaurant. At a wood table that could've accommodated six comfortably, two men sat on benches and drank oversized beers from curved glasses. A family with older kids pushed away mostly empty plates.

A couple shared an appetizer. A group of twentysomethings laughed loudly at the bar. Her gaze flitted across them all in seconds.

Then her gaze landed on Julia, seated at a table in the far corner, alone, and her breath caught. The two-seater next to her was unoccupied. Fate or luck, it didn't matter which. It would be foolish to squander the opportunity.

It would be equally foolish to stay too long. She checked her watch again—7:13 p.m.—and when she looked up again, a young woman with a high red ponytail was approaching. She reminded Ren vaguely of a girl whose boyfriend Ren had killed in Des Moines.

"How many?" the young redhead asked.

"Two. My sister will be joining me."

In Ren's experience, servers were more likely to remember the diners who ate alone.

The redhead began to steer her in the direction of the men with the tall beers, but Ren pointed to the empty table next to Julia.

"Mind if I sit there instead?"

The redhead flashed her best tip-winning smile and pivoted.

As Ren drew closer to the empty table, she felt an unexpected and slightly uncomfortable buzz in her stomach, akin to the one she'd experienced upon first meeting Nolan. The pulse that rarely broke sixty now raced. Ren grew more aware of the hard knot the vial made in her pocket.

Julia sat in a metal-legged chair against the wall. Of course. The kind of woman who reacted calmly to a sniper attack wouldn't sit with her back to the front door.

Ren also took the chair against the wall, mirroring Julia, and accepted the pair of laminated menus offered for her and her fictitious sister. She willed her pulse to steady and matched the young redhead's smile even as she thought, *Just go already.*

A moment later, she did, leaving Ren and Julia alone at their separate tables. Ren glanced at her watch again. Her pulse hovered in the low seventies. Not optimal, but better. And 7:15 p.m. She would allow herself five minutes. No longer than that. She set a timer.

Rubbing her raw cuticle, Ren pretended to study the menu a moment before she turned toward Julia's table. Up close, she was quite pretty. Ren noticed a small bump on the bridge of her nose. Had she broken it? "Sorry to intrude, but I've never been here before," she said. "What do you recommend?"

Julia shifted sideways to face her, her eyes a green that reminded Ren of sea glass. "Last time, I got the burger with the chipotle aioli, but the schnitzel and sausages are good too."

"Sounds like you've tried everything."

Julia offered a small grin. "Pretty much."

So Ren's previous instincts had been right: unlike most of Ren's targets, Julia wasn't a creature of habit.

She corrected herself: Julia wasn't a target, and because of that, Ren shouldn't linger. A small voice reminded her that, actually, she shouldn't be there at all. It wasn't as if Ren could ask Julia any of the questions that mattered, like why she'd behaved the way she had after hearing the gunshots, or if she believed her ex-husband had paid someone to kill his wife.

But Ren had perfected the art of silencing voices she didn't want to hear. Even her own.

She checked her watch. Three minutes and twenty-two seconds left.

"The schnitzel sounds good. Thanks."

The young redhead returned, stopping at Julia's table to deliver a glass of water and to ask if she wanted to start with an appetizer.

Julia shook her head. "I'm fine for now."

The server turned to Ren. "How about you? Something to drink?"

"I'm still thinking." She tried a smile, hoping her resentment at the intrusion didn't corrupt her expression. After the server left, Ren risked another glance at her watch. Thirty-one seconds of her time with Julia had been stolen. She felt the corners of her mouth tug downward.

Julia misinterpreted the frown. "Someone running late?"

Sensing an opening, Ren nodded. "I'm meeting my sister." She usually envied the easy way Nolan had with strangers, but when Ren forced a chuckle—she wasn't usually the type to chuckle—it sounded genuine. "I admit, I'm a bit impatient tonight. I'm eager to get home and watch the second part of that new docuseries on philosophy and ethical dilemmas. It's on Netflix, I think. Have you seen it?"

Julia's sea-glass eyes glinted, jagged shards reflecting the overhead light. Ren reached into her pocket for the vial, holding it in her palm beneath the table like a talisman.

"Sounds interesting, but no."

"Wish I could remember the name because I'd recommend it." She rolled the vial gently in her hand and eyed Julia's water glass for a second too long. There was no reason to kill Julia—at least from what Ren had learned so far—but Ren couldn't stop her mind from wandering. What would it be like to go up against someone so quick-witted?

Julia noticed her attention on the glass and smiled. "Hydration is important."

"It is," Ren agreed. Her palm grew moist around the vial, and she felt the fluttering of the tiny stranger.

Would killing and framing Julia keep her family safe?

Ren dug the nails of her empty hand into her palm. What was wrong with her? She wasn't used to being nervous, and she'd never before thought of compromising her ethics.

Defend the family.

Ren shook off the thought. *No. Not like this.*

Still, she asked herself: if she killed Julia, here and now, how would she do it? What if she dropped her phone and kicked it under Julia's table— would that distract her? Or would Julia accept a drink offered to her by a stranger? She didn't seem the type, but she'd already surprised Ren several times.

A small potted cactus sat in front of Ren. Remembering Julia's quick reflexes, Ren had the crazy urge to nudge it off the table to see if Julia would catch it before it hit the floor.

There were so many things she wanted to try. To say.

Instead, Ren cleared her throat and checked her watch. Though only ninety seconds remained, she strained to speak slowly. "Anyway, on the first episode of that docuseries, they survey random people on the street about morality. They ask some interesting questions. For instance: when judging whether actions are moral, are intentions or outcomes more important?"

Julia leaned toward her, obviously curious.

"What did people say?"

As she watched beads of condensation roll down Julia's water glass, Ren tried to appear relaxed even as her muscles tensed. She'd never played this game with someone she didn't intend to kill. She felt unexpectedly giddy.

"The responses were all over the place." She found herself leaning in Julia's direction too. She told herself this was no different than her phone call with Lydia Baird, or her encounter with Voss's ex-wife. She was just gathering information. Still, the fizzy sensation in her head grew stronger.

"So…" She pursed her lips on the *J* of Julia's name and almost said it. She bit hard on her tongue. She hoped Julia hadn't noticed. "What do you think is more important: intention or outcome?"

The timer on Ren's watch buzzed, but she silenced it. Beneath the table, her hand tightened around the vial as she waited for Julia to answer.

CHAPTER 33

JULIA

The pregnant stranger with the dark hair and blue eyes stared at Julia. "What do you think is more important: intention or outcome?" she'd asked.

Julia swallowed hard and tried to place the woman. Did she know her? She didn't think so, but a moment earlier, it had seemed as if she had been about to call Julia by her name. And then there was that question, which left Julia's mouth dry and her tongue tacky, because she'd asked herself the very same question countless times before.

But Julia dismissed the thought. She was making too much of a casual conversation. She was certain they'd never met, and that it was only the other woman's intensity that made her seem familiar.

"Both intentions and outcomes are important, but that's not choosing, is it?" A small potted cactus sat at the center of each table. Julia cupped her hands around hers and twirled it as she thought. She was surprised to see a slight tremor in her own hands. "I'm guessing a lot of people would say intentions matter more. You can't control the outcomes, but you can try to do the right thing and hope it will go the way it should."

"So that's your answer?"

Julia wished she saw it that way, but she shook her head. "If you intend to save someone's life but your actions end up causing that person's death instead, they're still dead, aren't they? Doesn't really matter what your intentions were. So I'd say outcome matters more."

The stranger stared at her for several beats before smiling slightly. "Well, that got dark."

Julia smiled back. "Yeah. Sorry about that."

Her blue eyes glittered. "Not at all," she said. "I appreciate the candor. It's rare these days."

Across the room, Julia caught sight of Mike and waved. At the same moment, the other woman glanced down at her phone and sighed, her perfect eyebrows knitting together. "Looks like my sister got held up at her kid's soccer game, so no schnitzel for me." She pushed her chair away from the table and stood, thrusting one hand in the pocket of her jeans, the other clamped to her phone.

"You could always get it to go."

"I'm not that hungry," she said. "Enjoy your dinner."

On her way out, the woman passed Mike. When he sat across from Julia, he gestured to the spot the woman had occupied a few seconds before.

"Who's your friend?" he asked.

"Not a friend." Julia realized she hadn't gotten the woman's name.

"You looked pretty friendly."

She grabbed her water. The glass chilled her palm, the condensation making it slick.

"I had to make conversation with someone, since my date was so late."

She'd meant only to tease him, but Mike's face grew serious. *Shit.* She'd used the d-word.

Julia checked her phone but there were no new texts from Cora.

Mike gestured toward her phone. "She okay?"

Julia didn't have an answer for that. With anyone else, she would've danced around the question with the usual vague replies—*As well as expected* or *She'll get there*—but seeing Cora had left her shaken. When Julia had stopped by, Cora had held tightly to her, but she'd pulled away cleanly when the time came to say goodbye. The quick retreat rocked

Julia. It said, *I'll be brave.* It said, *Promise you won't leave too.* It said, *I can't be sure you'll come back.*

"Saying goodbye again was hard," Julia said.

Mike reached across the table and covered her hand with his. "You could've canceled."

"She wanted to catch a movie with Evie and her mom anyway, and you said it's important."

"It is, but—"

"So, why'd you want me to come all the way to Long Beach?"

Mike flagged the server, asked for a lemonade, a sausage platter, and an order of spicy brussels sprouts, then turned his attention back to Julia.

He released her hand, which felt abruptly cold. "I've got someone we should talk to. He lives about twenty minutes from here."

"Who?"

"Remember that young activist I told you about? Kamal Tallisi?"

How could she not? The story had horrified her. "He was doxxed and nearly beaten to death."

"He's still pretty active on the dark web, though he's much more careful now." Mike's brown eyes clouded. "He gets off at eight, and he wanted to talk to you. He said he's…learned some things."

"What things?"

"After what happened, he's understandably skittish about sharing information over the phone."

Julia felt a prickling along her neck.

The server returned with the appetizers and Mike's lemonade. When she left, Mike stuffed a couple of brussels sprouts in his mouth, swallowing them after only a couple of chews. Julia worried he might choke.

She ate a couple more slowly; they were tangy from the pecorino cheese and remoulade. Then a few more. Her stomach grumbled in gratitude, but despite the food and the company, she couldn't keep her thoughts from straying to Cora. The distance between them made her uneasy, but it still felt safest, until she figured out what was really going on.

"Anything new with the investigation?" Mike asked.

Julia filled him in on Detective Hoffman's visit while he started in on the sausage platter. As he listened, his frown deepened. When she finished her story, he took a long drink of his lemonade and mumbled, "Hmm."

"Hmm?"

"I can't imagine what Eric's going through."

Julia crossed her arms, waiting for the rest of it.

After another drink of lemonade, Mike wiped his hands on his napkin, then steepled his fingers on the table. "Any chance—"

Julia cut him off with a shake of her head. "Eric was inches from Brie when she was shot. Cora too. I know you don't much like him—"

"I don't like him at all." When she cocked her head, he shrugged. "You didn't expect me to say he's a swell guy, right?"

Of course she hadn't. It was Mike she'd called, venting, when Eric hadn't picked up Cora for that father-daughter day at the music festival in Joshua Tree. Mike who'd shown up with overpriced tickets so Cora and Evie could go instead. Then there was that disaster of a first date, when she'd overshared. But still. Mike's dark eyes studied her with a tender intensity.

"So, yeah, I think Eric's an asshole," he said. "But that has nothing to do with why I had to ask. The evidence seems to be pointing in that direction, and I care about you. *I* would be the asshole if I didn't at least ask."

Julia couldn't find fault with his logic, since she'd had moments of doubt too. She hoped they were both wrong—because if her ex-husband had put their daughter in danger, the police would be the least of his concerns.

Julia picked up another brussels sprout, then changed her mind, setting it onto her plate, where she began peeling each leaf slowly away with the tines of her fork. At last she looked up. Mike was watching her with interest.

"Okay. Let's go talk to Kamal."

CHAPTER 34

REN

R en had spent six minutes and twenty-seven seconds talking to Julia. She'd allowed herself only five. Nolan would've called that extra eighty-seven seconds inconsequential, but Ren recognized it as proof that she was slipping—especially since she'd fantasized about poisoning Julia too. Even if killing her might protect Ren's family, she couldn't justify it. Not yet.

Back in her car, Ren watched the front of the restaurant. A couple of storefronts down, a woman with faded jeans and a cardboard sign stood tucked behind a pillar, invisible to all who passed. Heading into the restaurant, Ren had missed her too.

Why had she let Julia get to her?

And what would her father say?

Anthony Petrovic's decision to kill people for money came from a series of injustices.

The first happened before he was born. His father tried to run his family like a fiefdom, but his mother refused to recognize her husband's rule. They divorced almost immediately, leaving her to raise their son alone. In Anthony's memories, his mom, Linda, was a stubborn woman who cycled through odd jobs, usually a couple at a time, and spent any spare moments reading. Luckily, she read to her young son too, books without pictures and with tales too advanced for him to fully understand. But he found meaning in the way she told those stories: face rapt, voice ranging from a whisper to a shout, gestures so exaggerated that she once shattered a table lamp.

Linda died in her early thirties, while her ex-husband still lived somewhere on the East Coast. That experience revealed to Anthony Petrovic that life wasn't fair.

So when Anthony married, he vowed to be a better parent than his own father. Unfortunately, his wife didn't swear the same. She quickly left him and their toddler daughter for an also-married neighbor. Ren couldn't remember her mother's face, and her father certainly hadn't kept any photos.

After that, Anthony realized that not only was life unfair, but families were inherently fragile—and in need of defending.

So he went to law school with the intention of doing just that. But after graduation, his sincerity couldn't compensate for a surprising lack of skill. When a housing discrimination case got away from him, another attorney at his firm stepped in to help. The facts were, for once, squarely on their side, and the woman was brilliant, an impassioned speaker, a meticulous researcher—all the things Anthony had hoped but failed to be.

They lost anyway. Leaving the courtroom, his colleague said something that finally stuck with him: *I don't know what to think. As hard as we try to shield the innocent, families still get evicted. Parents still lose custody. And kids still get hurt.*

Soon after, she moved into corporate law. Her parting words to him: *It pays better, and when I lose, I won't care quite so much.*

But Anthony couldn't not care. And all his righteous anger found a home one night over beers with an old friend. The man had recently lost a cousin to an intoxicated, and unrepentant, driver who had caused a separate fatal crash a couple of years before.

She'll get a year in prison, then she'll do it again, the friend said.

Anthony agreed. And then he wondered aloud, *Why should only the innocent pay with their lives?*

Then he'd suggested they simply kill her.

If the friend had looked at him in horror, Anthony would've claimed he'd been kidding. But the other man, grieving and angry, stared at him with something closer to awe. After a brief discussion, they decided that Anthony should run her over with his car. The execution was lacking—they acted on impulse and with little planning—but the woman was dead within the week.

After hitting the woman, Anthony had pulled over a mile up the road, expecting to be sick. The nausea never came. Instead, he was heartened by how many other DUI deaths he'd prevented. The euphoria had caused his whole body to tremble.

Grateful, the friend gave him some money: a modest sum, but enough for a month's rent. Anthony immediately quit his law firm, leased the gym as cover, and started researching a different career. One more aligned with his new mission. And with his new mantra: *Shield the innocent. Kill the guilty. Defend the family.*

From the time Ren was young, her father had trained her to share this mission. And even early on, it had become apparent to both of them that the daughter eclipsed the father in several ways. She was smarter. More meticulous. And her instincts were better.

Or so she'd thought until recently.

Ren wished her father was there to give her counsel. Throughout her childhood, he'd made mistakes, but he always knew the right thing to do in the end.

Finally, Julia and the man she'd been dining with emerged from the restaurant. Unlike the others who had passed by before, Julia stopped at the woman with the cardboard sign. She talked with her for a minute before handing over a folded bill. Ren leaned forward in her seat, watching the exchange. The gifted money didn't surprise Ren—but the conversation did.

What makes you different, Julia?

CHAPTER 35

JULIA

Kamal Tallisi wore his curls cropped an inch from his scalp. It wasn't until he turned that Julia noticed the horseshoe-shaped scar, ropy and pale, where no hair grew along one side. There was something magnetic about Kamal, despite his patchy stubble and long, thin face—cheeks hollowed, the skin beneath his dark eyes sinking. Julia wondered what he'd be like if he hadn't been beaten nearly to death. He seemed the kind of person others would easily follow.

When Kamal opened the door to let Julia and Mike into his Garden Grove apartment, Julia couldn't help picturing that version of him: a college student not much older than Cora, passionate about dismantling the system and optimistic that he could.

This Kamal led them to the balcony, large enough for only two plastic chairs. Kamal and Julia sat, while Mike stood.

To Julia, Mike said, "I asked Kamal to look into the shooting."

"Anything for Mike." An expression of reverence flashed on the young man's face, which led Julia to wonder exactly how much Mike had helped during Kamal's recovery. It occurred to her that Mike might have secrets he kept even from her.

Kamal pulled a pack of cigarettes and a lighter from the pocket of his track pants. He shook out a cigarette and lit it.

Mike crossed his arms and leaned against the railing. "Appreciate the help, Kamal. What'd you find?"

He shook his head. "People are talking a lot of crazy shit." He took a long drag on his cigarette, careful to blow the smoke away from his guests. He turned his attention toward Julia. "I dug into Baird's daughter, but there's not much online. Some of the conspiracy nuts are saying that's so no one will discover the truth: that she's that girl who was killed thirty years ago."

This ridiculous theory again. "Melody Weaver? We read that too."

He half laughed. "But they've got *evidence*." He flicked ash onto the concrete. "They claim only a few photos exist of Brie before she was four, and they reveal a mole she didn't have as an adult."

Julia shook her head in disbelief. If that had been true, Baird would never have allowed those photos to exist.

"They've also posted receipts showing Baird was on a business trip in the area where the Weavers were camping." Kamal held up his hand to cut off Julia's protest. "Obviously doctored. But that's the thing about conspiracy theories: they don't have to be true to have power. I know a guy who would swear on his life that a certain pop star is the clone of a satanic cult leader." He took another pull on his cigarette. "They're also saying Baird's a human trafficker. Or even, on some boards, that Baird and his friends are aliens, and Brie was sacrificed to bring on the apocalypse."

Of all the things Julia had thought Kamal would tell her, she would never have gotten to this. At her look, Kamal shrugged. "People believe what they want to believe."

Julia remembered what Mike had told her earlier. No matter how outrageous, the rumors increased the chances that the story would linger in the news cycle, or at least on the dark web. And anything that drew interest to the Anderson Hughes shooting was bad for Cora.

What if one of these nuts comes for my daughter?

As if reading her thoughts, Kamal said, "No one outside the fringes is going to buy most of this shit. Why it matters is it makes the less crazy stories sound more plausible." His focus on Julia burned as hot as the tip of his cigarette. "Most people agree that your ex-husband paid someone to kill his wife."

"That's just not true," she said too quickly. It was one thing for her to think it, and another for it to become reality to these conspiracy theorists.

Kamal regarded her, not unkindly. "The truth often comes disguised as rumor, doesn't it? Especially if it's too dangerous to share any other way." He breathed in more smoke. "But I thought you should know, in any case. That people are calling for his head."

"Thank you," Julia said sadly. "I should."

"People are also saying that before her death, Brie Bennett met a man at a hotel in San Clemente."

Julia's breath quickened. She'd let herself forget about that. *Now they were getting somewhere.* "Are they suggesting he might've done it?"

Kamal shrugged. "Or given Eric a reason to. Sometimes the appearance of guilt is enough. You understand."

She stiffened. Was he talking about her parents? Cordelia? Her attention shot to Mike, but he shook his head as if to say, *He didn't hear anything from me.*

Kamal gestured toward Mike with his cigarette, scattering ash. "Mike's a vault. But all it takes is two people whispering too loudly at a bar, or someone seeing you where you're not supposed to be. The only way to stop the spread of information is if people don't care enough to share it."

He wasn't talking about her specifically. He was only proving a point, but still her hands shook. There was a static in her head she hadn't heard in many years. To steady herself, Julia tried to find distractions. A crack in the leg of her chair. A dried leaf near Mike's shoe. A trick Cordelia had shared with her: *If you don't want to see something, look away.*

Julia had spent half a lifetime looking away.

"You got a name for the boyfriend in San Clemente?" she asked, digging her nails into her palms to center herself.

Kamal shook his head. "Not yet, but I'm working on it." He brought the cigarette to his lips again, his eyes growing more intense. "But it seems the police are officially focusing on your ex-husband. Who else would've wanted her dead?"

"Brie wasn't exactly likable. She had enemies."

"Ones who hated her enough to pay a hundred grand to have her killed?"

A hundred grand? The amount missing from Eric's account. She managed to keep her voice steady. "Maybe if it meant getting to her father?" Kamal seemed to consider that, at least, so Julia continued. "Look, I didn't know her well enough to say either way. But if it wasn't random, then my money's on the boyfriend. Or someone connected to Oliver Baird."

In any case, it can't be Eric.

Kamal arched one thick eyebrow. "I'm only reporting what I've heard. My source in the police force is pretty reliable, but I understand. You don't know me. But Mike here told me you were a reasonable person, so just consider how the killing went down. She was shot in the head, in public. Doesn't it make sense her husband might want an alibi, but also to watch her die? People are sick like that."

Again, Eric's words came back to her: *I had to convince her to come to Cora's move-in day.*

Kamal continued. "Sure, the sniper took an extra shot or two, tried to cause enough confusion to make the police think it was random. Just another senseless shooting, like all the others, right?" Another quick puff. "Then there's the location: a college. Not just a college, but a rich kids' college. The shooter probably intended for the response to focus on gun violence. If Brie had been just your average soccer mom, maybe. But she wasn't."

Kamal took one last drag before tossing the cigarette onto the balcony floor. He ground it into the concrete with the toe of his sneaker. Julia noticed the scattering of butts around his chair.

"Since Brie and her dad weren't close, my guess is the hired gun really didn't know she was Baird's daughter. Suddenly, this quick, lucrative job turned into a high-profile shit show. And that's why your ex-husband needs to die."

Her gut twisted, but Mike beat her to the question. "What the hell are you talking about?"

Kamal held out his palms in a placating gesture. "There's probably no immediate threat to him, because it's early stages. But as soon as the investigation heats up, even a little, whoever your ex-husband hired won't want Eric arrested. He'll want him at the bottom of the El Capitan Reservoir. Because rich white guys are really good at cutting deals."

Mike straightened, coming off the railing. "Kamal, thank you. We'll tell the police."

"Tell them what?" Julia asked. "That unnamed sources heard rumors that Eric might be in danger? The police have access to all the same information we do. More."

"There's no harm in giving them a heads-up. For Cora..."

She exhaled in frustration, and fear. "I *am* thinking about Cora. So, fine. I'll call Detective Hoffman. Just tell him...I'm worried." She touched her pocket to confirm she still had his card, feeling the faint rectangular outline.

Kamal's phone dinged and he glanced down at the screen. "You're not gonna like this either."

"What?"

Kamal looked back up, face solemn. "The media's confirming that only two people have died. Not three. So it's out there now."

Julia leaned forward, needing him to say the words. "What's out there?"

"Bruce is dead, Brie is dead, but the student is still alive."

Kamal's eyes held hers for a long moment, and Julia understood: he was talking about Cora.

All of Julia's nerves buzzed, like a thousand stinging hornets. She thought of the man she'd seen at the bar, and the dark sedan that had followed her. There was no hope of misleading them now.

She pulled out her phone, calling her daughter. Cora immediately declined, then texted: in theater. call later.

Julia texted back: Stay there. I'm coming to get you.

This was Julia's fault. She should've trusted her instincts. She should've locked Cora in her bedroom and posted a guard outside. Now her daughter was out in the world—and her would-be killer was too.

Hand unsteady, she punched in a second number. Eric didn't answer either. She tried again. When he didn't pick up the second time, she texted Call me.

Then Julia stood and pushed back her chair, her whole body shaking. "I need to get Cora."

"I'll come with you," Mike said.

"We took separate cars here, remember? Meet me at the theater. I'll text you the details." With her hand trembling, it took her a couple of attempts to send the link to Mike.

"I've got them," he said finally, clapping a hand on Kamal's shoulder in farewell.

"Okay." Julia took a deep breath, brain whirring. "Then you can take Cora home with you," she said, voice shaking. "She can't go with me to Eric's house. Or to ours."

She couldn't take her daughter anywhere the man in the dark sedan might know about.

Mike frowned. "I don't want you going to Eric's either."

"Kamal said there's no immediate threat to Eric."

"*Probably* no immediate threat," Kamal chimed in from his seat.

"And what if Eric lashes out?" Mike countered, eyes on Julia.

"We were married. I've known him since college. He won't hurt me."

"You say that about the man who might've had his wife killed."

"He didn't do it." He *couldn't* do it. Not with Cora right there.

Even as she said it, she thought, *Even hired killers make mistakes.* She grew nauseous, and every muscle in her pulled her toward the door. "We don't have time for this, Mike. Meet me or don't."

As Julia passed Kamal, he touched her arm, and they locked eyes.

"Be safe," he said. He turned his head so Julia could see the horseshoe-shaped scar again. "I know better than most people what can happen if you aren't careful."

230

CHAPTER 36

REN

By the time Ren got home, Nolan was at the stove sautéing shredded carrots, broccoli, and diced chicken. Good food for growing a baby, but Ren craved a burger. She should've gotten takeout as Julia suggested.

"Smells good," she said.

He gestured toward a pan on the unlit back burner. "Rice is done, and this'll be in a minute. Grab a couple of plates?"

She got the plates down and handed them to Nolan. As he scooped up the chicken and vegetables, he glanced sideways at her.

"You were gone a long time." He added rice to the first plate and handed it to her. "Any problems with the surveillance?"

"None."

She placed her plate and two sets of utensils on the small kitchen table. Then she filled a tumbler with tap water and grabbed a can of lime LaCroix from the refrigerator for Nolan. He preferred sparkling, but the carbonation gave her heartburn. Everything gave her heartburn these days. She reached for the bottle on the table and popped a couple of preemptive Tums.

Finally, she sat down. "Did you or my dad learn anything more?"

Nolan finished filling his own plate and joined her. "Eric Bennett's our guy." He took a bite, smiling as he chewed. "I was able to track the money."

"The second payment?"

He shook his head. "The *real* money. Apparently, Brie had a trust, which reverts to her husband upon her death. And remember, there's talk that she may have already been cheating."

"That explains the wife, but what about the daughter?"

He shrugged. "Haven't pinned that down yet, but my guess? She found out about the hit. Maybe not directly, or she probably would've told someone. But maybe she overheard something she shouldn't have, and Bennett was afraid she'd put it together." He took a drink of water. "Or it could really be about the trust."

Ren picked at the cuticle on her thumb. Despite their earlier conversation, she wasn't fully convinced. It felt too easy.

Nolan must have read the doubt on her face because he leaned forward and pinned her eyes with his. "A hundred million. That's the size of the trust."

Ren exhaled sharply. A hundred million was definitely motive. And if Brie Bennett had been cheating…"You get a look at the paperwork, or is this secondhand?"

"I verified it, Ren." Annoyance seeped into his voice.

"So there's no provision about length of marriage before he can collect? They've been married less than a year."

He seemed to relax. "Oh. That. No. No provisions. The money's all his."

Unless they killed him. Then the inheritance would probably revert to the daughter he'd paid to have killed. Ren found that poetic.

Ren reclined in her chair and folded her arms, resting them on the shelf of her stomach. "Tell me about Jim Usoro."

"Who?" Nolan shoveled rice into his mouth, then talked around it. "The guy we killed a couple of years ago?"

Three years. "That would be him."

"What do you want to know?"

232

"Everything."

Nolan speared a broccoli floret with his fork. "It's like I told you back then. He was an asshole who got off on hurting kids and women."

Her hand fell to her stomach and she glared at him. "That's not all, though, is it?"

"No. He also had some dirt on Baird. But that had nothing to do with why Baird ordered the hit."

Ren pushed her plate away and leaned forward as far as her stomach would allow. "What dirt?"

"Doesn't matter."

"It matters."

He rested his fork on his plate, broccoli still impaled on its tines. "Baird bribed someone to rush an inspection at the Shearwater, or to sign off on some repairs that weren't quite complete. Something like that. Usoro was angry because Baird had backed out of a business deal, so he asked around. Found out about it." He waved his hand dismissively. "It wasn't that big of a secret. It's how business is done sometimes, you know, and it probably wouldn't even have hurt Baird if it came out."

Even as the comment angered her, she knew it was true. There were different rules for people like Baird.

Nolan emptied his water can and crushed it nearly flat. "You've met Baird. You know how he can be. Notoriously competitive, and unwilling to yield." When she nodded, he went on. "So Baird did his own digging into Usoro, intending to ruin him. But what Baird found…I didn't exaggerate what Usoro did." He tossed the aluminum disk toward the recycling bin but missed. "Baird's investigator found cable ties and soiled sheets in Usoro's stepson's bedroom. The boy had taken to getting up in the middle of the night and sneaking into the kitchen for snacks, so Usoro started tying him to his bed frame."

Her cheeks grew hot. "Why didn't you tell me all this then?"

He looked confused. "That's never been how we've operated. You trust me to do my job, and I trust you to do yours."

You didn't this time, she thought.

He leaned in, his gaze hardening. "What we need to talk about is how we're going to get rid of Eric Bennett."

"I wasn't aware we'd settled on killing him."

"You know we have to. To protect our family. You and me."

Ren noticed his definition of "family" hadn't included the baby.

Nolan continued. "There are some other things you should know about Eric Bennett. He fits your criteria." She made note of his wording. *Your* criteria. Not *our* criteria.

Nolan seemed not to notice the slip. "He embezzled from a previous company, but they didn't report it because he paid the money back."

Her still-tight shoulders jerked in a shrug. "So he's not someone you'd want to do business with."

"Okay. You don't care that he cheats in business, but what about in his personal life? He cheated on his first wife, when she was pregnant with the daughter he tried to kill."

Ren immediately thought of a dozen different poisons she'd like to use.

Nolan's eyes grew fevered, his mouth settling into a tight line. "I'm telling you, Bennett's our guy."

Though she was nearly convinced, she hesitated. "Even if we kill him, it doesn't fully solve our problem."

"You mean because someone else still had to pull the trigger."

"Which brings it back to us." *To you.*

"I've got that handled." He moved the plates out of the way and reached across the table. "You've always been able to read people, love. You've got to know I'm telling the truth here, and that we need to kill Bennett."

Ren cupped the bottom of her stomach, stroking it with her thumb. *That's where the head will be,* she thought. Though the tiny stranger was now smaller and lighter than Ren's hand, all fragile bones and translucent skin, it was starting to grow muscle. In a year, it would be sleeping in a crib and eating mushed banana.

After a few minutes, Ren nodded. Though she usually took great care planning jobs, this time the risk was greater—and personal. Baird had demanded quick results, and the rumors she'd planted had almost too effectively set up Bennett as a suspect. They didn't have much time before law enforcement took action.

Ren felt a pang for Julia and her daughter, but killing Bennett would be best for them all. It wasn't just about the money the daughter would inherit. No one should be raised by a monster.

"If we're going to do it, it needs to be tonight," she said.

CHAPTER 37

JULIA

With lighter than usual traffic and her foot heavy on the gas, Julia made good time on the drive to Oceanside, yet each quick glance at the clock showed that only a minute or two had passed.

Kamal's warning had lacked urgency: Cora *might be* in danger. There was probably no *immediate* threat against Eric. Still, as soon as Julia had gotten in the car, she'd smoothed out Hoffman's card, which she'd inadvertently crumpled in her rigid fist, and called. Hoffman had been guarded in his responses. In a high-profile case like this, there were likely hundreds, if not thousands, of tips, so Julia had no idea how seriously the detective took hers. He might still believe the shooting was random, his interview with Eric a formality. Hadn't she been told they had to consider all angles?

Besides, as much of a priority as the Anderson Hughes case was, Hoffman and his team had other demands. They had other cases, other leads, and loved ones of their own.

Julia had only Cora.

She pressed harder on the gas pedal and checked the clock again, then the speedometer, doing the math in her head. If traffic continued to cooperate, she would pull up to the theater in about eleven minutes. The fiftieth-anniversary screening of the classic *Cabaret* that Cora and Evie had gone to see had already ended.

Julia called her daughter but it went right to voicemail.

She said a quick prayer: *Please, Cora, stay inside the theater.*

But she knew that even if Cora did as her mom wished, there were no guarantees she'd be safe. For proof of that, Julia had only to think back to the courtyard. Julia's foot grew even heavier.

She thought again of how reckless she'd been to ignore her instincts. With what she'd endured to develop them, she should've known better. What would Cordelia say? She'd never have let Cora go off alone.

When Cordelia first invited Julia to share her tent, less than two weeks after Julia had run away from foster care, the young woman was already an addict, though she didn't yet show the obvious signs Julia would learn to identify: bad teeth, leg ulcers that seeped, arms gouged from incessant scratching.

Instead, Cordelia dazzled Julia. She was lovely and brash, with skin that perpetually peeled because she refused to stay out of the sun. She had calloused hands and a smirk she weaponized. *Don't get close,* it warned. But that never applied to Julia. Cordelia's yellow hair with its dark roots had instantly reminded Julia of the black-eyed Susans her mom grew one summer. Her friend also had a thing for vintage clothes. Julia never saw her as excited as the day she found an old pair of plaid bell-bottoms in a donation bin. The only thing Cordelia remained shy about were her "street feet," as she called them.

They're hard to avoid when you live out here long enough, Cordelia finally admitted to Julia, who saw it firsthand: when Cordelia was on the hunt for drugs, or floating from the effects of them, she would walk, often for hours, in worn-out sneakers. Abscesses formed on her right foot. Even months after her foot healed, she still limped. But when she was clearheaded, it was Cordelia who'd introduced Julia to the bins, and to the shelter in the Midway District, where a minor like her was almost guaranteed a spot if she got there early. *Always be first in line,* Cordelia would say. Clothes, clinics, shelters—whatever it was, there were never enough. There were more shelters for animals than for kids, and not nearly enough of everything else to go around. Julia usually preferred staying in the tent with her friend, though later she'd come to regret that.

From Cordelia, Julia came to understand that listening was what saved you. Hearing that shuffle of feet on concrete. Paying attention to that hitch in an addict's voice. Recognizing the click of a belt unbuckling, or a pistol being cocked.

Or the sound of a zipper in the dark.

Julia learned to listen to her instincts. When it was okay to accept a meal someone was offering, and when it was better to turn it down even when the hunger gnawed, its teeth so sharp it kept her from sleeping. There were worse things than hunger.

Later, Julia would wonder what might've happened if that initial kindness had been offered by someone other than Cordelia. If it had been attached to expectations—of drugs or sex or some other trade she was ill prepared to make. The kind of trade forced on Cordelia early on.

But for Julia, it hadn't come with a cost. She'd been offered friendship instead, and that was what had saved her.

As Julia sped down the highway, she thought again of her parents, as well as Cordelia. Two tragedies she should've seen coming. She might've prevented both if she'd been paying closer attention. And now, with Cora…*No.* She wouldn't think about that.

By the time Julia pulled in front of the theater, her spine felt as if it had been carved from ice. She saw no sign of her daughter and released a long breath. Cora had listened to her. She'd stayed inside.

Unless she hadn't. What if she'd ventured out of the lobby to check for Julia? What if the man in the dark sedan had been watching her and—

Julia stopped herself. She called her daughter again. This time, she answered.

"Mom? What's going on?"

Mike pulled in a few spaces in front of her. "You still inside?" Julia asked.

"Yeah. We're in the bathroom. Why're you freaking out?"

Mike was out of his car, tapping on her window. She climbed out too. "I'm not freaking out."

Mike smiled at that and grabbed her hand. The gesture steadied her. "Come to the main entrance. Mike will take you home."

"But what about Evie and her mom? And why can't I go with you?"

"Just come to the door, Cora."

She disconnected and looked at Mike. He squeezed her hand. "I've got this. I'll keep your girl safe."

Despite her previous sense of dread, Julia allowed herself to believe him: Cora would be all right, and Eric would be too. And she would find a way to get to the bottom of whatever was going on.

She'd wait for one hug, and then she'd return to Encinitas.

CHAPTER 38

REN

Nolan was better at picking locks, so he took the back door at Eric Bennett's house. Ren was better at looking harmless and pregnant, so she took the front.

With shadows gathered on the porch, Ren stood in the corner where the streetlights didn't reach. She glanced at her watch, worn over a glove. Though it was past ten, she thought it likely that either grief or guilt would be keeping the recent widower awake. Figuring she'd given Nolan enough of a head start, she rang the doorbell.

While she waited, she wondered if they'd made the right call. Not about killing Bennett—she understood that Bennett needed to die—but about the method. She and Nolan had engaged in their usual debate: Nolan's Glock or Ren's syringe? Nolan had argued that a bullet to the head was the most efficient method, and nearly impossible to hear thanks to his Osprey suppressor. Ren had pointed out that while the Osprey was quiet—the sharp *clack* always reminded her of a staple gun—the syringe was truly silent.

Come on, Nolan had argued. *No one's hearing a single suppressed shot in a house as well insulated as Bennett's.*

To which she'd responded that on such a warm night, there was no way to guarantee that the windows wouldn't be open.

He'd rolled his eyes and reiterated that a bullet would drop Bennett in an instant, as opposed to the thirty seconds it might take for the toxin to stop his heart.

A lot can go wrong in thirty seconds, he'd said.

Ren had countered, *And if things do go south and we need to track down shell casings or patch the drywall from a stray bullet, how long will that take?*

They needed it to look as though Bennett had disappeared. Like the guilty husband fleeing before he could be caught.

A slug buried in the wall would contradict that narrative.

That had won Ren the argument. But now as she rang the bell a second time, she worried they'd made the wrong choice. Nolan would approach from behind, so he had the syringe, while she had her backup Walther, secured in its new belly band holster. She would've felt more comfortable if she'd been the one in charge of the poison.

The porch light flashed on and the door squeaked partially open. Through the crack, Bennett regarded her with a mix of confusion and suspicion. Eyes bleary and crusted with sleep.

So no guilt, then.

The smudges beneath Bennett's eyes had darkened since she'd surveilled him that afternoon. His knuckles were white as he clenched the door. She remembered how those hands had grabbed Julia's arm.

The man's eyes narrowed. "Yes?" His breath was sour, his stubble peppered with flecks of dead skin.

Ren forced a smile. "Eric Bennett?"

"Yes."

"I need to come in."

He positioned himself so he better blocked the door. "Why?"

Ren could've manufactured a reason, but there was no need. He wasn't letting her in no matter what she told him, and she was just the distraction anyway. "So I can kill you."

Bennett cocked his head, obviously doubting what he'd heard, but then seemed to understand. He pushed against the door, panic rising, but Nolan already stood behind him, syringe in gloved hand. Nolan snaked an arm around the other man's waist and yanked him backward. Ren wanted to shout *Not like that,* to remind him stealth was better than force. But he'd already committed, and she couldn't risk distracting him. Even though she knew exactly how it would play out.

Darn it, Nolan.

Ren slipped inside, locking the door, her mind and heart racing, even as Nolan remained unaware of his mistake. Nolan used his free hand to push on Bennett's forehead so his chin tilted, exposing his neck, as if Nolan intended to either slit Bennett's throat or give him a really close shave.

Ren's eyes darted between the empty hand pressed against Bennett's forehead and the syringe Nolan held in his fist at Bennett's waist.

Unless he sprouted a third hand, Nolan wouldn't be able to inject Bennett without first releasing him. Even had Nolan had the angle, injecting the toxin in the stomach would greatly increase the wait before it took effect.

If a lot could go wrong in thirty seconds, it would totally fall apart in a minute.

Ren took a step forward but she couldn't risk getting close enough to take the syringe. The Walther pressed against her side.

She reached for it, even as she tried to think of another way. She went to the shooting range regularly, but she hadn't used a gun to kill someone since that first job a decade before.

Her hesitation filled only the space between heartbeats. She drew the gun. Aimed it. Her pulse slowed.

Nolan released Bennett and stepped back, one swift and fluid movement, giving her a clear shot. But Bennett took advantage of his sudden freedom. He sprang sideways, moving erratically but with a clear goal: the back door.

She didn't dare shoot at a moving target. She didn't have that level of skill.

Nolan understood this too. He moved toward her at the same moment she reached for him, and they traded weapons. Without exchanging a word or gesture, they fell back on instinct, the rhythm learned through other jobs and years of marriage. Working together, the push-pull of the hunt, felt nearly sexual to Ren. Together, they assessed weakness. Flanked their prey. Forced the target to their center.

Bennett ran, an awkward and unsteady gait, while their own steps were careful but quick. When Nolan cut off Bennett's path to the back door, he pivoted, but Nolan already had the Walther raised, his hand as steady as if it were his own Glock.

But this time, Nolan was the distraction. Ren jammed the needle in Bennett's neck, depressed the plunger, and stepped aside.

Bennett swatted at his neck and stumbled, either the toxin or the last drips of adrenaline making him sway. He opened his mouth, and Ren froze, anticipating a scream. But Bennett only slurred, the words as soft and ill-defined as a toddler's. Ren could make out only one word: "Cora."

A moment later, his forehead puckered. His eyelids drooped. Then he pitched forward, his foot catching the edge of a planter on his way to the ground. He landed hard.

Ren clearly marked the moment he gave up. Not quite dead but past saving, Eric drew a long breath, lungs heaving with the effort of filling a final time. When he exhaled, it was in surrender. Ren moved toward him again, kneeling to grab his hand, close enough to get another blast of rancid breath.

"What the hell, Ren?" Nolan anger-whispered. When she looked at him, his forehead was pinched. She'd broken one of the core rules: avoid unnecessary contact with a target.

The stare she returned to him was glacial.

One final, guttural sound rose from Bennett's throat. When Ren glanced down again, his face had relaxed. His eyes flat. His chest still.

Ren examined the planter. Though the dying man had only grazed it, she worried he had chipped it, or pushed it an inch, leaving a telltale ring on the floor showing where it had been before. Some sign that a struggle had taken place. But there wasn't so much as a stray particle of dirt. Ren cocked her head as she studied the plant, touching one of its tendrils with her fingertip. She didn't know this one.

She swiped a gentle finger along the waxy leaves and then stood to help Nolan check the rest of the living room, retracing the steps Bennett had taken in his attempt at escape. Other than an area rug that needed straightening, the living room appeared as they'd first found it.

That's a bit of luck, at least, Ren thought. *He didn't break anything.*

While Nolan left to retrieve the body bag he'd left on the back porch, Ren went into the kitchen and started opening drawers. In the third one, she found what she'd been looking for: among the jumble of loose keys, bag clips, and hardware parts, she found several loose coins. She selected one of the quarters.

She pressed it between her thumb and index finger and rubbed the raised image of Washington's profile. She squinted to see the date. When she couldn't make it out, she moved to the edge of the window, tilting the coin until the moonlight illuminated the lettering. At first, she could tie no memory to the year it had been minted. Then she seized on one: it was the year she'd killed Usoro. She traced the date with her fingertip.

Funny all the ways our lives can connect.

A sound outside caught her attention. She glanced out the window but saw nothing. Just Nolan dragging in the body bag, she decided.

Ren slipped the quarter in her pocket, then left the kitchen to pack Bennett's suitcase.

CHAPTER 39

JULIA

Julia pulled up to Eric's house and immediately checked her phone. While there were still no texts from Eric, there was one from Mike: Cora with me at my place. Come as soon as you can.

There were also nearly a dozen from Cora, along with a missed call from her, all of which must have come in when she'd been trying to call Eric.

What's going on?

Why aren't you responding?

You didn't answer the phone.

What if I've been abducted by cats?

Cats may seem nice but they can be shifty.

What the hell mom?

So Mike says you're checking on dad. Why?

Mike says you're just worried but I know he's lying.

Lying's bad. Bit of a double standard don't you think?

Seriously why aren't you answering?

We're coming to dad's. If you're not there I'm turning you over to the cats.

At all the talk of cats, Julia flashed to Cilantro, and the greenhouse where she lived. A sanctuary for them both. If not for the shooting, Julia would've spent the next day there, making sure everything was in order before the start of classes on Monday. Now she had no idea when either of those things might happen. The start of the semester had been officially delayed at least until the following week.

Julia texted Cora: I'm at dad's now. No need to come. And please don't involve the cats.

She called Eric one last time, then put her phone away and got out of the car.

Unlike earlier, Eric's car was no longer in the driveway. Sometimes if he planned on being home for a while, Eric would park in the garage, especially if he didn't feel like socializing with a salesperson who thought he should upgrade his windows or with a neighbor interested in a game of golf.

Or with police who might show up for another round of questioning.

Julia walked tentatively toward the front of the house. This close to the beach, the town house didn't have much of a front yard, but it did have that garage. She stopped on the sidewalk and scanned the property. She thought she caught a faint glow coming from a side window in that garage. She wished the roll-up door had windows too—something that might've given a hint of what caused that glow—but it was a solid wall of insulated steel. Julia decided to start with the garage. Check to see if Eric's car was inside. If his car wasn't there, she could call Mike. They could make a plan. And if his car was there? Then she would have to decide if the conversation could wait until morning, and if she was even the one to be having it with him.

Despite the slight breeze off the Pacific, the night remained mild. Julia moved closer to the side of the garage, toward the glow, which as she got closer spread and grew indistinct. She squinted. Had she imagined it? With the LED lights of the streetlamps and the moon waxing gibbous, had she simply seen a reflection?

Then the glow took shape again. There were no curtains on the garage window, so she immediately identified the glow's source: a small night-light plugged into a wall. Inside the garage, there was no movement.

And Eric's car was gone. *Shit.*

Though she'd planned on calling Mike, Julia found herself drawn to the front of the house first. She climbed the steps, and even though she didn't expect a response, she lifted her fist to knock. But then she noticed the door wasn't flush in its frame. It hadn't quite latched. When she pushed the door with her fingertips, it creaked open. Though Eric was prone to leaving his door unlocked, this seemed especially careless.

Naturally wary of the dark, once inside, Julia flicked the light switch next to the door, then pushed the dimmer switch to the top. The canned LEDs overhead cast the room in cold, bright light.

She called out, "Eric?"

As she moved farther into the house, her gaze flitted across the living room, landing first on the corners, then on each of the objects in turn. Looking for signs of what might've happened since her last visit. The remote seemed to be in the same place. She didn't see his cell phone or keys on the coffee table. There were no dirty dishes to indicate he'd eaten, at least not while seated on the now empty sofa.

She turned her attention to the open concept kitchen and dining area. No dishes there either. Everything seemed exactly as she'd last seen it.

Flipping on lights as she went, she moved through the house quickly—until she got to the bedroom Eric had shared with Brie. Julia remembered how he'd emptied drawers and closets in his search for clothes for burying Brie. There was a smaller mess now. But this time, it was composed of Eric's clothes.

She walked into the attached bathroom. On the counter there was one electric toothbrush charging. She didn't know if he'd already gotten rid of Brie's. There was no toothpaste or deodorant on the counter, so she started opening drawers, searching for them. Her search came up empty. Had he gone somewhere?

Other things struck her as odd. He flossed regularly, but he'd left the floss behind. He'd taken his cologne, which he only used on date nights, but he'd forgotten the sports cream for the slight but chronic pain in his back.

Leaving the master suite, she checked the guest room before crossing the hall to the third bedroom, which Eric kept as an office. The room was pristine. On the shelves, the books were carefully aligned. On a simple wood desk was what looked like a business card.

She approached the desk and picked up the card. ERIC BENNETT. SENIOR FINANCIAL ANALYST. BAIRD ENTERPRISES. Also listed: Eric's cell phone number and a Los Angeles address.

Julia ran her finger over the embossed lettering. Eric was working for Brie's father? He'd told her about the job, but he hadn't mentioned it was at Baird Enterprises. What would happen now that he was no longer Brie's husband?

Julia tucked the card in her pocket, next to Detective Hoffman's, and returned to the living room. On edge, her gaze returned to Anya, the carnivorous plants she and Cora had potted. The pitcher plant and sundew. Her attention lingered. Eric hadn't asked her to care for anything in his absence, and Cora had dropped off the plant only the day before. When Julia had checked Anya earlier, she'd been healthy. The plants would be fine until—

She cocked her head, the light catching the bare tentacles of the sundew. She stepped forward and squatted beside the plant.

The sundew got its name from the glue-like secretion at the tips of its tentacles. To survive, sundews relied on the mucilage drops to lure and trap insects. But the tips of Anya's tentacles were bare.

That didn't make sense.

She scanned the plant for pests and darkening leaves, which might indicate humic acid buildup. But she and Cora had planted the sundew only the morning before, and Julia had checked on it that afternoon. Most of the causes for the missing mucilage drops—root rot, an infestation, environmental factors—she quickly discounted.

A few hours earlier, the sundew was healthy. Now it wasn't. Which meant the plant had likely been traumatized. Her guess: the pot had been jarred. During a sudden, frantic exit? While sundews were fairly hardy, a sudden hard knock to Anya's pot could've released the mucilage drops.

With proper tending, the sundew would bounce back. But she no longer worried about the plant.

She worried about her ex-husband.

CHAPTER 40

REN

Nolan drove Bennett's Mercedes to San Diego International Airport, and Ren followed. After dumping the Mercedes in the long-term parking lot, Nolan climbed in beside Ren in her Prius. Though obviously unhappy, he waited until they were on the road before he began complaining again.

"We should've left the body in the trunk."

Ren merged onto I-5 and engaged cruise control. They would be on the road awhile. She hoped her bladder wouldn't give her any trouble. "We've covered this. If the police realize Bennett's missing, they're going to put out an alert on the Mercedes. The airport is one of the first places they'll look."

Out of the corner of her eye, she caught Nolan glowering. "By the time they know he's gone, it won't matter if they find him right away. Our problem will be fuckin' solved." She scowled at the profanity, and he apologized. "Sorry. But it will be. We won't have to worry about it anymore, because they'll think the other guy did it to cover his tracks."

"What *is* the plan on that?"

"I'm still putting it together, but soon. I promise." He had the earnest tone he got when trying to persuade her. He'd been using it more often lately. "Anyway, the police aren't going to find out that Bennett's gone for at least a couple of days, like we planned. Eventually, some nosy neighbor will notice his front door's not latched, or the police will come back wanting to talk. But he lives alone. No one's going to start asking questions for a while."

Ren put on her blinker and got into the right-hand lane to take the Martin Luther King Jr. Freeway. "What if his daughter stops by? Or his ex-wife?"

Nolan turned to stare out the side window. "I still think it would've been safe to leave him in the trunk."

"Sure. Leave him in the trunk. Because a decomposing body in a hot car won't attract attention."

Nolan continued to glower. "It's just so fuckin' far." This time, he didn't apologize.

Ninety minutes later, they pulled off the road and into the desert of eastern San Diego County, a spot far beyond the light pollution of the city and too remote for even the stargazers. Nolan usually rode a high after a job. Manic conversation. Sexual overtures. But not that night. The silence between them grew charged, but not in the usual way.

Eric Bennett's last word had been his daughter's name. Rasped out of guilt? Ren didn't think so. It felt like…love. A father like that didn't kill his daughter, not even for a hundred million dollars.

Ren parked near a stand of Joshua trees and pointed to a rock formation not far off the road. "There."

She hit the button to pop the trunk and then got out, leaning against the driver's door. Nolan got out and moved to the back of the car.

Ren folded her arms across her chest and watched him struggle with the body bag. She supposed she could've helped. Supported the weight of the body's lower half. But she wanted him to work for it. The Anderson Hughes job had turned out to be a huge headache for them both. Right now she should've been at home, researching alternative medicine and frequent urination in her copy of *What to Expect When You're Expecting,* not helping her husband dump a body in the desert.

Having freed the body from the trunk, Nolan started dragging it toward the nearby rocks. Watching him, Ren was reminded of that first time she'd disposed of a corpse with her father, who was always quick with his advice and judgments.

Lift with your legs.

Then: *Hold tight to the ankles or calves, not the feet. If a shoe slips off, you might drop the body.*

And finally: *You need to trust your partner. Always.*

Nolan continued dragging while she scanned the landscape, enjoying the darkness. From previous visits, Ren knew that the rocky hills that rose in the distance were made of granite, striped with pale bands of quartz and feldspar and darker ones of biotite. In the daytime, the brush at their feet would be brown or green, and if it had been the season for it, there would be flashes of color: a smoke tree with its tiny blue flowers, yellow poppies, the red tubular flowers of the hummingbird bush.

But night robbed the desert of its hues. A nearby cactus resembled a cluster of obsidian knives, the distant hills painted black. Everything was silhouetted beneath an ocean of stars.

In the distance, Nolan stumbled and swore. "Can I get a little light over here?"

Ren thought the moon and stars provided adequate illumination—it was always better to do their kind of work in the dark—but she retrieved the flashlight from the glove box and clicked it on. She supposed the beam had the added benefit of keeping wildlife at bay. There were mountain lions out here, and coyotes. That had been part of the appeal. Coyotes were opportunistic eaters.

An unwelcome thought seized her: would the poison in Bennett's body break down before the coyotes discovered him? She wished she'd thought to research that. She wouldn't want her actions that night to have a negative impact on the desert's ecosystem.

Ren spoke, only slightly louder than normal, trusting the desert to carry her voice.

"Before you, I dated only one other guy. A month in, I found out he'd once been engaged. When I asked him why he'd never mentioned it, he said he didn't think it was important." Ren shifted, and for a second, the flashlight beam danced on the sand. "After I learned he'd kept that from me, it was all I could see about him."

Nolan paused, wiping sweat from his forehead. "You've never seemed the jealous type."

"It wasn't about the other woman. It was about him, and the fact he'd lied."

At the rocks now, Nolan froze. She thought he might tell her then—whatever secret he still kept—but he regained his composure and unzipped the body bag. He positioned himself near the head, grabbed the body beneath the shoulders, and pulled it free of the plastic. They would dispose of the bag separately on the way home. Roll it up and toss it in a random restaurant's trash bin somewhere north of San Diego County. A body found in the desert told one story. A body found in the desert in a body bag told quite another.

Nolan paused to adjust his grip and looked at her. "So this guy you were dating. You killed him?" Only half joking.

She didn't answer, not directly. "You know what I've always found most interesting about toxins, Nolan? In small amounts, some can be therapeutic. Lifesaving, even. But too much..." Her lips stretched into a semblance of a smile, but even she felt the wrongness in it, her cheeks too tight. "It's all in the dose."

When Nolan released the body, stashing it behind a boulder, he was breathing heavier than usual. "What the hell are you talking about?" He avoided her eyes, and Ren knew she was right: he was hiding something. He had been for days.

"Whether a toxin is fatal also depends on what part of your body it attacks. How easily the targeted tissue can repair itself. Whether it's reversible, or whether you just have to treat the symptoms and hope to ride it out. The liver is pretty resilient, for instance. If the liver were attacked, you would have a pretty good shot." Her face settled into stone. "But again, it all comes down to dose. You throw enough toxin at any part of the human body, and it dies. Even the resilient liver won't be able to regenerate."

Still averting his eyes, Nolan wiped his dusty hands on his pants and started to walk back, but Ren shook her head. "Strip him. We need to take his clothes with us." When he hesitated, she sighed. "It's not like you have to take his underwear, Nolan. Just everything else."

They couldn't risk trace evidence being found on Bennett's clothes. Those would go in another trash bin, separate from the body bag.

Nolan looked unhappy about his new task, but he returned to the body. Eager to be done, he finished quickly. After he'd stashed the clothes and the body bag back in the trunk, he stood in front of her.

Ren forced herself to make eye contact. "Lying is a little like that, don't you think? You omit a detail, keep one tiny secret, and at first it seems fine. Maybe you even tell yourself you're doing a good thing—protecting someone you love. But then you start keeping the big secrets too, and this relationship you thought was so resilient—it's damaged irreversibly. It's toxic, and beyond saving." She paused, staring. "How close are we to that, Nolan?"

The silence grew thick between them, but to his credit, his gaze didn't waver. He squared his shoulders, decision made.

Finally, Ren thought.

"I didn't mean to keep it from you as long as I have," he said. "I've been trying to tell you since last night. Ever since I saw Brie's photo on the news and realized who she was. What I'd done wrong."

Her skin prickled. She crossed her arms and waited.

"When I was hired, I had the photo. A name. The time and place. And Brie was there, at that time, at that place, standing next to Eric Bennett and his daughter. A happy little family." His voice grew fevered. Trying to convince her again? "When I looked through the scope, it was the three of them, clustered together." He sighed. "Anyone could've made the same mistake. They look so much alike."

The desert air seemed abruptly cold. The stars too bright.

"You killed the wrong person." It hit her like a landslide. "On top of missing your second target."

His jaw tensed. "I didn't miss. The bullet hit its target."

"The second bullet, you mean. The first hit that Murphy guy."

"I didn't miss," he repeated, angry. At Ren's expression, he dropped the scowl. "Anyway…Brie Bennett was never the target. Julia Bennett was."

The news sent Ren back a step. Though she'd guessed that was where his confession was headed, his admission left her unsteady. She'd come to care what happened to Julia, and now they might really need to kill her.

As if reading her thoughts, Nolan said, "If Julia Bennett knows something that could blow back on us, she's a threat. And Baird can't find out I killed his daughter by accident. Last night, when I told you I'd followed Eric Bennett to that bar in San Clemente? I'd just found out I'd killed the wrong woman, on top of the girl still being alive. I intended to correct my mistake, and take care of the real targets, but conditions weren't optimal." He paused, jaw twitching. "So I followed Julia Bennett, hoping she'd lead me to her daughter, and then I could kill them both."

Ren's balled fists throbbed. "Did she see you?"

He hesitated. Less than a second, but the pause troubled Ren. "Of course not. But I lost her on I-5."

The effort of still holding her gaze made Nolan squint.

"There is no trust, is there?" Ren asked coldly. "The hundred million dollars you offered as motive?"

The reason the body now lay before them, awaiting scavengers.

Nolan's silence answered for him. Another deceit, spun to justify his failures.

Nolan took a step closer to her, his eyes clear, his face earnest. "Without someone to give to Baird, we weren't safe. And I knew you needed to be sure before we struck." His voice grew weary, but it held no regret. "So I made the hard choice. I gave you a reason to be sure. You may resent me for it, and that's okay. I can be the bad guy if it means you and our child are no longer in danger."

Nolan finally broke from her stare, letting his eyes drift down to her belly. Then he climbed into the car without saying more.

Before getting in beside him, Ren scanned the landscape one final time. She imagined the predators that would soon skulk out of the night to investigate the intriguing new smell of the body. Predators sensed weakness, and opportunity.

Nolan was showing weakness too. How long before Baird caught the scent?

CHAPTER 41

JULIA

The steel-and-glass tower stretched nearly a thousand feet into the sky, one of the highest points in the iconic Los Angeles skyline. Julia double-checked Eric's business card to make sure she had the correct address before noticing a small silver plaque bolted to the building. BAIRD ENTERPRISES.

She was in the right place, but still, she hesitated before entering. Was showing up at Eric's new job the right move?

It had seemed that way on Saturday night, when Julia had found his house empty. She'd decided she'd wait until Monday afternoon, give Eric a chance to call. Answer her texts. Explain things. When he hadn't, she'd spent another several hours debating how much to tell Cora. But what had she really seen? A tangle of clothes on his bed. The sundew with its bare leaves. The abandoned floss.

She left a message on Hoffman's voicemail anyway.

When Cora had asked about her dad, Julia only said he hadn't been home. On Sunday, while Cora hid out in her room, Julia spent the day stress baking, triple-checking every lock, and peering out at the street. Later, Mike brought pizza, and she could tell that he too was comforted when Cora finished her second slice and one of the toffee chip cookies Julia had baked.

257

Now, though, Julia doubted herself. She knew Cora was safe, once more with Evie and her mom, but she wanted that normal day back: Mike and pizza and toffee chip cookies.

But nothing was normal. Not really. Classes should've started that morning. She should've been preparing to grade papers, doing research in her greenhouse, connecting with students. But Julia's hesitation wouldn't help Eric or Cora. She pushed hard on the revolving door that led into Baird Enterprises.

The lobby was all white stone and tinted glass, and several degrees too cold. Goose bumps rose on Julia's exposed arms, her toes instantly chilled in her sandals. She approached the reception area and the young man in a headset seated behind the plexiglass, his neck bowed. In the aggressive air-conditioning, she envied him his lined suit jacket.

Rubbing her arms, Julia asked if she might be escorted to Eric Bennett's office. She had a whole speech planned—how Eric had accidentally taken their daughter's cell phone—but when the man looked up, his expression made her forget every word.

"You're…? I thought…?" He cleared his throat and tried again. "Name please."

"Julia Bennett."

He visibly relaxed. "Sorry." He fiddled with his headset. "I've only seen Mrs. Bennett a couple of times, but you look an awful lot alike. Or looked. I mean…let me see if I can get someone down here. If you'll take a seat."

The young man waited until she was out of earshot before he pushed a button on the side of his headset and started talking. A few minutes later, he gestured her back to his desk, and handed her a visitor's badge.

"Tenth floor. Conference room will be the first door on your right. Ms. Roberts will meet you there."

At the bank of elevators, Julia pushed the button, aware that the young man and a wiry security guard both watched her. The car couldn't come quickly enough, but when it did, the surge upward pulled her stomach closer to her throat. A few seconds later, the doors opened on a suite with floor-to-ceiling windows, beyond them an endless sky as blue as it ever got in L.A. Julia stepped closer, taking in the entire city. From above, the streets looked safer, the tiny people and their toy cars less significant. She turned away and headed into the conference room.

Before her stretched a long table—satin glass, metal base—holding stacks of iPads and bottles of water arranged in tidy rows. A woman reclined at one end in a gray high-backed chair. She wore a navy blazer and skirt, her hair a glossy chestnut except for a blond stripe that framed her face. She wore thick-rimmed glasses that she removed when Julia entered the room.

The woman stood, closed the door, and gestured toward the chair across from her, which Julia took.

"I'm Samantha Roberts. Call me Sam." She pointed to the bottles at the center of the table. "Water?" She didn't wait for Julia to answer before pushing one in her direction.

Sam perched back on the edge of her chair, her brown eyes unblinking. She wore two large diamond earrings that, if real, would've cost more than a year's mortgage on Julia's bungalow.

"It's a pleasure meeting you, Julia. Eric's talked so much about you."

This surprised her. How long had Eric been working here?

As if reading her thoughts, the other woman added, "Eric brought me along, from our old firm, when he started here. We've known each other for years."

Julia picked up the bottle of water, cold enough to make her fingers feel frostbitten. Shards of ice floated inside. She shook it as if it were a snow globe, watching the ice chips swirl. "I can't decide if I should drink it or mount a little figurine inside. Maybe a tiny log cabin? Some pine trees."

Sam smiled. "When you work here, you learn to favor wool suit jackets. So how can I help you?"

Julia opened her mouth, but beyond her lie about Cora's phone, she wasn't sure where to start.

A moment later, Sam continued in a softer tone, "I'm concerned about Eric too." But the extreme angle at which she inclined her head seemed practiced.

Julia shook off the thought. She had no reason to doubt this woman's sincerity.

"Why are you concerned?" Still holding the water bottle, Julia's palms had grown icy. She held on, the chill a tether that helped her focus.

Sam's eyes found the door, as if confirming it remained tightly closed, before leaning in.

"Of course, with everything last week, we didn't expect Eric to put in a *full* day today." Her tone certainly suggested otherwise. "But he had some important documents he was supposed to sign. We were expecting him by nine."

"I take it he didn't show."

"Not so much as a text."

The cold of the bottled water seemed to be seeping into her bloodstream. "That *is* strange. But he does have a lot on his mind."

"It just doesn't seem like Eric. And this is a new job, for both of us. You don't disappoint a new boss." She glanced toward the closed door and then back again. "Especially if that boss is Oliver Baird. You haven't heard from Eric either?"

Julia saw no reason to overshare. "Not since Saturday afternoon."

"You must be worried too, or why would you be here? You're not like the other Mrs. Bennett. You don't just stop by unannounced."

Julia stiffened at being referred to as *the other Mrs. Bennett,* but she didn't correct Sam. Instead, she remembered her story. "Our daughter misplaced her cell phone. She thinks she might've left it in Eric's car." Before Sam could push for details, Julia asked, "So Brie stopped by here a lot? I was under the impression she and her father were estranged."

"They are. Were." She shook her head. "Honestly? I don't know anymore. Her father can be a tough man to please." She made the last part sound like a compliment. "Brie visited Eric more at our old firm. She'd bring him a latte, or swing by for an impromptu lunch."

"How romantic," Julia said dryly.

"She was checking up on him."

"Did she have reason to think she needed to?" Eric hadn't ever seemed coy about Sam, but that didn't mean anything, not really.

Sam's face remained passive. "Not that I'm aware. How about you?"

Julia drew back, staring hard at the other woman. "What about me?"

"I got the impression that Brie thought you and Eric might still be involved."

Shocked that a stranger might ask this, Julia couldn't shake her head fast enough. "No. Just…no."

Sam finally smiled. "I didn't think so. You never stopped by, after all."

Julia stifled an inner groan. She hesitated, then asked, "What about Brie? Suspicion begets suspicion, right? Do you know if she was seeing someone?"

The smile turned chilly. "It wouldn't surprise me. I'd imagine Brie would want the scales balanced, as it were." Her eyes narrowed to slits. "You sure nothing was going on with you and Eric?"

"Completely."

"You two are close, though, aren't you? He talked about you."

"He's Cora's father, so we make the effort. How about you? You followed him here. You must be good friends."

Sam lifted her shoulders. "Eric mentioned the opening here, and I took it. He's always looked out for me. And Mr. Baird is a generous employer."

"How well do you know Baird?"

"Well enough to know he wouldn't want me answering that question." In the pause that followed, she picked at the label on her own water bottle before uncapping it and taking a sip. She looked again toward the door. "You're not here about your daughter's cell phone, are you? You're worried about him, just like I am."

The goose bumps rose again on Julia's arms.

"Nope. Just here about the phone."

The door finally opened, and a man entered quickly, without knocking. His dark beard was worn short and shot through with silver. His suit was sharply pressed. When he walked across the room, his strides were long and confident. If there had been a crowd, it would've parted. And, Julia thought, maybe bowed.

Julia recognized him from the news. Oliver Baird. In person, she saw some of Brie in his face. The nose, she thought, and the way his eyes narrowed.

She looked sideways at Sam, who was already standing.

"Ah," Julia said in sudden understanding. "You were babysitting me, weren't you?"

Sam smoothed her skirt. "It's been a pleasure," she said simply, and slipped from the room.

Baird smirked into the silence that followed. "Don't be too hard on her, Julia. I figured you'd be more forthcoming with a woman. Some people find me intimidating."

Julia couldn't fault his logic. If he'd come at her with the same questions Sam had, she probably wouldn't have answered. She was glad she hadn't given much away.

"Come." The word wasn't an invitation. Baird spun on his heels, obviously expecting her to follow.

Julia crossed her arms and remained in place. Glancing briefly at her phone, she unlocked it and started tapping. When Baird cleared his throat, she lifted her head.

"Letting a friend know I'm here." She hit send and pocketed her phone.

"Why? Are you frightened?" He seemed pleased by the idea.

"Not at all. Just covering my bases."

"Then are you coming?" Though phrased as a question this time, it was no less an order.

"Where?" she asked, stalling, even as her concern grew. Why was Baird even here, with her?

Where are you, Eric? she thought. *What have you done?*

"We're going to Eric's office. Let's see if we can find your daughter's phone." Baird's tone made it clear he didn't believe her story. Out of options, Julia followed anyway.

CHAPTER 42

REN

Ren was seldom nervous, but that afternoon, her stomach rumbled as if she'd sampled some of her own baneberry. She watched as people trickled in and out of the unassuming gray building. Not a lot of traffic today. That was good, at least. She wished she'd had more time to scope out the office, but she'd been distracted, worrying she might have to kill Julia.

Nolan had been insistent: Julia still had to die. Even if they'd killed the client and dumped his body in the desert, it wasn't like them not to finish a job.

If we let her live, it'll reflect poorly on our brand, he'd said.

Remembering, she wrinkled her nose in distaste. He'd actually said that: *our brand.* As if they sold sneakers or auto insurance.

Nolan had offered to finish the job, or at least accompany Ren, but she'd shut him down with one of her most arctic stares.

I've got this, she'd said.

Julia didn't deserve to be shot like a rabid animal. Especially after what had happened to her parents. So it had been decided that Ren would take care of her.

But Ren wasn't killing the girl. At least not unless she got in the way. Ren had made that clear.

Nolan had understood. *The girl isn't the one asking the questions,* he'd agreed.

Before they'd moved into their condo, in their old home, Ren had procured poppy seeds from Southeast Asia, which she'd planted in the loam in the hidden corners of her beloved garden. It was illegal to grow *Papaver somniferum,* the root of opium, in the United States, but it was also illegal to kill people. Life was risk.

From seed to fruit-bearing flower, the poppy's growth cycle lasted about four months. Each year, when the plant had matured, she'd used a scalpel to slice open a pod, about the size of an egg, which released milky beads of sap she'd allowed to dry to a rich, sticky brown. Then she'd halved the pods, removing the seeds and allowing them to dry in the sun for the following year's planting.

With the right solvents, she could make that sap into heroin, morphine, whatever she wanted. Now that she no longer had her full garden, Ren was running low on her homegrown morphine, so she didn't use it often. But Julia was entitled to a death as painless—and as euphoric— as Ren could offer. So she began her next poison with the last of her morphine.

As she selected her other ingredients, she considered their toxicity and their taste. For poetic license, she would've liked to add a little belladonna—translated as "beautiful lady"—but it would be too bitter. She wanted a morsel that was delicate, and sweet.

The ingredients she'd ended up mixing were expensive, the dose overly generous, but Ren didn't want Julia to suffer. She was fairly certain the taste would be subtle, though she couldn't exactly verify that. More importantly, once ingested, the mix would kill quickly.

That was, if Ren went through with it. She still hadn't decided. The poison was back home, tucked in among her socks.

In front of her, the door to the office opened, a couple emerging mid-argument. Something about window coverings ordered in the wrong size, which would set back the completion of the nursery remodel. Ren waited for them to pass. Then, to center herself, she performed a quick breathing exercise—just as she'd learned in her pregnancy books—and entered the building.

Dr. Kari Jordan was a tall woman with gray-blue eyes and blond hair she wore in a loose braided knot. When she smiled, she exposed rabbitlike incisors.

"Not waiting for anyone?" she asked.

Ren tried to relax as she reclined on the table, stomach exposed in her hospital gown.

"No."

Ren hadn't told Nolan about the appointment.

He had lied to her about the trust. Worse, he'd made a mistake that threatened her baby.

How had that happened, anyway? How could he have mistaken Brie for Julia? True, they looked a little alike. They both had dark hair and light eyes, and their builds were similar if you weren't paying close enough attention. But Brie's arms were scrawnier. Sticklike, really. She wore more expensive clothes and had a flashier smile. She reminded Brie of ethylene glycol: sweet to the taste but common and unreliable. An amateur's poison. In contrast, Julia was more like tetrodotoxin, a sodium channel blocker carried in some fish. Elegant and extremely potent. A more interesting choice, in Ren's opinion.

Though angry at the mistake, Ren was also secretly glad. It brought an unexpected sadness to think of Julia dead. Even if her death still proved necessary—a likely outcome—at least Ren would have known her for this short time, and given her a few last days with her daughter.

Dr. Jordan squirted warm gel on Ren's stomach. "This will help the sound waves travel more easily into the uterus."

She moved the wand over Ren's skin as she studied a monitor, occasionally tapping on the keyboard. Still looking at the screen, she said, "I noticed this is your first appointment." She'd made the comment earlier too, but Ren hadn't responded then. Apparently, the doctor wasn't ready to let it go.

"Work's kept me busy lately."

"I understand work is important, but make sure to take care of yourself too." The doctor continued swiping and one-handed typing. "Rest and regular checkups are a part of that. We want a healthy mom and a healthy baby."

Ren tensed, craning her neck so she could see the screen. "Is something wrong with the baby?"

Dr. Jordan smiled. "The baby's fine. Let me show you."

She moved the wand slowly, pointing out various body parts. "Here are its legs. Its stomach. And this? That's the heartbeat."

Ren squinted to see. When she noticed the slight fluttering, her own heart did the same.

Applying a continuous pressure, Dr. Jordan swiped the wand. She stopped and smiled again. Even before the doctor spoke, Ren knew what she was seeing. The tiny stranger's face, in profile. "And that's your baby's head."

The doctor left the wand in place for several moments, allowing Ren to study the slope of the tiny stranger's face, the tilt of its nose.

"Do you want to see if we can identify the gender?"

Ren started to shake her head and then, tentatively, nodded instead.

The pressure from the wand intensified, triggering Ren's full bladder. She clenched to stop herself from urinating right there on the table. Briefly, she considered asking Dr. Jordan if it was normal to have to urinate so much that early in the second trimester, but she stopped herself. She didn't feel comfortable sharing her symptoms with this stranger, medical degree or not. Better to search on an encrypted browser at home.

Dr. Jordan adjusted the wand and then pointed. "Sometimes the baby's in an awkward position and we can't tell, but your daughter is being very cooperative today."

Daughter. Though Ren couldn't make out the shapes in the swirls of light and dark, she studied the screen with a fierce intensity.

"Have you thought of any names?" Dr. Jordan asked.

As with most expecting couples, she and Nolan had discussed the topic at length. To honor Ren's father, she'd considered Anthony for a boy, Antoinette or Antonia for a girl. Toni for short. She and Nolan also liked Lily and Elizabeth and Tessa.

Impulsively, Ren said, "Julia's a nice name."

"Derives from Jupiter, king of the gods in Roman mythology. Strong name."

King of the gods. Ren liked that.

CHAPTER 43

JULIA

Eric's office was located midway down the corridor on the tenth floor of a building that topped out at fifty-two. Not a corner office and a long way from the penthouse. So why was Oliver Baird, the occupant of that penthouse, bothering with someone like Julia?

Baird pushed open the door onto a smaller version of the conference room: glass desk, floor-to-ceiling windows, and a high-backed executive chair, this one in blue leather. Behind the desk, an accent wall covered in rough graphite tiles ended at a flat eight-inch baseboard. Across from the textured wall stood a dark cabinet. Boxes still sealed with tape were stacked next to it. It took Baird only three strides to reach the windows. When he did, he spun to face Julia. His expression seemed one of curiosity.

"You knew my daughter." He spoke with a slight brogue.

"Not well, I'm sorry to say." A silence grew between them, and Julia rocked on the balls of her feet, abruptly uncomfortable. "And I'm so sorry for your loss."

He waved off her condolences, impatient. "Why might someone want Brie dead?"

"Shouldn't you know that better than me?"

"I should, but I don't." No apology. Just a statement of fact.

His watch buzzed, and he glanced down at his wrist before returning his attention to Julia.

"Tell me about your ex-husband."

"Eric?"

"You have more than one?"

"You know I don't."

He smirked, shallow dimples interrupting his black-and-silver beard. "And why would you say that?"

"Because Eric married your daughter, and now he works for you. With your resources, you've thoroughly vetted him and, by extension, me."

His smirk disappeared, lips tightening. "Even the most thorough investigations don't uncover everything, Julia. People are remarkably adept at hiding their worst secrets."

Julia managed to keep her gaze steady. "If he had secrets, I'm not the one he would've shared them with. Obviously. We've been divorced for years."

Baird's watch vibrated again. He ignored it.

"What kind of man is Eric?"

"Not the kind who would hurt your daughter." Even as she said it, she remembered the hastily packed bag. The online rumors. The detective's interest. She strained to keep her expression neutral even as her jaw pulsed.

"How about you, Julia?" Baird's expression hardened. "What kind of person are you?"

Her palms sweated despite the blast of air-conditioning. "The kind who doesn't share her secrets just because some rich guy asks."

His watch buzzed a third time. The slight grooves in Baird's face deepened with his scowl.

"Have your look around. For the phone. And then see yourself out," he said at last. Then he strode across the room, his phone in his hand as soon as he hit the corridor.

*   *   *

With Baird gone, Julia figured she had only a couple of minutes before security came to strong-arm her into leaving. She moved to the boxes across from the desk, but when she got close, she noticed the fraying of the cardboard near the tape. They'd already been opened and resealed.

That explained why Baird had no qualms about leaving her alone. If there had been anything to find, he'd have it already.

Julia peeled back the tape and separated the flaps of each box anyway, surveying the contents. A stapler, tape dispenser, and scissors. Several notepads. A plain blue mug. A box of pens. File folders that were creased but empty. Framed photos of Cora and Brie tucked into bubble wrap. Julia moved on to the drawers.

It was only when she reached the bottom drawer that she noticed it. Not in the drawer itself but near it, where the textured wall met the baseboard. The two boards were misaligned. Probably less than an eighth of an inch, but an obvious flaw in an otherwise meticulous space.

Hesitating only briefly, Julia closed the office door and quietly moved back to the corner of the room, then dropped to her knees. Her fingers grazed the flat wood. Because the baseboards were taller than her hand, she couldn't get a full grip, so she pushed hard with her fingers. It held firmly in place.

She switched to the second baseboard, and immediately noticed a thin seam. When she pushed near the wall, the wood flexed.

She wedged her fingernails underneath and lifted. The panel shifted, but she didn't have enough leverage.

The scissors.

Julia returned to the boxes and grabbed the scissors. She ripped a couple of sheets from one of the notepads, triple-folding the paper into a long but narrow strip, then separated the scissor blades to wrap the paper around the sharp edge. She secured it with a long strip of tape as best she could.

Moving to the baseboard again, Julia jammed the point of one blade between the wood and the tile floor. She wiggled the scissors until the metal hit wall. She applied pressure, careful that the paper protecting her hand didn't slip. Finally, a section of wood popped off to expose a small hole.

She discarded the scissors and used the flashlight of her phone to peer inside.

Empty.

She put her phone back into her pocket, then traced her index finger on the floor inside the hole. She rubbed her finger against her thumb. No grit. The small space was free of dust. Clean.

The door opened, and Julia looked up, expecting to see security. She saw Baird instead. A moment later, a large man with a meaty neck appeared beside him. Hugo? Rocky? He'd surely have one of those names you might also give your Rottweiler.

"Looking for the money?" Baird asked.

Julia cocked her head, confused. *Money?* She stood. "What are you talking about?"

Baird folded his arms across his chest. "I was curious to see what you would do if I left you alone." His brogue was thick. "You certainly found that hiding spot quickly."

So he'd been watching her. The office was so sparsely furnished, she wondered where he could've hidden the cameras. She glanced up.

"The lights?"

He didn't reply, but the twitch at his jaw told her she'd guessed correctly.

She gestured toward the exposed hole. "Eric couldn't have done that. He only just started working here."

"Of course he didn't. The building was designed with many such hiding places. Some of my executives can be quite paranoid." His gaze turned glacial to match the chilled air. "I was unaware he even knew about it, actually. But when he didn't show up this morning as scheduled, I checked this office. That's when I found the cash. Stacks of it."

Remembering the money missing from Eric's account, she couldn't stop herself from asking. "How many stacks?"

Baird let the question linger between them, unanswered. "Don't misunderstand. There are stashes of cash like Eric's all over this building. Most of my executives aren't creative in that regard, though I did once find nude photos a partner took of his wife." He shook his head. "His girlfriend, I'd understand, but his wife? To each his own, I guess."

When Julia took a step, the guard shifted so he filled the doorway. Even in her wedge sandals, Julia came only to his collarbone. She rolled her eyes at the display of machismo and straightened her spine to show she wasn't intimidated. Even if maybe she was.

"What did you and Brie fight about before she died?" she asked.

"We fought quite often. You'll have to be more specific." Baird managed to sound both exasperated and weary.

"Last Tuesday."

He laughed. "If I answered that, you would be quite amused." The smile he offered seemed genuine, as if he took great pleasure in keeping this secret from her. "Now about the money."

"I don't know anything about that."

His eyes narrowed, obviously unconvinced. "Here's my theory. You and Eric had started up again, and you wanted Brie out of the way."

Julia recoiled. "You think I would have my own *daughter* shot?"

"A minor wound, I've heard. A nice misdirection."

Julia had the sudden urge to *misdirect* her foot into his shin.

Baird gestured to the baseboard. "You found the hiding spot in less than a minute."

"That's only because whoever replaced the baseboard did a crappy job."

When the guard's neck reddened, Julia snapped her fingers. "Ah, that would be you." For the first time, she was grateful for the air-conditioning. At least she wasn't sweating. "Better stick with the security gig, because you definitely wouldn't cut it in construction."

Julia tried again to brush past the guard, but he grabbed her arm. His fingers were tight, but not so tight they would leave bruises. Smart. The only other time someone had grabbed her like that, when she'd been living in Cordelia's tent, she'd had finger-shaped marks on her skin for a week.

Luckily, she'd been shown what to do so it wouldn't happen again.

Julia wrapped her entire hand around Hugo's pinkie, even his tiniest finger the size of an engorged banana slug. Pressed her thumb to his nail and jerked. Adrenaline made her twist harder than intended. She heard a soft pop, and he immediately released her. But the only sign she'd broken his finger was his slight grimace.

"Changed my mind, Hugo," she said anyway, breathing heavily. "You suck at security too."

CHAPTER 44

REN

D r. Jordan removed the wand from Ren's stomach, and her baby disappeared. Ren felt a momentary pang of loss.

The doctor replaced the wand in its holder and grabbed a paper towel. She offered it to Ren. "So, I'd like to—"

Ren's phone rang, cutting off Dr. Jordan mid-sentence. Ren snapped to sitting, reaching for the clothes she'd left folded on a nearby chair. She found her phone quickly and checked the screen, ignoring the look of disapproval on the doctor's face.

"So everything looks okay?" Ren asked.

Dr. Jordan frowned. "You didn't completely fill out the health history questionnaire, so there are some questions—"

"But the baby's good?" Standing now.

"Your blood pressure is a little high."

Ren shed her gown, no trace of modesty. "Like I said, work stress."

Dr. Jordan's frown deepened. "Remember what I said about finding time to relax."

Ren grabbed her pants. "It's fine. My project at work will be ending soon."

The phone went silent, but Ren knew it would start ringing again soon. Oliver Baird wasn't the type of man who let his calls go unanswered.

Ren slipped on her pants, then started to wriggle into her T-shirt, snug on her gel-slick belly. She really needed to buy some new shirts.

"I can see you're in a hurry, but remember to stop at the desk and make a follow-up appointment."

"I will." She wouldn't. At least not with Dr. Jordan. With everything that had been happening, she and Nolan likely needed to leave town for a while. For a moment, she grew wistful at having to leave the condo, just when it was starting to feel like home, but she and Nolan had already stayed too long.

It's just real estate, her father would've said.

Still scowling, the doctor left Ren to finish dressing. It was only then that Ren realized she hadn't thought to ask for a photo of the ultrasound.

Ren managed to use the bathroom and exit the building before the phone rang again. Baird calling back.

When she answered, Baird sounded irritated. "Your husband just called while I was in a meeting. Several times. I was forced to leave the room. And then I call you, and you don't answer." He paused. Expecting an explanation? Apology? Ren offered neither. "It all feels a bit disrespectful."

Surprised, Ren needed two tries to unlock her car. "What did he want?"

"He gave me a name. The task I assigned *you*." Another pause. "Tell me, Ren, why was it your husband who called me?"

She settled in the driver's seat, but with no one else around, she left the door cracked. So Nolan had come through after all. "Of course I told him. We're partners."

"I don't give a fuck." Ren's jaw clenched at the expletive. "I told you to leave him out of it. Yet you didn't. That concerns me. Or, rather, that should concern *you*. I'm not certain you want to be lumped in with your husband right now."

"Why do you say that?"

On the other end of the line, someone in the background was speaking—keening, really—but too softly for Ren to make out the words.

Baird's voice grew momentarily distant as he spoke to someone in the room: "Shut up about your damn finger." His attention returned to Ren. "We just had a visitor at the downtown office. Julia Bennett."

He let the name settle. Ren was glad it was a call and not an in-person chat. If they'd been face-to-face, her expression would've betrayed her.

"She broke my guard's pinkie."

Ren allowed herself a smile but swallowed it quickly. Inappropriate.

"How unfortunate," she said.

"That bitch is stronger than she looks. And nosy as hell." Ren bristled, but Baird kept speaking. "But the good news is, I found stacks of cash in my former son-in-law's office."

"How much cash?"

"Fifty thousand dollars."

The money they were owed. Not that Ren could ask for it.

"Half your going rate, yes?"

"That seems thin. There are other things he might've wanted to do with fifty thousand. Hide it from the IRS. Buy a car."

"You can't buy a car worth driving for that." He paused, then let out a low chuckle. "No need to worry, Ren. I've confirmed you and Nolan weren't involved."

Ren's head buzzed. *Confirmed? How?*

"Of course we weren't involved," she said.

"My point is my former son-in-law was stashing cash, which means he was hiding something from Brie." Baird's brogue grew thicker with irritation. "We still need to do something about Julia Bennett."

Ren's spine snapped erect, her neck stiffening. While they both spoke on encrypted phones, she was taken aback that he would state his intentions so boldly. She was also worried: had whatever Baird found shown that Julia was the intended target?

"That's not necessary. You said Nolan gave you a name, and the husband appears guilty. So everything's resolved."

Several seconds ticked by. When Baird spoke, he no longer sounded irritated. He sounded amused. "I admit, I'm surprised you're not disturbed by all this."

A couple approached a nearby truck, and Ren reluctantly pulled her car door closed. "Why would I be?" she asked, even as suspicion crawled along her spine.

Baird chuckled. "With all your talk about family, I would think you would be more…protective. I mean, it *is* your father we're talking about."

The name Nolan had given Baird was her *father's*?

Ren's cheeks flamed, but she couldn't show weakness. Her father had taught her that. Ren touched her stomach and filled her lungs to keep the anger from her voice. "Is there anything else?"

Baird chuckled again, a cold and mirthless sound. "I think it's time we have another chat, Ren. Tonight. In person."

The pulse in Ren's jaw throbbed, at both the request and his casual use of her name over the phone. "Where?"

"The Shearwater. It's sealed up tight, but I'll text you the passcode for the garage. Bring our nosy little friend too, so we can find out how much she knows." Ren doubted Julia knew anything of value. Still, it wouldn't hurt to find out before Ren administered her dose.

"And Ren? Bring Nolan too. I still have a few questions for him."

After ending their conversation, Ren returned home. She retrieved a small tin from her sock drawer, and carefully packed up the rest of her stash. She also packed two bags: one for her and one for Nolan. When she left the condo, she paused in the doorway. But she didn't look back. No reason to be sentimental. *It's just real estate.*

Two hours later, she was in Julia's house. She set the timer on her watch for fifteen minutes and allowed herself a quick tour. Kitchen. Both bedrooms. Bathroom. But it was in the garage that she lingered. On the shelves were gardening supplies arranged in haphazard rows: bags of peat moss, perlite, and washed sand; trowels and buckets; ceramic pots; and jugs of distilled water. She opened one of the bags of sand, took off a glove, and let the tiny grains slip between her fingers.

When the alarm on her watch vibrated, she returned to Julia's bedroom and sat cross-legged on the floor of her closet, the door closed. Hidden in case Julia's daughter came home first. Ren hoped she wouldn't. She didn't want it to come down to that.

CHAPTER 45

JULIA

Despite her bravado, the conversation with Baird left Julia shaken. She hurried away from the building and toward her car. On her way over, she hadn't been able to find a parking spot in the shade. Now she was glad for that. In the heat of the car's interior, she still shivered. She couldn't lock her car doors fast enough.

How could Baird think she was sleeping with Eric? And then there was that money he claimed to have found in Eric's office. Eric hadn't actually paid to have Brie killed—had he?

No. No way.

Julia kept coming back to the bullet that grazed Cora, and her daughter's proximity to Murphy and Brie. She still couldn't believe Eric would endanger their daughter.

But if he wasn't involved, then why had he fled his home? And why wasn't he returning her calls?

Julia texted Cora. Have you eaten?

When Cora didn't respond right away, Julia typed, I make a mean boxed macaroni.

Though she tried to keep it light, Julia needed her daughter home, under her protection, until she could figure out what it all meant, and what the hell had happened to Eric.

Julia stared at the phone for several minutes, willing the dancing dots to appear, but none did. The once-welcome heat grew stifling. She started the car, pulled onto the road, and called Mike through the Bluetooth connection.

For a moment, she thought he might ignore her too. But after several rings, he picked up.

"What's with texting me your location?" he asked.

"Just wanted someone to know where I was." Now that she was on I-5 and headed home, it seemed a ridiculous precaution. What was Mike going to do for her all the way down in San Diego, other than report her last known whereabouts to the police?

"So you went to Eric's office." When she'd mentioned the idea to him the night before, he hadn't wanted her to go. Irritation seeped into his voice. "How'd that go?"

"I broke a man's finger."

At least he laughed. "So it went well."

"Baird asked if I had anything to do with his daughter's murder."

"Making friends all around."

"He also found money in Eric's office." She couldn't bring herself to add what that likely meant: that Eric was involved in Brie's death.

But Mike understood. "I'm sorry, Jules."

For several seconds, she listened to him breathe. Then she said, "I wish you'd been there."

"You didn't ask me." Irritated again.

Would he have come if she'd asked? Probably, but he wouldn't have been happy about it. Which was why she'd gone by herself.

"And truthfully? I wish you hadn't been there either." His voice husky. "You're going to get yourself killed if you keep poking at this."

She felt twin spots of heat bloom on her cheeks. "When you were a reporter, would you have stopped if someone demanded it?"

"I would never demand anything of you." He sounded offended.

Why was a conversation with Mike suddenly such a challenge? "You know what I mean."

Julia heard a soft clatter. "You there?" Her question was met with silence. "Mike?"

Deep breathing. "Sorry about that. I was buttoning my shirt and the phone got away from me. Slippery little sucker."

"Truce? Why don't you have dinner with me and Cora?" she asked. "I can make pasta."

"Mac and cheese, huh?"

"If I add a bagged salad, it's a balanced meal."

He exhaled sharply. "Sorry, Jules. They're holding that vigil tonight to mark what should've been the first day of classes, and I really want to be there for my students." He paused. "Assume you got the email too?"

She had, and of course she wanted to be there for the Anderson Hughes community. But the thought of being in a crowd in that courtyard again made her queasy. "Forgot about that."

Mike didn't call her on the lie. "Unless you need me? If you do, you know I'm here. Always."

Julia didn't want him to go. She parted her lips, a second away from asking him to stay with her and Cora. But that seemed selfish. He'd already done enough for her, and the students needed him too.

"No. Go. We'll talk tomorrow."

Silence stretched on the other end of the line. If not for his breathing, she might've thought he had disconnected. Then he said, "I'm glad it was his finger that was broken, and not yours. You'll have to tell me about it over Bloody Marys."

And with a quick goodbye, he was gone.

A mile from home, Julia stopped at the grocery store. She decided she would make Cora a real dinner, with real pasta. Not something from a box. Well, the pasta would be from a box, but the sauce would be from a jar. She might even sneak in some extra vegetables. And there would be garlic bread. She needed to do this for Cora, but even as she tried to distract herself with dinner plans, her mind still reeled after what she'd learned at Baird's offices. She shot Eric another text, more direct this time.

What the hell?

Julia had just picked up a loaf of French bread when her phone rang. Expecting Eric, she connected. In the background, a rock song played low. She heard the hum of traffic. Her daughter's heavy breathing.

Cora was supposed to be at home with Evie and her mom. Why wasn't she at home?

Julia dropped the bread into her cart. "Where are you?"

"I'm with Evie and her mom. At Balboa Park." Before Julia could ask why the hell she'd left the house, Cora released a ragged breath.

"Dad—"

With that, her daughter broke. Her sobs competed with her efforts to breathe until it sounded as though she might choke.

Julia abandoned her cart and walked toward the exit. "I'll come get you."

"It's okay. I'm okay." The way her voice continued to hitch suggested otherwise. "Evie'll drop me off." Another sob. Another gulped breath. "We're headed to the car now."

Julia stopped near the corral of shopping carts outside the store. "What happened with your dad?" She resumed walking.

"He's dead." An ocean of grief held in two words. "They found him in the desert. They think…they think someone killed him, Mom."

Julia froze only a few feet from her car. She had a flash of Cora at twelve, when she'd come home red-faced in an outrage that had quickly dissolved into tears. It had been about the time Eric had left them, which had combined with Cora's hormones and the casual cruelty of middle school girls like gas to a match.

Cora had cried for hours. Refused dinner. Blasted songs about betrayal. But what Julia remembered most was her daughter's face later, after the crying had finally stopped, when her eyes had grown heavy with sleep and grief. When she'd looked up at her mom from her nest of blankets and asked, *Why don't we matter to him anymore?*

That wasn't true, of course. Cora had always mattered to Eric, even if he sometimes struggled with the best way to show it. Kind of like Julia's own dad.

Julia could hear Cora struggling for breath.

"A couple of days ago, that detective, Hoffman, called me. He wanted to talk about where Dad was Tuesday night, and about Brie's second phone. So when I saw the police were calling back, I thought it was about that. But they—" She tried again. "They told me…"

She could go no further. As Cora sobbed, Julia heard Evie's soft words of comfort in the background. She was grateful for that, at least—that her daughter was with someone she loved.

"They're sure it's him?" Julia wanted to believe they'd gotten it wrong. She held that hope tightly.

"Fingerprints."

With that, the last thread of hope snapped. Julia's legs threatened to buckle. When Eric had started working in the finance industry, he'd been fingerprinted as part of his background check. He'd been so excited when he'd come home that day. They would have a brighter future together now, he'd said. She'd believed him, even if he'd already been sleeping around at that point. Julia remembered the excited professional who thought his fingerprinting warranted a celebratory bottle of pinot. The cheap kind that was still Julia's favorite.

For a moment, she couldn't breathe.

"The detective said he'd been dead for days. Why didn't you tell me that Dad was missing?" Another ragged breath.

"I didn't know." She hadn't—not for sure, anyway—but it felt like a lie. She was pretty sure it sounded like one too.

On the other end of the line, Julia heard a car door shut.

"How am I supposed to believe that?" Her daughter's voice dimmed, faded.

"I'm the one person you can always believe, Cora." She sent the words with force, hoping each landed.

"I don't think that's true." In the silence, she sniffled. "What happened to Grandma and Grandpa?"

"What does that—"

"What happened?"

"They died."

"Yeah. Right. What about that girl I'm named after—Cordelia? You've mentioned her a few times, but when I ask who she is, you blow me off. *Just some friend from a long time ago,* you say, and then you start talking about something stupid, thinking I won't notice."

Each new accusation cut more deeply than the last. "Now's not the time—"

"It never is." Cora's voice had an edge to it now, as if she'd found someone to blame for her dad's death: Julia, for not reporting him missing. For keeping too many secrets. "We're in the car now. Be home soon."

Julia's arms tightened with the frustrated urge to hold her daughter. She started to tell Cora how much she loved her, but she was already gone.

Julia's mind wandered to the day she'd lost her own parents. Stroking her mom's hair even though she could no longer feel it.

She tried to call Cora back, needing her daughter to hear the words, to *feel* them, but she didn't answer. The two currents of grief, past and present, tugged at Julia, until she dropped to her knees in the parking lot.

CHAPTER 46

REN

If Ren hadn't followed her father into the trade, she would've been a florist. She'd always loved flowers. As a child, she'd picked daisies and forget-me-nots and braided them into bracelets. She'd keep a sunflower or a sprig of tiny roses in a small vase until the leaves withered and the petals crumbled in her palm.

When she was in her teens, her interests grew more serious. She spent her time researching flowers, visiting nurseries, taking garden tours, and eventually she'd developed a list of favorites.

Then she'd planted her garden at the duplex, the only place she'd ever lived alone. She'd started with hemlock. The seeds were easy to germinate, the plant was hardy, and the bursts of tiny white flowers with their lacy leaves provided a nice contrast to her darker rhododendrons. She'd read that Socrates's death by hemlock had been peaceful, but Ren would learn firsthand that this was a lie. That target had endured a slow death marked by paralysis, which left him lingering in consciousness but unable to move.

Next came wolfsbane. Hood-shaped blue-purple blossoms jutting from erect stems. When ingested, its roots caused a fatal paralysis of the heart and respiratory center. Nothing went wrong with her usage there.

Ren had grown up around guns, and the austere death they brought. Guns served a single purpose: to fire a bullet toward a target. Guns were a tool. Nothing more. But the wolfsbane and rhododendron and belladonna—they brought joy. That was their true purpose. They were deadly only if you didn't leave them alone.

For a while, Ren's favorite flower had been oleander, so it was a poison made from the juice of crushed oleander stems that Ren brought with her the night she met Nolan.

Ren's father had tasked her and Nolan with surveilling a man accused of killing his ex-wife, but Ren recognized the assignment immediately for what it was: busywork. The man lived in Cerritos, across from a community park, in an area not quite suburban but not so shady that the police did routine patrols. No doubt the reason her father had picked the location, and his fake target.

Despite the late hour, she'd insisted they stop for coffee on the way. What good would her poison be if he didn't have a drink to slip it in?

They'd both ordered lattes, hers served hot, his iced. He'd told her he always took his coffee cold—"Instant gratification, and no scalded tongue."

He'd grinned, and she'd felt heat rise in her cheeks. When they both reached for their drinks at the same moment, they'd nearly touched. Ren had pulled back and shoved her empty hand into her jacket pocket, where it'd tightened around a tiny plastic bag, like one for an extra button. She'd hoped the oleander would dissolve in the iced latte. She'd only practiced with room-temperature water.

Ren got a bit of luck when Nolan declined the straw the barista offered. Easier for her to spike if he removed the lid.

They left her car in a strip mall lot and walked the few blocks to the park. On the way, he asked the usual questions—*What kind of music do you like? Where did you grow up? Favorite season?*—and she told the usual lies: *classical, Cedar Rapids, and definitely summer.*

Then his questions grew more intriguing. *Smith & Wesson or Remington? How old were you when you saw your first dead body?*

Ren didn't have much experience with men. She'd caught herself stealing glances at Nolan's profile: too-sharp nose, thin lips, the sparse stubble that grew along an angular jaw. She had to remind herself that that's what Nolan was too: a target. Just that. By the time they'd reached the park, he'd finished half of his coffee without her noticing.

They chose a picnic table with a clear view of the target's house, perching on the tabletop with their feet on the bench. At first, a couple of feet separated them. Then Nolan scooted closer so that their thighs touched.

"We'll make a more convincing couple like this," he said.

Ren didn't object. His nearness put his cup in reach.

She popped off the lid of her cup and blew on the coffee before taking a sip. She feigned a look of discomfort. "Hot," she said.

He held up his cup in a mock toast. "Told you. Iced drinks are the way to go."

She blew on her coffee again, slowly, watching as Nolan's eyes drifted to her mouth. With him distracted, she used her other hand to retrieve the tiny bag of poison from her pocket. It was only later that she realized how much easier tiny glass vials were.

She took another sip, then scrunched her face. "Care to share a couple of your ice cubes?"

"For you, anything." His voice grew husky as he took off the lid. He poured a splash of coffee and several ice cubes into her cup.

Before he could replace the lid, she kissed him. He set his cup on the table and used both hands to cradle her head as the kiss deepened. Ren grew light-headed. She nearly fumbled the tiny bag, but managed to empty the poison into his cup without him noticing. Then she slipped the empty bag into her pocket.

When they pulled apart, Nolan's eyes were all pupil.

He breathed heavily. "After that kiss, I need to hydrate."

He finished his coffee in a couple of long gulps. When she made no move to drink hers, he motioned to her cup.

"Something wrong with your latte?"

"I need a second to recover too." Having left her own coffee exposed, she had no plans to take another drink.

Nolan laughed, a deep, rumbling sound. He tilted his head in the direction of the house across the street.

"It doesn't look like our guy's coming out tonight." His voice was hoarse. "Want to head back to my place?"

"Very much." Ren was surprised when her own voice rasped. She hoped he didn't pick up on the regret there too.

Ren wasn't sure how long it would take for the poison to kill him. At least an hour, she guessed. But even if she had time, she didn't dare kiss him again, in case some of the toxin remained in his mouth.

On the way back to the car, Ren almost risked it anyway. It was like the mad honey made by bees who fed off certain species of rhododendrons. A taste would be mind-altering and, if she was careful, it probably wouldn't kill her.

Two hours later, Nolan showed no signs of poisoning. When Ren laid her ear on his bare chest, his heartbeat was strong too, if a little fast. She expected that, though, given the ferocity of their sex. She would've been insulted if his pulse had been slower.

Half an hour after that, they extracted themselves from the tangle of sheets, and headed to the gym to meet her father. When he saw Nolan, he pursed his lips. Ren was sure he was furious—she'd never defied him before—but when Nolan excused himself to use the restroom, her father offered a slight smile.

"You didn't kill him."

Her stomach knotted. "Timing wasn't right."

"That's not it, though, is it?"

Despite the smile, his eyes were hard, but Ren didn't look away. To look away would've been weakness, which to her father was among the greatest sins. Maybe even a greater one than failure.

Her father took her silence as confirmation. His face softened. "The real reason you didn't kill him is because you've been listening." He sounded…proud. "You shouldn't kill someone without a reason, and I didn't give you one, did I?"

So it had been a test. He'd meant her to challenge him, and now he believed she had, when all she'd done was screw up the dosage. She couldn't tell him his pride was misplaced.

That experience taught her two lessons. Always make the poison a little stronger than you think you need. And always question your orders, even if they come from someone you trust.

Now Ren remembered something Nolan had said after the shooting: he'd been hired because his target had killed someone. She was a horrible person. Ren hadn't looked at her husband's explanation as closely as she should've—probably because the closer she looked, the more it sounded like a lie.

Sitting cross-legged in the closet, Ren pricked her ears at the sound of a car, feeling a pang of regret that it would all be over soon. She would've liked to take Julia's botany course, or ask her for parenting tips. But even if she no longer believed Nolan told the truth about why Julia needed to die, that didn't change Ren's plan.

Julia was a threat to Ren and her baby. And as much as she respected Julia—as much as she would've liked to be her friend—Julia would never be family. And family always came first.

CHAPTER 47

JULIA

Julia paused on the threshold of the bungalow. Though Eric had never lived there, it seemed emptier after Cora's news, and after their argument.

She opened the door and drew a deep breath. The faint scent of that morning's breakfast lingered. Coffee and sausage grease, now congealed in the pan. The faint sulfur of cold eggs in the trash. She should've washed the pan and taken out the garbage before she left for L.A.

Julia considered waiting outside for Cora to return home. But eventually she would have to get used to being alone there. There was no reason to be afraid of her own empty house.

She stepped inside, where even her slight breath seemed to echo, and locked the door behind her.

Julia had been hiding behind a locked door for so long, she'd allowed herself to forget what it was like to be truly vulnerable, but Brie's and Eric's deaths had brought that all back.

The night the man came to their tent, Cordelia was off chasing a high. It was late—Julia hadn't owned a watch, but it was probably after midnight. The zipper's teeth had started separating, slowly, slivers of night seeping in between the nylon flaps. At first, Julia thought it might be Cordelia returning.

But then she saw the top of the man's head—hair short and gelled into place—as he slipped into the tent. He entered quietly, with shoulders hunched, sneakers planted toe first. When he glanced up and saw Julia watching, he grinned, as if they were friends meeting at a party.

The easy way he looked at her made Julia wonder: *Do I know him? I must, if he's in my tent at this hour. Or maybe he thinks this tent is his.*

Who are you? she'd asked. Still trying to be polite.

The bloated moon of the man's face hung above her. His cheeks flushed. Then she recognized he wasn't one of them. He was too well-fed, his jeans too crisp, and his sneakers too new.

Surprising her with a burst of speed, the man zipped the flaps closed behind him and covered Julia's mouth with one long-fingered hand, the other circling both of her wrists. His eyes were too wide, and his limbs jittered, but he was strong.

When he leaned in, he smelled of the drugstore lotion her mom used to buy. Julia fought an urge to vomit. With his palm pressed against her lips, she knew she might choke on it.

She squirmed and his grip on her wrists tightened.

Where's the other one? The blonde? His voice rasped. His breath smelled of cigarettes and mint. *I've got something for her.*

Drugs. He was looking for Cordelia to offer her drugs. For a moment, Julia thought that not being Cordelia would save her. Then she realized drugs weren't what he intended to offer. At least, not without payment.

Beneath his hand, heart racing, she mumbled an answer. *She's gone.*

As if that wasn't obvious. In a space that small, there was nowhere to hide.

The man sighed, obviously disappointed. He pushed harder with the hand that covered her mouth, which caused his fingers to creep against her nostrils.

Suddenly, she couldn't breathe. She struggled and tried to suck air. Cheeks puffing in, out. Trapped against his palm, her breath whistled.

Her jaw worked as she tried to bite into his flesh. She tried to twist free, but his body kept her pinned. When nausea welled again, she didn't fight it. If she threw up, he might release her in disgust.

His power over her aroused him. As he swelled against her, Julia's head grew dizzy. Her heart thrashed. She thought he might release her to reach for his zipper, and Julia prepared to breathe, scream, fight.

Instead, he flipped her over roughly. Pressed his knee into her back. Face mashed against the ground, compressed under his weight, she felt her lungs burning. She tried to scream but couldn't. Pain radiated along her spine. Hot, angry tears formed.

The man yanked his zipper to free himself from his jeans. Julia's scream came suddenly, sharp and full of rage.

Only it wasn't *his* zipper, and it wasn't *her* scream.

The man released Julia, his howl joining the other one. Julia scuttled toward the corner of the tent, and she turned to see the flaps of the tent unzipped and Cordelia riding the man's back, her fists buried in his hair, mouth wide as she continued shrieking. Her pale face radiated anger, and something else too. Julia thought it might be regret—that she hadn't been strong enough to do the same for herself as a child. That no one had been there to fight for her as she now fought for Julia.

The man shook off Cordelia, and she landed on the ground. He took a step toward them. But outside a curious few had gathered. Julia could hear them whispering.

He rubbed his scalp and ambled out of the tent.

They watched him go, but Julia knew men like him always tried again. There were always plenty of opportunities for men with violent urges.

Jerked back to the present, Julia rubbed her wrist where Baird's guard had grabbed her. Where the man with the gelled hair had once left bruises. Anxious, she checked her phone. She called Cora again. No response.

Julia moved to the kitchen, getting a plastic tumbler from the cabinet and a pitcher of lemon water from the refrigerator.

She paused, frowning at the pitcher. She'd thought it had been nearly full, but apparently, Cora had finished most of it. Still, there was enough left to fill her tumbler.

She drained the cup in a few seconds. Her nose wrinkled at the slight aftertaste. The lemons must've turned.

Her phone dinged. A text from Mike letting her know that Kamal was able to track down the first name of Brie's lover. Julia felt a fission of excitement, and terror. Progress at last. But she was also disappointed that Brie really had been cheating. Eric had deserved better.

Then Julia read the name. *Nolan.* She sighed in frustration. The name meant nothing to her.

Julia twisted the lid off the pitcher and dumped the lemons from the infusion chamber into the trash. She caught another whiff of egg. Queasy, she stripped the full bag from the trash can, tossed it in the outside garbage, and returned to the kitchen. There she knelt to grab the Lysol from under the sink, intending to spray the inside of the trash can, but she stood too quickly and vertigo surged. She grabbed the countertop to keep from stumbling.

Damn stress. She hadn't slept much lately, and her diet had been crap. Unless she'd caught a virus?

No. Not possible. She didn't have time to be sick.

Julia pushed back her shoulders and continued her tasks, half listening for Evie's car. After she sprayed the can and lined it with a new bag, she checked her phone again.

Cora and Evie must've hit traffic.

From a bowl on the table, she picked the largest lemon, washed and sliced it, and then realized she hadn't washed the pitcher. She returned to the sink and turned on the water.

That's when she heard it, the creak of her old floorboards. Had Cora come home and she'd missed the sound of the door? But after that night in the tent, her instincts weren't as easily misled. In Cordelia's voice, they screamed.

Run.

And even more urgently: *Warn Cora.*

Julia started to turn, water still running, but she grew dizzy, the bright light of the kitchen turning gray at its edges.

She closed her eyes and held tightly to the countertop. Reached for her phone. Head fuzzy, she tried to call Cora. It went to voicemail.

A body pressed against her back.

A woman's body, followed by a woman's voice. "You're not one for routines, are you, Julia?" The voice sounded familiar. Julia was usually good with voices, but her head grew light, her limbs like rubber. "But I've noticed one habit of yours." The woman reached around Julia in an almost lover-like gesture, her arms a vise that kept Julia in place. She tapped the acrylic pitcher with one unpainted nail. "Hydration is so important."

Thinking of Cora, Julia tried to move, but her rubber body betrayed her. The woman tightened her arms to keep Julia upright. Julia caught the woman's reflection in the window. The stranger from the restaurant.

The woman reached around her to turn off the water, whispering in Julia's ear, "You should cut back on the lemon, though. All that acid can be hard on your teeth."

The woman noticed her phone and went still. She tapped the screen. "What's this?"

Julia couldn't have answered even had she attempted it. Outside, a car door slammed. She heard the faint goodbyes between Cora and Evie. She opened her mouth to shout but her numb tongue wouldn't cooperate.

In her head, she shouted, *Cora...*

She had only seconds. She could feel the truth of that in the greasy churning in her stomach, and the way the darkness bloomed at her vision's edge. But mostly, she felt it in her muscles, which trembled like leaves in a brisk wind.

She knew her only shot at escape was to alert Cora, who still possessed a clear head and a phone. If she could scream, she would have a chance.

To submit to this woman meant death.

Julia swallowed around her useless lump of a tongue and, her voice hoarse but clear, she managed to speak. But her voice was a whisper. "Leave her. Please."

Then, in case her meaning wasn't clear, she stumbled in the direction of the back door, willing her rubber feet away from the kitchen. Away from her daughter.

She managed a few shaky steps. Distantly, she heard the click of a key in the lock.

Then, only inches from the back door, she tumbled into darkness.

CHAPTER 48

REN

Julia didn't need to answer Ren's question about the phone. All the information was right there in the text thread from some guy named Mike.

Kamal found the guy Brie was hooking up with. Only got a first name. Nolan.

A flash of acid burned in her chest.

Really, Nolan?

Ren turned off the phone and aimed for the trash. She threw it with more force than she'd intended, and it thwacked against the hard plastic.

Once Julia was in her trunk, Ren pulled out two heavy-duty zip ties. She used the first on Julia's feet, then moved on to her wrists. She positioned Julia's hands so the palms faced against each other—she couldn't allow her the opportunity to wriggle free—and then cinched the band tight. Ren hated the way the plastic cut into Julia's skin, but there was nothing to be done about that.

The maps app estimated that the drive from Kearny Mesa to Malibu would take just short of three hours. Because of this, she'd kept her water intake to a minimum. She couldn't very well stop every thirty minutes for a bathroom break. Not with Julia in her trunk. While Ren had considered

296

letting Julia regain consciousness in the back seat—it would've been nice to talk with her on the drive—she knew that even with the restraints, she couldn't risk that. She and Nolan had already made too many mistakes. Ren injected a mild sedative into Julia's arm to make sure she remained unconscious and gently closed the trunk.

Most of the drive to the Shearwater passed in silence. Before a job, Ren often listened to classical music—Finzi's *Dies Natalis* was a favorite—but that night, she didn't want the distraction from her plans. She also didn't want to miss any sounds that might rise from the back of the car.

As Ren passed the tagged sign announcing her entrance into Malibu, she focused her ears again on the space behind her. If Julia had awakened in the trunk, she gave no indication. No thumping came from the rear of the car. No screams for help. Then again, Julia didn't seem the type to exhaust herself with fruitless pleas. If she regained consciousness, Ren thought she would occupy herself with quiet planning, as Ren herself would. Despite her lingering irritation over the text on Julia's phone, she allowed herself a slight smile at the thought.

This stretch of Highway 1 cut between the hillside to her right and the Pacific Ocean to her left. A pedestrian bridge of rock and concrete connected the smaller homes perched along the slope—which was dotted with spiked plants, jagged brush, and the occasional palm—to the beach. Oceanfront homes blocked the view in most spots, but every once in a while, Ren caught a glimpse of water. While Ren didn't care for the beach, she appreciated the ocean's beauty, especially at night, with its black-glass waves and a roar to rival any of Finzi's compositions.

Not far from the hotel now, Ren checked in with Baird, and with Nolan. She bit her tongue to keep from mentioning the text on Julia's cell. Better to talk in person. Each call lasted less than ten seconds. A few minutes later, she rolled into the parking lot of a Jack in the Box and got out of the car. She risked a quick run to the bathroom before leaning against her car and pulling out her phone. Ren could've connected through Bluetooth, but for the next two calls, she didn't want to chance that Julia could overhear—even if Julia would be dead within the hour.

Ren's first call was to Darien. Aware she didn't have much time, she skipped the greeting and got straight to the point.

"We're not coming back," she said, bracing for the questions Darien was sure to have.

Instead, he said, "Okay."

Okay? "You're not surprised?"

"I had an uncle in your line of work. You're too smart to leave the business the way he did."

Ren shifted to get a better view of the trunk, where Julia remained, hopefully, unconscious. "And what way was that?"

"Suddenly."

So Darien knew? Or thought he did. "What kind of work did your uncle do?"

He laughed, deep and low. "The kind you don't want me talking about on the phone."

Ren nodded her approval, though Darien wasn't there to see it. For a second, she wished he was. "So. You want the gym?"

"Hell yeah. Although I'll be ditching that couch."

Despite the circumstances, she smiled. "Paperwork's already in the drawer. It's locked, but I'm guessing you know a locksmith."

"My aunt's good with a lock. But a crowbar's quicker."

"Well then. I'm glad it'll be in good hands."

"Pleasure doing business with you, Ren."

Ren hung up and, inhaling deeply, made the call she'd been saving for last. The one she'd been dreading. Her father.

"Hey, kiddo." He sounded tired.

Ren released her breath and, feeling off-balance, widened her stance. She still worried she might topple. "Hey, Dad."

"You're safe?" That was always part of his usual greeting. It meant, *Is this line secure? Can you talk openly? Any threats I should be aware of?* Ren thought maybe this time, it meant more too.

"I'm good." She touched her stomach. "We're good."

Her father cleared his throat but said nothing for several seconds. The silence swelled. Was he angry with her? Disappointed? Finally, he said, "You know Nolan framed me?"

More frank than he would've usually been on the phone. Maybe he thought he had nothing left to lose now.

"I heard."

"Wasn't your idea, though?"

"Of course not." There was no heat in her reply. She knew he had to ask.

"It was a smart play."

Ren knew what he meant. Anthony Petrovic would protect his daughter, even if it meant also protecting the man who'd betrayed him.

"I'm going to confess."

Ren scowled into the phone. "No."

"I can't risk you and my grandchild getting caught up in this."

"I had no part in that shooting." Her caution was gone now too. "Even if it leads back to Nolan, I'll be safe. I can even give you an alibi. Maybe we were out shopping for a crib?" While she would hate to lie, sometimes the wrong thing had to be done for the right reason. Hadn't she built her entire career on just that?

"If you turn on Nolan, he'll turn on you," her father said.

"He won't." Even now, she wanted to believe that.

"He doesn't share our code, Ren." He blew out a breath. "Besides, there's evidence."

Her entire body grew cold. There couldn't be. "What evidence?"

"Apparently, Brie's father found a phone in Eric Bennett's office. One that had texted a single number dozens of times."

"But you didn't—" She stopped when she realized just how far Nolan had gone to set up her father.

"Yeah. Apparently, the whiskey wasn't the only thing Nolan had in that paper bag at my house."

Ren cursed herself for not checking that sack.

Her father continued, "He slipped his burner phone and a round from his gun into my bedroom closet." His voice grew thick. He'd never sounded so weary. "I shouldn't have trained you to follow my path."

"I'm good at what I do."

"You're the best. Better than me, and definitely better than that asshole."

She winced. "Dad."

"The baby can't hear me, Ren. If I was right there talking directly into your stomach, even then it wouldn't understand."

"It's about establishing habits now for when the baby can hear you later."

He sighed, and even through the phone, she heard the sadness in it. "You know I won't be around when that happens, kiddo."

Ren wanted to contradict him, but he had a point. Even without the evidence Nolan had planted, there would be proof enough in that bedroom closet to convict her father—if not for Anderson Hughes, then for a dozen other crimes. In the beginning of his career, especially, he hadn't been as careful about covering his tracks.

"I've spent my adult life holding others accountable for their sins, and I'm proud of the work I've done. Whatever happens, I'm okay with it, especially if it means you're safe." Despite his reassurance, her father didn't sound okay. He sounded beaten. "It's just that I never expected it would be family who ended it for me."

In her head, Ren composed what she would tell him. She would apologize on behalf of Nolan. Encourage her father to run. Assure him she would help as much as she could. It wasn't as if either of them had an employer-funded pension or lifetime medical to fall back on, so Ren had been smart about setting money aside.

Her father spoke before she could say any of that. "There's something else. One of my old colleagues reached out after he heard that fingers were being pointed in my direction." He paused, and Ren picked at her cuticles. *This can't be good.* "Apparently, about the time Nolan was hired, this old friend also heard rumors about this job. That someone was looking to contract. That's the problem when you deal with clients who are motivated by anger. They're not always careful. They talk."

"Did this friend know Brie was Baird's daughter?"

"He did. He told me this whole thing was always destined to be a huge clusterf—mess."

Her bones vibrated, the way they did when a crucial detail fell into place. "Were you able to confirm whether Eric really was the one who hired Nolan to kill Julia?"

"You've got it half right." Her father chuckled. "And Ren? You're going to love this."

CHAPTER 49

JULIA

J ulia awoke in the dark, her wrists and ankles restrained. A dull ache bloomed in her right temple, and her tongue felt chalky.

Where—?

A trunk. She'd been taken.

A second later, she remembered the rest. How she'd volunteered herself to save Cora.

Cora.

Her daughter's name bounced around in her head, piercing each of the spots that ached and creating new ones. In her mind, she screamed it.

Cora!

She tried to part her lips to scream for real, but tape sealed them.

Her half-open eyes seeped at the corners, and she became aware of a crust that had formed there. She blinked them slowly open, then brought her bound hands to rub each eye in turn. She worked at the tape with shaky hands. "Cora?"

Her voice rasped. She cleared her throat and tried again.

"Cora." Fear and anger gave her voice weight.

A car door slammed, and she winced at the fresh pain in her temple.

A second later, the trunk popped open. She glimpsed a woman's face half in shadow before her head was lifted, almost gingerly, and her eyes were covered. She caught the faint scent of sweat. Memory tingled, but it was lost in the lingering effects of whatever sedative had knocked her out.

"I'm going to cut your ankle restraints so you can walk," the woman said. "Screaming will do you no good, and I'd prefer you not, anyway. I'd hate to have to gag you."

When Julia spoke, her throat stung. "Where's Cora?"

She heard the plastic at her ankles breaking. She moved her feet an inch, testing her freedom.

"Where's Cora?" she asked again, growing more insistent.

"She's fine."

Julia wanted desperately to believe her. "Is she in the car too?"

The woman helped her to a sitting position, guiding her legs out of the trunk. "She's actually quite lucky, your daughter. If she'd looked left instead of right, she might've seen me. She might've tried something stupid, and I wouldn't have had a choice." She sounded genuinely regretful.

"What did you do with her?"

"She's sleeping off a mild sedative." The woman pulled Julia to a standing position, supporting Julia's weight when her knees threatened to buckle. The ground felt hard, and the woman's voice echoed. Were they in a parking garage? "Well, not that mild. I had to make sure she was out for a few hours. But when she regains consciousness, it won't be any worse than a hangover."

Julia tensed, ready to run if given the opportunity. Her captor must've felt her body go rigid, because she clicked her tongue in warning. "Now Julia. You want Cora to stay safe too, don't you?"

All fight left her body. She nodded.

The woman guided Julia slowly by the elbow. They rode an elevator up several floors—Julia guessed three or four—before walking down what felt like a hallway. An office building? Julia had a moment of panic that she might be back at Baird Enterprises. But this elevator had risen much more slowly. And there was the faint odor of fresh paint.

Julia heard the soft *tick* of what she thought might be a key card inserted into a reader. A moment later, a door opened.

Inside, they walked a few steps on carpet before turning to the right, onto tile, where the woman lowered Julia to the floor, again with care. A moment later, Julia heard a sharp clicking as her ankles were secured with a new zip tie.

A door slid shut and she was alone. Fighting panic, she tried to focus on her surroundings—but with her eyes still covered, she couldn't find purchase. Breathing harder and harder, Julia felt the past pushing back in on her.

This time, she didn't try to stop it.

If we don't get to Humboldt County, you should go back into the foster system. Cordelia's voice rang as though it was in the room. Julia had heard her say it over and over again, whenever she'd talk about leaving the streets. She'd daydream aloud about heading north to someplace like Eureka or Garberville, where it was cooler but cheaper. They could get retail jobs or maybe work at a casino.

Julia had always responded with the same thing. *I'm not leaving you alone.*

Until one night, one of the very last, when they'd been lying in the dark. Julia had again refused, but for once, Cordelia hadn't let it drop. Instead, she'd rolled to her side, unexpectedly clear eyes gleaming in the tent.

Okay. But if I die, then you'll go. She'd grinned, teeth still intact, face only just starting to turn gaunt. Later, Julia would think a lot about that grin. Obsess over what she might've missed.

Two nights later, Julia was forced from the tent with a painfully full bladder, careful not to wake Cordelia. She didn't go far. After that night with the intruder, they tried to stay close after dark. A few minutes later, when she'd pulled back the tent flaps, a strip of streetlight fell across her friend's face.

Not asleep.

In a heap in the corner of the tent. A needle jutted from Cordelia's leg. She was limp, unresponsive. Face clammy. Too cold. Lips blue. The paramedics came, but the shot of naloxone didn't revive her.

If I die, then you'll go.

It was too late to take it back.

Julia had lived up to her vow. Though she was tossed out the week she turned eighteen, the extra time in foster care allowed her to finish high school, and to apply for college and the scholarships that were her gateway to a better life. To Eric. And really, in the end, to Cora.

Once more trapped in the dark, she made that vow again.

I'm getting the hell out of this place.

Julia brought her bound hands to her face and worked off the mask. She was in a bathroom. She scanned for sharp edges or breakable objects. Anything she could use to saw through the zip ties. But if there ever had been anything useful, there wasn't now. Her captor had been thorough.

Julia closed her eyes again and thought about how carnivorous plants grew in environments too hostile for other vegetation. Lacking soil nutrients, they'd evolved to feed on insects instead. Some, like the cobra lily, had grown large enough to digest rats.

It was the same for her now: she had only two choices. Adapt or die.

Julia wouldn't dishonor Cordelia's sacrifice by making the wrong choice now.

CHAPTER 50

REN

Nolan looked angry. "Why'd you bring her?" he asked, gesturing toward the bathroom that held Julia. "We're assassins, not baby-sitters. You should've killed her at her house. Made it look like a suicide."

"Baird wants to question her."

Ren also understood that she was stalling. She didn't want to kill Julia.

That didn't mean she wouldn't do it, though for different reasons than her husband's. He wanted to tie up loose ends. Get in good with Baird again. Nolan saw no problem with killing someone just to save himself. She understood that now.

But maybe she was being too hard on him. In a way, it was the same for her, though it wasn't herself she was protecting. Inside her womb, the tiny stranger fluttered.

Actually, not a stranger. My baby. My family.

Ren took a small tin from her pocket and selected a mint, popping it in her mouth. As he always did, Nolan held out his own palm. He crunched his, impatient, while she let her own dissolve on her tongue.

"After Baird gets what he wants, we'll dump her body in the ocean. Fewer questions that way." She glanced sideways at the bathroom. "Even if she eventually washes ashore, she'll be scrubbed of evidence. If we're

306

careful, they won't be able to tell whether it was an accident, suicide, or murder."

"You should've called me in to help."

She locked eyes with him, thinking but not saying, *I couldn't risk you making another mistake.*

"I handled it," she said coldly.

His face softened. "You can handle anything. But why here, at Baird's hotel?"

"It's what Baird wanted."

He was visibly relieved. "Well, that's great. If we play this right, he might still throw jobs our way. We've proven we're good at cleaning up messes."

Of course Nolan focused on the money.

He must have noticed a shift in her expression, because he said, more kindly, "I know the killing has started to weigh on you."

A sudden and unbearable sadness descended. He didn't understand her as well as she'd always believed.

She was fine with killing. If it was a righteous kill.

"She's a girl, by the way."

Nolan's face wrinkled in obvious confusion, but a moment later, he got it. He touched her stomach. "How long have you known?"

"Since this afternoon."

"What do you think about naming her after my mom?"

She hoped he didn't read the melancholy in her smile. "I'm not naming her Gladys."

But her smile had tipped him off, and he exhaled deeply. "You know."

"About my father? Yes. I know."

"You understand I had no choice?" When she remained silent, his voice grew more urgent. "If I'd set up someone else, we would've had to kill them too. A dead client *and* a dead assassin? That wouldn't have convinced the police, and it certainly wouldn't have fooled Baird."

Her father's words returned to her: *It was a smart play.*

Nolan cupped her face in his hands. "There was no one else," he said.

His gaze intense, his stubble more unkempt than it had been a couple of days before. "Your dad won't deny it. *Defend the family* and all that. Maybe the evidence won't be enough to convict anyway."

Every muscle in her stilled—that he would dare use her father's mantra against him. "He's going to confess."

Not that it mattered. That was the one thing she hadn't dared tell her father: Baird would never allow the man who'd killed his daughter to make it to prison.

"I'm sorry, love. But we're safe now." His eyes dropped to her stomach. "All of us."

She tried to smile, but the corners of her mouth refused to lift.

CHAPTER 51

JULIA

Julia's palms faced each other, the zip tie cutting into her wrists. She wriggled to see if she might be able to slip out. Too tight.

She studied the strip of heavy-duty plastic. While there was no way she could get through the tie itself, the lock that secured it might break. If she applied the right kind of pressure.

Julia scooted across the tile, then pressed her back against the vanity cabinet. She inched her feet toward her butt and pushed upward until she was finally standing. Then she used her teeth to reposition the locking mechanism between her wrists. The hard plastic abraded her skin as it twisted. Still, she pulled it a little tighter, creating more tension.

She rolled her shoulders and blew out a breath. Preparing.

This is going to hurt.

In her mind, she worked through the steps she'd learned in her self-defense classes. Raise arms. Push elbows out. Bring hands down in one quick, violent motion, into the stomach. Watch the locking mechanism break.

She closed her eyes and went through it again. Arms. Elbows. Hands into gut. Bye-bye, zip tie.

She raised her hands over her head, elbows out slightly, and pulled her forearms into her stomach. She grimaced.

Yeah, that hurt.

But the zip tie remained in place.

With her teeth, she tightened the zip tie even more and tried again, hitting her midsection with enough force that she knew she'd bruise the next day.

If there was a next day for her.

Damn it, Julia. Do you want to be the pitcher plant or the ant?

Without thinking again, she raised her arms, exhaling and throwing her shoulders back at the same moment she thrust her hands into her stomach. The gesture knocked the air from her lungs, and she felt her vital organs surge up into her throat.

But the locking bar shattered. The plastic ring fell to the ground.

Hands freed, Julia snatched up the broken strip of plastic. She pinched the ridges just below the V-shaped tip. Then she sat, bent forward at the waist, while also drawing her feet toward her, knees out. Rocking and reaching to close the gap between her right hand and her bound ankles. The angle was awkward and her back spasmed. Her stomach hurt like hell too. But she gritted her teeth.

I'm not going to be a fucking ant.

She pushed the tip of the plastic strip into the locking mechanism that secured her feet. She jiggled the plastic tip, which acted like a shim. As she pulled her ankles apart, the tie unlocked and fell to the floor.

Julia rubbed her wrists. Then she walked quietly to the bathroom door, and slid it open an inch.

CHAPTER 52

REN

S weat had started to bead on Nolan's forehead. "Remember how we met?" he asked.

Ren felt an unexpected warmth in her chest. "My father never wanted you dead, you know. He just wanted to test me."

He laughed, but his voice rasped, and he had to clear his throat before he could speak. "If you'd failed his test, I would still have been dead. But I understand. Trust has to be earned."

She circled his waist with her arms and rested her head against his chest. His heartbeat was faster than normal. She looked up at him, remembering that first meeting. He'd suspected what her dad had asked of her but had showed up anyway. *Worth the risk,* he'd said. They'd had sex twice that night, and every night for the next week. He was so handsome, and charming. Her heart seized. She touched his face.

"I'm still glad you didn't kill me." He said it as if it were a joke. As if he understood that for her, such a thing wasn't possible.

"I meant to, you know. I just didn't get the dosage right."

"My lucky day."

She released him and stepped back. "When we talked earlier, my father told me something else. An old friend of his knew early on that this contract involved Baird's daughter."

Nolan licked his lips, then brushed his finger across the skin between them and his nose, wiping away a slight sheen. If Ren hadn't known better, she would've attributed the sweat to nerves. "How? I already told you there was no indication—"

She cut him off. "I believe you." That's why planning was so important. If you rushed a job as Nolan had, details could be missed.

His face relaxed but then immediately wrinkled into a frown. "But wait: Brie wasn't the target. Julia was." He paused. "I didn't get that wrong, did I?"

"No. Julia was the target."

"Then I don't understand."

"Right target. Wrong client," she said. "When my dad said the job involved Baird's daughter, he didn't mean she was the intended victim. Brie was the one who hired you."

At first, she'd thought the text she'd seen on Julia's phone meant that Nolan and Brie had been having an affair. She'd put it together a second before her father told her.

The hotel was the location for the money drop. Nothing more.

But it was sloppy. Some guy named Mike had Nolan's name, as did someone else named Kamal. And Ren suspected the something that Baird had found in Bennett's office was Brie's burner phone, the match to the one Nolan had planted in her dad's house. There would be texts connecting her to Nolan.

His mistakes had endangered them all.

Understanding dawned on Nolan's face. "She used her father's accounts to make initial contact," he said. "She must've known I wouldn't say no to Baird."

"That's my guess."

He laughed, one sharp bark. "So that's why I never got that second payment," he said. "I killed the client. Man, I really screwed this one up, didn't I?"

But his handsome face betrayed no more shame than if he'd been a child caught helping himself to a second piece of cake.

Ren tamped down on her displeasure. "I still don't understand, though. Why the girl?"

He shrugged. "I got a text saying to add her to the contract. She was a liability that could expose the client, and us."

The shrug nearly undid her. That he could be so casual about killing an innocent girl. Funny how he hadn't shown her a Polaroid of that text exchange. "Brie wanted her stepdaughter dead because she was a liability?"

"Looks that way."

"That's just…" Her voice trailed. For the first time ever, she felt like swearing. "That's wrong."

"It's *business*." His tone grew sharp. "You should understand Brie better than anyone."

Her rage twisted into an icy knot at the base of her neck. "How so?"

"Baird has a problem, he calls us. Why wouldn't the daughter he raised do the same?" He waved his hand in dismissal. "An artist's son becomes a sculptor. An angry man raises an angry child. For better or worse, we're the product of our childhoods, aren't we, Ren?" He shot her a knowing glance. "It's why you're a hired killer too."

"It's not the same."

"You're right. Baird doesn't hide behind all that ethical bullshit." There was no anger in his voice. No judgment. Only, it seemed, exhaustion.

She wanted to debate him more, but there wasn't time.

"Can I ask you a question?" she asked.

"Of course."

"What's your definition of evil?"

"I said I was sorry." He sounded sincere, but she'd been fooled before.

"That's not what this is about."

He wiped sweat from his forehead and blinked rapidly. "We all have evil in us. What matters is how we balance it with the—" He stopped. In his eyes was something she hadn't seen there before. Fear. "Why did you ask that?" His eyes widened. "That's one of those questions you ask before…"

His voice trailed off as his body started to twitch. Not yet a seizure, but that would come soon enough.

She felt a moment of regret but no guilt. Though she found her father's code too rigid—too naive—she'd always agreed with him on one thing: the importance of family.

Plus her father was right: eventually, Nolan would've turned on her. Better for the baby if she acted before he did. "I wasn't sure I could go through with it. I even packed you a bag. But I didn't screw up the dosage this time, Nolan. I've learned a lot since the night we met." She took a few steps back. "I'll take good care of our daughter. I won't name her Gladys, but I'll always put her first."

Like I'm doing now.

"The mint," he hissed. "You bitch."

Ren didn't take offense. It was hard on her, watching him die, so it had to be even harder to be the one dying.

Nolan lunged for her, or tried, but his motor functions had been compromised. He fell to the ground. She hoped she'd given him enough that death would come quickly. She didn't want to see him suffer. Even more, she didn't want Julia to suffer, since Ren planned to give her the same dose.

After Nolan had finally stilled, she reached into his pocket. She found only his wallet filled with cash. She took out all the bills, separating one wrinkled bill from the others. Then she felt the familiar quickening in her stomach.

She didn't need a coin for her jar this time. She had something far better.

She tucked the small bundle of cash into her pocket.

Ren checked her watch—she expected Baird soon—before turning her attention to the bathroom. Time to take care of the next problem.

CHAPTER 53

JULIA

Julia lingered on the threshold. Apparently, the woman who intended to kill her was named Ren.

Her voice carried to Julia: "Brie was the one who hired you."

Brie?

As she'd listened at the door, details clicked into place. Julia thought of how Brie had been bothered by her haircut, which made her look a little less like herself. Brie had allegedly gone to move-in day to appease Eric, but maybe that wasn't it at all. Maybe she'd decided it would be better to have an alibi. Or maybe she wanted to watch.

Other memories crowded in. Brie scanning the crowd in the moments before the first shot. The money hidden in the wall—hers, not Eric's. Probably meant for the hotel in San Clemente, where the first installment had been dropped.

So Brie *hadn't* been cheating on Eric. When Cora read the texts saying it would be over soon, Brie hadn't been referencing her marriage. She'd been referencing Julia's *life*. The toxic relationship she'd wanted to end had been Eric's, with Julia. Their renewed *friendship*.

And because Cora had read those texts, Brie had targeted her too. Julia's vision tunneled. Her skin burned. Brie had actually *paid* someone to kill Cora. And Murphy had died solely because he had picked the wrong spot in line.

Julia heard the man hiss, "The mint. You bitch."

Julia hoped he suffered.

Minutes later, when Ren stooped to pull something from his pocket, Julia took the chance to slip out of the bathroom. She quietly opened the door to the hall.

Once outside the hotel room, Julia grew less stealthy. She sprinted down the carpeted corridor, squinting in the dim light. She looked for a staircase that would take her down and found it quickly, holding the chrome handrail as her sneakers slapped against the brown tile.

In the lobby, the front door was boarded shut. She slammed against it with her body, hard enough that pain shot through her shoulder. She took a step back and kicked it, more out of frustration than because she thought it would do any good. The boards didn't even flex.

The windows were boarded too, but she pounded them with her fists anyway. She checked the reception desk. No phone. She spotted a fire alarm. Ran to it. But when she pulled it, nothing happened. Not yet connected.

She fought an urge to scream. She didn't have time to wallow. She turned toward the glass door that led out into the parking garage and pushed, expecting resistance. It swung freely. She closed her eyes, took a hopeful breath, and stepped out onto concrete. She moved to her left, away from the wall of glass. With no windows or obvious exits, darkness pressed against her. She squinted to locate the garage door.

Farther to the left. About ten feet away.

She raced in that direction. Tried to force the door up at the same instant she spotted the keypad. She swallowed a curse.

Moving forward again, she fast-walked between rows of numbered stalls. She passed only three vehicles. Ren's Prius. What looked to be a work truck. And an Audi she didn't recognize. Without the keys, they would be useless to her, and probably had alarms that would give away her location anyway. Julia's eyes had started to adapt to the dark, but she steadied her breath and listened too. Somewhere, she heard a thumping she couldn't identify. Above her? She stopped and tilted her ear upward, toward a ceiling crisscrossed by ducting and red piping, but the sound was quickly lost to the low mechanical thrum.

As Cordelia had taught her, listening was what saved you.

CHAPTER 54

REN

Ren saw the broken zip tie on the bathroom tile and couldn't decide which was stronger: her annoyance or her admiration.

She knelt, picked up the scraps, and inspected the broken locking mechanism. Rolled it between her fingers. She'd figured Julia might try to twist free, even at the expense of the skin on her wrists, or find a shim. But Ren hadn't realized her prisoner was strong enough to break the zip tie on her own.

Ren wished anew that she didn't have to kill Julia, and for a moment, she wavered. Then her stomach tightened, reminding her of the stakes. There was nothing more important than her daughter. On some level, Julia would understand that too.

Feeling better about the situation, Ren straightened to standing and checked her watch. Baird would be arriving soon, if he hadn't already. She'd planned on meeting him in the hotel room, but with Julia gone, she would have to pivot.

She left the room and went in search of Julia.

CHAPTER 55

JULIA

Julia began moving again, walking faster even though her path was cloaked in shadow. She couldn't be sure what lay in front of her, but she knew what was behind. She started to jog.

Staring hard at the ground, Julia passed more construction supplies, and rolling bins and carts. When her path curved, she slowed. A ramp sloped downward. She turned the corner to her right and heard it behind her—the click of the glass door closing.

She hugged the wall as she hurried down the ramp. At the bottom, a faint, flickering light pushed against the shadows, casting its strobe on metal drums and buckets of paint. A slight chemical odor hung in the stale air. When she inhaled, it burned.

As Julia raced across the open concrete, skirting the cinder block walls and weaving between concrete posts painted white, her breathing grew more labored. She sensed that someone else shared the dark with her. When her sneakers squeaked, she winced but kept moving. Her steps thudded, but behind her, there was only silence now.

Julia turned another corner, descending another level. Ahead of her loomed a white wall with two doors, both open. On the left, a storage closet or small office. On the right, a lit stairwell. The stairs led upward.

No good. Still, she was grateful for the light. She stopped, for just a few heartbeats, trying to get her bearings.

There. Another door. With a green exit sign.

She started moving again. The chemical smell grew stronger. Ahead of her, a wall signaled a dead end, and the floor no longer sloped. There was nowhere left to run. The open concrete reminded her of the courtyard at Anderson Hughes, and she sucked in a breath. If the door was locked, her only choice would be to return the way she'd come or to hide. Both choices would only delay fate. All hope of escape now rested in that small round knob.

She sprinted the last few steps. Stopped in front of the door. Reached out with a moist palm. Twisted the knob. It turned freely, and she released a long breath into the chemical air.

Hand still on the metal, she heard a voice echo from behind her. "Glad to see at least one of those assholes can follow directions."

Julia turned to see two men. Sweat dripped into her eyes, stinging. Even in the dim light she recognized him. Oliver Baird.

The meaty-necked guard she thought of as Hugo stood beside him, a splint on his pinkie, his gun already drawn.

CHAPTER 56

REN

As she entered the lobby, Ren felt an icy finger trace her spine. This was where the four workers had died. Death had been part of Ren's life for so long, but somehow the thought of the workers suffocating where she now walked made her shiver.

Ren walked with renewed purpose into the parking garage.

A minute later, she found her fugitive had slipped outside through an exit door on the lowest level, where cement steps led down to a tiny strip of beach. Beyond it lay only the sea.

Julia hovered halfway down the steps. Oliver Baird loomed over her, wearing a dove-gray suit that looked to be fine merino wool and a white dress shirt with two buttons undone. No tie.

Next to Baird, a thick-necked bodyguard glowered at Julia. His arms were crossed in front of him, right hand tight around a Ruger. She recognized his ruddy face.

Ren ignored both of the men, already annoyed, and addressed Julia. "Impressive trick back there."

Julia gave a half-hearted shrug. "I aim to entertain. If you close your eyes, I can show you my disappearing act all over again."

Ren released her own gun from its holster, holding it with a deliberate casualness. "I think just the once is enough."

Baird stepped forward, forcing Julia farther down the concrete steps and onto the sand.

"You brought the woman, but where's Nolan?"

The bodyguard stepped closer too, blocking Ren's view of Julia. The final concrete slab was too small to fit even the three of them, so Ren reluctantly gestured for them to move onto the beach too. The tide swallowed all but a strip of wet sand, and foam reached between the sharp rocks with milky fingers.

As the bodyguard got out of her way, Ren saw that Julia had managed to sneak closer to the water's edge.

"Nolan is in the hotel room," Ren said.

She studied Baird's waistline. There wasn't an obvious bulge, but there were plenty of places to hide a weapon.

Baird's thick brows shot together. "He needs to get his ass down here. I have some questions for him."

She frowned at the expletive. "That will be a challenge, considering he's dead."

His face relaxed, as she'd hoped it would. "I'm pleased you decided to clean up your mess, though you'll forgive me if I want to verify—"

Ren shot the bodyguard twice. He tumbled heavily onto the sand.

Baird's expression darkened, and Ren watched him closely. If he had a weapon, this was the moment he would go for it.

Instead, he raised his hands, palms out.

"That was a mistake, Ren." Despite his posture, there was no surrender in his voice. She thought of what Lydia Baird had said: *When people consider themselves untouchable, they can be arrogant. And careless.*

Taking a step forward, Ren said, "You've relied on others for so long, you've lost the ability to protect yourself."

As if to prove his autonomy, Baird took a step away. Ren split her attention between him and Julia. She wasn't letting Julia escape again.

Gaze darting between the two, Ren bent down for the bodyguard's weapon. She emptied it of bullets and tossed it aside. "By the way, yes, Nolan did kill your daughter."

Baird nodded curtly, growing more relaxed, even smug. "No surprise there. Brie had asked if I knew someone who could take care of a problem for her." He gestured toward Julia. "That woman. We fought about it. I thought I'd convinced her to leave well enough alone. Then this morning, I found that damn burner phone and all that cash."

"Like father, like daughter. Your agenda has never been any better. You had me kill Voss so he couldn't expose you. Usoro too." It wasn't a question, but still she waited for his response. When he gave none, she added, "Janice Stockwell. Juan Gomez. Teresa Reyes. Ray Osman."

"Who're they?"

"The workers who died here."

Baird looked confused, but she saw it there. His guilt. No, that wasn't right. He felt nothing close to that. What she glimpsed was more of his trademark arrogance. It shouldn't matter if he knew, because he was Oliver effing Baird.

"What the fuck does—"

Ren shot Baird in the head.

CHAPTER 57

JULIA

Julia watched in horror as Baird crumpled. Ren quickly checked him for weapons, then trained the gun on her.

"The day we met at that restaurant, I thought about poisoning you. Just for a second. For my family. I had a worry it might come to this." Her voice was conversational—no different than when she'd asked for menu recommendations.

How long had this woman been watching her?

By the tilt of the other woman's head, Julia guessed she wanted a response. "I'm glad you didn't."

This seemed to please her. "You understand that tonight, it has to happen. But because I like you, I'll give you a choice." With her gun still trained on Julia, she pulled a small tin from her pocket. Whatever was inside rattled. "Mint or bullet?"

The ocean rumbled behind Julia and the whole earth seemed to shake. Could she make it into the water before being shot? If she screamed, would anyone hear?

She put her odds at less than 50 percent. And even if someone heard, a bullet would silence her faster than help would arrive, or than she could swim.

An abandoned surfboard floated on the surf. The waves threw it against the posts of a distant pier with enough violence that chunks were missing. Julia couldn't stop herself from picturing its previous owner being tossed in the surf like that broken board. With the waves tugging at her sneakered feet, Julia feared the same might happen to her.

She took a step, but Ren had anticipated it, moving closer.

"Come on, Julia. You're smarter than that." She sounded disappointed. "Bullets can travel faster than the speed of sound."

"Well, I *was* on my middle school track team."

Ren laughed. "You must have a preference. If it were me, I would prefer the mint. It takes longer, but it's fairly painless."

Julia motioned toward the gun, trying to find common ground. "A forty-five, right?"

Ren nodded solemnly. "A Walther. But I don't much like guns."

Julia looked from the gun back to Ren. "Me neither." Her mouth dry.

"Because of what happened to your parents?"

It should've surprised her that the other woman knew, but it didn't. "You said this has to happen. But why?"

"You know why." Ren touched her stomach. Then she asked, more softly, "Did you have to urinate all the time when you were pregnant?"

Confused, Julia worried she might give a wrong answer. "What?"

"I don't have any female friends to ask. When I looked online, it says it's normal, but you can't always trust what you read online."

Julia tried not to stare at the gun. "At the end, it felt like a small horse was sitting on my bladder."

The corners of Ren's upper lip twitched. "For me, it feels like an elephant." She shook the tin again. "Now which is it? I'd hate to shoot you if that's not your preference, but I also need to get out of here."

Julia's temples pulsed. The air drained from her lungs. Her heartbeat was a thunderclap.

My preference *is to stay alive.*

But despite the other woman's friendly tone, her expression made it clear she'd decided Julia's fate long ago.

Ren sighed, reluctance mingling with the first hint of impatience. "I've never killed someone who didn't have it coming." She paused and cocked her head. "Or maybe I have. Recently, I've come to realize my husband was less than honest with me about the jobs he contracted."

Still looking to buy time, Julia asked, "Is that the guy you killed up in the hotel room?"

"It was. I've got to say, you surprised me back there, escaping like you did. You're stronger than I gave you credit for."

"I've had to be."

Julia hoped Ren would ask about that. For now, the plan was to keep Ren talking until Julia could figure out a better plan. But Ren didn't take the bait.

"You've surprised me a lot, Julia. Looks like you're leaving the choice to me." She raised the gun.

"Mints." If she could draw Ren closer, maybe Julia could disarm her?

Ren tossed the tin over. Julia intentionally fumbled it. Could she run? Would Ren be able to hit a moving target? Ren had said she preferred the poison, but that didn't mean she wasn't a good shot. She hadn't missed Baird or his bodyguard.

Ren sighed, her gun arm steady. "My life has been about making the guilty pay. You might not deserve this but—"

"Maybe I do."

Ren's hand lowered, just a couple of inches. "No. I've been watching you. You're a good person."

Julia risked a step backward, into the surf. Legs tensed. "We're actually a lot alike."

Ren shook her head. "I'm not a good person," she said. "I try to be, but it's hard, trying to make the world a better place." Her left hand settled on her stomach. "It's worth it. For her. For your daughter too."

The mention of Cora turned Julia's stomach.

"You misunderstand. I'm not saying you're a good person. I'm saying neither of us is." She pinned Ren's eyes. *Keep talking.* "The man who killed my mom was named Walter Brooks." At his name, Julia's nostrils flared involuntarily. She hadn't said it in twenty years—had tried not to even think it. And she'd never told this part of the story to anyone before. Not even Cordelia. Not even, really, herself.

"Earlier that day, Walter and his cousin decided to go into the crack-dealing business together." It was easier to say the name the second time. Julia closed her eyes, remembering the details that had come out during Brooks's confession. "They figured since they used, they would be naturals. You can see they were wrong about that. Walter'd killed his cousin within hours."

When Julia opened her eyes again, Ren still had the gun raised, but she was listening.

"The best guess is that my dad was in the bedroom when Walter knocked. My parents had fought that morning, and my dad would have either gone to the lake or retreated into their room. But the lake was especially ripe that summer."

Julia could still smell the decomposing algae and the rotting fish. To chase away the memory, she filled her lungs with the crisp, salt-tinged air. What she still wouldn't say were the questions that haunted her: what if she'd lingered at the bookstore, or never left home at all? What if her parents hadn't fought, or there had been more urgency in the neighbor's call to the police? What if her mom hadn't turned on that damn fan, making the curtains flutter, or Julia had unplugged it on her way out?

"When I came home, the front door was open." In reflex, she lifted her palm, remembering the scratch of the peeling paint, the slight warmth of the vinyl. When she'd first entered, she'd seen no signs that anything was wrong. Then she'd noticed the fan on the floor, its cage and blades separated.

"The back door was open too. I didn't stop in the house. Didn't call out for my parents." She took another pull of salty air, and exhaled violently, willing the memories to leave her body too. But they remained lodged in her chest, choking her. Now that she'd started, she had to see this through. "I wonder if it would've been different if I had. If I'd found my dad before I found my mom."

Out back, her mom's torso had been twisted one way, legs another. Her skirt had been hitched mid-thigh, exposing a flash of blue cotton underwear. Julia had smoothed her mom's skirt. That close, with her eyes wide and her mouth agape, her mom had looked surprised.

Julia had touched her hair. *Love you, Mom.*

"She'd been shot." Dark blood on the steps. Dark blood on the dandelions. Dark blood on Julia's hands. Then the sun had flashed on metal a few feet away. "And Walter Brooks had dropped his gun. I picked it up."

Crushed dandelions in her left hand. Cool metal in her right. An old Smith & Wesson.

Remembering, bile surged in her throat. The most haunting what-if of all: *What if he'd just remembered to run with his gun?*

"I went inside, intending to call the police. I think. I might've just been wandering. In shock." She looked toward Ren again. The other woman's face was rapt. When Julia brushed her hair back, her hand trembled. "That's when I saw my dad." Later, Julia would learn how close she'd come to encountering Brooks too. He'd left only a minute before Julia entered the house, throwing the fan on his way out. That's what had likely roused her father: the crash of it hitting the wall.

"It happened quickly, all of it. Finding my mom. Finding the gun. Coming back inside." She estimated about forty-five seconds. Certainly no longer than a minute. "My dad ran out of the hall, toward me. Reached for me." Julia blinked quickly. "I remembered my parents' fight. My mom on the grass beneath the dying palm. And I thought, *Who else could've killed her?*" Julia shook her head. She'd never told the story before, and she wasn't getting the details right. "No. It wasn't a thought. Nothing as solid as that. It was more a feeling. And the way he came at me…"

Julia stopped to catch her breath. Ren continued to study her, gun lowered to her side now. But Julia suspected that was only because the weapon had grown heavy.

She locked eyes with Ren, both of them standing deathly still. The only sound was the crashing of the waves.

"I shot him."

At her confession, her entire body shuddered. She could still feel the gun's recoil, so fierce that she'd finally dropped her clump of dandelions.

"He died without knowing my mom was dead." Another pause, thick with decades of suppressed guilt. "But maybe, because of my expression in that moment—my terror—he did?"

There was also the gun she'd held. No hiding that. Ren's weapon seemed to twitch in response.

Julia forced herself to finish. "The police came a few minutes later. At first, like me, they thought my dad had killed her. Then Brooks confessed. To killing my mom, at least. While they also convicted him for killing my dad, he never admitted to that one." The waves lapped at Julia's sneakers. The tide was coming in. "I realized my dad was innocent before the police did—that my dad had reached for me only because he meant to embrace me."

She blinked against the tears. If she had any chance to get back to Cora, she needed to forge this connection. "Do you know what my dad did in the seconds before he died?" A few tears fell, and she swatted at them angrily. "He took the gun from my hand." He'd pressed the dandelions back into her palm. Rasped her name.

Julia.

His last word, and what nearly broke her now. She puffed out a breath and threw back her shoulders.

"That's how we're alike, Ren," she said. "We've both killed someone we love. You, your husband. Me, my dad. You may say I'm a good person. I'm not. But that doesn't mean we can't both try to be better."

Ren stared at her before speaking. "Nolan said the target had killed someone. I guess he didn't lie about that, at least." Her eyes grew soft for several seconds before snapping back into place. "That's not the only way we're alike, Julia. We both have fathers willing to sacrifice for us." She raised the gun. Was it Julia's imagination, or did Ren's hand shake slightly? "And we're both willing to do the same for our own daughters."

The scent of brine was strong. Smoke too, though she couldn't see a source for it. The smoke reminded Julia of the ash snakes she would light for Cora on the Fourth of July. An invisible hand made a fist around Julia's heart and squeezed.

"I can keep your secret," Julia said. "I've kept that one for decades."

"You won't. You'll go to the police." She studied Julia's face. "Tell me I'm lying."

"Judging by what you did to your husband, you don't much like liars." *Stall, Julia, stall.* "But why did you go through his pockets?"

"I like to remember the people I've killed." Ren tilted her head in the direction of the two dead men. "Guess I should check theirs too."

"You've got one from my ex-husband, then." Julia fought the impulse to gag. "That's pretty messed up."

"You should never forget the lives you've taken."

A second later, the soft pop of gunfire split the night.

CHAPTER 58

REN

Ren had just decided to let Julia go when she heard the shot. Strange that the sound registered before the pain.

But then the wound began to burn. In her side. Inches from her avocado-sized daughter, protected by only an amniotic sac and her mother's fragile body.

Anger flared hotter than the pain. Ren turned and saw Baird's guard— on the ground, raising the gun. Probably grabbed from an ankle holster she'd forgotten to check.

Maybe Nolan had been right: pregnancy had made her soft.

The guard narrowed his eyes, and she brought up her own gun. She acted a second behind him. He got off his shot first.

But his hand shook, and his shot went wide.

Ren's hand was steadier. She'd aimed slightly to the left to account for wind. Clenched her teeth and pushed her pain to the background. The bullet struck the guard in his chest. The impact rolled him face-first into the sand.

Ren closed her eyes and dropped her gun. She fell to her knees, resting her weight on her left hand as she probed her wound with her right. She searched for the bullet's entry point. Panic rose, but she fought against it. The palm she used to support her weight sank into muck, salt water licking her fingers. She grimaced, as much from the slimy feel of it as from the pain.

She grew dizzy. Light-headed. She looked for Julia, but Julia was gone. She'd taken advantage of Ren's distraction to escape. It was the right move. She tried to nod in respect, but her head felt as if it had been filled with rocks. How could her head feel so light and yet so heavy at the same time?

Ren closed her eyes. When she opened them again, she saw her. Julia. She was with the guard, fingers pressed to his neck. Then Julia grabbed the gun, emptied it of bullets, and threw all of it into the water. The throw was impressive. Julia definitely had an arm. Ren should've gone with metal cuffs instead of the zip ties.

She exhaled, the sound swallowed by the wind. She hated that her death would come from a bullet on the beach. Apparently, she'd been right to despise both.

Suddenly, Julia was beside her. Ren released a long, rattling breath. Julia's face, inches from her, wore a concerned expression.

"The asshole's dead," she whispered. And for some reason, Ren didn't mind the profanity.

Julia bent to examine the wound. Ren was glad Julia had stayed. It confirmed that she was a good person. Ren had been right to decide to let her go, even if Julia would never know her intentions.

Ren had already decided this was going to be her last job. She had enough money saved for her and her daughter to start a new life. One that wouldn't require Ren to kill unless she wanted to.

Her last job. She sighed again.

Sand scratched her neck. The water stung her eyes. Her brow furrowed. She was on the ground, though she didn't remember lying down.

Julia's face had grown too earnest. "You'll be fine," she said. "The baby too. The bullet just grazed you, and missed the baby entirely."

Ren tried to smile. "You know I hate liars," she said.

A nearly full moon passed behind the clouds. The world dimmed. Julia's breath warmed her face. Ren wished she'd been able to save her daughter, but maybe it wasn't such a terrible way to die after all.

CHAPTER 59

JULIA

Julia and Cora had the patio at the restaurant to themselves. Though it was January, Julia needed only a thin sweatshirt to stay warm. But another chill ran deeper, and was less easy to shake. She hadn't been back to the restaurant since that day a stranger sat beside her, asking what she recommended.

Something on her face must've tipped Cora off, because her daughter asked, "Do you still think of her?"

Every day. "Sometimes."

After that night in Malibu, all the violence had intertwined in Julia's head: Serena Bell, black drops beading like oil on the grass. Brie Bennett, a smear of rust-stained concrete. Ren Petrovic, blood crimson even in the moonlight.

And, of course, Eric. Five months later, Julia still reached for her phone to text her ex-husband some bit of news about Cora before remembering.

Julia tried to bury the past deep, but that was proving harder than it had once been. So she didn't sleep much.

Baird's name remained in the news. The latest story was about the hacking of his estate's account. Julia wondered if Ren had taken the money—

a retirement gift? Or, more likely, a gift to the families of the people he'd had killed? That screamed Ren.

Overall, though, public interest in Baird had waned. Even his widow had already remarried. She'd sold Baird Enterprises too, which had been quickly renamed. While the world didn't know all that Baird had done, Julia thought the renaming was a form of justice. Baird was disappearing, one rebranded building at a time.

When Julia had stumbled off the beach that night, she'd found her way to the road, and flagged down a man on a bike, using his phone to call 911. She'd brought the police straight back to the beach, where they'd found only two bodies. Oliver Baird and a large man later identified as Percy.

They'd never found a third.

The tide had been coming in, and at first Julia thought the current might've taken Ren. But that didn't explain Ren's car going missing too.

The police remained confident they would find her. Julia was equally certain they wouldn't.

The clatter of plates on the table broke the memory's spell. She focused instead on her daughter's face.

For so many years, when Julia looked at Cora, she saw her vulnerability first. The premature baby in the NICU. The twelve-year-old abandoned by her father. The granddaughter robbed of the chance to know her grandparents. How had Julia missed the woman her daughter had grown into? The strength in the set of her jaw. The intelligence in her eyes. The ferocity that had once terrified Julia, but which she finally recognized as her daughter's greatest strength.

"Anything else?" asked the young man who'd served them.

"No, thanks." Julia smiled at Cora. *This is enough.*

When they were alone again, Cora took a bite of her burger, large enough that Julia worried she might choke.

"So much for the myth of the starving college student."

After taking a semester off, Cora was starting spring classes the following week. But not at Anderson Hughes. She had enrolled at San Diego City College and planned to move in with Evie. That last part was proving hard to process. But if Cora was ready, Julia had to be too. That was the deal with being a mom.

When Julia's eyes started to burn, she long-blinked and took a bite of her own burger.

Cora wiped the corner of her mouth with a napkin. "I might add another science class," she said, taking a drink of her soda. "What do you think about geology?"

"I think it rocks."

Cora groaned before grabbing a French fry and dipping it in ketchup. "I'm already taking physics, but I think I can handle both."

"You know what they say about atoms."

Cora ate her fry while giving her mom the side-eye. "I don't think I want to know," she said. But Julia was patient, and after a couple of beats, Cora sighed. "Okay, fine. What do they say?"

"Never trust them, because they make up everything."

Cora's reluctant smile was worth the corny joke. "Love you, Mom."

"Love you too, Cora."

When they'd finished their burgers and the server returned to clear their plates, he brought with him a small package. It was wrapped in plain silver paper.

Cora's eyes lit up, but Julia's mouth went dry. She took a drink of water, but memory made it bitter.

"Did you get me a back-to-school present?" Cora asked.

She had: a pair of Doc Martens platform boots Cora had been coveting for a month. But she hadn't brought the boots to the restaurant.

Julia shook her head, just as the server placed the box on their table.

"This was dropped off earlier, but there were instructions to wait until after you were done eating."

He grinned, likely thinking he was taking part in some romantic gesture.

Cora seemed to think so too. "It must be Mike. An anniversary gift." She poked the box, then pushed it toward Julia with her fingertip. She rolled her eyes playfully. "I mean, it's only been a month, but it's Mike, so it totally makes sense."

They'd actually been dating officially for six weeks. Even Mike wouldn't celebrate that.

Julia leaned back in her chair, away from the table and the silver-wrapped gift. She stared up at the young man who'd delivered it. "Who dropped this off?"

Her voice came out sharper than she intended, and he backed up a step. "Just some woman. Came in right after you were seated."

So over an hour earlier. Plenty of time to make it to Castaic or Thousand Oaks—or toward a plane to another country.

"What did she look like?"

The server seemed flustered. He'd likely been expecting a larger tip, not an interrogation. "Blond, I think. She wore a hat, and sunglasses."

Julia knew the woman wasn't a blonde, at least not naturally.

"Oh—and she had a baby." He looked pleased that he'd remembered. Probably trying to salvage his tip. "A tiny thing. Couldn't have been more than a month or two old."

The server grabbed the empty plates and scuttled away before Julia could ask any more questions. But she didn't need to.

Cora cocked her head, curious, while Julia continued to stare at the box. When Cora reached for it, Julia snatched it from the table. It weighed less than a pound. When she turned it on its side, something inside slid, hard. Tentatively, she shook it. Something rattled. Glass?

Julia hesitated, then tore off the wrapper and opened the box.

Inside, a glass mason jar contained a single penny. Tied around its lip was a note. It bore only four words: *It's better to remember.*

Julia reached for her water but, remembering a bitter tang, pulled back her hand. After a moment, she picked up the jar.

Following her confession on the beach, Julia had often dreamed of her father and that look on his face, the one she'd first mistaken for anger. More recently, though, she'd been having a different dream: her dad holding her arm while she wobbled on roller skates, his face bearing the same fierce expression. The one she now knew was a mix of love and a sometimes paralyzing fear. She recognized it because she felt it too as she stared into Cora's face, bright and shiny across the table.

"That's from her, isn't it?" Cora asked, craning her neck to see better.

"Yes."

Cora wrinkled her nose. "Why a jar?"

Julia didn't answer, instead rolling it in her hands so the coin clinked against the glass.

Ren had survived.

She felt an unexpected surge of relief, followed immediately by a swell of horror.

Julia tossed the jar back in the box. She wadded up the silver wrapping and stuffed that in the box too. Then she laid some cash on the table and stood. Her eyes remained fixed on Ren's gift.

It's better to remember.

"Let's go," she said to Cora, leaving the box at her seat.

Outside, Julia held tightly to Cora's arm, much as her dad had that day he'd taught her how to skate, even as she understood she would soon need to let it go. Let *her* go. Despite all that had happened, Cora was ready to take her place in the wider world, and as her mom, Julia needed to be at least that brave too.

Julia took a breath and started speaking, her voice unexpectedly strong.

"The man who killed your grandma was named Walter Brooks…"

ACKNOWLEDGMENTS

Authors are always thanking their agents and editors, but in this case a simple appreciation seems inadequate. My consistently amazing agent, Peter Steinberg, and brilliant editor, Helen O'Hare, have been fierce advocates for this book, and overly generous with their time and insight. So though a thank-you seems not enough, I'm still saying it. Thank you for loving this book, and for making me a better writer.

Thank you, too, to everyone at Fletcher & Company, and the talented team at Little, Brown / Mulholland: Josh Kendall, Ben Allen, Gregg Kulick, Marie Mundaca, Nell Beram, Gabrielle Leporati, Anna Brill, and the others in publicity, marketing, production, sales, design, and editing whose names I don't yet know but who worked tirelessly to make this book the best it could be. I'm humbled to be working with all of you.

To the booksellers, librarians, and readers who've supported my work: You are the reason I keep at this. Thank you also to the members of the International Thriller Writers, Sisters in Crime, Redwood Writers, the 2020 Debuts, and all the members of the writing and reading community I've met online. I've especially loved connecting with the Bookstagram community, with a special shout-out to Magen Mintchev, who probably posted about my debut nearly as much as I did.

There are few people I trust with my early, messy pages. Thank you, Crissi Langwell, Ana Manwaring, Jan M. Flynn, Gina Blaxill, and Mary

Keliikoa. And to my amazing book coach, Dawn Ius: Your notes have been invaluable, your friendship even more so.

There are other authors, too, who have been so generous with their support and time. Though this list could easily run as long as this book and I'd still likely miss someone, I'd like to thank Tessa Wegert, Sam Bailey, Natalie Jenner, Alison Hammer, Vanessa Lillie, Jaime Lynn Hendricks, May Cobb, Barbara Conrey, Wendy Walker, Samantha Downing, Hannah Mary McKinnon, Lyn Liao Butler, Georgina Cross, Elena Taylor, Megan Collins, Anika Scott, and Heather Gudenkauf. This list grows daily, so by the time this sees print, there will no doubt be another dozen names to add to it. The author community is the most generous one I know, and I'm incredibly grateful to be a part of it.

Now a confession: I kill plants. Even the fake fiddle leaf tree in my living room lists to one side. And yet some foolish impulse led me to make Julia a botany professor with a thing for carnivorous plants. Thankfully, Lisa Bentley and Mike Wilder filled in the gaps when it came to greenhouse biomes and mucilage drops. They weren't alone in their generosity. In the writing of a book, hundreds of questions come up, and I'd like to thank all who provided the answers: Retired Lieutenant Tom Swearingen of the Santa Rosa Police Department. Daniel Hunt. Eric Wittmershaus. Mike Murphy. Kari Kincaid. Your insights were invaluable, and any mistakes in these pages are my own.

For an introvert who spends a good chunk of each day in front of the computer, I'm also fortunate to have many wonderful friends and colleagues who celebrate this journey with me, help me brainstorm when I'm stuck, and are just generally excellent humans. Thank you, Holly Clarke, Lisa Ostroski, Patty Hayes, Dean Derosa, Denise Barredo, Karen Jacobsen, Willy Linares, Andrea Garfia, and Alena Wall. And to everyone in my hometown who has rallied around my books—neighbors, book clubs, readers I've met only in passing or not at all, and even my dentist—you make me proud to live in Santa Rosa.

To my stepdad, Rob, my extended family of Middendorfs and Harringtons, and the entire Chavez family, I'm blessed to have you in my life.

ACKNOWLEDGMENTS

Above all others, my deepest gratitude goes to my patient and supportive family. To my children, Jacob and Maya, you amaze me every day with your brilliance, empathy, and strength. (And thanks, Maya, for making sure my younger characters don't sound too "mom-ish.") Alex, you make me laugh even on the bad days, and you are singlehandedly responsible for most of the good ones. You three are the reason my characters always fight so hard for their families.

ABOUT THE AUTHOR

Heather Chavez is a graduate of the University of California, Berkeley's English literature program and has worked as a newspaper reporter, editor, and contributor to mystery and television blogs. She lives with her family in Santa Rosa, California. She's the author of the thrillers *No Bad Deed* and *Blood Will Tell*.